THE GOLDEN OCEAN

By Patrick O'Brian

THE
GOLDEN
OCEAN

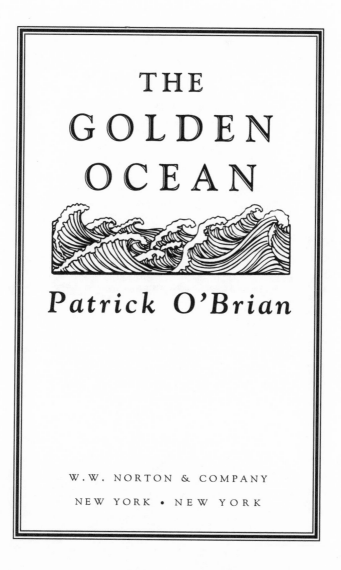

Patrick O'Brian

W.W. NORTON & COMPANY

NEW YORK • NEW YORK

The text of this book is composed in Goudy Oldstyle
with the display set in Goudy Handtooled
Composition by ComCom
Manufacturing by The Haddon Craftsmen, Inc.
Book design by JAM Design

ISBN 0-393-03630-8

W. W. Norton & Company, Inc., 500 Fifth Avenue, New York, N.Y. 10110
W. W. Norton & Company Ltd., 10 Coptic Street, London WC1A 1PU

1 2 3 4 5 6 7 8 9 0

for Mary
with love

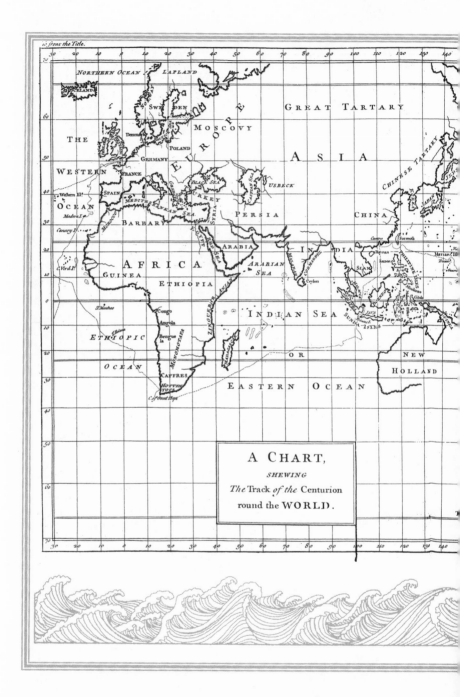

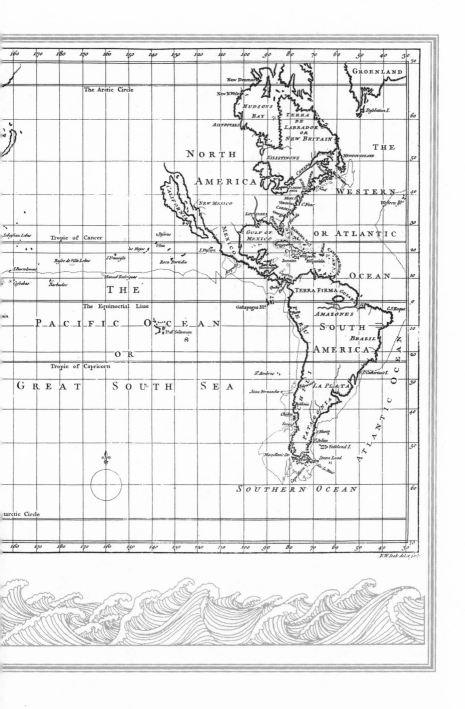

The Arctic Circle

GROENLAND

New Denmark

New N.Wales

HUDSONS
BAY

ASINIPOVALS

TERRA
DE
LABRADOR
OR
NEW BRITAIN

Desolation I.

KHISTINONS

THE

NOUVEOUNLAND

NORTH

AMERICA

CALIFORNIA

NEW MEXICO

WESTERN

Western I?

Sebastian Lobos

Tropic of Cancer

Paxaros

OR ATLANTIC

GULF OF
MEXICO

MEXICO

Paxo de Villa Lobos

Ulva

las Mojas

S.Francisco

Roca Partida

I.Passion

S.Bartolomeo

Manuel Rodriguez

OCEAN

Barbados

Carbobas

Jamaica

Hispaniola

THE

The Equinoctial Line

Gallapagos Is?

TERRA FIRMA

C.S.Roque

AMAZONES

PACIFIC OCEAN

I.ºof Solomon

SOUTH

BRAZIL

AMERICA

OR

Tropic of Capricorn

GREAT SOUTH SEA

St.Ambros

S.Catherines I.

Juan Fernandes

LA PLATA

ATLANTIC OCEAN

Baldivia

Chiloe

Socos

C.Blanco

S.Julian

Falkland I.

Magellanic Str.

Staten Land

Str: le Mair

SOUTHERN OCEAN

tarctic Circle

R.W.Seale del.et sculp.

THE GOLDEN OCEAN

1

'GOOD-BYE,' THEY WERE ALL CRYING. 'GOOD-BYE, PETER. Good-bye, good-bye.' And he meant to call out 'Good-bye' again to all of them, but the lump in his throat choked the cry to no more than a squeak.

'Good-bye, Peter,' they were calling still; and clearly came after him the voice of old Turlough, 'Peter, come home soon, with your pockets full of the Spanish gold.'

At the bottom of the hill, where the turning came, he looked round and saw the handkerchiefs waving white on the hillside and he held up his hand to wish them farewell: and he watched the twinkle of their waving, though it swam in his eyes, until the bend of the road and the long stack of turf hid them all from his sight.

Then it was the soft green of the crossroads by Joseph Noonan's cabin and the women waving their blue shawls, and he had to collect himself to smile and call back.

'And let you bring us the King of Spain's bright crown,' cried Pegeen Ban behind him.

'Well, it has begun,' he thought; but although he had looked forward to this day so much, the reflection that the adventure was now beginning left him strangely unmoved. The pain of leaving them all was so much greater than he had ever expected, and it almost daunted him: it quenched all the excitement that had kept him from sleeping these many nights past; and it left him quite desolate.

He stole a sideways look at Liam, but Liam, in delicacy, feigned to be absorbed in the buckle of his reins, and he said nothing. They rode on in silence, with nothing but the creak of leather and the deadened thrum of their horses' hooves on the soft and grassy road.

After a long while Peter said to himself again, 'Well, so it has begun,' and again he wondered that the words should feel so commonplace and flat. Perhaps it was because he was still on such familiar ground, he thought, looking up from his horse's mane: when you start out on a great adventure perhaps you expect everything to change all round you at once, and there is a feeling of something wrong in going over the country you know so well. He looked round, and indeed it was the same country that he had seen every day of his life: they were coming across the bog of Connveagh now, by the inland road, and already the sea was far away on the right hand: on the left the blue mountains of Slieve Donagh and Cruachan ran up, smooth against the huge pale sky; and he knew that if he turned in his saddle he would see the far ash-trees that sheltered the Rectory of Ballynasaggart, where they would be sitting down to breakfast now. Before him the road ran on, faint through the dim rushes and the grass, to the sudden fall in the land where the bog of Connveagh left off and the Moin bog began; where the world stretched out, far and flat, to the edge of the sky, and over the Plain of the Two Mists there was a white haze never moving and not a single cabin, let alone a farm or a house, to be seen in the whole vast expanse—nothing but the pale flash of the water in the turf-cuttings and the shine of the creeping river.

It was a huge and a wild landscape, and one that a stranger might have found inhuman and desolate; but it was Peter's own country, and he thought it no more saddening than the long cry of the curlews passing over behind them. And yet although it was so familiar, today he looked at it so hard that for a while he almost saw it with a stranger's eye; but then the soft sea-rain drifted in across them and the distant country was lost in its fall.

It was not a cold rain; nor did it drive: they hardly noticed it weeping gently out of the sky, as it did for so many days in the year; but it matched with Peter's state of mind and the song that Liam was half humming, half singing under his breath—the lament for the wild-geese, the exiles who never returned—and it made him, if anything, lower in his spirits than he was before.

They went on: on and on steadily through the small rain, and Peter was so wrapped in his thoughts that a figure leaping up at the side of the road brought the heart almost out of his mouth—a tall figure in a blue coat, springing out of a hole with a screech and flapping the sides of its cloak.

'T'anam an Dial, omadhaun,' cried Peter, quietening his horse; and, speaking still in Irish, he said, 'What are you doing here at all, Sean? And have you no more sense than to be leaping out of a great hole, screeching and waving the sides of your cloak, which is not your cloak anyway but Patrick Kearney's?'

'You great fat thing,' said Liam, frowning at his nephew. 'What manners are these? Why are you carrying the shoes?'

'I am coming too,' said Sean with a grin, taking Peter's stirrup-leather and urging the horse forward.

'You are not,' cried Peter and Liam together: the first said it in a wondering tone; the second without much conviction.

'I am, too,' said Sean, trotting evenly by the horse's side with the shoes bumping rhythmically against his broad chest as they dangled from their string.

'You are not,' said his uncle again, but only from a spirit of contradiction.

'I am,' said Sean; and Peter, who knew that otherwise this conversation might continue indefinitely, interrupted with, 'Did your father say you could go?'

Sean turned up his big open face and said, 'And would I be so wicked and undutiful as to go off from my own country without my father's permission and his Reverence's blessing? Would I not think it the great shame for ever, to be stealing away like a polecat?'

At the sight of so much righteousness Peter was almost certain that Sean was lying, and he said directly, 'Did your father truly say that you might go? And did my father approve?'

'Ah,' said Sean with a leap and a jerk that made Placidus stagger and change step. 'Oh,' he cried, 'it is hard to be after running twenty miles across the mountain and over the bog and then to be called a renegado, no less.'

'It is no more than seven,' said Liam, 'and he has no leave of anybody but the empty wind.'

'Listen, Sean,' said Peter. 'Did your father say you could go?'

'Am I not telling you?' cried Sean, boiling with frustration and shaking the patient horse until it tottered. 'Did I not say to my Da, "Will I go?" and did he not say, "You will"? And did not his Reverence encourage my heart with his noble description of the free and magnificent life in his royal Majesty's imperial fleet? "Sail forth young man," cries his reverend honour and he pacing back and forth in the small parlour itself. "Sail with the royal navy into the golden ocean, far into the golden sea." '

' "The golden ocean, the golden sea",' cried Peter. 'Did he say that indeed, Sean, now?'

'He did,' said Sean, pleased with the reception of his words. ' "Sail on the golden waves of the west until you can touch the sun with your hand," says he, "and my younger son Peter, that elegant boy, will give you his protection if you attend to your duty." '

'It does not sound like my father—God bless him—at all. . . .'

'God bless him,' they cried, Liam raising his hat.

'. . . except for the ocean, the broad, golden sea.' Peter went on. 'He was saying a word of the same kind to me, about a golden voyage and a place called Colchis—he was saying that I must make my way there myself.'

'It is to Cork we are going,' said Liam in a pragmatical tone—'to Cork by way of Derrynacaol: and not to any Colchis at all.'

'Where is this Colchis?' asked Sean, intensely interested.

'Oh, in Greece, sure, or somewhat behind it,' said Peter. 'It is all in the book. But I do not have it clear in my mind—there was this gold in the tree, and a dragon and a wise-woman who was beautiful, the king's daughter. It is William who would tell it: he can read the Greek and the Latin like any archbishop.'

'It was long ago, I am sure?'

'Why, surely it must have been.'

'Before Saint Patrick, maybe?'

'Perhaps so, Sean—very likely indeed, from what I recall.'

'In the time of the Tuatha De Danaan, perhaps it was?'

'Ah, Sean, I cannot tell you. You should ask William—he is the great scholar, with his podarkees Achilles and his hic hac horum.'

'I wish,' said Sean, looking down for a while and watching his bare feet running—'I wish I could read the Greek.'

'Read the Greek, is it?' cried Liam with strong indignation. 'Oh, the serpent. The impudent toad. Many and many a time have I said to my poor sister—and she quite demented with tales of his misconduct—I have said to her, "If you will not cut the comb of that young cock he will end on the gallows, like many another unpromising reptile, and then we'll hear of him going for a soldier in King Lewis's army of Papists, where he will be knocked on the head out of hand and shot through the body with flintlocks and pikes. He will be brought back and tried for foreign enlistment and treason and they will hang him at the four roads of Ballynasaggart. Let him be put to a respectable master," I said, "and let us hear no more of this running up and down and playing the fiddle and making of rhymes or jingles in Irish—it is bad enough to be speaking it in private the way no one can hear us, but to write it in sheets . . ." '

'What is wrong with the Gaelic?'

'It is a language of servants. And it is not good enough even for them. What kind of a place can a servant get and he speaking nothing but Irish like something that has come in out of the bog?'

'It was once the language of kings.'

'I spit on your kings. It was never the language of commerce.'

'It is the language they are speaking in Paradise.'

'It is not. Some few very poor and ignorant angels with hardly a feather on them yet might still speak a few words of it in the dark corners of Heaven; but the language that is rightly spoken there, is the English.'

'Well,' said Peter, 'Irish is good enough for me.'

'Your honour will please himself,' said Liam sharply, 'but when we meet the young gentleman in Derrynacaol I hope that your father's son will not make me blush by speaking the servants' language.'

'But Sean now,' cried Peter, returning to the point that had been at the back of his mind, 'if my father said all this, why did he not tell me? And why did you not start with us? You might have borrowed Clancy's mare, and your uncle Liam would have taken her back with Placidus. And what is your baggage apart from Patrick Kearney's cloak for such an enormous voyage—and I wish you may have got it from him fairly. Have you a letter at least to recommend you to Mr Walter, Sean?'

'I have the shoes,' replied Sean, 'and before Derrynacaol I will be putting them on.'

Derrynacaol: it was two full days' journey from Ballynasaggart to Derrynacaol, far out of the country of Peter's knowledge, but they were to try to reach it in a day and a half, for the great horse-fair was held at that time of the year and it would have been the world's pity to pass by without seeing anything of it. They would arrive in the afternoon of Wednesday if they travelled by moonlight, and they would be in time for the races.

'It is the race they call the Town Race that we must see,' said Liam as they went up the white road of Slieve Alan, 'for that is the great race and the town gives a silver bell to the winner.'

'Are they very fine horses, Liam?'

'Are they very fine horses? They are the best in the world,

16

my dear, fit for Julius Caesar or the Lord Lieutenant, and there is half Ireland lining the course and cheering the winner. Why, even the worst and the last of the creatures that run there would be like a comet in Ballynasaggart and it would put the mock on Cormac O'Neil's brown gelding, the ill-shaped thief.'

'I wish I could ride in a race like that,' said Sean, who was up behind his uncle for a rest from the road.

'Pooh,' said Liam. 'A great long-boned, tick-bellied slob of a thing like you? Those tall and stately magnificent horses would bend to the earth. No indeed: unless the gentry who own them are as light as may be they have little jockey-boys who weigh no more than an owl. For they are mad to win this race, do you see? And not an ounce will they carry that they can spare. It is not only the honour of bearing the bell away, but each gentleman pays five guineas to enter and each lord ten, and the winner takes all—and there are the side-stakes too, and the betting: but I'll say no more of that.'

'And why will you not?'

'Because it's there is the evil side of racing. Did his Reverence never tell you how wicked it is to gamble? And do I not tell you it is foolish as well, and I the best judge of a horse in the County Galway, if not in the whole of Connaught, *whatever* Cormac O'Neil may say. No: it is a fine and laudable sight, the glorious creatures, and then there is the piping and the dancing; but the betting and the wickedness—there's folly for you, and under his Reverence's command there will be none of it; nor any truck with the thimble-riggers and the common coney-catchers. And while I have it in my mind I will warn you against the pick-pockets that swarm at the fair. You must keep your hands in your pockets, or they will certainly steal the teeth out of your head. Indeed, they may do so even then, for there was a man from Dungannon who had the wig snatched from his poll in the hurly-burly by the winning-post, and he holding his pockets with might and main; which I had from his aunt in Dungannon itself: so if you have any money or valuable thing upon you at all, give it to me and I will carry it in the purse, God shield us from harm. For you cannot conceive of their wickedness.'

'God between us and evil,' they said, and Peter handed him a thick cart-wheel of a crown piece which had been trundling round the family for several years, going from John to William to Sophia to Rachel to Dermot to Hugh to Laetitia; and Peter had it now from William, it being given to each on his birthday by the previous holder and kept for the next, a treasured possession, too valuable ever to spend yet giving a most agreeable feeling of wealth, rare in a country clergyman's family; and Liam pulled up the purse by the string round his neck—the purse where the few hard-saved guineas for the journey lay warm and bright in their leather bag—and put the crown piece in. He looked at Sean, who avoided his eye, and then at Peter again. 'There are your buckles,' he said.

'Faith, so there are,' cried Peter, clapping his hand to his throat. 'But come, Liam,' he said, after a moment's thought, 'they'll not be stealing the buckles off my shoes or my breeches, I'm sure, for they are only cut steel. But will I give you the one from my stock?'

'A fig for the glass bauble: but your shoe-buckles look like silver almost, and you had best take them off. And the ones from your knees.'

'Sure, Liam, I won't. How can I go into Derrynacaol— which is like Nineveh that great city, no doubt, from all that you tell me—to meet Mr FitzGerald without a buckle at all?'

'They will steal the ears off a rat.'

'Well, they may steal the coat off my back, but I'll not go into Derrynacaol naked for all that. And so I defy them, Liam.'

'Prudence, Mr Peter, is——' began Liam, but at this moment they reached the gentle top of the round green hill and there below them lay the green plain all open to the watery sun, and the shining river far below.

'There it is,' cried Liam, pointing away to a dark mass in the middle distance, where the haze of smoke drifted over the houses. 'There's Derrynacaol.'

'*That?*' asked Peter.

'It's a little small place, so it is,' said Sean.

'It's a village, is it?' cried Liam in a passion. 'It's a huddle of cabins, is it? A claddach, perhaps? Are there no eyes in your head to see the pompous great steeple and the elegant court-house? Though it is true,' he said more coolly, 'that not much of it shows from here. But there, look now, on the other side of the river—do you see in the bow of the river?—that great round of green half the size of America. Well, that is the race-course alone!'

'Is it, then?' cried Peter, astonished.

'It is, too,' replied Liam, appeased, 'and the best race-course in Heaven is scarcely more handsome or vast.'

'Oh, it's I'll be there first,' cried Sean, slipping down and starting to run.

Sean was the best runner for twenty parishes—and it was said in Ballynasaggart that if he desired a change in his victuals he had but to run at full speed to catch a snipe in the one hand and a cock in the other—and he took a great start on them. He was quite out of view for a while, although they travelled on briskly: there were some people on the road now, which was a change after the bare and mountainy country, and they were all hurrying, pressing forward with their faces towards Der-rynacaol; there were donkey-carts and horsemen and nearer the town many people on foot, but never a hint of Sean did they see until they were close to the very door of the inn. He had put on the shoes well outside the town, not to disgrace his company; but they were the family shoes of a numerous clan or sept whose members differed much in size, and although they increased Sean's outward glory they added nothing to his comfort at all and the last half-mile had flayed the hide off his spirit as he minced along on tip-toe. Indeed he was so reduced that he was glad to hobble into the stable, and all the while Peter was changing he lay on a heap of straw with his feet in the air while a compassionate ostler from Tuam pumped a jet of cool water over them.

This changing was Liam's idea, and he insisted upon it

although Peter was boiling to be at the fair. 'It may very well be that you will meet with Mr FitzGerald,' he said, 'and you would not wish us all to be shamed with your old frieze coat: besides, there are the lords and the gentry from all the country and their ladies like peacocks for glory—it will never do to show like a scrub.'

As he spoke he unpacked, spreading Peter's best coat and polishing the buttons on his sleeve, breathing heavily to make them shine: so Peter made the best of it and when it was over he was glad he had done it, for not only was Liam's satisfaction plain on his face—and it is always pleasant to please your own people—but for his own part he felt more confident and worldly: and indeed he was a creditable figure to come from an isolated parsonage at the remotest edge of the poorest diocese in the western world. His long-skirted blue coat (handed down from Cousin Spencer), his embroidered waistcoat and his buff breeches (William's by rights, but pressed into his Majesty's service for the occasion) were all the product of devoted cutting-down and needling and threading at home, but they looked quite as if they had come from a tailor's hands; and his gay waistcoat, which represented seven months of loving toil on the part of Laetitia, was finer than any tailor could have produced, particularly as her affectionate zeal had carried the pattern as far as his shoulder-blades, whereas embroidery usually stops at one's ribs. And as for his linen, that had been grown and retted and spun and woven and tented and bleached entirely at home, and Solomon had no finer linen than that of Ballynasaggart, nor finer lace (if Solomon ever wore lace, which is doubtful indeed) than that which came from the bobbins and pins of Pegeen Ban to hang in a spidery web at Peter's throat and his wrists.

'Your mother would be proud,' said Liam, tying Peter's hair in the black ribbon behind.

'But fine clothes are a vanity,' said Peter, looking with furtive approval into the glass.

'Sure it's the coat that makes the man,' replied Liam, holding his head on one side. 'Why you might be the son of a bishop, or at least of a dean. I'm glad now that I did not take the buckles away, so I am.'

'Ah, the buckles,' said Peter, putting his hand to his throat. 'I wish you may not be right about the thieves at the fair.'

'Pooh,' said Liam, 'they'll not take that thing, for sure. Why will you wear it at all, the green glass?' He peered at the kind of a buckle in Peter's stock: it was there more by way of an ornament in his jabot than a thing of utility, and Liam thought it looked incorrect.

'Mother Connell gave it me for a luck-bringer,' said Peter, with an obstinate look.

'The old dark creature,' cried Liam. 'She should be burnt on a faggot.'

'She should not,' cried Peter.

'Yes she should,' said Liam. 'The witch.'

Peter made no reply for the moment, while he thought about the old strange yellow-faced woman who lived in a desolate cabin beyond the round tower by the sea: in a curious way they were friends; sometimes he brought her fish from the sea, and although she talked to nobody else—even hid when the Rector came by—she would tell him long tales of Cromwell's time, when she was a girl, and of ancient kings.

'She had it from her grandmother,' he said, 'and she thought it came from the Spanish ship. And I tell you what, Liam, she'll hear what you say if you do not take care.'

Made bold by the distance Liam snapped his finger and thumb. 'Little I care for all she may do, the black witch,' he said, 'and that green gawd is only some fairing she stole as a girl if ever she was one and not born as old as a crow, which I doubt.'

A distant roaring came through the low window. 'They are beginning a race,' cried Liam, on fire to be gone. 'Will I wait by the door while you put on your shoes?'

At the door he may have waited for a time that seemed long to him, but he was gone when Peter came down, though he had been upstairs only the time it took to ram his feet into his shoes, to rip the left one off in order to remove the shoe-horn,

and to put the shoe on again: there was Sean still there however, hovering on the door-step and peering impatiently back
into the hall and then out over the heads of the crowd.

'There's the Lord-Lieutenant's own cousin has just gone
by,' he cried on seeing Peter arrive, 'in a coach and six with
outriders and footmen galore.'

'Where?' asked Peter, staring into the river of men and
horses and asses and carts.

'There,' cried Sean, darting into the throng as a coach-horn
brayed out loud and high, and Peter saw him no more.

Peter hesitated for a moment, but the tide of people was
setting strongly down towards the church and he joined in the
wake of a party of butchers, who were marching down the
middle of the street, clashing their marrow-bones and cleavers
and from time to time uttering a concerted shriek.

'*They* must know where they are going,' observed Peter to
himself, as he stepped over a blind-drunk soldier lying at
peace in the gutter: and he was right, for in a few minutes they
had traversed the little town and he was in the tight-packed
jostling crowd that lined the green race-course. They were all
waiting on the edge and staring away to the right, and Peter
wriggled and thrust his way through until he could see the
green grass from under the arm of a gigantic seller of tripe; he
was half-deafened by the talk and the shouting, but above it all
he heard a great roar that swelled, mounting and mounting
until it was caught up by the people all about him, and in
another moment he saw the horses all close together racing
down like a wave of the sea. Then they were passing him with
a thunder and pounding and the green turf flew from under
their hoofs and Peter found that he was shouting at the top of
his lungs and although he could not hear a sound of his voice
he could feel the vibration. And they were gone, leaning in on
the curve, the beautiful horses, and there was nothing but the
brown earth where they had passed and the shouting died
away.

Peter began to recover his breath. 'The roan won,' he was
crying to the world in general when the words were jerked

back down his throat and his hat banged down over his ears as the tripe man brought down the arm that he had been waving these ten minutes past.

'Did you see him?' cried the tripe man, picking him up and abstractedly straightening his hat. 'Did you see Pat in his glory a-riding the roan?' He screeched out a kind of halloo and quietly observed, 'He's my own sister's son, the joy, and I am a ten-pounder this minute, a propertied man. However, I am sorry I beat down your honour's fine hat: and will you take a piece of the tripe—it was Foylan's young bullock and one of the best—or a craubeen for love, with the service of Blue Edward, your honour, the propertied man?'

Peter did not wish to seem proud, still less to offend the good man, so he accepted the pig's foot, wrapped the end of it in his handkerchief to keep it from his flowered waistcoat and wandered away into the dispersing crowd. It was now that he found the stalls of fairings and gingerbread, the fire-eater and the sword-swallowing marvel from the County Fermanagh, for they were placed in irregular lanes on the outside of the great expanse of grass, all trodden now into a dun-coloured plain, smelling like all fairs in the open and resounding with the cries of the men with raree-shows, two-headed calves, the great hen of the Orient, admired by the Pope himself and the college of Cardinals, performing fleas and medicines for the moon-pall and the strong fives. He also saw the pea-and-thimble man against whom Liam had warned him, and a gentleman who promised a guinea for sixpence, if only you could pin a garter in a certain way, which seemed quite easy—so easy that Peter regretted his crown. 'For,' he thought, 'there are ten sixpences in a crown, and with ten guineas I could buy such fairings for Sophy and Rachel and Dermot and Hugh and the rest.'

However, nobody ever seemed to win the guinea, except for an old little wizened man, who was strongly suspected of being the garter's father.

'Sure the old thief is the garter's own Da,' said an indignant grazier from Limerick, who had lost three shillings clear, and in the momentary silence that followed these ominous words the gambling man cried, 'Fair, fair, all fair; fair as the Pope's election and the course of the stars: come, who's for a nobleman's chance at a guinea? Pin him through, pin him fair and the guinea is yours—will you watch how I do it and do the same, so?' And catching Peter's eye he said, 'Let the young gentleman have a try for his craubeen alone—I'll not ask a penny, but accept of the elegant foot, always providing he has not bitten it yet.'

'Ha ha ha,' went the crowd, forgetting its wrath, and Peter, with all eyes upon him, started back, feeling wonderfully and undeservedly foolish.

'Why, young squire, never blush; come up and never show bashful,' cried the showman, and Peter felt his face growing redder.

'Down with the gambling,' he thought to himself; and leaving the crowd he hurriedly veiled the trotter and thrust it down into his pocket.

He walked quickly away past the fortune-tellers and the double-jointed prophetical Hungarian dwarf from Dublin, then more slowly through the real business of the fair, the long lines where grooms led and ran horses up and down before the gaze of knowing, horse-faced men; and so, forgetting his vexation, he drifted on to the blue booth where a shanachy was telling a story, accompanying himself with twangs on a harp, fierce or pathetic as the matter required.

He had seen everything, and two races more, including the last, when it occurred to him that he might find Sean over where the dancing was, and the pipes. But though he scanned the rings of dancers in the ceilidhe, admiring their steps, he saw nothing of Sean; nor did he find him at the big enclosure for the wrestling; and now that the main events of the day were done the shebeens with their whiskey were beginning their trade and already there were men drunk on the ground. Yet it would have been strange if Peter had not been used to that; and tranquilly avoiding two fights and a small riot he made his way slowly back to the inn.

It took him some time to find it, for there were more people than he had ever seen in the world quite filling the streets, and everywhere there was the confusing babble of voices, English and all the accents of Irish and even the dark speech of some horse-dealing strangers; but suddenly he was facing the open door of the courtyard, and right in front of him were his two missing followers.

'Listen, Peter a gradh,' said Sean, much agitated; 'listen, you'll not be angry now?'

'Why would I be angry, Sean?' asked Peter, frowning and staring after Liam's hurrying back.

'Sure my uncle's the great judge of a horse,' said Sean. 'It is in his nature to judge them with skill.'

'Oh,' said Peter, doubting the worst.

'And there was this grand spotted horse as tall as a church,' said Sean, 'and he, regarding its legs and considering their strength, said the horse could run faster than the others. And sure it ran like the wind.'

'Did it, Sean?' cried Peter, brightening. 'But there was another ran faster, maybe?'

'Not at all, not at all. My uncle Liam was right and the great spotted horse ran—it flew, never touching the earth. The other horses, you would have said it was assess they were, barely creeping along.'

'Well then?'

'But—you'll never be furious now, nor wicked?—*they* crept in the right direction, while the great spotted horse went away through the crowd to the river, for he scorned to compete with them, and the little jockey-boy sawing at the bridle in vain in vain. They are probably in the County Tyrone by now.'

'Did he lose a great deal, Sean?' asked Peter.

'He did not,' said Sean: but from something in his manner Peter took no comfort from his words, and after a second Sean went on, 'He could not, indeed: at that time he lost nothing at all, the way he had—but you'll not grow outrageous? Sure you'll be kind to my uncle and he broken-hearted?'

'Sean,' said Peter, laying his hand on his arm, 'you'll not tell me that they had his pocket picked?' In that moment Peter had divined the fact; and as if Sean had replied he went on, 'And yet it was hung round his neck.'

'He had brought it out to be flashing the gold,' said Sean.

'Well——' said Peter; but instead of finishing his remark he took a turn up and down the yard.

'Well,' he said at last, 'there is only the one thing to do. On the eighteenth day of this month I must be in Cork: there is no time to go back, and besides my poor dear father—no, what we must do is to sell Liam's horse; and I believe that if we find the right man and you ride with care to show him to his best advantage, the creature, we may get two guineas per-haps. It is a grave step to take—why, Sean, what's the matter?'

'Gone,' whispered Sean. 'Pawned.'

'And Placidus too?'

Sean nodded. 'With the gombeen-man of Athy,' he said. 'But not sold.'

Peter opened his mouth; but closed it again and paced up and down in the yard.

'And the baggage too, I suppose?' he asked after a dozen turns.

Sean nodded. 'It was his last stroke to win it all back,' he said.

Peter renewed his pacing. 'Well,' he said, pausing on a turn, 'at least Placidus is not sold: that would have wounded my father's heart.'

Three turns later he said, 'And with the luck of the world—thanks be to God——'

'Thanks on high,' said Sean.

'I had shifted into my best clothes, so they are not lost, and I can face the Commodore.'

And after another three turns he suddenly cried, 'I have it, Sean: I have our salvation. This Mr FitzGerald I am to meet in the evening; he's sure to be rich—I'll ask him to lend me five guineas or six. That will bear our charges and unpawn Placidus. Ha ha, Sean—that's the way of it,' he exclaimed, clapping Sean on the shoulder.

'Hoo hoo,' cried Sean, with a hoot of triumph and relief, his spirits mounting directly. 'Sure he'll be delighted to oblige a companion and he the richest man's son in the West, no doubt, if not close kin to the Deputy.'

'You have not seen him come to the inn?' asked Peter, reflecting.

'I have not,' replied Sean, 'but will I ask of the grooms? He'll surely have servants before and behind, and his horses may be filling the stables at this very minute, the valuable beasts.'

'Do that thing,' said Peter, 'and if you have news of him come and whisper to me privately. I will sit in the great room of the inn.'

2

HOPE HAD DIED BY SIX O'CLOCK; BUT STILL PETER SAT ON IN HIS corner seat, watching the continual coming and going through the wide-open door. There were farmers and graziers of the richer sort, gentlemen of all sizes and shapes and of every age but his own, red-coated officers, periwigged medical men, black lawyers, snuff-coloured merchants and the clergy in cassocks; footmen in liveries of every colour hurried on errands; parties of young men roared through the windows to their acquaintances within; indeed, half Ireland seemed to be in the great room of the Royal George and Harp. But alas it was the half that did not include the one person he really wanted to see; this person, Mr Peregrine FitzGerald, was unknown to Peter except by reputation and name, but he had a clear notion of what to expect and for hours and hours he had been looking for the arrival of a young fellow about his own age and size, a midshipman in the Royal Navy, who would, Peter supposed, come in and gaze about to find his travelling companion, and who, by his looking about and searching, would advertise his presence.

It would have been easier, Peter reflected when first he took his seat, if they had both been in the land service, for a red coat would show up at once: but in the Navy the officers wore what they chose, and apart from the King's cockade there was no way of recognising them at all. But that reflection had taken place a long while ago. The sad change from lively expectation to no hope at all had taken place by six in the afternoon, when the rain began: but when the tall clock coughed and said eight, Peter was still looking earnestly at the door; he was still spinning out his mug of tepid porter and making it last, and he was still assuring himself that clocks in public places were very often made to run fast on purpose.

'Mr Palafox?' asked a voice at his side, and the dregs of the porter splashed on the floor as Peter jumped up. 'Your servant, sir,' said the thin figure before him, with an elegant bow. 'My name is FitzGerald.'

'Servant,' cried Peter, making a leg, and quite red with pleasure. 'May I beg you to sit down and take—and take——' He had meant to add, 'a glass of wine,' but the sudden recollection that he was quite unable to pay for a small pot of ale, let alone a bottle of claret, pierced into his mind, and he finished with a wave of his hand to an empty chair.

'You are very good, sir,' said FitzGerald, sitting down. 'But first I must make my excuses . . .' And while he explained why he was so late—no idea the time had been running so fast— much taken up with seeing the races, the town, various friends—Peter gazed at him with the utmost attention that civility would permit. FitzGerald was nothing like what he had expected: for one thing he was wearing a bottle-green coat, and for another he was very much older. And yet on closer inspection he was not so ancient in fact: he wore his own hair (which was red), but it was powdered, and powdered

28

hair, like a wig, made a man appear of an indeterminate age. On second thoughts Peter judged FitzGerald to be about his own age, though indeed his urbane and fashionable air, his very rich clothes and his general ease, made him appear five years older at least.

FitzGerald talked on in the most agreeable way; but there were two things that prevented Peter from taking much share in the conversation, or indeed from absorbing much of what FitzGerald said. The first was extreme and raging hunger: Peter had had nothing since breakfast, and what with the excitement of the races, the disaster and the long-drawn-out waiting he was so hollow within that if he had been anywhere else he would have gnawed his craubeen with unspeakable joy. The second was the manner and form in which he should frame his request.

It had seemed so easy when he cried, 'I'll ask him for five guineas or six,' but now it appeared insuperably hard.

'. . . and then Culmore assured me on his oath that the filly was sore of the near fore-foot—said his groom had it from hers, they being twins of a birth—and so I did not back *her*, either, ha, ha.'

'Ha, ha,' echoed Peter, suddenly aware that a response was called for, and wondering what FitzGerald's topic had been.

'But the truth of the matter, you know,' said FitzGerald confidentially, 'is that those stables are quite unfit to be used. I know my father would not even put one of the tenants into them, and . . .'

'Now if I were to say to him, "Mr FitzGerald, please will you lend me some money?" ' thought Peter; and he was still thinking when the explosion occurred.

He did not see the beginning: there was a crowd filing along by their table, a great deal of talking, noise, laughter. And he was bent over the table, trying to hear FitzGerald through the din, and trying to think at the same time. Then there was a sharp cry, the crash of FitzGerald's chair as it fell; the crowd was spread open, and a wig fell plump into Peter's little puddle of porter. FitzGerald was out there on the wide floor, holding a young officer by the nose. The officer was pulling madly at his sword, but FitzGerald, with wonderful promptness, had his other hand on the hilt.

From the wild hubbub of voices Peter gathered that Burke—the officer's name—had trodden on FitzGerald's foot. 'Pull harder, your honour,' cried Sean, with boundless delight, and then the two were heaved apart by a surge of violent peacemakers. For a moment FitzGerald and Burke were still attached, the grasping hand of the one extended to its utmost and the nose of the other to a great deal more than the usual length: then there was a wall of men between the two and FitzGerald, with a flush on his face and a brilliant gleam in his green eyes, was sitting down.

'As I was saying,' he said, 'the course was entirely too soft for a horse with an action like that, so . . .'

'My wig, sir, I believe,' said a frosty-faced gentleman to Peter, very sharply.

'. . . so although there is not his match over a measured mile on high, champaigne country,' continued FitzGerald, 'it would scarcely be wise to lay evens when he is to run in a plashy bottom like Derrynacaol after a week of rain.'

'Just so,' said Peter earnestly. 'I am of your opinion entirely.'

At this point two red coats approached the table. 'We are from Burke, of course,' said the elder, after the exchange of formal politeness.

'My friend here will act,' said FitzGerald. 'Allow me to name Mr Palafox, of the Royal Navy—Captain Marney.'

'Shall we discuss the details in an hour's time?' suggested the soldier. 'I propose the Butler Arms.'

'Charmed,' said Peter, with a creditable appearance of phlegm, and Captain Marney walked away with his companion, humming the tune called Greensleeves.

'I am sorry to wish this on you,' said FitzGerald. 'But I promise you it will not be long. We will come out at dawn: I will line his vitals with steel: and in five minutes we shall be on our way—it will serve to get us up early, which shows that even an oaf like Burke has his uses. Let's have a bottle and drink to his slow recovery.' He called the waiter.

'I did not see what he did,' said Peter.

'Trod on my foot.'

'So you must get up at half-past five and push a sword into him?'

'Exactly so. He did it on purpose, you know. He has been seeking a quarrel with me ever since I fought his brother, and that was the only thing his boorish mind could find to do. However let us not talk about him. There are much more agreeable subjects.' He paused. 'So we are to be companions on the road? Well, I am very glad of it.'

'So am I,' said Peter, wondering if FitzGerald were really quite the ideal fellow-traveller. They sat contemplating one another, and after a pause FitzGerald repeated, 'I am very glad of it, not only for the pleasure of your conversation, but because we have some desperate lonely country ahead of us, with a desperate number of thieves in it. But you have two servants with you, sir, I believe? And a band of four should be safe from any attempt.'

'Not exactly——' began Peter, meaning to set this misunderstanding straight right away; but he was interrupted by the coming in of a servant.

'Mr Lyon's compliments,' said the man, 'and he regrets he cannot oblige Mr FitzGerald.'

'Oh,' he said, looking a little blank. He felt in his pocket, and the servant's smile grew. 'However,' he said, bringing his hand out again and waving it, 'it does not signify. Thankee.'

A long silence followed the servant's departure, and eventually FitzGerald broke it by saying, as he filled his glass with a mixture of water and wine, 'Let us drink to the confusion of Timothy Lyon. Do you know,' he added, drawing his chair nearer, 'that man has made his fortune out of my family, and now he has the monstrous assurance to decline an advance of a small note of hand.'

'Well,' said Peter, thoughtfully sipping his wine, 'that's very bad, I am sure.'

'It is the blackest ingratitude,' said FitzGerald. Then, fiddling with the stem of his glass, he said, 'Mr Palafox,' and stopped. Peter was surprised to detect a nervous tone in his voice, but he was so much occupied with his own problems and with his hurry of spirits at the recent quarrel and its approaching result, that it came as a complete surprise when FitzGerald continued, 'Mr Palafox, it would oblige me infinitely if you could let me have ten guineas, just until we reach England.'

He gaped at FitzGerald, hardly believing his ears, and Fitz-Gerald hurried on, 'You see, I made a foolish mistake at the races today, and I have left myself quite high and dry. It would be——'

'But I was just going to ask you,' broke in Peter. 'I was going to say the very same words.'

'Oh,' said FitzGerald; and there was a short silence.

'I am very sorry, indeed,' said Peter, hesitantly.

FitzGerald smiled. 'It is of no consequence,' he said. 'But I confess I had hoped you would be rich, being so well attended.'

'It is only Liam and Sean,' said Peter; then, feeling the necessity of an explanation, he went on, 'Liam farms my father's glebe at Ballynasaggart: he is not what you would call a servant at all, but he does all kinds of things, like selling the pig, and he was going with me as far as Cork and he would take back the horses. And Sean came of his own notion, to see the world: he is Liam's nephew and the son of my nurse. It was Liam who had the purse, you see, being cautious and used to the world: but it went at the races, and the horses are pawned.'

'My poor shipmate,' said FitzGerald, shaking him by the hand very cheerfully. 'What a sad way you are in. And there was I imagining a Croesus—I was ill with expecting you. But tell me, you could not send home?'

'I could not,' replied Peter, 'for I know very well there is not a gold piece left in the house. We are quite poor, you know,' he added, simply.

'I beg your pardon,' said FitzGerald, flushing. 'I did not intend to be impertinent. For myself I cannot send home either, and for much the same reason.' He carefully shared out the last of the wine. 'I cannot accept such ingenuous candour,' he said, 'without offering my explanations in turn.' And Peter learned that he was the son of Edward FitzGerald of Ardnacruish, a gentleman who had almost ruined himself by pursuing three law-suits at once about a right of way through his demesne. 'It was not so bad until the first affair came to the House of Lords,' said FitzGerald. 'But when that failed the poor old gentleman (who was in the wrong from the start, by the by) came to me with tears in his eyes and said, "Terence, my boy (my name is Peregrine, but he was thinking of my brother), Terence, my boy, I am vexed to the soul, but I cannot buy you the pair of colours I promised. Not even in a marching regiment," says he, shedding tears. "So I suppose you will have to be a crossing-sweeper, if we can find someone to sell you a broom on credit." "Stuff," says my Aunt Tabitha. "Why will you not write to Cousin Wager, as I have said these five years gone?" "Sure, Tab," says he, "it would be kinder to the boy to drown him in a stable bucket than to have him cooped up in a ship. There never was a FitzGerald who could do anything if he was not on a horse; and sweeping his crossing he will at least be within nodding distance of the creatures." "Stuff," says my aunt—and so it went on; but in the end the letter was written to Cousin Wager, who is something grand in the Admiralty, and the answer came back and my father borrowed twenty guineas from the tailor to carry me over. It is true that he had to order clothes to the tune of nigh on a hundred to do it, but they will always come in. And if only that slug of a horse had run faster this afternoon I might have been able to pay for them all out of hand: still, I have my appointment, and once I am aboard the *Centurion*——'

'The *Centurion*?' cried Peter.

'Yes. You'll not say it is your ship as well?'

'It is, though,' said Peter. 'My father's old friend Mr Walter is chaplain, and he begged me the place.'

'Well, that is capital,' said FitzGerald, shaking his hand again. 'So we are to be shipmates in fact. But tell me,' he said, pausing thoughtfully, 'you are a great sailor, I dare say?'

'No,' said Peter, shaking his head. 'Not at all. I have played about in our boat, and in the fishermen's curraghs, but I have never set foot in a ship—a brig was the biggest I ever sailed in.'

'Is a brig not a ship?' said FitzGerald, with a smile. 'But still, I see that you are sailor enough to answer a question that has been puzzling me ever since Cousin Wager wrote back and I began to read voyages. What is this larboard and starboard they are always talking about?'

'Well,' said Peter, 'the starboard is the right as you look towards the front of the ship and the larboard is the other side. Some people say port. Yes, Sean?' he said, breaking off.

'If his honour is Mr FitzGerald,' whispered Sean, bending low over the table, 'he had best fly like a bird. And you too, a gradh. Will you slip out by the back now, before it's too late?'

'Why, what is the matter?' cried Peter, amazed.

'Sure, there's information against you. Someone has sworn the peace against Mr FitzGerald, and the constable is coming to take you both up before the justice, Sir Phelim O'Neil, bad luck to his house.'

That night they lay out on the mountain, on the crest of the line of hills that divides the County Galway from Roscommon, and they slept secure, for, as Sean said, 'Wisha, your honour, the magistrate's word goes no further than the edge of the county, and although the dear knows you cannot go back, you may go forward as far as ever you please.'

They slept secure from arrest, but not from the rain: and in the sodden dawn Peter thanked his kind fate for a follower so foreseeing as Sean, who in their hurried departure had had the wit to whip up the wooden bottle that Mrs Palafox had provided for Peter's morning draught. Now the fiery whiskey bored down his throat and lit up his stomach, preserving him from the noxious damp.

'That is far better,' he said, wiping his mouth with the back of his hand. 'But I wish——' His words were cut short by the sight of Sean, who appeared suddenly on a naked rock above them: the wind was holding his long cloak straight up in the air, increasing his already considerable height to ten feet and more: his black hair also streamed up, and his blue eyes were glaring down in a hard, inimical, piercing way at a stranger far below them; and the reason for this was that the hare which had hitherto been concealed under his cloak was now entirely open to view. The inoffensive, uninquisitive stranger passed on his harmless way, and Sean came down.

'If you did that on my father's land,' said FitzGerald, picking a clean bone of the half-smoked hare (it is hard to light a good fire when even your flint and steel drip wet on being shaken), 'you would find yourself transported before you could very well bless the Pope. He is a Papist, I suppose?' he asked Peter, nodding towards Sean in the manner typical of his kind.

'He is not,' said Peter, shortly.

'Well, he is a wonderful poacher for a Protestant,' said FitzGerald.

'The mist is lifting,' said Peter. It was: it tore and parted as they watched, thinner, and at last so sparse and rare that it was no more than a few wisps between their hilltop and the great plain of Ireland with the white road winding away, far below.

'What shall we do now?' asked Peter, more to himself than FitzGerald or Sean, after he had gazed at this sight for a while.

'What we ought to do is go down there to the road and walk steadily towards the south,' said FitzGerald. 'It will dry us, perhaps, if the rain does not come back; and at least I am sure it will diminish the distance between us and Cork.'

'I tell you what, Palafox,' he said again, when they were down out of the sopping heather and the patches of rust-coloured bog and on the dry road, 'it is an infernal thing not being able to go back to Derry: I have just thought of a prodigious fine notion, if only we were there. You could go round to all the parsons' houses and tap them for five guineas apiece.'

'Listen,' said Peter, in a pitying voice. 'Do you really think there is a parsonage in all the West with five guineas in it at one time?'

'There are two in Derrynacaol,' said FitzGerald. 'My cousin is the Bishop of Clonfert, and I know the value of the livings there. There are a couple of charming snug places in Derry: I wish I had gone into the Church. But not hereabouts, 'tis true,' he said, looking forward to the thin and deserted country that lay far before them. 'Here they live somehow on twenty or thirty a year.'

'Perhaps I should go back and try,' said Peter, standing in the road.

'No,' said FitzGerald, 'it would not do at all. They would nab you at once and then it would be days and days of finding surety of good behaviour and all that. You would never reach Queenstown in time, to say nothing of being arrested for debt at the inn. I am sorry, upon my honour, for it is all in my quarrel: but a second is as much troubled as a principal in a duel.'

They walked on in silence. Peter thought of Placidus. He thought of Liam. And he thought, with a sudden gasp of realisation, that his whole prayed-for, cherished, unexpectedly lucky chance of a career in the Navy was at stake. If he could not reach Queenstown in time to sail on the transport in which he was ordered to sail, everything would be lost. He knew little about the Navy, but he did know that a midshipman's appointment was made by a captain to the ship he commanded—to that ship and none other. He knew that it was not a general commission, but a particular and a revocable appointment: if the *Centurion* sailed without him, he would no longer be a midshipman, and he would no longer have any way into the career that he longed for.

There was a sudden, strangely unexpected thrumming of feet behind, and a man passed them, running with a steady, high-paced gait: he was dressed in a yellow-and-scarlet livery, and he carried a long, silver-headed cane.

'Good day, Thomas,' cried FitzGerald, as he went by, and

'Good day, Mr FitzGerald, sir,' called the man, waving his hat but never wavering in his stride. Peter was too desperately worried to take much notice, yet he did say, 'What's that?'

'It is Culmore's running footman: and I think it means good news.'

'What is a running footman?'

'Why, a footman that runs. That stands to reason. But come, let us not break our winds racing along like this. Sit down on this stone.'

'No, no, no,' cried Peter. 'I will not. How can we sit down when every minute counts for so much?'

'Why, what a fret you are in,' said FitzGerald coolly, sitting down and resting his feet. 'But listen to me for a minute. That was Culmore's running footman: he runs in front of his master's coach. So that means Culmore will be along in a little while. If I cannot borrow twenty guineas from Culmore, you may call me an ass—after all, I know how well he did at the races. Therefore I can see no point at all in blazing along the road and making it more difficult for our salvation to catch up with us.'

Peter hesitated. He was extremely unwilling to stop for a moment: but FitzGerald seemed so calmly certain that he was almost convinced. He hesitated. Then Sean said, 'There's the dust of a coach far behind us, so there is,' and Peter sat down.

Now he saw the dust himself, white, a slowly-travelling plume. He took off his battered shoes and cooled his feet in the grass. They were all very tired, and they sat quite still.

The coach rolled up. On the box the coachman gathered the reins in one hand while he disentangled a horse-pistol: behind, one of the footmen had a blunderbuss ready. A face with its wig awry peered out of the window.

'Good day, my lord,' said FitzGerald, advancing and making a beautiful bow.

'Why, upon my soul, it's young FitzGerald,' said Lord Culmore. 'What are you doing in this horrible place?'

'I am airing my friends,' replied FitzGerald. 'May I name Mr Palafox, of the Navy—Lord Culmore.'

'Your servant, my lord,' said Peter, making a leg.

'Your most humble, sir,' said Lord Culmore, bowing to the sill. 'How is your father?' he asked FitzGerald, coming out of the coach. 'I hope you left him well?'

'Not as well as I could wish, but low in spirits. He was talking of hanging himself on the Boyne apple-tree.'

'That is the old crooked one, ain't it, in front of the house?'

'Yes, that's the tree.'

'Then it will not serve his purpose. I would lay seven to one that the branches would break under fifteen stone. Ten to one,' he added, after consideration.

'No takers, my lord,' said FitzGerald, 'for I am of your opinion.'

'Where are your horses?' asked Culmore, looking about. 'Do you still ride that chestnut?'

'Oh, we left them—we left them some way behind,' said FitzGerald, 'and as for the mare, I let Stafford have her at last. Johnny Stafford.'

'I know him' said Culmore, smiling. 'I won five and twenty guineas from him a month ago. He thought some young fellow among his tenants could run against my Thomas. Ha, flesh. I would back my Thomas against any two of them—any two men in the kingdom. But can I take you with me? Can I be of any service? Command me. There is all the room in the world in the coach.'

'You are very kind, my lord,' said FitzGerald in a low voice, 'and you can put me exceedingly in your debt if you wish . . .' They moved a little way along the road, Lord Culmore wearing a perturbed expression. Peter withdrew in the other direction, whispering fiercely to Sean, 'Don't stare, for all love, you ill-shaped great cow.'

'Well,' said FitzGerald, as the dust rose again behind the vanishing coach, 'now you may call me an ass if you wish.'

'Oh?' said Peter, closing his eyes.

'Yes. The sordid old screw would not part with better than ten.'

'Ten guineas? Hoo! Glory above,' cried Sean.

'Will you close your mouth now?' said Peter, with a great smile spreading in spite of all he could do to look sober and grave.

But Sean would not be quiet yet. He continued, 'Had I known his honour could lay a gold piece, sure I would have begged to run against that Thomas at even odds.'

'Why, and so you could, too,' said Peter, reflecting.

'Can he run?' asked FitzGerald.

'Can he run?' said Peter, dusting his hands. 'Can he run? He could run that poor stick-carrying creature into the earth and back again without drawing breath.'

'Is it true?' cried FitzGerald.

'Yes, it is,' said Peter, with staggering positiveness. 'And have I not seen him take up a hare in his hand, and the hare running on a hill the way hares go their fastest?'

'To think I have let such a match slip through my hands,' said FitzGerald, beating his forehead. 'Culmore would have laid a hundred—two hundred. And we might have gone to Cork in our own coaches. Oh, it is very hard to bear.'

'Still,' he said, after a silence, 'there is our next dinner for sure. Which is something.' And he laid the ten pieces in a row on the milestone.

They considered the disposal of the sum, reckoning up their expenses with anxious addition. But it became apparent that once their bills at the inn were paid there would not be enough left to unpawn both horses—FitzGerald had sold his outright.

'Then it must be Placidus,' said Peter, charmed with the certainty of redeeming the creature.

'But come,' said FitzGerald, 'did you not say that Liam's nag was a stout beast that could carry two?'

'Yes.'

'And this other one can't?'

'He could up to ten years ago, but truly he does not care for a pillion now.'

'Ten years ago? Good heavens, how old is he at all?'

'Oh, he was long past mark of mouth when I was a little boy,' said Peter. 'I suppose he must be rising twenty-five or so.'

'Oh,' said FitzGerald, and he muttered something in which the words 'knacker's yard' and 'museum' could just be distinguished.

'He is a remarkably fine horse for his age,' said Peter eagerly, 'and if you know how to ride him, and if he likes you, he can trot very well. You only have to take care not to bear on his withers, and to talk to him all the time, encouragingly, you know, and he will go on amazingly.'

'You have to talk to him all the time?'

'Yes. In Latin, of course. My father has always recited Virgil aloud as he rides about the parish, and Placidus is used to it. Then when my father goes to sleep, which he does sometimes, Placidus stops so that he will not fall off. So you have to keep talking, or he thinks it his duty to stop. Oh, and I had almost forgot: when it is your turn to ride you must never menace him, or he bites you and then lies down. But apart from that and his bowl of bread and milk in the morning——'

'Bread and milk?'

'Yes,' said Peter earnestly. 'Just sufficiently warm; not hot, you understand, but just loo-warm. He cannot digest oats or hay in the morning. Nor beans.'

'I see,' said FitzGerald. 'No beans in the morning.'

'Just so,' said Peter, with an approving nod.

'You're not codding?'

'No,' said Peter. 'Whatever makes you think that?'

'Do you seriously propose that we ride and tie—for if he cannot carry two there's no help for it—that we ride and tie through the length of Ireland, alternately walking and then riding on this remarkable animal, perched up on its rump and haranguing the countryside in Latin?'

'You do not have to harangue—just quietly reciting will do.'

'Do you know how long my Latin would last?'

'Oh, as for that, I have found the declensions will serve to fill in the gaps. I believe that he does not really distinguish the odds.'

'But seriously,' said FitzGerald, 'to go along perched up on an antediluvian screw—oh come, let us get a guinea for his hoofs and hide and buy something a little less antique.'

'Sell Placidus!' cried Peter, 'Now it's you that are codding.'

'I take it,' said FitzGerald, after a thoughtful pause, 'that he is, as I may say, a kind of pet horse?'

'That's the way of it,' said Peter firmly.

'Well, in that case,' said FitzGerald, 'I suppose there is nothing to be said. Only I pray to Heaven that no one I know ever sees me.'

'Upon my word, I do not see why,' said Peter warmly. 'He was by Bucephalus out of a country mare, and Bucephalus' sire was the Godolphin Barb.'

'That entirely alters the whole affair,' said FitzGerald, 'and I should be proud to walk by his side. With the Barb's own grandson as our mount, we shall cross the country like a couple of kings, if rather more slowly.'

3

IN THE LATE AFTERNOON OF THE EIGHTEENTH DAY OF THE month two foot-sore, thin, weary and travel-stained midshipmen limped hurriedly over the stones of Queenstown to the water where Sean held a boat.

'Where did you get it, Sean?' asked Peter, getting in.

'Sure I borrowed it—now, your honour, make haste, for she sails on the evening tide,' he said, heaving FitzGerald bodily in. He shoved off, set the sail, and in a moment they were scudding on the stiff breeze, and the noble city of Cork sped from them backwards.

'Sean,' said Peter, sitting in the sheets with the tiller under his knee and listening to the bitter roaring of a pair of natives on shore, 'I wish you may have borrowed it fairly.'

'The day was not seen on the face of the earth when I would be stealing a boat,' said Sean. 'But we being so pressed, the way she is sailing with this very tide, and they being wishful to delay us for their own profit, I said your honour would leave the boat hire with the boat. And the rightful fare is fourteen pence. Behind the island she is lying, the *Mary Rose*: will you go on to the other tack, so?'

'No. We'll lie a little longer on this,' said Peter, bracing himself against the heel of the boat as the wind laid her down and the water raced gurgling under the side. 'Now,' he said, having put her shaving round the stern of the wherry, 'now over—sit down, FitzGerald,' he cried.

'Well, upon my honour,' said FitzGerald, rubbing his head where the boom had rapped it, 'what strange things you do.'

Presently he sat up again, settled his hat upon his head, and gazed about. 'So this is the sea,' he observed. 'I say, there is a vast great deal of it.'

'No it an't,' said Peter. 'This is only the Cove of Cork. The brig lies behind the island there. The main sea is beyond.'

The next tack showed them the far side of the island, and Sean said, 'There she is, and her topsails are loosed.' As he spoke a thin white line of sail on the brig spread suddenly into a rectangle, bellying out in the wind and straightening as they sheeted home and hauled away.

'We shall be lucky if we catch her,' said Peter, edging the boat a little nearer the wind.

'Would it not be quicker if you went straight, rather than dodging about in this fashion?' suggested FitzGerald as they went about again.

'But the wind is straight from her to us,' said Peter. 'Sean, give her a hail as soon as you can.'

They were now coming up towards the brig's starboard quarter, sailing as near the wind as the boat would bear. 'We shall do it,' said Peter.

But as they came under the lee of the island the breeze grew lighter and full of flaws. The brig was gathering way and now the water between them was wider.

'Oh go on, go *on*,' urged FitzGerald, wringing his handkerchief between his hands.

Sean put up his hand, and his deep, sonorous hail boomed over the sea; but as if in answer to it there was a burst of white triangles as the brig's jibs were set and she moved faster away.

FitzGerald groaned. 'Never mind,' said Peter, glancing up at the sky, 'I'll follow her to England if need be, by the powers.'

'She's backing her topsail,' cried Sean. 'Hallelujah.'

The brig's foretopsail yard came round: the sail shivered and filled again. Her speed slackened, and as the boat cleared the island the wind took her true. In another three minutes they were alongside.

'There,' said Peter, as he laid the boat along, just kissing the brig, 'that's neat, though I say it myself. Up you go,' he said to FitzGerald, who was gaping at the chains of the brig. 'There,' he said, quickly guiding FitzGerald's hands and propelling him up the side, while Sean struck the sail and laid fourteen pence on the thwart.

'You Navy chaps are always cutting it fine,' said the mate of the brig as they came over the side. 'Now I suppose some poor unfortunate soul will have to take your shallop in tow. Vast heaving, you lubbock,' he roared in parentheses, and added, 'The master is below in the cabin.'

The master of the *Mary Rose*—she was a victualler, chartered by the Admiralty, from Cork for Portsmouth—was no more pleased to see them than his mate, and he spoke sharply about almost missing the tide while some folks disported themselves on shore; but they were both so utterly triumphant and enchanted with having accomplished their care-ridden journey, at having caught up with the brig when all seemed lost at the very last moment, and with being aboard a vessel that would carry them all the rest of the way without any planning or contriving on their part at all, that they were wonderfully cordial to the master; who afterwards confided to the mate his private opinion that 'the midshipmen came aboard as boiled as a pair of owls'—in which he betrayed a grievous lack of discernment.

'This is very fine,' said FitzGerald, with enthusiastic approval, as they stood on deck watching the green hills recede. The steady north-easter sang in the brig's taut rigging; the sun came out, low under the clouds, lighting the green of the land with an extraordinary radiance. Somewhere behind the haze that hung over Cork, Placidus would be moving composedly along the road to Mallow, carrying Liam away to the north and the west, all over the green country that they might never see again: the thought came into Peter's head in spite of his excitement; and the same thought was clearly with Sean, who looked long and gravely towards the shore, as so many of his countrymen have done. But FitzGerald, also like many other Irishmen leaving their country, was in tearing high spirits. 'I am wonderfully pleased with the sea,' he cried. 'It was a capital idea, writing to Cousin Wager. I am sure the Navy is far better than the Army in every way. Why, it will be like a boating picnic on the lough, without the troublesome business of going home in the evening. I say, this is famous, is it not, Palafox?' he said as the *Mary Rose* lifted to the send of a wave. The wind was blowing across and somewhat against the tide, and a little way out from the land was a line of rough water, chopped up on the invisible swell from the Atlantic: when they crossed Crosshaven, now a sprinkling of white on the loom of the land, the *Mary Rose* entered this zone of cross forces, and began to grow lively. In an inquisitive manner she pointed her bowsprit up to the sky, then brought it down to explore the green depths below, and her round bows went thump on the sea.

'This is famous,' repeated FitzGerald, staggering to keep his footing. 'Famous,' he said again, swallowing hard.

'Do you see that ship?' cried Peter. 'No, not that—that's a

ketch—there, right ahead. I believe she's a man-of-war.'

FitzGerald stared forward beyond the heaving bowsprit, which had now added a curious corkscrewing motion and a sideways lurch to the rest: he groaned, and covered his eyes with his hand.

'Palafox,' he said, 'I don't give a curse whether the thing is a man-of-war or not. Isn't it cold?' A little later he said, 'Palafox, I am feeling strangely unwell. We should never have eaten that pork at Blarney. Are you feeling unwell, Palafox?'

'Never better,' said Peter, still trying to make out the ship.

'Then perhaps it is the motion of the vessel,' said Fitz-Gerald, gripping the rail with both hands and closing his eyes. Peter looked at him quickly, and saw that his face had turned a very light green.

'Come over to this side,' he said, taking FitzGerald by the elbow, 'then you can be sick to the lee.'

'I will *not* be sick,' said FitzGerald, without opening his eyes: he pulled his arm away pettishly and shivered all over. 'And I beg you will not say such disgusting things. Oh.'

'You will feel better directly if you are,' said Peter. 'Some people swallow a piece of fat pork on a string. Come, make an effort.'

'No,' said FitzGerald, feebly striking out sideways.

Peter and Sean looked at him with easy compassion. *They* were not transfixed with perishing cold; *their* brains and eyes were not heaving; *their* mouths were not unnaturally watering; *they* did not wish the world would come to an end, nor that they could instantly die: indeed, they were having a most enjoyable time—were healthy and disgustingly cheerful.

'Oh,' said FitzGerald. He could say no more: Sean plucked him from the rail, to which he clung as the only solid thing in a dissolving universe, and half carried him, half led him below, where Peter stuffed him into a bunk, too far reduced even to curse them, and covered him with blankets.

The wind began to get up in the night and backed round into the west; it brought rain with it, and the next day Peter and Sean, in borrowed tarpaulins, kept the glistening deck to watch the cruel coast of Cornwall drift by in the late afternoon. From time to time they went down to comfort Fitz-Gerald as he lay, utterly void and longing for the death that he saw approaching, but at all too slow a pace. There was nothing to be done for him, however. He would take nothing; and if ever he could be roused to speak, it was only to say, 'Palafox, you said fat. You should never have said fat—oh.' Sometimes he said that he almost hoped he might live to have Peter's blood for it: at other times he said he forgave him, and wished to be remembered at home.

On Thursday the wind, as if it had been specially ordered, shifted into the south-west and south: they sailed gently up the Channel on a milk-and-water sea that rippled playfully in the sun, the innocent element; on either side there sailed in company with them a great number of vessels, near and far; and as the sweet evening gathered in the western sky, Fitz-Gerald appeared on deck in time to see five ships of the line with two attendant frigates and a sloop of war pass within a cable's length, close hauled on the wind and in a formation as precise as a regiment of foot-guards on parade. With their towering height of gleaming canvas—their royals were set—and with their long sides exactly chequered with gun-ports, they gave an instant impression of immense strength and majesty, a moving and exhilarating feeling that made Peter wish to cheer. FitzGerald was moved too; a tinge of colour came into his face and some animation to his extinguished eyes.

'It would almost be worth while going to sea to be aboard one of those things,' he said.

'Hullo,' cried Peter, turning round. 'How are you?'

'Thank you, the worst is over.'

'It took you pretty badly,' said Peter, with a grin; 'you should have tried—you should have tried my recipe. But how do you mean, it would *almost* be worth while?'

'Palafox,' said FitzGerald earnestly, 'you do not seriously suppose, do you, that once I have got my feet on dry ground, any mortal persuasion will ever get them off it? If you do, you are mistaken; for the minute I leave this ship—or ketch or brig or whatever you choose to call the horrible machine—nothing, *nothing* will induce me to get on to it again, nor any other floating inferno. No: my talents lie in another direction, I find.'

'I am very sorry for it,' said Peter. 'But you know, it is never so bad again. Have you eaten anything yet?'

'No,' said FitzGerald, 'and I do not believe that I ever shall eat again.'

'That is a pity,' said Peter, 'for I passed by the galley just now and I saw the cook making a prodigious broth, with a hen in it. Indeed, there's the steward now. Will you not come down and watch us eat, at least? The smell alone would revive a dying man.'

FitzGerald hesitated, allowed himself to be persuaded—would just peck at the soup to be companionable—went down, begged the master of the *Mary Rose* would excuse him, had been much indisposed of late, on account of over-indulgence in pork at Blarney—ate soup, ate more soup, attacked venison pasty—pasty excellent, sea-air capital for giving an appetite—demolished a raised pie—ate solomon gundy, ate lemon posset, ate cheese, ate more cheese—varieties of cheese discussed, all excellent in their kind—ate more cheese. And at the master's invitation he drank to his future lieutenant's commission in muddy port; he then voluntarily proposed Peter's appointment as master and commander, as post-captain, as rear-admiral of the blue, red and white; as vice-admiral and full admiral of the same squadrons; and to himself as first sea-lord; he earnestly promised them his protection and countenance from the moment he reached that high office, and was removed, exceedingly talkative, to his bunk.

When Peter next came on deck darkness had fallen. His head was proof against the master's port, for he had been weaned on poteen that would burst into blue flame a yard from the fire—it was usual in Ballynasaggart to employ whiskey as the universal medicine, and indeed it was almost the only thing that kept the inhabitants alive under the perpetual drizzle of rain.

It was a profound darkness that filled the warm night—no moon, no stars but the riding-lights of other vessels near at hand. He stood against the rail, and the brig worked silently in on the tide past St Helen's; scarcely a ripple moved her, but the black water gleaming along the side in the reflection of the great stern-lantern showed that she was under way. There were lights on shore, scattered like a necklace broken, and lights at sea, moving steadily to their unseen destinations: voices in the dark, mysterious in their invisibility, and once a ghostly form, pale whiteness reaching into the sky, swept by them, a man-of-war bound for the Jamaica station. He heard the order 'Hands to the braces' and a pattering of feet: then the ship was gone.

'Joe!' hailed the mate of the *Mary Rose*, shattering the enchantment.

'Ho!' answered a very loud voice from out of the night.

'Where's *Centurion* lying?'

'How come you're so soon?' countered the unseen Joe. 'We did not look for to see you this tide.'

'Is she at St Helen's yet?'

'Nor this week neither,' said Joe, apparently right under their stern.

'Joe!' hailed the master.

'Ho!' replied the voice, which had secretly moved quite round the brig.

'Spit-ed,' said Joe, sulkily; and was heard no more.

'She's lying at Spithead,' interpreted the master, 'and that being so, young gentlemen, you had best lie aboard tonight and take a pair of oars over in the morning, after a good breakfast—which you won't see many more of them.'

'That is very kind of you, sir,' said Peter.

'Which it is agreeable to my sentiments, sir,' said the master of the *Mary Rose*, with a profound inclination, 'to be of service to the gentlemen of the Navy.'

He left the rail, and Peter heard him recommend the man at the wheel to keep to the middle of the channel if he wished to retain his blazing head on his flaming shoulders. 'I had better prepare everything tonight,' thought Peter, and he went below. There he found Sean before him, brushing clothes as well as he could by the light of a small swinging lamp. A considerable heap of dried Irish mud showed the pitch of his zeal.

'Listen, Peter a gradh,' he whispered, with anxiety filling his voice. 'Your honour will never forget my petition? Sure you will keep it in mind?'

Peter's reply was lost in a sudden rumbling din that vibrated solemnly through the brig as they let go the anchor, but he nodded, and when it was over he said, 'I'll do all I can, Sean my dear, indeed I will: but I wish you had brought a paper of recommendation.'

The *Centurion*. His Majesty's ship *Centurion*: she lay with her yards across, trim, shining with cleanliness even under the grey sky of the morning, her decks a scene of intense activity; parties of seamen in canvas trousers hurried with buckets and mops; a half-company of red-coated Marines performed their exercise with a rhythmic stamping and crash to the beat of a drum.

'I say, Palafox,' said FitzGerald, who was first up the side, 'do you see that——'

'You, sir,' cried an angry voice behind them; 'you there! Who the devil are you?' It was the officer of the watch, who knew very well who they were, but who nevertheless stared down upon them with a fierce and disciplinary eye. 'What is your business? What do you mean by wandering about his Majesty's ship like a pack of geese on a common?' These last words were addressed to Peter, who had unhappily made three paces in the wrong direction.

'I was looking for Mr Walter,' he replied in a faltering voice.

'Roaming up and down the ship like a parcel of apes,' continued the officer of the watch. 'Get off this ship directly, and come back and report yourself to me in a proper manner. And salute the quarter-deck when you come aboard, do you hear?'

FitzGerald was scarlet with anger: he took a hasty step

forward as the officer turned, but Peter seized him by the arm and pulled him away. 'Don't be an ass,' he hissed, dragging him to the side. 'You can cut his throat later.'

They vanished and then reappeared. Peter took off his hat as he set foot on the deck and advanced towards the officer of the watch, who returned his salute.

'My name is Palafox, sir,' he said.

'Reporting for duty,' prompted the officer.

'Reporting for duty,' said Peter.

'Mr Palafox,' said the officer, holding out his hand, 'I am happy to welcome you aboard.'

FitzGerald in his turn was made welcome to the *Centurion*, and the officer said, 'Have you your dunnage with you? Your sea-chests,' he added, seeing their blank expressions. 'Those are your things, are they?' he asked, looking beyond them to where Sean stood with FitzGerald's portmanteau on his shoulder and a little leather parcel that belonged to Peter. 'Those are your things, eh? You have left your sea-chests ashore? Unwise. Never part with your chest—ordered to sea in five minutes—never see it again. Jennings, take the dunnage and show the gentlemen their quarters. Master-at-arms, seize that man. Pin him. Collar him before he's over the side. He has not got a certificate, has he?' he asked Peter, who stood there appalled at the sight of poor Sean immovably wedged in the grasp of two powerful sailors and a Marine.

'I am sure my father would have given him one,' said Peter, 'and I assure you, sir, he bears the best character of anyone in our parish.'

'Your servant, is he? Well, I'm sorry for it,' said Mr Saumarez, with his eyes gleaming with greed; 'but it's all one, you know.'

'Oh sir,' cried Peter, 'I can vouch for him, upon my word I can. I was going to beg your interest with Mr Anson to have him admitted to the ship. He is a first-rate seaman, and he is very eager to serve in the fleet. If a certificate is necessary, I will write home at once.'

For a moment Mr Saumarez appeared to suspect that Peter

might be presuming to make game of him, and bent a very ominous look upon him; but his brow cleared, and he said, 'Very well, Mr Palafox. I believe I can assure you that your request will be granted. Master-at-arms, take the man below. Mr Dennis will read him in.'

'Thank you, sir; I am extremely obliged,' said Peter, fervently shaking the officer's hand; and Sean, blessing his honour's magnanimous heart, hurried the wondering master-at-arms below while the sailors stood around gazing with wild surmise.

'What the devil,' cried Mr Saumarez, slowly recovering; 'is there no work to do in this ship? Mr Bowes, why are those hands standing about like a parcel of in-calf heifers? Mr Walsh, your party is at a standstill. Good heavens, this is not fiddlers' green. Has nobody ever seen an honest man ask to serve his country, as a privilege, in his Majesty's fleet?'

'No sir,' said an unfortunate gunner's mate, who conceived that these words were addressed to him. 'Only the officers, sir.'

'Hold your tongue, sir,' cried Mr Saumarez; 'and get on with your work, or by the living . . .'

'I wonder when the fellow is going to show us our quarters,' said FitzGerald, as he crouched under a beam in the half-darkness.

'I believe these *are* our quarters,' said Peter, uncertainly, feeling with his hand for something to sit on.

'Nonsense,' said FitzGerald. 'You could not decently mew up a cat in this horrible booth.'

'Beg parding, sir,' said Jennings, appearing again, 'but I can't find your sea-chests nowhere.'

'Never mind,' said FitzGerald, fishing out their last half-crown. 'There's for your trouble. Now just show us our quarters, will you?'

'Thankee, sir,' said Jennings, spitting on the coin, 'but I have shown you your quarters; no codding, I have. This here is the midshipmen's berth.'

'Oh,' said FitzGerald.

'Do you know if Mr Walter is aboard?' asked Peter. 'I should like to wait upon him, if he is.'

'Chapling, sir? Oh yes, sir, he's in his cabing. Shall I show you the way?'

'If you please.'

'Not been to sea before, sir?' asked Jennings, hurrying along.

'No,' said Peter.

'Which I thought not,' said Jennings, with a grin that reached to his ears, 'from the way you talked about your man's certificate.'

'Did I say something wrong?' asked Peter, stopping under a grating that let through the light of day.

'Well, you mistook of the lieutenant's meaning, if I may say so,' said Jennings. 'He meant a certificate, a paper of writing, to say as how your man was *exempt* from the service. And you meant a character to get him *into* the service. Hor, hor,' laughed Jennings, leaning against a standard in honest mirth. 'Lord bless your innocence, there's the hottest press out in twenty year—not a officer aboard but Mr Saumarez and the fifth and the chapling—all the rest is out with gangs as far as Lyme and Seaford—and you begging and pleading to have him took aboard. Oh, hor hor hor hor!'

'Oh,' said Peter, not very pleased at being thought innocent, 'I see.'

'All what we've got from the bridewells and gaols is shut up in the orlop in case they escapes—tinkers and mumpers and half-wits, not a seaman to be had for love or money, and the ship wanting of two hundred, and them all running to the inland counties for fear of the press, and hiding in barns. Oh, hor hor hor!'

'Well, that will do,' said Peter, quite sharply, and without more than a muffled heave Jennings brought him to the chaplain's cabin.

'Good morning, sir,' said Peter into the gloom. 'I am Peter Palafox, and I have brought you a letter from my father.'

'I am very happy to see you,' said Mr Walter, and Peter had a vague impression of a tall figure rising among the shadows: he heard a thud as Mr Walter struck his head, not on the ceiling, for ships do not possess them, or at least not where you can hit your head on them getting up, but on the place which a mere landsman would call by that name. He also heard something that sounded wonderfully like a stifled oath, and then Mr Walter said, 'I always hit my head on that—on that disagreeable spot. But come, Mr Palafox, or Peter, as I think I may venture to call you, for I knew you before you were born, let us find somewhere where you can sit down and make yourself comfortable. How is my excellent old friend, and your mother? No, you cannot move that. That is a gun. Here, shift the papers from my sea-chest, and sit on that. It is rather dark in here,' he added.

'So you have arrived from Ireland,' he said as they settled down.

'Yes, sir,' replied Peter, handing him his father's letter.

'Thank you. You will forgive me if I open it at once: it is not every day that I have the pleasure—you see, one can read quite well by holding the paper so, where the light comes in through the crack. When the port is open you can see the whole extent of my domain, of course—remarkably spacious. One might almost think oneself in a hundred-gun ship: though naturally my stores take up a good deal of space. But, however, they are doing something to the port, and it has to remain closed. Ha, ha. Your father remembers our days at the university. He reminds me of our avidity for sausages—for maids of honour. Ha, ha. Sad dogs we were. Roaring blades. But we were not in orders then.'

He read on in silence, bent sideways to catch the single shaft of light; and Peter, his eyes growing used to the dimness, made out the shape of a table, two chairs and a hanging canvas cot piled with books; these and the chaplain would have filled the cabin too full for comfort, but in addition there was an immense gun, like a couchant elephant, right in the middle, and the sea-chest, as big as a coffin, upon which he was sitting, embowered in more papers and books. It already called for uncommon agility to move from one side of the cabin to the other, and Peter tried to imagine what it would be like in a hollow sea. 'And how,' he wondered, 'do they ever come at the gun to fire it?'

'Well, well, well,' said the chaplain, folding the letter and putting it aside with an affectionate pat. 'It seems no more than yesterday that we two walked the High, discussing the Church and State. Dear me.'

'Sir,' said Peter, nervously beginning the speech that he had prepared, 'I have to thank you most heartily for your great goodness in obtaining——'

'Not a word,' cried the chaplain, removing his wig and waving it with a courtly air, 'not a word, I beg. Your father has already expressed himself in the most handsome way. I only hope that you and the service will suit. The Navy is not always what might be called a bed of roses. There is hard lying, short rations sometimes, and always the perils of the sea.

> Illi robur et aes triplex
> circa pectus erat, qui fragilem truci
> commisit pelago ratem
> primus—

I am sure that your father's son is familiar with Horace?'

Peter cautiously said that he was pretty well acquainted with the gentleman, but he did not commit himself any further.

'Now,' said Mr Walter, 'I dare say that you have a good many questions to ask?'

'If you please, sir,' said Peter, 'first may I ask how they fire that gun, and then what a sea-chest is, and why do they keep asking me where mine is?'

'Why, in action,' said the chaplain, indicating the walls of the little room, 'they knock down these bulkheads. The cabins disappear and the whole deck is one long open space, so that they can come at the guns and run them out of the ports.

That is called clearing for action. As for your sea-chest, that is the chest that contains your belongings, your slops, your tarpaulin jackets, your nautical instruments, your uniforms—in short everything but your personal stores, which you can entrust to the attendant on the midshipmen's berth, a very good honest fellow named Jennings.'

'Uniforms, sir?' cried Peter with extreme dismay. 'But we thought the Navy called for no uniform. The King's cockade in your hat, sure, but no uniform at all: and at home we all said how fortunate it was I was going into the sea-service, for my father could never have set me up in the Army, regimentals costing the teeth from your head—being so very dear, sir.'

'Why, to be sure that was the case until these last years,' said Mr Walter. 'But now most officers wear the same clothes as the gentleman who received you—you took notice of him, no doubt, in his blue laced coat and his white breeches. All the officers in our squadron wear the same, and many commanders insist upon their young gentlemen being so dressed. Mr Anson is most particular. But it is the other things in your sea-chest that are even more important: your navigating instruments, quadrant, parallel rulers, scales and all the rest; your linen; your bedding . . . Our first lieutenant is rigorous in these matters, and only the other day, only on Thursday I say, he turned away a wretched boy who had the effrontery to appear without so much as his Necessary Tables, to say nothing of a proper supply of other things. Mr Saumarez said, very rightly, that on a long voyage a youngster's welfare depended essentially upon his equipment—he must be provided with clothes for the tropics and for the high latitudes, quite apart from his weapons and in course stores and money for his mess and for the schoolmaster. That is what we mean by the term sea-chest: the sum total of a young gentleman's equipment, as well as the brass-bound wooden envelope that contains it.'

'Sir,' said Peter in a low voice, 'I have no sea-chest.'

'No sea-chest?' cried the chaplain.

'No sea-chest, sir; nor anything in it at all.'

'Dear me, dear me,' said the chaplain in a shocked undertone, gazing at him in the dim light. 'No sea-chest whatsoever?'

'None whatsoever, sir, upon my honour. Only a little small kilageen, as we say, made of leather. From Seamus Joyce's old cow, that died.'

'And pray what is in it?'

'Six shirts and some stockings, sir. And a spare coat, with my handkerchiefs laid in the one pocket and my Bible in the other.'

'A quadrant, perhaps?'

'Never the ghost of a quadrant, sir. We were sure—indeed my mother was positive—that the service provided these things . . .'

'My poor boy, my poor boy,' said the chaplain, shaking his head sadly. 'What a great way off you do live, to be sure. Six shirts for a voyage that may last two or three years? Oh dear me, dear me. Do you know where we are bound?'

'Yes, sir. We are bound for the Great South Sea, there to cruise upon the Spaniards, and confound 'em unawares.'

'You know that? Good heavens above! It is supposed to be a secret. Who told you?'

'Oh,' said Peter vaguely, for his mind was too much taken up with the dreadful news to be much concerned with the question, 'oh, everybody said so, at home. Michael Noonan the excise man, Patrick Lynch the sow-gelder—everyone.'

'Even in that remote waste,' said the chaplain to himself. 'That is how State secrets are kept in this degenerate age. I must tell the Commodore. How long have the Spaniards been aware of the plan, I wonder?' He paused. 'However, we must get back to the matter in hand. So you have no sea-chest, Peter, I collect?'

'No sea-chest, sir,' said Peter again, looking so wan that even in this dim light the chaplain could make out his distress. They remained silent for some moments, Peter's heart dying within him—so near to his goal, the ship actually stirring under his feet at this minute, and then to be turned back—and Mr Walter's mind busily turning over the meagre resources of a lean, lean purse and an overloaded credit.

'Peter,' he said, 'you must know that unhappily I am not a rich man, and that my own provision for this great voyage has quite exhausted what wealth I had. I cannot tell what to do, upon my word. To equip you very modestly might cost as much as twenty pound . . .'

'Oh sir,' said Peter faintly. In Ballynasaggart twenty pounds kept the whole family for twelve months of the year.

'Twenty pound . . . Tell me, did your friends not give you somewhat to bear your charges—something for contingencies unforeseen in Ballynasaggart?'

'Yes, sir,' said Peter. 'My father gave me a purse of gold. Six broad pieces, sir, no less.'

'Why then,' cried Mr Walter, flinging out his hands in relief and knocking down a pile of books, 'why then, there you are! O what a relief to my mind this is! It is not enough, to be sure, but with some pinching and contriving and with the advice of my good friend the purser—a most experienced sea-provider—we may rig you out creditably enough to pass muster. So your good father gave you a fine round plump purse, bless him.'

'He did, sir,' said Peter, and he hesitated for a moment before adding, 'But it was all lost at the races.'

'Lost at the races?' said Mr Walter, in a wondering, dubious voice.

'Yes, sir. I grieve to say that at the races it was lost.'

'Lost at the races!' cried the chaplain, now flushed with anger. 'Do you presume to tell me that it was lost at the races? Profligate boy!' he cried, striking the table an ominous blow.

'Oh sir, by your leave . . .' began Peter.

'No, sir, not a word: no, no,' cried the angry chaplain. 'The brisk intemperance of youth may excuse much; but not this. You know the value of a gold piece to a clergyman with a living like your father's as well as I do: you know, or you should know, the self-denial and privation needed to put by a single half-guinea. To squander his substance in this manner is an example of heartlessness such as I have rarely encountered. I am disappointed in you, sir; I am profoundly displeased with your conduct; and I wish you good day.' Mr Walter was a man of high principle, opposed to violence, and he had meant the interview to end with these words. But his unprincipled right hand (much given to generous indignation) rose of its own volition, and swinging forward in a pure arc it struck Peter's left ear, knocking his head against the gun so briskly that the metal rang again; and Peter fell off his stool, quite amazed.

It took him some moments to collect his wits. In the meantime the chaplain picked him up, straightened his sprawling limbs and put him back on his stool; and Peter heard the words, 'Dear me, dear me . . . never should have done it . . . poor boy . . . temptation, no doubt . . . there, now . . . why, he looks but palely . . .'

'By your leave, sir,' cried Peter suddenly, 'it was not the betting. Oh sir, it was not the betting, but a cutpurse, a rapparee, an unlucky black thief of a pickpocket that did be stealing it in the crowd. Will I tell you the way it was, sir?'

'Do, my poor boy, do: for I fear I have done you an injustice,' said the chaplain, dusting Peter's face with his handkerchief. And Peter told him the way it was, in very great detail, right through Connaught and the greater part of Munster, through the chops of the Channel and to the very deck of the *Centurion* herself, that noble ship, ending with the heartfelt words, 'but never did I truly miss the purse until this moment, sir.'

'Oh dear, oh dear,' said the chaplain heavily, sadly. 'So you were robbed, and I have beaten you for being robbed. You must forgive me, Peter. But what is to be done? What are we to do? I am at a stand. I protest,' he said again, after a pause, 'that I am quite at a stand.'

At this moment there was a great rumbling groan, and the port opened upwards and outwards, letting in a blinding light and a blast of fresh sea air.

'Mind the ink-well!' cried the chaplain, as he and Peter darted about after the flying papers, 'and for the love of Heaven cling to my sermon.'

'Beg pardon, sir,' said a bearded face, upside down in the opening. 'We've just opened the port, like.'

In time everything was picked up, sorted, squared and made fast under heavy books. They sat, gasping and dazzled, gazing at one another through narrowed eyes; and all that Peter could see in Mr Walter's face was doubt and anxiety. 'I might,' said the chaplain at last, 'I might give you a letter to Mr Shovell. He hopes he may be given the command of a cutter, a hired cutter, for service in the Channel . . . but I don't know, I'm sure.'

He went on musing aloud in this way for some time, and Peter's gaze wandered to the brilliant sea-scape on the far side of the square gunport: he saw boats passing to and fro between the guardships and the squadron, and for a brief moment the whole of the foreground was filled with the bulk of an eight-and-twenty-gun frigate running before the wind, with studding-sails aloft and alow on either side. The brown faces on her quarterdeck were turned towards the *Centurion* and he could see them laughing as they looked up. She vanished, and his mind returned to Mr Walter's discourse: he found that the chaplain was explaining the various categories of 'young gentlemen', the King's Letter Boys, the volunteers, and those who appeared on the ship's books as captain's, lieutenant's and even boatswain's servants, but who in fact walked the quarterdeck like the other midshipmen; yet he was aware that Mr Walter was not really talking to any purpose. And as time went on he also became aware that Mr Walter was staring at him in a very curious way—staring with a fixed, unwavering gaze at his throat, sometimes half closing his eyes and sometimes leaning his head to one side. In the brilliant light that now filled the cabin there could be no possible doubt of his unwavering stare, nor of its direction. The explanation continued, somewhat at haphazard: the gaze grew even more intense. Peter began to feel uneasy, and at length he put his hand to his cravat to see whether it was undone, or whether perhaps it had dipped into the ink.

'Peter Palafox,' said the chaplain, 'pray reach me that

buckle.' And when he had it in his hand he leant back until he was in the sun, holding it to his eye in a very knowing and professional manner. 'So there you were wandering about Ireland,' he said, after a long considering pause and countless inspections of the buckle in different lights, 'wandering about like an Egyptian, I say, with an emerald pinned to your throat. A handsome emerald, though a little flawed, of course, and scratched: but a fine generous colour. At one time,' he went on, still peering deep into the stone, 'I taught English to a Dutch jewel-merchant. I loved to see his baubles, and perhaps he taught me more than I taught him. I must not call myself a phoenix—oh, no—but I can tell a true stone when I see one. Look, this is what we call the garden of an emerald—beautiful, is it not? Now if it were not for this unlucky hole bored at the edge—Indian work, for sure—it might fetch two or three hundred guineas. But even so, I am very much out if it is not worth a year of your father's living at the very least. How did you come by it?'

Peter, his heart's blood flowing again and a delightful tide of joy surging in his stomach, told him; and the tale was interrupted by the meaningless chuckles of happiness in its purest state.

The chaplain said, 'Your good old lady was right, I am sure. It must have come from some ship of the Spanish Armada— many were wrecked on your shores, as I understand. What a curious reflection, that it should have come from a galleon to fit you out to serve against that same contumelious nation. If you choose, I will turn this stone into a sea-chest, and a reasonable purse besides; for otherwise the merchants might be tempted to take advantage of your youth and inexperience; and we must never expose others to temptation, in case they should fall. But now I believe we must eat a piece of cake and drink a glass of Madeira, to welcome you aboard, and to repose our minds after their anxiety.'

Back in the midshipmen's berth, with his mind duly reposed, Peter found it empty except for a very large cat and a very small boy. FitzGerald had gone. The hatch was now open, and the very small boy sat on a locker, looking up it and singing, in a remarkably high-pitched soprano,

'The secret expedition ho
The secret expedition hee,'

over and over again. Peter stood, contemplating the pink-cheeked singer and wondering first where FitzGerald was and secondly how this child could have got aboard; and presently the song came to an end.

'Tell me, my boy,' said Peter kindly, 'have you seen . . .'

'Who the——do you think you are?' asked the child, with an unflinching stare.

'You should not use such words,' said Peter, quite shocked.

'And you should not use such an infernally impertinent form of address to your seniors,' piped the very small boy. 'I suppose you are one of the new horrors that the Admiralty in its wisdom has inflicted upon us. What the——do you mean by addressing me as your boy? Eh? Damn your impertinence,' and growing pinker with wrath the child went on. 'Five years seniority, and to be called "my boy" by something that has crept up out of the bilge when the cat was asleep. Rot me, by——, I've a month's mind to have you keel-hauled.'

'I am sorry,' said Peter, much taken aback. 'I was not aware.'

'In future you will address me as Mr Keppel,' said the child severely, and returned to his song.

Peter, to preserve his countenance, stroked the cat, a shabby animal, black where it had any hair, and dull blue where it was bald. The cat suffered this for a minute, lashing its tail; then with a low growl it seized his hand and bit it, like a dog.

Peter recoiled and bumped into a large, yellow-haired, florid, thick man, whose ordinarily good-humoured face was clouded with discontent.

'Nah then, cully,' said he, in a hoarse whisper, seeing Peter and the cat so closely joined; 'don't you tease that cat.'

'It's the cat won't let go, so it won't,' cried Peter, waving it in the air.

'Don't you go a-teasing no animals here, for I won't have it. And that's flat,' said the newcomer, detaching the cat with a powerful heave. 'Poor Puss,' he said, sitting down on a locker to comfort it. 'Pretty Agamemnon.'

'I was stroking it,' said Peter.

'You don't want to go around a-teasing of animals,' was the only reply. 'Puss. Poor old Ag. *Pretty* Ag.'

'Ransome,' said Keppel, 'did you have any luck?'

'No,' said Ransome. 'I took the gig's crew to a wedding at Fareham, thinking to snap up a few as they came out of the church. But the women set on us in the churchyard—knocked us about something cruel—while the men all got out of the vestry. Who's this been stowing all this stuff on my locker?' He looked crossly at FitzGerald's portmanteau, and after a moment he pushed it off with his foot.

'That is my portmanteau, sir,' said FitzGerald, who unfortunately appeared just as it fell, 'and I will thank you to pick it up.'

'Nah then, cully,' said Ransome, still in the same hoarse whisper, 'keep your hair on.'

'Another Teague, so help me,' said Keppel; 'the wretched island must have sunk at last.'

'You are an offensive boy,' said FitzGerald, 'but I imagine you do not know it. If that fellow is your servant, tell him to pick up my portmanteau.'

'How can you be such a blackguard?' cried Keppel, with real indignation.

'If you mean to check me with coming in through the hawsehole,' said Ransome, growing suddenly very red, 'I'll learn you good manners.'

'I do not understand your jargon,' said FitzGerald, 'but if you want a threshing, sure I'll help you to one.'

'That's right,' said Ransome, peeling off his coat.

They had equal courage: it was weight and skill that decided the matter. FitzGerald weighed ten stone to Ransome's fourteen; Ransome had great skill in boxing; FitzGerald had none, and in ten seconds he was flat on his back with the blood running fast from his nose. He gasped, took a deep breath and sprang to his feet. He kept upright for much longer this time, and hit Ransome one or two good blows before he went down. Peter propped him up against his knee and wiped his face. 'You can't go on,' he whispered; 'the fellow is twice your size.'

'Can't I?' said FitzGerald. 'Let me go.'

He got up, and with a ferocious rush he shot under Ransome's guard, smashing in one right-handed hook that jarred Ransome's head on his shoulders. Then he was down again; but with scarcely a pause he leapt up, hitting madly: for a second the blows followed fast, hard bare-fist blows like the sound of a mallet on wood. One of FitzGerald's got home, and Ransome with an instinctive reaction hit him really hard. The uppercut did not travel six inches, but it lifted FitzGerald a foot, with his chin in the air, and he fell as if he had been dropped from a steeple. He fell oddly crumpled, and he did not move.

'What is this appalling din?' snapped a voice behind Peter. 'Fighting like a lot of snivelling schoolboys? Who is this?'

'Mr FitzGerald, sir.'

'New midshipman? The Irish one?'

'Yes, sir.'

'I might have known it. Well, pour some water over him.'

'Aye-aye, sir.'

'We was playing,' said Ransome, with heavy invention.

'Playing? Then you—what is that infernal racket? Yes, Settle, what is it?'

'Beg pardon, sir, but some of the pressed men in the orlop has gone mad, talking foreign and carrying on horrible.'

'Did you put the Irishmen in separate bays, as I told you?'

'Yes, sir. But they got out,' shouted the quarter-master to make himself heard above the mounting volume of furious sound that welled through the grating.

'Mr Saumarez' compliments, sir,' said a ship's boy from the quarter-deck, 'and he would be glad of a little less noise.'

'My compliments to the first lieutenant, and it will be attended to directly.'

'The Commodore's compliments, sir,' said a second messenger, bumping into the first. 'The port-admiral's barge is coming alongside, and he would like to hear himself speak.'

'My duty to the Commodore,' said the harassed lieutenant, 'and I will see to it myself.'

'If you please, sir,' said Peter, 'I believe it is my servant. May I go down?'

'You'll hear from me, Settle,' said Mr Dennis, shaking his first distractedly. Then to Peter, 'Come on, if you can do anything.'

As they reached the orlop they entered an almost tangible hullaballoo; howls and curses in Irish shattered the heavy air, and in the gloom they could see a small band beleaguered in the aftermost bay.

'Connacht! Connacht!' came Sean's voice high above all, as he and four tall Connaughtmen fought off the attacks of a pack of men from Munster and Leinster, while a party from Ulster assaulted both sides indiscriminately.

'Sean, Sean, for the glory of God,' cried Peter in Irish, 'will you stop your murderous noise, and the Commodore asking are there savages in the heart of the ship and the Admiral no less himself advancing in splendour like a king to make us a compliment?'

At the sound of his voice and the tongue that he spoke they all turned to see, and he continued passionately, 'It is the fine figure we make now to the Saxons, we the most polished and elegant, most ancient of people. Where should the world look for an example if not to us? And the moon-calf Sean shaming us all in the face of the people, his soul to the devil.'

'Now listen,' said Sean, scratching the back of his leg and blushing under the blood that flowed from his forehead; but his explanation was lost in Irish cries of 'Shame,' and 'Ignorant peasant,' and 'Violent fellow that does be putting a mock on the nation'; and in the righteous peace that ensued Peter called him aside. 'What was the trouble?' he asked.

'It was some question about the birth of Saint Patrick,' said Sean. 'The Munstermen said—faith, I never heard what they said; but they were certainly wrong.'

'Let them say, let them say: and I tell you this, Sean—and listen, now—if once again you ever do this, I will cast you off and wipe out your name.' Pushing Sean crossly away, Peter said to Mr Dennis, 'Sir, I think the trouble is finished. It was a religious disagreement.'

'Good,' said the lieutenant, wiping his forehead. 'You speak the lingo, so tell them from me that the first man to mention a church, or *any* moral subject whatever, will be hanged and lose a month's pay. Where are those flaming Marines? Oh, here you are at last, Gordon. Now you go back to the cockpit,' he said, patting Peter's shoulder, 'and sit perfectly still. For if there is the least sound from there while the Admiral's aboard you will every one of you be disrated and finish the commission cleaning the heads.'

Peter made his way back and entered the berth as the Admiral was piped up the side. There were several other midshipmen now, and they were obviously discussing FitzGerald, for they stopped as Peter came in.

'This is the other Teague,' said Keppel.

'My name is not Teague,' cried Peter. He had had a trying day, and he was in no mood to be joked at.

'Be calm, Teague,' said another midshipman, and fell to whistling Lillibullero.

'Take it easy, Teague,' said another.

But Peter would not take it easy: he hesitated, trying to quell the wild indignation; but he failed; it possessed him, and with a furious shriek he hurled himself upon his country's oppressors.

4

'MY DEAR PETER,' SAID MR WALTER, 'I HAVE ASKED YOU TO come here because I think it my duty to your father to speak to you seriously. You are not making a good impression, neither you nor your friend.'

'I know it, sir,' answered Peter, hanging his head.

'You are very ignorant of the service, but at least you know that a midshipman's whole professional future depends on his captain's report?'

'Yes, sir.'

'Peter, are you quite sure that you are suited for the Navy? Mr Saumarez tells me that you and your friend know no more about the work of a ship than, as he says, a pair of female Barbary apes; and I am sorry to say that the master finds you stupid.'

'Sir, I am stupid with the master's questions about navigation: I try very hard, but I can't find out the answers. I never learnt the mathematics at home, not beyond the Rule of Three.'

'It is true,' said the chaplain, shaking his head. 'I did my best to help your poor father to some knowledge of Euclid, but it was labour lost; though as a Grecian he outpaced us all.'

'And as for knowing nothing about the sea,' cried Peter, red with the humiliating recollection; 'it is *not* fair, indeed it is not.'

'Quietly, quietly.'

'I beg pardon, but it is not. I can sail a boat with any of them and 'tis I can put a curragh through the surf at Ballynasaggart and it roaring as high as the church. Only I do not know the names of the things in English, so they think me a fool and a landsman.'

'Have you tried to improve your knowledge of the English sea terms?'

'Sure the Dear knows I have——'

'Say "Yes, sir".'

'Yes, sir. It was only yesterday FitzGerald and I were in the beakhead asking some of the men——'

'At the time of that distressing scene with the Commodore?' said Mr Walter, frowning, and Peter nodded.

'Tell me exactly what happened. I heard only the words on the quarter-deck.'

'Well, sir, we had been asking these men the names of the rigging and I had thought for some time that they were gammoning FitzGerald. One said, "And that is the mainbrace. Do you see how badly it wants splicing?"

' "Where?" says FitzGerald.

' "There," says another. "It needs a good splice, but we don't like to say it. The captain has let it slip out of his mind, and with the first puff of wind the mast will come down."

' "He would be very grateful for being reminded," says the first one, "but we daren't go aft, being only ratings, you see."

' "How very glad he would be," says another. "Why, it might be the saving of the ship." And before I could say anything FitzGerald was gone.'

'Yes,' said the chaplain, 'and with a bow—quite out of place—he said to the Commodore, "By your leave, sir, the men up at the sharp end of the boat consider that the mainbrace needs splicing." It was a very shocking piece of effrontery, and although the Commodore passed it off as being accountable to your friend's inexperience, I really thought Mr Saumarez would have him confined. I understand that Mr FitzGerald enjoys the highest protection; but if he thinks that that will allow him to take liberties with Mr Anson, he is wrong. Mr Anson is not the kind of man to be influenced by such a consideration for a moment. By the by, who were the men who led him to such a monstrous impertinence?'

'I could not say, sir, I am sure,' said Peter, with a glazed look coming over his face. 'All I remember is that they left the beakhead very suddenly when FitzGerald went aft.'

'Hm. Quite so,' said the chaplain. 'But now I am on the subject, my boy, I must tell you that this friendship of yours makes me very uneasy. As I take it, he borrowed an important share of the money I brought you?'

'Yes, sir; we went snacks. But he bore my charges all the way here. He would have done the same thing for me.'

'And then there was that very discreditable affair with Ransome.'

'Yes, sir,' said Peter uneasily.

'It appears that your friend still bears malice.' Peter was silent. 'And if that is the case, he is not playing a gentleman's part.'

Peter was still silent. He was keenly aware of the strong disapproval that surrounded them in the midshipmen's berth—a disapprobation that extended to him, because although he could not feel that FitzGerald was right, yet he could not possibly not take his part.

'I may have heard a distorted account,' said the chaplain, 'but from what I have gathered, he insulted Ransome with his birth and Ransome knocked him down. I would have done the same. And now he has not the good feeling to make his apology.'

'It was not quite like that, sir,' said Peter. 'He did truly think Ransome was a servant: I thought he was a seaman myself. We neither of us knew that midshipmen were so old and big. FitzGerald did not intend to insult him, and indeed afterwards he said he would have cut his tongue out rather than say it. He said he meant to express his regret, only it was so difficult. He said, "How can I go to the fellow and tell him I am sorry I mistook him for a servant or a common seaman when he has been one in fact—the apology would be worse than the offence." But since then the others have been so unpleasant that he has got on his high horse, and whatever I say only makes it worse.'

'It is bad blood. He has only to go to Ransome and candidly admit that he was wrong. Ransome is a very fine fellow: he behaved extremely well on the lower-deck: he is an excellent seaman and he has a courage that Homer would have mentioned with honour: Mr Anson made him his own coxswain, and then, to reward his merit, rated him midshipman. If I thought your friend had a tithe of Ransome's merit, I should feel very much happier for you, Peter. Life is not very pleasant for Ransome: there are many of his former shipmates aboard, and it is the nature of low minds to grudge at another's rise—I do not say that they do, mark you; but I believe he feels his position acutely, far more acutely than ever he need. Certainly there is not a gentleman aboard, not one in the squadron, who would have thrown his origin in his teeth, or who, having done so by inadvertence, would not have apologised in the most full and public manner. No, no. It is very bad, and by associating with Mr FitzGerald you are tarred with the same brush. Believe me, my boy, the Commodore is not a man to be trifled with. He is unceasingly engrossed with the business of preparing the squadron for sea; he has a thousand cares of which you can know nothing—you may have heard, however, of the criminal decision about the invalids?'

Peter nodded. The squadron was undermanned: seamen could not be had, nor soldiers for the military side, and it was said that Government intended to fill out the numbers with pensioners from the Royal Hospital at Chelsea.

'You have? Well, that is but one of a thousand matters that call for his instant attention. But for all that he knows that his prime duty as captain of the *Centurion* is the welfare of the ship and her company, and he is certainly informed of all that happens aboard. What kind of opinion will he have of you, Peter? Not only because of this unsuitable friendship, but because of the innumerable scrapes you have got yourself into from the moment you arrived. Do not think to shelter behind my frail protection. I am a very unimportant person here, although Mr Anson honours me with his friendship. But if I were a flag-officer and the Commodore's own brother, that would avail you nothing if he were to judge you unfit for the service. I put this to you very seriously, Peter; and I put it to you urgently, because at dinner yesterday he mentioned your name: I did not hear what he said; but he mentioned your name.'

Peter walked soberly away. He wanted to think: but in a ship filled with more than four hundred men, all of them active in one way or another, it is not easy to find a place for quiet meditation. He was wondering whether he might presume to go into the tops, or whether that might be a crime, when he heard his name. It was far off, and mixed with a jumble of sound, but one catches one's name very quickly. 'Mr Palafox. Pass the word for Mr Palafox.' Then another voice, a little nearer, and another. His name, shouted, followed him up the ship, growing vastly in sound, and he hurried aft to report himself. But before he reached the quarterdeck he ran into the Commodore's steward.

'Wait a minute, young gentleman,' said the steward. 'What's the hurry?'

'The Commodore has passed the word for me,' said Peter, trying to get by. 'I must run.'

'You can save your breath, sir,' said the steward, 'for I am on the same errand. The Commodore sends his compliments to Mr Palafox and would be glad of his company at dinner today: he regrets the short notice.'

'My compliments to—to the Commodore,' said Peter, suddenly ill with apprehension, for dinner was no distance away at all, 'and I shall be most happy.'

He dashed into the midshipmen's berth and forward to the odd, dark kind of cupboard against the jear-capstan casing where he and FitzGerald slung their hammocks. He flung off his coat and rummaged wildly among his possessions in the brass-bound sea-chest, found a clean shirt and his best new coat. He dressed with particular care, but it took longer than he thought, for in his haste he was clumsy, and he was still wrestling with a cross-grained buckle when he heard the ship's bell go 'One-two, one-two, one'. Certain that he must have miscounted he shouted into the berth, 'That was four bells, wasn't it?'

70

'Why?' asked a voice.

'I have to dine with the Commodore,' said Peter, forgetting their dislike in his hurry. He emerged, buttoning his coat.

'It was five bells. You will be late,' said Elliot coldly.

'Still, he can't go like that,' said Hope. 'You've forgotten your dirk and you've trailed your coat in the dust. Here, stand while I get it off you.'

Keppel fetched his dirk and Peter buckled it on while Hope brushed his back. It was kindly done, and although he had barely time to gasp out a thank you before he raced away aft, Peter felt a strong pleasure from it.

'They could have been wicked,' he thought: but this reflection was instantly effaced by the sight of the first lieutenant at the half-deck. Mr Saunders looked over him quickly. 'That will do,' he said, nodding. 'Come along.'

It was a defect in Peter's upbringing that he had rarely, almost never, been used to paying formal visits or to dining out; but it was an unavoidable defect, for not only were his parents too poor to entertain, but in the neighbourhood for fifteen miles around there was nobody to entertain. Lord Magher, who owned a vast tract of land that included Ballynasaggart and seven villages beside, had never even seen his Irish estate; his agent, a Scotch Presbyterian, had alienated the Reverend Mr Palafox by his rigid treatment of the tenants; the squireen of Connveagh was a disreputable creature, permanently drunk and of more than doubtful loyalty; and of the two livings that bounded the parish, one was held by a rich pluralist in Dublin and the other by a clergyman even poorer than Mr Palafox and with a family that outnumbered his by four. It is not to be wondered at, therefore, that at first Peter saw little of the noble stateroom, its gleaming cloth and silver, and the decanters glowing in the sun that came pouring through the great stern-gallery. He had a vague impression of being greeted by an expanse of buff waistcoat and a blue coat afire with gold, of being introduced to various people, and then he was sitting down before his plate and scalding his mouth cruelly with boiling soup.

But he neither dropped his spoon nor hurled his plate into

his lap, and in time he began to take more notice of his surroundings. At the head of the table sat Mr Anson: he was a broad, strongly-built man with a fine head, a Roman face accustomed to command: at the moment he was listening to an anecdote of Marlborough's wars with an expression of polite interest, but his face was tired, and a man who knew him well could have told that his mind was far away. The speaker, on the Commodore's right hand, was Colonel Cracherode, commanding the land forces: Peter had seen him before. There was another red coat farther down the table—a young officer of the Marines, who was as rigid with awe as Peter, but who, to keep himself in countenance, fiddled incessantly with the stem of his wine-glass and drank such a very large quantity that by the first remove his face was as red as his coat. Next to him was the captain of the *Wager*, one of the ships of the squadron, and opposite Peter one of the *Wager*'s midshipmen, Mr Byron. Mr Saunders, first lieutenant of the *Centurion*, sat at the farther end.

The Commodore had a French cook on board: the food was excellent—quite unlike the usual fare of midshipmen—and Peter was beginning to enjoy himself in a quiet way when his peace of mind was shattered by his captain's voice.

'Mr Palafox,' said the Commodore, 'a glass of wine with you.'

Peter bowed and drank to him: he neither choked nor spilt his wine, but now he felt that his security was gone—he might be spoken to and called upon to reply at any moment. His forebodings were right. His neighbour, a post-captain, turned to him and said, 'Palafox? I know that name. Yes. It was in the year '21 that Miss Dillon married a gentleman called Palafox, in spite of all that I could say. I was first of the Falkland then and thought no small beer of myself; but the parson carried away the prize.'

'That was my mother, sir,' cried Peter.

'Indeed? Indeed?' said the captain, looking at him with lively interest. 'Then when next you see her, pray mention my name with—what would be proper?—with my kindest regards, and tell your father that I still bear him an undying grudge. I trust they are both very well?'

'Thank you, sir, very well indeed.'

'And where do you live now? I seem to remember that your father had a living somewhere on the west coast. Bally——'

'Ballynasaggart.'

'That was the place. So he is still there. I know just where it is, although I could not precisely recall the name. Terrible great seas, and the current sets inshore round the headland. An ugly place to be caught on a lee-shore with a westerly gale and the tide making.'

'Is that by the Blaskets?' asked Captain Kidd of the *Wager*, across the table. 'I was wrecked there once.'

'No, far to the north,' said Peter's neighbour. 'Far to the north, with no Dingle Bay to run for. A much worse coast.'

'The Baskets are bad enough for me,' said Captain Kidd. 'The natives knocked us on the head one by one as we came ashore.'

'What do you say to that, young man?' asked Peter's neighbour.

'Why, sir,' said Peter, 'they are only wild men from Kerry. We call them firbolgs, sir.'

'Do you? I would tell you what we called them,' said Captain Kidd, 'if it were not for the respect I owe to the Commodore.'

'Are your fellows any better?' asked Peter's neighbour, with a wink.

'Yes, sir, they are,' said Peter. 'Only last autumn there was a brig on the reef by Maan Point, and we drove the boats out through the surf although it was breaking up the way it washed the cows off the top of the cliff.'

'How did you manage that?'

'Why, sir, we carried the curraghs about two miles to the cove that is sheltered a little, and so we launched them and brought off every man alive, although Michael Tomelty and Seamus Colman were drowned.'

'How many oars do they pull?'

'Eleven sir, counting the one at the back,' said Peter, who knew very well, having held it on that occasion.

'And you say they carried a ten-oared boat for more than a mile?'

'Yes, sir,' said Peter, with the uncomfortable feeling that he was not believed.

'They must be strangely built boats in your part of the world,' observed Mr Saunders.

'Yes, sir,' said Peter, looking down. It would not be right, he knew, to launch into a long explanation, particularly as the whole table was listening now: but it was hard to be set down as a wild teller of tales—and an unconvincing one at that. He ate a little more, but without much appetite, and presently the cloth was drawn.

The port went round; they drank the King, and after that Peter relapsed into a meditation; he sat upright, not touching the back of his chair, as trim, neat and silent as a midshipman should be in such august company, but his spirit was far away in the warm drifting rain of his own country, where the land falls sheer to the western sea.

'Wake up,' said his neighbour, and with a jerk Peter realised that he was being addressed.

'I was saying,' said the Commodore, smiling at him, 'that Mr Palafox will decide the question.' The thought of deciding any question at all froze Peter to the spine. 'Colonel Cracherode says that your boats are not made of wood: I maintain that they are.'

'Sir,' said Peter, 'we do have wooden ones, but they are made of skins entirely.' 'What's the merriment?' he thought angrily, as the table burst into a general laugh.

'You had better tell the Commodore how they are built,' said Mr Saunders.

'There is a frame, sir,' said Peter, 'of wood that will bend, and that we tie together: then we sew bull skins to that for the very best boats, and dress them with the oil from the sharks that we catch.'

'And you put to sea in those?' asked Captain Kidd.

74

'Yes, sir,' said Peter, wonderingly; for to him it was an everyday occurrence.

'In those seas,' said the Commodore, 'it must be a very fine apprenticeship for those that survive.'

'But sir,' said Peter, made uncommonly bold by the Commodore's affability, 'there is the disadvantage that we call the things by Irish names; and although a man may be able to work one of our boats through the sea and it standing straight up to the sky, he sounds but a sad looby in a man-of-war when he calls the mast the tree, as we do at home.'

'Never mind,' said the Commodore. 'When I first went to sea I could not make out why the half-deck was so small compared with the quarter-deck. It will all come in time, if you have a seaman's right resolution. By Heaven,' he said, breaking off, 'I wish we had a few score of your villagers here. Kidd, have you heard of the shabby trick the guardship played on poor Legge, after he had been promised ten able seamen?'

The conversation drifted away to the manifold difficulties of manning the fleet, and Peter spoke no more; but he was very much happier than he had been, and when dinner was over he went on deck with a much lighter heart.

'Mr Palafox,' said the first lieutenant, looking upon him with an unwontedly favourable eye, 'you may go with Mr Keppel in the cutter: he is taking a party up the coast to see if he can press a few men. Look lively now, and tell them not to hang too much cloth on the tree,' he added, with a curiously human smile.

The cutter was alongside, still hooked on in the chains, and Peter dropped down as the boat reached the top of a wave.

'Mr Saunders said I was to come,' he said.

'I see,' said Keppel, with chilling indifference. 'Give way,' he ordered, and the boat pulled away into the eye of the wind.

Half-way to the shore they passed the liberty boat, and in the sheets Peter saw FitzGerald huddled in his boat-cloak. He looked ghastly pale; and he made no sign as they passed.

'Do you know what the other Teague has done?' said Hope to Keppel, meeting him on the Hard.

'No?'

'He has fought with an ensign of the 43rd and has a ball through his leg.'

5

'FORTY-FIVE DEGREES, OUGHT MINUTES NORTH, AND FIFTEEN degrees thirty-one minutes of West longitude,' said Keppel, making a decorative flourish under his answer.

'Mr Palafox?' asked the schoolmaster.

'I have not quite worked it out yet, sir,' said Peter, breathing heavily over his slate.

'Mr Hope?'

'It does not seem right, sir,' said Hope, looking doubtfully at his reckoning. 'I have 20° 1' South and 143° 50' East.'

'Mr Hope intends to discover the great southern continent,' said the master grimly. 'Now, sir,' he said, taking Peter's slate. He studied it for a while, then observed, 'And Mr Palafox would have us sailing through the northern suburbs of the city of London.' Mr Pascoe Thomas, the schoolmaster of the *Centurion*, was a patient man, but even his patience had limits, and now he burst out, 'Simpletons, loobies, dullards, jolterheads, witlings. Never have I had such a miserable set of midshipmen. Every year it gets worse. I thought the *Pembroke*'s midshipmen were humanity's lowest dregs, but I was wrong: this class beats them into a cocked hat for wilful, malignant stupidity. It is enough to make a man throw up the service. The ingenious Mr Hope calculates our position by a system of his own, unknown to the rest of mankind; and this depraved numbskull'—indicating Peter with his thumb—

'makes his by adding the date to the dead-reckoning and hoping for the best. Mr Palafox, let us have your definition of a rhumb-line, if you please.'

'A rhumb-line, sir, is——' quavered Peter, but before he could commit himself eight bells struck, and the watch was over. The master skimmed Peter's slate at his head and hurried below to refresh his spirits in the wardroom, where he had been invited to the feast the first lieutenant was giving to celebrate their true departure. They had sailed from St Helen's nearly a fortnight before, but they had had to convoy the merchantmen, and it was only now that the Turkey fleet had left them, a great mass of vessels, a hundred sail and more straggling down to Gibraltar: now the squadron was alone, free of the responsibility of guarding the slow, vague, wandering merchantmen; they stood away for the south-west with a fair wind, and the squadron was in high spirits. They made a brave show on the grey sea, five men-of-war in line ahead: the *Pearl*, of forty guns, the *Gloucester* fifty, the *Severn* fifty, the *Wager* of only twenty-eight, but looking more like a ship of the line, being an East-Indiaman bought by the Admiralty to carry stores and land artillery, and the *Centurion* of sixty, wearing the Commodore's broad pennant. In the middle of the line, but away to windward, sailed the *Tryal*, eight, a sloop of war; and to the lee the victuallers, the *Anna* and the *Industry*, two little chartered pinks that were intended to accompany the squadron part of the way, carrying stores until the men-of-war should have room for them. It was a brave show, and it was a formidable armament as well: some two thousand men were in the ships, more than two hundred guns, and deep down, far below in the carefully laden magazines, each ship carried ton upon ton of black, gritty sharp-smelling and immensely potent gunpowder, every ounce of which was meant to be used, as the Fighting Instructions said, to take, burn, sink or destroy the King's enemies—in this case the ships and the cities of the power of Spain.

A great deal lay behind them: for the senior officers, the almost interminable delays with the dock-yard and the Admiralty's changing plans, the insuperable difficulties of finding hands to man their ships, and the impotent exasperation of knowing that every single delay would make their voyage still more hazardous for the whole crew, the false starts that had begun early in August—contrary winds that forced them back again and again, six weeks of it—and then the tedious tiding down the Channel. But now it was all over at last: the sailors, after so much dockyard and harbour work, were in their element again; the landsmen had had time to grow used to the sea, and even to enjoy it—at least they were no longer very sick every time a wave went up or down. It is true that the squadron's black shame was still there, a piece of administrative bungling so grossly cruel that even the most hardened pressed men from the gaols had been revolted: the shocking rumour about the Chelsea pensioners had proved to be true. Five hundred of the poor old men had been ordered to Portsmouth, and although all those who were capable of shifting for themselves had immediately crept off towards home—not without the tacit consent of some of the officers—still two hundred and more had been brought forcibly aboard. Some of them were now sunning themselves in the waist of the ship, resting the old bones that had been battered as long ago as King William's wars: and it must be admitted that on this fine day at least the ancients were remarkably cheerful.

For Peter, too, a great deal lay behind. He was no longer lost anywhere in the ship; he could distinguish a crowfoot from a catshead without a moment's hesitation, and his long-splicing had won the bo'sun's praise. He now had a real place in the ship, whereas before he had been little more that a nuisance to people already busy to the point of distraction (the temper of the quarter-deck had grown comparatively mild since they had cleared the chops of the Channel, against what it had been at Spithead and St Helen's), and now he was assigned to a watch, a division—the foretop—and a station, where he was useful, if not of any great importance.

If it had not been for the navigation lessons, given both by Mr Thomas, the schoolmaster, and by the august Mr Blew, the *Centurion*'s master or chief navigating officer, which were a sore trial to Peter, and the uncomfortableness of the midshipmen's berth, he would have been ideally happy. It was not the physical discomfort that Peter minded, for he had been brought up hard, and of the two, his present circumstances were a little less Spartan than those at home, even in the article of food, for Mrs Palafox, though good and kind and an excellent hand at embroidery, had but the remotest notions of cooking, in which she closely resembled the succession of vague women who wandered in and out of the Rectory kitchen. So Peter did not mind the hard tack, the burgoo, the burnt offerings, the biscuits in which the weevils were already making their interesting little burrows, or the junk: but he did mind the feeling of unfriendliness, the knowledge that he was not accepted as one of the group. This was not a bullying, hazing mess, the kind that can make a new midshipman's life an unspeakable misery: it was not that kind of berth at all; for one thing, there were no very young fellows in it—and for another, the general tone was quite against that kind of thing. But he and FitzGerald had started off on the wrong foot, and Peter felt the results of it keenly.

FitzGerald himself was still unfit for duty. His wound was clean and the bone untouched, but the combination of three days of continual sea-sickness, the wound and the fever produced by the wound, had kept him below until they sank Rame Head behind them on the north-eastern horizon. Since then he had been assigned to the larboard watch—Peter belonged to the starboard—but he had been excused watchkeeping duty. At first, on getting up, he had appeared quite restored, his old self again. He had confided to Peter his intention of calling Ransome out when they next touched land. 'It is the only way of clearing the matter up,' he said. 'I obviously cannot batter him about like a footman in a pothouse brawl; but with a small-sword it is a different thing entirely.'

Peter knew that that was true. He was no mean hand with a sword himself (the Rectory of Ballynasaggart was the bloodiest abode of peace in the West, with Peter and his brothers lunging by day and night), but he had found himself an untaught bumpkin when he tried passes with FitzGerald.

'Still and all,' he said, 'it is the strange way of making an apology to a man, to be running a blade through his vitals.'

'I have no intention of apologising. I may have had once, but then I was wrong. Do you expect me to stomach a beating?'

Peter had shrugged, saying no more. He knew the trait only too well, the black inveteracy of his countrymen in a quarrel, right or wrong: it was the origin of so many of the feuds at home, some of which had lasted so long that the first cause was lost to all recollection.

But then had come FitzGerald's interview with the Commodore. This had had more effect on him than his duel, and he came away pale and silent. He never told Peter what had happened, but for days and days he stayed below, saying very little, sometimes poring over the manual of seamanship in a hopeless, bewildered fashion, and sometimes writing letters that he afterwards tore up.

'We may part company at Madeira, Peter,' he said once— they had grown very familiar during his illness, when Peter had spent all his watches below at his side. 'I don't know: but I am afraid we shall.'

However, that was days ago, and the sombre impression of it had left Peter's mind, which tended to be volatile and to enjoy things as they came. At this moment he was enjoying his escape from the master's inquisition, and he went forward to the fo'c'sle, where Sean awaited his appearance.

'I have been plotting the ship's position, Sean,' said Peter, importantly.

'Have you, your honour, dear? Sure and it's grand to be learned.'

'Yes,' said Peter.

'And I have been reasoning with the steward and the butcher,' said Sean.

'Ah now, Sean, I hope you have not hurt them,' cried Peter anxiously.

'I have not, Peter a gradh, though I may do so in time. Listen, your honour, while I tell you. I joined his Majesty's noble fleet to fight; I joined it for glory, did I not?'

'It's as true as the sky is above us,' said Peter, 'and the sea is below.'

'I did not join it to work,' said Sean, his eyes growing dark. 'Why would I join it to work? I have never liked work at all; nor does my father; nor did his Da, may he rest.'

'God have his soul,' said Peter.

'Nor did his father, nor his, who was the Mac Dermot's own harper and lived at Coolavin.'

'It is a family disliking: it runs in the blood.'

'It is very well for the women, I think,' said Sean. 'It keeps them busy and makes them attentive: but is it right for men? It is not.' He paused. 'I came for glory,' he said again.

He stood thinking for a while, and then he said, 'They put me to work. Well, so they may too, for a while, until we find out the enemy. But I will not mind the pigs. I will not mind any pig on the earth or below it, nor if it were the great pig of Mac Datho king of Leinster, the heathen, which three hundred cows fed for seven long years.'

'And do they want you to mind the pigs, Sean?'

'They do. "Mind the pigs, Sean, honey," they say. And the steward comes and he lays a great compliment on his speech how it is the way the pigs will love me and prosper; and the butcher says, "Sean, mind the pigs, for your dear country's honour." But I reply, "You verminous steward and butcher, I will *not* mind the pigs. Did I embark in this gorgeous imperial fleet to be minding of pigs, when I could have stayed in my own country to do the same thing, with the pigs running free on every hand and at large? Your souls to the devil, you butcher and steward." '

'But you will mind our little sow? Sure, you will never desert our own pig now, Sean?' cried Peter, referring to the

animal they had bought at Portsmouth together with two
likely young sheep, and which now led its thoughtful existence in the bowels of the *Centurion* with the rest of the
officers' livestock and all the hens that did not live in coops
on deck.

'I will not,' said Sean passionately. 'I will not tend a pig by
way of labour or work. As for the little sow, I will mind her
for love; but only in my watches below, when I may do what
I please. I will cherish her, for diversion and joy, by way of
delight; but never by way of labour nor work—still less in
compliment to the steward or butcher.'

'Mr Palafox. Pass the word for Mr Palafox: to the cabin.'
The cry came forward. Peter could hear it around him and
under his feet as it passed in the 'tween-decks.

'You'll tell the Commodore, your honour?' cried Sean after
him. 'You'll tell him that Sean will not mind the pigs?'

'Oh, Mr Palafox,' said the Commodore, 'I had meant to
have a word with you the other day—do not fidget, if you
please—but there was no suitable opportunity. Mr Walter
tells me that before you left home you had already heard of
the expedition.'

'Yes, sir.'

'What did you hear? Try to remember exactly what was
said, without adding anything that you may have learnt subsequently.'

'Aye-aye, sir.' Peter thought for a minute. 'The common
people thought that an English fleet was going to attack the
Spanish main,' he said, 'but the clever ones, like the gauger,
said there was an expedition fitting out to pass into the South
Sea by Cape Horn and attack Manilla; but it was all a great
secret.'

'A very great secret,' said the Commodore bitterly. 'Tell
me, what did the clever ones say about the ships of the squadron?'

'Sir, they told them as they are. But one of the preventive
men said the *Argyle* instead of the *Gloucester*.'

'There's close counsel for you,' cried the Commodore, hitting the table with his fist. 'Is there any more that you can tell me, Mr Palafox?'

'Yes, sir. They named Mr Anson as the commander, and it was thought that the squadron would round the Horn at mid-summer.'

'I see. I see. Was there any more, Mr Palafox?'

'Well, sir, it was only a rumour,' said Peter, hesitantly.

'Go on. If this rumour is as near the mark as the others, it will not be far out.'

'They said the Spaniards were sending away a squadron too.'

'Any particulars?'

'Yes, sir. But, sir,' said Peter, racking his memory, 'I cannot remember the Spanish names.'

'Do you remember anything of their number and force?'

'Six ships, sir, some said. But some said eight. They all said two ships of the line and the rest smaller. There was the name of the admiral too: something like Bissado.'

'Pizarro. Yes. A most capable, seamanlike officer. I am very glad to know it, if it is true. What is your estimate of the truth of this information, Mr Palafox? What is its probable source?'

'It comes from the owlers mostly, sir—the smugglers. There is always a Spanish lugger or a Portugee somewhere up or down the coast. And then, sir, there are many people with relatives in Spain, in the Spanish service, or studying to be priests at Salamanca, like Padeen Mc—like several I know: and news comes home.'

'Two ships of the line and four others at least: perhaps six,' said the Commodore, thoughtfully. 'Is there anything more you can tell me?'

Peter reflected, staring down at his feet. 'No, sir, I don't think there is,' he said.

'It is a great pity that you did not retain the names of the Spanish ships. However, perhaps they may come into your mind: if they do, write them down at once and bring them to me. That will do for the moment, Mr Palafox.'

'Aye-aye, sir,' said Peter, retiring.

83

'Did you tell him, your honour?' asked Sean, in the gang-way.

'Sure I told him every last thing that I knew,' said Peter absently; and vaguely he wondered why Sean should dart below with such speed, armed with such an unholy weapon to crush the butcher and steward.

Peter thought and thought through the forenoon watch, trying to relive the time when Patrick Leary, the best smuggler of Mallagh, had told him about the Spanish ships: but it all seemed so long ago now. He tried to remember the letters he had read for some of the villagers—letters from sailors and soldiers in the service of Spain (illegally, like the men of the Irish regiments in the French army; but taken very much as a matter of course at home) and from the seminarists far away. But the exact details would not come.

He thought hard during his watch below with no better result; and in the dog watch he tried to combine reflection with the exercise of his duties, which, the wind coming round contrary and fitful, required all his concentration. This earned him a very well-merited rebuke from Mr Brett, and five minutes later he was ordered to the mast-head to expiate the crime of sluggishness and incomprehension.

Mast-heading on a fine day, however, was little punishment to Peter: the tremendous cliffs—they fell fifteen hundred feet in one appalling drop, and he had been accustomed to walking about them, like a fly, from childhood—the cliffs at home made his present height seem trivial, and from his perch he phlegmatically gazed at the unbroken horizon.

'Goposco? Goposco? Poposco?' he murmured. High in the pure air, but still below him, the main-topgallant staysail made a huge triangle that swelled in a lovely curve under the thrust of the wind, blindingly white in the sun and almost black by contrast where the curved shadow of the fore-topsail fell upon it: peering down between the main-topgallant staysail and the main topsail he could see a good deal of the waist of the ship, far, far below, holystoned and gleaming, with small figures moving about down there.

'Giposco?' he said; but it did not sound right. 'That bowline is slack,' he observed, watching the windward leech of the foretopgallantsail beginning to shiver. A furious roar from the deck showed that Peter was not the only one to have seen it, and before the roar had died away the bowline tightened guiltily and the bridles plucked the trembling sail like so many fingers, taughtening the leech to take the wind.

The *Centurion* was sailing close-hauled with the larboard tacks aboard upon a breeze something south of east: she could have carried far more sail, but tacking as she was obliged to, and with no more than sixty really able seamen in a watch, the Commodore dared not set more, although every league lost meant a later and more stormy passage round the Horn.

Looking forward now, Peter saw the *Gloucester*, the next in line ahead, pay off half a point: the signal to tack must have run up the *Centurion's* mizzen, and looking windward to the *Tryal*, Peter saw the repeated signal flying; it was too far for him to make it out without a glass, but it could be nothing else.

'Hands to tack ship,' he heard below him, and the shrilling of the bo'suns' calls, as the *Centurion* paid off to gather the little extra way that should carry her through stays, and he saw the hands race aft.

He watched them with a kindly interest, as ignorant as a child unborn of his duty, which was to proceed with all possible despatch to his station. He watched them as they hauled the lee tacks, weather sheets and lee bowlines through the slack and stretched along the weather braces in readiness for putting her about.

'The *brace*, you crimson beast,' came the despairing bellow of a bo'sun's mate, and Peter guessed that some frantic landsman had clapped on to a lanyard, or perhaps a stay. Then he heard the cry 'Helm's a-lee!' and the *Centurion* began to come up into the wind. There was a steady succession of orders—'Fore-sheet—fore top-bowline—jib and staysail sheets let go—off tacks and sheets'—and the yards groaned in their slings as the braces brought them round, while the blocks

85

made their wooden shriek, leaping up and down under the unsteady pull of inexpert hands. The staysails shivered, the main and mizzen square sails lay becalmed by the headsails, her backed forecourse and foretopsail clapped untidily against the mast and shrouds, and now the whole array of canvas, so taut, orderly and beautiful a few minutes ago, was a mass of vaguely flapping, meaningless cloth, like Bridget Hanlon's washing-day magnified a hundred times. The *Centurion* was in stays.

Her impetus tended to carry her round, and her backed head-sails had something of the same turning effect; but at the same time they checked her advance, giving her stern-way, and it was possible that she might ignominiously fall off again, back on to the old tack. In his anxiety Peter stood on tiptoe, gauging her state by glancing now at the vane and now at the line of her deck: they were no longer exactly parallel—she was beyond the wind's eye. At the same moment he heard the strong voice of the officer of the watch cry 'Mainsail haul!' and again the main and mizen yards creaked round: her stern-way increased, and now came the word 'Let go and haul!' followed by a sharp and indeed somewhat tense 'Bear a hand there, damn your eyes.' Now the head yards came round, the hands at the braces singing out 'Hey yo, one for Jo; hey yo, hey yo, haul-o the blackamoor, haul-o the blackamoor,' and at the third *blackamoor* the jib and fore-staysail filled together, and she was round. Immediately afterwards the square sails filled and the hands were called to brace them up sharp and haul on the bowlines. The *Centurion* heeled to the wind again and gathered way on the starboard tack: Peter relaxed—it would have been dreadful for the *Centurion* to have disgraced herself in the sight of all the squadron. But still there was a flapping somewhere aft, and angry voices were to be heard desiring various works to be accomplished with very great rapidity: however, in spite of the united efforts of the quarter-deck, the warrant-officers, the petty-officers and the blue-water sailormen, it was a long while before the *Centurion* was moving under well-trimmed sails—a much longer time than seemed to please Mr Saunders, who had now joined Mr Brett on the quarter-deck, and whose displeasure could be heard a mile away. The ship was undercanvassed; but for all that she had twelve sails abroad—no, thirteen, Peter corrected himself, catching sight of a corner of the mizzen-topsail staysail, which had been set since his disgrace—and handling them with instant exactness was impossible when half the crew was still incapable of telling a halliard from a horse.

It was some time, then, before Peter resumed his familiar easy swoop. 'Suppose this is a roll of twenty degrees,' he said to himself, settling comfortably on the cross-trees, 'and suppose she is pitching five degrees, and suppose I am a hundred and fifty feet up, I ought to be able to work out how far I travel sideways and how far I go to and fro,' for some primitive notions of trigonometry were beginning to dawn. 'But,' he thought, having ruminated for some time, 'I should have to look at the tables.' He tried to make a rough estimate by facing aft and then leaning forwards to look as perpendicularly as he could between his feet as they dangled in space. In the middle of the roll the main-topgallant stay came just between his shoes; then he saw the main-topmast stay, the main-stay below it and below that the deck, sweeping steadily away to the right, then the ship's side, the fore-chains, and after that the sea—a great deal of sea. Deliberately the *Centurion* began her backward roll: the sea moved to the left, the side of the ship reappeared between his feet, the deck, the stays, in reverse order: the mast, and Peter with it, reached the vertex, passed it, and leant over to the lee, where his clear view was spoilt by the sails.

'Probably fifty feet,' he thought, 'with some to add, of course, on the leeward, seeing that the wind lays her over.' He gazed down for some time longer, for the pendulum-like motion had a curious fascination for one who was impervious to sea-sickness and the dread of height; and he might have gazed indefinitely if he had not been aroused by four bells and the piping up of the watch below. He leant out, seized a backstay, wrapped his legs round it and slid down without a stop, reaching the deck with something of a thump and with his stocking worn through where the rope had rubbed it. He talked with FitzGerald for a moment at the gangway, and then went below to attack their private ham, for he found that his airing had given him a violent appetite.

He was darning his stocking when FitzGerald came in. 'I say, Palafox,' he said, 'you're in a pretty high state of grease.'

'I have been eating the ham,' said Peter.

'Anyone would think that you had been sleeping with it,' said FitzGerald. 'What are those stripes in the fat?' he asked, absent-mindedly cutting himself a slice.

'That's where I drew my wool through it,' said Peter, 'to make it pass into the eye of the needle, you know.'

'You should have licked the wool,' said FitzGerald, stowing the ham away. 'I have just come from the surgeon.'

'Oh? What did he say?'

'He said I was fit for duty, which is what I have been telling him for days. Tomorrow I shall turn up with the larboard watch. But I tell you what it is, Palafox,' he said, sitting next to Peter and speaking in a low voice. 'Now that these fellows are so cursed unpleasant, upon my word I hate the idea of displaying my ignorance. I may not be here very much longer, but even so I should hate to be a laughing-stock for these oafs. I have been reading in this,' he said, tapping the manual that protruded from his pocket, 'and I would take it very kindly if you would hear me and tell me when I am wrong.'

'Of course,' said Peter, putting down his stocking directly.

'I'll begin at the front of the ship,' said FitzGerald. 'Just the essentials, you understand. What I want to avoid are the absurd, ludicrous errors like—like——'

'Like taking a sheet for a tack?' suggested Peter.

'Exactly so,' said FitzGerald. 'By the way, the sheet is the thing on the right and the tack the one on the left, isn't it?'

'Well, no. Not really,' said Peter. 'It depends on the wind.'

'But it is in this,' said FitzGerald, pointing to the diagram in his book. 'Look: it says sheet and tack.'

'Yes, but in this picture she is sailing with her larboard

tacks aboard. The wind is coming from that side, you see? Now when she goes about they brace round the yard, like this, and then the sheet is this side and the tack over there.'

'Oh.'

'Look, the sheet always goes aft.'

'Towards the flag at the blunt end?'

'That's right. It holds the after end of the sail tight round to the wind, when the wind comes sideways. And the tack holds the other end of the sail tight for'ard—the tack must go from the clew—the bottom corner—of the sail for'ard, you see?'

'Yes. Oh, I understand now. So whichever side the wind is blowing from, those tacks are aboard. Why didn't the dunderhead say so in the book? What a capital teacher you are, Peter: I puzzled over that for hours. Now what are these——'

Bailey, Preston and one of the master's mates came in: FitzGerald broke off, and a moment later he said, 'Shall we take a turn on deck?'

'Five minutes later Peter was saying, '. . . you can't see it properly from here. The foretop would be much better—let's go up there. An't you coming?' he asked, hanging in the ratlines.

'It scarcely seems worth while,' said FitzGerald.

'You do not mind the climb, do you?' asked Peter, looking down at him.

'What the devil do you mean?' said FitzGerald, with an anger that surprised Peter very much. 'Do you mean to imply that I am afraid? If you think you may presume, because you happen to be able to climb, you will find yourself mistaken. It is an accomplishment common to every monkey born, after all.'

Ignoring this civil reflection, Peter said, 'Come on, then,' and ran up the shrouds. When he had been in the top for some minutes he saw FitzGerald's face appear; he was pale, and he was breathing hard.

'You have come through the lubber-hole,' said Peter. FitzGerald made no reply for a while, but stood looking about him. The roll of the ship, exaggerated by the height, sent him staggering off his balance against a swivel-gun. He held on to it with both hands. 'What other way is there of getting here?' he asked. His face was expressionless; his tone unnatural: Peter wondered why on earth he had become suddenly so unfriendly.

'You ought to come up by the futtock-shrouds. These ones,' said Peter, walking to the edge of the broad platform and leaning over to point out the ropes that ran in a sharp diagonal from the edge to the upper part of the foremast. 'It is quite simple going down: you hang by your hands, wait for the roll and then bring your feet up and feel for the hold. Look,' he added, pointing up at the topmast, 'those are the futtocks, coming out from the ordinary shrouds at the top.'

'What is the point of hanging upside down,' said Fitz-Gerald, not looking up, 'when there is a square hole specially made to allow for a much safer passage? At this height it is madness.'

'Well, I cannot say, I am sure,' said Peter, but I know they make game of you if you use the lubber-hole. And as for the height, this is nothing. You should have been where I spent my watch, in the fore-to'garn crosstrees. Mr Brett mast-headed me. Shall we go up there? You get the view of the world, for seeing the headsails.'

'You are showing away, Palafox,' cried FitzGerald. 'You always do. Or at least, you always have since the Commodore took notice of you. With your futtocks and crosstrees. You are a confident scrub.'

'I am not,' cried Peter squeaking with indignation. 'And you asked me yourself to show you the things. You are a scrub yourself to say so, and so you are too.'

He swung himself over and shot down on deck in a fuming huff. There was a grain of truth in what FitzGerald said: Peter had played second fiddle on land, and now that they were at sea, where he was so much more at home than FitzGerald, he rather enjoyed the reversal, and he was somewhat free with his nautical terms; but it had nothing to do with his being distinguished by Mr Anson, and the manner of the accusation was unjust and wounding.

Peter went below in a rage, tripped over the cat and fell heavily on his nose.

'What a clumsy brute that Teague is,' said Preston.

'You will not call me Teague,' cried Peter, getting up and dusting himself.

'Why not, Teague?' asked Preston. 'And you ought not to blunder about, Teague, disturbing your seniors' rest. Why do you do it, Teague?'

By way of reply Peter drove his left fist into Preston's face and followed it with a right hook that flattened that young gentleman's ear against his skull.

'Ow,' said Preston, retreating, 'I'll pay you for that.'

'A mill,' cried Hope and Keppel simultaneously, swinging out of the hammocks in the dog-hole where they spent their watches below.

'Let him get his coat off,' said Hope.

'Let me go,' cried Peter, struggling madly.

'Come, mill in decently if you must,' said Hope, restraining him still. 'Here, I'll be your second.'

They stripped to their shirts while Keppel and the grinning Marine sentry cleared the ground.

'Now, young cock,' said Hope, 'go in and win.'

There was never any doubt of the outcome. Preston was only fooling: Peter was in furious earnest. He battered poor Preston to a standstill in two minutes, knocked him flat, and with a murderous shriek leapt upon him and hit him sharply in the stomach.

'Hey, wo, the man's down,' cried Keppel and they both tried to prise Peter off. But the notions of fair play current in England at that time had not yet penetrated to the West of Ireland, and Peter would not let go. He had Preston's throat, and he was determinedly throttling that unfortunate youth when Clowes, a young Marine officer who had come running at the sound of a fight, added his strength to that of Keppel and Hope, and wrenched Preston away.

'What a fellow you are,' he exclaimed. 'You should have retired to your corner.'

'T'hanam an Dial,' cried Peter, spitting in his eye, 'come on,

91

the three of you. Blackguards. I'll rip out your heart,' he cried, banging the redcoat's nose.

'Cool off, Teague,' began Keppel, but Peter was on him, and they went down in a flurry of arms and legs.

'Lash him into a hammock,' said Keppel, nursing his jaw while the others sat on Peter and he threshing about under their weight with tears of rage in his eyes.

'God help us, what a fury,' said Hope, 'Keppel, sit on his legs.'

'Is Mr Palafox here?' asked Mr Walter in the doorway.

'Yes, sir,' said Hope. 'I beg pardon for not getting up, but he will be the death of us if we cease to oppress him.'

'For shame,' cried the chaplain, seizing Hope by the collar, 'four against one? Where's the sport in that?' He heaved the midshipman aside with unclerical vigour and grappled the next, but Peter, getting to his feet, called out, 'It was only a game, sir.'

'A game? Do you call this a game?' said Mr Walter, pointing to Preston, still dazed and white, sitting on a locker, and to Clowes, with a scarlet handkerchief to his nose. 'I believe you have been fighting,' he said sternly.

'Oh no, sir,' mumbled Peter.

'Come with me,' He preceded Peter to his cabin, and there he said, 'Peter, I charge you directly with having been fighting.'

'Sir,' replied Peter, his wits sharpened by the battle. ' "An, si quis atro dente me petiverit, inultus ut flebo puer?" '

'Ha, ha,' laughed the chaplain, 'very well answered, my boy. But do not let it occur again. It is not a bullying mess, I know; and you must not get yourself a fire-eater's reputation, like your unfortunate friend. Never forget that you will in all probability be cooped up with these young men for a year or more: there must be give and take in all parts of the ship, and nowhere more than in the cockpit.'

'I won't be called Teague,' said Peter, sullenly.

'What is this?' cried the chaplain with an ominous frown. 'How do you come to speak so petulantly to me, sir, as to say, "I won't be called Teague"?'

'I beg your pardon, sir. I meant no disrespect.'

'For the sake of a foolish name, will you sow discord? Will you show malignant, unworthy resentment?'

'I won't be called Teague,' said Peter.

'For shame,' said the chaplain. 'Such doggedness does you no credit. Go away. Leave the room, sir. And I do not wish to see you again until you show a far more amenable disposition in every way.'

'The Teagues have parted brass-rags,' said the midshipmen's berth; and it appeared to be true. Peter and FitzGerald were barely on speaking terms, and very uncomfortable Peter found it.

'He can be such an amiable creature,' said Peter to himself, thinking of his companion, 'but in some ways he is such a jackass. He has been aboard for ages now, and over a month at sea, but he knows nothing—seems to have observed nothing at all. And then he is as proud as Lucifer.'

It was an uncomfortable time altogether that followed, with baffling winds that destroyed their hopes of a quick passage to Madeira and kept both watches heavily at work, sometimes for no more gain than a league of southing in four and twenty hours of strict attention.

An uncomfortable period, with tempers getting frayed and many hands up for punishment: there were days when the mastheads were quite festooned with midshipmen, and sometimes, when he was aloft with a glass, Peter could see that it was the same with the other ships in company, for his telescope would show him disconsolate colleagues arranged, like ornaments, high above the sails of the *Gloucester* and the *Severn*.

However, the wind came fair at last, and they ran three days and nights under a press of canvas before it fell into a dead calm. Here, in the silent sea the Commodore had a chance to engage the crew in one of his favourite exercises: at the break of the quarter-deck the seamen, division by division, took their turn at blazing away at a bottle hanging from the fore yard-arm.

'It is very well,' said Colonel Cracherode, 'but if I may be permitted to say so, it would not do in the Army.'

'Why not, Colonel?' asked the Commodore.

'Why, sir—not that I imply the least criticism of naval methods—' said the Colonel, meaning that he condemned them root and branch, 'but we consider a musket too deadly a weapon to be handled as any fellow takes it into his head. Like that, for example,' he cried, instinctively ducking as the foretopmen took up their arms.

'Mr Palafox,' said the Commodore.

'Sir?' cried Peter, turning round.

'Do not point your musket at Colonel Cracherode. Point it at a midshipman, Mr Palafox. They can better be spared.'

'Hor hor hor,' went Peter's division, like a lot of false traitors.

'You was pointing it into his stomach over your shoulder, sir,' whispered Hairy Amos, the ablest seaman in the division.

'So we do it by numbers,' said the Colonel, 'obtaining thereby safety for ourselves, and the effect of a concentrated fire upon the enemy.'

'Yes,' said the Commodore, 'I have often seen the Marines perform their exercise, with excellent results. But our intentions are different: for whereas the Army requires an annihilating volley to break up a cavalry charge, for instance, what I want is a body of sharpshooters, so that I always have plenty of hands in the tops, each one of whom can hit his mark on the enemy's deck. Look, now,' he cried, as a sly, long, gipsy-looking foretopman shattered the bottle, to the rapturous cheers of his mates and the watch below. Another bottle appeared, and the sly fellow hit it. A third bottle: the foretopman raised his musket, sighted it, lowered it to fan away the smoke, and then shot the bottle fair and clean, looking round with a secret leer while his mates clawed him on the back.

'The fellow's a poacher, I make no doubt of that,' said the Colonel. 'And anyway, sir, it would not do for the Army. Very wild and irregular, sir.'

'It may not do for a soldier,' said the Commodore, 'but if he downs three enemies as he has downed those three bottles, it will do for a sailor, although he does not stand to attention or know his musketry drill.'

Then it was the turn of the great guns, and Mr Randall, the gunner, came into his own: the gun-ports opened, the massive twenty-four pounders on the main deck were run out, and their crews stared out under the low port-lids. At the word of command the lanyard jerked, the gun roared with a vast crash, a great orange tongue of fire and the thunderous rumble of the carriage hurtling back: the gun-deck was filled with the acrid fighting smell of powder, and Peter, hurrying along behind Mr Randall, saw the second gun go off. He was less amazed by the shattering noise, and watched the gun with particular attention: in the very instant of firing the whole gun leapt, actually left the deck; it was quite fascinating. Soon the gun-deck was darkened by the heavy cloud of smoke that lay in a swathe upon the sea: the sun pierced in shafts through the open ports, and in the shafts the smoke swirled thick. The men were stripped to the waist, for it was hot, and the heavy work of loading, swabbing, running the guns up, made them gleam.

'Mr Palafox,' said the first lieutenant, pausing in his walk along the gun-deck, 'what are you doing here?'

Peter could not think of a reasonable answer.

'Do you think this is a holiday? A raree-show? Bartholomew Fair? Go back to your station immediately. You will hear from me this evening.'

But as Peter, in guilt-stricken haste, returned to his rightful position in the ship, eight bells sounded and the watch below took over with uncommon eagerness, ousting the reluctant larboard watch at the guns and the stands of arms. The cutter was lowering away, and Peter, with a boldness that surprised himself, asked Mr Brett if he might go in her.

'Eh?' said the lieutenant, and turned away to give an order.

Peter wanted no more: in another moment he was in the cutter, explaining his presence to Mr Stapleton, the fifth lieutenant, by the somewhat disingenuous remark that, 'Mr Brett had desired him to go.' His land-conscience pricked him faintly, but his deep-sea-conscience instantly replied that Mr Brett would certainly desire him to take every opportunity of improving himself in his profession; and he tranquilly enjoyed the sight of the *Centurion* growing smaller in the cutter's wake. It was a long time since he had seen her as a whole—had seen her from outside, that is—and he was struck again by her towering beauty. Her royals flapped now and then in the faint movement of the air, and she still had a very little way on her; but otherwise she was in suspended animation, alive, but in a trance. He looked back at her now with a very much more knowing eye, and his glance ran up and down the rigging—no longer an unmeaning bewilderment of rope, but a well-known and fascinating combination of counteracting forces in equipoise as well as a series of aerial paths. Her open gun-ports made her look strange, however: he noticed them particularly, and turning to the lieutenant he said, 'Sir, how do they open the gun-ports in a wind, if you please? I mean, when the wind is on the other side, laying her over?'

Mr Stapleton did not answer for a moment, because he was meditating the form of his reproof: but then he said, quite mildly, 'They cannot. She is very deep-laden, and if we meet with the Spaniards in anything of a sea we shall have to fight with the upper tier alone. Do you know where the keel is, Mr Palafox?'

'Oh yes, sir,' said Peter, amused.

'And do you know what keel-hauling is?'

'Not exactly, sir. But Mr Saunders has promised to show me this evening. Pray, what is it, sir?'

'It is when they bend a line to your neck and another to your heels and pass you under the ship's keel from the starboard main-chains to the larboard main-chains. It takes a long time, and when there is a good deal of marine growth on the bottom it is very uncomfortable. It is the usual punishment for midshipmen who speak to their betters without being spoken to. ''Vast that talking there,' he cried. 'Silence in the boat. Give way, you sons of——. Chattering like a floating hen-coop.'

Somewhat appalled by this intelligence, Peter looked away from the *Centurion* and sat meekly with his eyes inboard. Almost at once his gaze met that of Sean, who for some time had been trying to attract his attention by sundry nods and becks.

'Why, Sean, my dear,' he cried, 'and what are you doing here, at all?'

'Sure, they wanted a real seaman, your honour,' began Sean, with a beaming smile. 'Will I tell you the way——'

'*Will* you be quiet, Mr Palafox?' roared Mr Stapleton. 'You, O'Mara, stow your gob. Cox'n, let it go.'

'It' was a floating target: it splashed over the side, and the lieutenant turned the boat. 'Pull now,' he said, 'if you value your hides.'

'A few moments later there was a white puff in the *Centurion*'s waist, almost instantly followed by the deep note of one of the upper-deck nine-pounders, and the high splash of the ball fifty yards beyond the target. The ball leapt from the surface and went skittering on like a gigantic game of ducks and drakes: Peter was still staring after it when the second gun banged out.

'Straddled it,' said Mr Stapleton with satisfaction, as the ball pitched short of the target, but in the true line. 'That must be Mr Randall pointing the guns.'

After a few more shots, some of which fell very near the target, there was a long pause.

'Give way,' said Mr Stapleton, who knew what was coming. He took the cutter a good distance from the target, and his friends on the *Centurion*'s quarter-deck, smiled. 'He is not going to linger,' said Mr Norris, the fourth lieutenant.

'I would go farther off still,' said the master, 'with the gun crews in their present——' But his remaining words were utterly engulfed in the tremendous thunder of the broadside: the ship heeled from the blast, and the target vanished in the shattered sea. And not only the target; for a wide area all round it the water was lashed into a violent second's life, bearing out Mr Stapleton's judgment of the raw crew's aim. In the moment of stunned silence that followed, Peter looked at the *Centurion*, and saw nothing but her topgallant-sails and royals rocking above the rising smoke.

The cutter's crew were lying on their oars close by the ship; the cloud of smoke had drifted half a mile down the light air. Two pensioners were leaning over the side, staring down and talking of the cannonade that had preceded the battle of Blenheim: the cutter was waiting for orders, and Peter was vaguely listening to the old men's talk when he saw FitzGerald appear in the main-shrouds, immediately above the boat, and he heard an authoritative voice saying, 'Up you go. Up and ride the main-royal. And you will find yourself at the mast-head every single day of your life until you learn that in the Navy you obey an order at the double and with no argument whatever.'

'He has caught a Tartar this time,' thought Peter, not without a certain satisfaction, 'and has been mast-headed.'

FitzGerald cast a haggard look downwards: but it was obvious that he did not see him, and with a sudden pang of anxiety Peter remembered his unaccountable behaviour in the foretop a little while ago.

'He has never been mast-headed before,' he reflected. 'And I do not think I have ever seen him aloft.' He remembered the early days in the Channel, when some wretched landsman had been flogged for refusing duty aloft, and how some of them had been driven almost mad with the terror of the height.

FitzGerald was climbing slowly, with a strange, almost wooden motion. Peter watched him approach the futtock-shrouds, pause a long time, and then grip them for the outward climb to the top.

'Oh, he's all right, then,' he thought. 'Sure I was mistaken.'

But looking down again his glance happened to fall on Sean, who was still looking fixedly upwards. Sean was in Fitz-Gerald's watch, and although his duty usually lay below, it suddenly occurred to Peter that Sean would know more about FitzGerald in this respect than he did himself.

FitzGerald waited a long time in the maintop, and when he came into sight again in the topmast shrouds Peter noticed that he had kicked off his shoes, presumably to get a better hold.

'But it is so absurd,' said Peter to himself, trying to allay his anxiety; 'the sea is as calm as a pond, and the ratlines are like a flight of stairs.'

FitzGerald was going up and up, but more slowly now, and often he looked down. After every downward look there was a long pause before he recommenced his painfully clumsy and laboured ascent.

When he reached the topmast futtocks he missed his footing and hung by his hands alone. Peter saw his white face, very small in the distance, looking down between his drawn-up shoulders: he sprang up in the boat.

'Sit down at once,' snapped the lieutenant, and, 'Aye-aye, sir,' he shouted in reply to an order from the quarter-deck. The cutter shot away from the side.

'Mr Palafox,' he said in a low tone, with real irritation, 'you must learn how to behave yourself in a boat, or there will be serious trouble.'

'Aye-aye, sir,' said Peter. 'I beg pardon.' But he managed, by screwing himself round, to keep his eyes on the *Centurion*. FitzGerald had clawed his way up to the crosstrees, and he appeared to be crouching there in a queer, hunched attitude. Now he was moving again, climbing the topgallant shrouds; but even from the cutter his movements seemed all wrong, like the movements of a wounded animal. Once or twice he stopped for so long that Peter thought that he would go no higher: but he did; slowly and uncertainly he went up and up towards the topgallant mast-head. He seemed to be staring upwards now: it was too far away to see his face at all, but his head appeared to be thrown back.

'He has still got to get on to the royal-yard,' thought Peter, as FitzGerald reached the topgallant crosstrees. 'Will he ever manage the royal? God be with him: will he manage the royal?'

'Keep your eyes in the boat,' cried Mr Stapleton, and Peter straightened himself with a jerk: but the order was addressed to Sean, whose stare at the main-royal was more obvious than Peter's.

Peter cautiously looked again, and to his surprise he saw that FitzGerald had gone on directly, and that he was well on his way to the yard, which the *Centurion* (like most men-of-war) carried on the pole of her topgallant mast, not far below the tuck. Peter saw him make the last few feet and settle himself, then, with a significant look and an imperceptible nod to Sean, he turned away.

'Then I was wrong,' he thought. 'He was just going up slowly to put a mock on the first lieutenant.' But he wished he felt a little more certain of the truth of the statement.

'In oars,' said Mr Stapleton. 'Bowes, step the mast.'

Peter had not noticed the breeze getting up, but it had, and there away to the east was the dark patch of ruffled sea that showed the shape of the little wind: behind it, and stretching away to the clouds on the horizon, there was more wind by far.

The cutter ran straight down to do her errand aboard the *Tryal*; and that was very pleasant—the crew sat demurely and watched the sea go by, faster and faster as the breeze freshened. But the return was another thing again, a long, tiring pull into the wind. Half-way over Peter remembered, with a thrill of disagreeable anticipation, that his watch would have been called an hour ago, that he had not in fact obtained leave to absent himself, and that Mr Saunders had already a bone to pick with him in the evening. This occupied his mind enough to keep him silent during the rest of the pull; but it did not occupy him exclusively, and when the cutter hooked on he vanished up the side with such rapidity that the lieutenant, already busy, had only time to say, 'Where's that midshipman?' before he was gone.

Darting over to the windward shrouds in the hope that he might escape the notice of the officer of the watch, Peter raced up to the maintop, up again, up and up to the main-royal yard.

'You are all right, an't you?' he asked.

'Peter,' whispered FitzGerald, 'for God's sake tie me on. I cannot hold much longer.' His face was rigid and ghastly: it shocked Peter to the heart: and his voice was barely human. The ship was rolling now, and Peter had to move with care as he cut the pennant halliard in two places, made the loose ends fast, and passed three turns under FitzGerald's arms.

'Mr Palafox,' came from the deck nearly two hundred feet below, for the second time. 'Mast-head, there.' It was impossible to ignore it now.

'I'll come back and get you down,' said Peter hastily; 'you're quite all right now—firm as a rock.'

'Don't let them know,' whispered FitzGerald; and Peter, with a reassuring nod, shot down towards the deck. As he went he noticed that the shrouds where FitzGerald had passed were red with blood.

'Now, sir,' said the incensed Mr Stapleton: and he treated Peter to a pretty long statement of his views. 'Junior officers *in* first, *out* last. Do you understand that?' he concluded.

'Aye-aye, sir,' said Peter, starting away.

'Now, sir,' said Mr Dennis, the officer of the watch, 'what is the meaning of this?'

Mr Dennis had finished at last, and Peter really thought it was over: he had almost reached the shrouds when a ship's boy came running and said, 'Mr Palafox, sir, Mr Saunders' compliments and would like to see you directly.'

Peter was running aft when he saw Ransome. 'Ransome,' he said, gripping him tight by the elbow and pouring the words into him at close range, 'I've got to go to number one. Fitz-Gerald's riding the royal. In a horrible state. Can't get down. And listen; I've cut the pennant-halliard, to lash him on.'

There was no change of expression on Ransome's big, heavy face, nothing except amazement that anybody could possibly cut the pennant-halliard. He was still staring as Peter left him, and Peter could not tell whether he had understood, or, having understood, would do anything about it.

Mr Saunders, first of the *Centurion*, was a disciplinarian; and there was no man of his seniority in the Navy List who could be more unpleasant when he chose. He did choose, on this occasion: but Peter, with the image of his friend hanging up there, barely noticed anything but the pauses where he was to say 'Yes, sir,' and 'No, sir,' and 'Aye-aye, sir'.

FitzGerald was up there, gripped by some awful horror that Peter could see but could not entirely understand: he was physically helpless—there was no need for him to have held on with any force at all: he would have been perfectly safe without, but he had torn out his living nails—helpless and exhausted, yet his courage was not destroyed, nor his pride. Peter strained his ears in an absurd attempt to distinguish some noise that might mean that Ransome was going aloft. The first lieutenant spoke very grimly about the Articles of War, and Peter stood mute and submissive while his mind hovered in the rigging above.

'Discipline, young man . . .' said Mr Saunders, and at the same moment, high above their heads, Ransome said, 'Nah then, cully. Handsomely does it. Just catch a hold rahnd my neck. And don't ever you look down.'

'Ransome,' said FitzGerald, a little later, 'please let me try the last stretch by myself. I'd give the world not to be disgraced.'

'Try it, cully,' said Ransome, doubtfully, 'but I'm afeard it's no go. You're all shook to pieces, like. It ain't no disgrace, cock; anyone can have a spell of the topman's horrors.'

'. . . and if you reflect upon what I say,' said the first lieutenant more kindly, feeling that he had been a little too hard, that his severity had cowed the poor boy's spirit, 'you may make a seaman yet. I believe you have the makings of one already. That will do, Mr Palafox.'

'Aye-aye, sir. Thank you, sir.'

Peter regained the deck in time to see Ransome carrying FitzGerald like a child. 'It was just that Mr FitzGerald was took with a cramp in his wounded leg,' he was explaining to the officer of the watch, 'so I give him a hand down the last bit, like.'

'Very well. Help him below,' said Mr Dennis. 'Damned awkward place to have a cramp. Here, Mr Palafox, you can make yourself useful: his Majesty does not pay you for your beauty alone—take Winslow and Cheetham and see to the frappings of the number two quarter gun.'

It was dinner-time on Sunday. The muster and the reading of the Articles of War, the high ceremony of the naval week, had passed off with creditable regularity; and indeed, the men were beginning to look something like a man-of-war's crew, rather than the heterogeneous sweepings of the press-gang. Even the invalids, as the pensioners were rightly called, made a fairly alert and respectable appearance. Mr Walter had preached on being contented with one's lot, and they had listened with becoming attention: at least they had not openly resented his remarks.

The midshipmen's berth was in a state of strong and pleasureable anticipation: Sunday always brought some change in their diet, and from early in the morning it had been rumoured that there was to be drowned baby after the junk.

'How is that baby coming along, Jennings?' asked Keppel, attacking his meat.

'She's nicely swole, sir,' replied Jennings, 'or at least she was a little while ago.'

'If she bursts her cloth,' said Hope, with his passion somewhat muffled by an intervening turnip, 'I will haul the sailmaker before the Commodore myself.'

'I don't mind it, even if the cloth *is* burst,' said Keppel. 'I *love* drowned baby, however old and sodden.'

FitzGerald was sitting silent and withdrawn, eating very little: once or twice he had seemed on the point of speaking, but each time the mess-attendant had come in and he had sunk back.

'There, sir,' cried Jennings, in honest triumph, putting down a battered pewter dish in front of Ransome, the senior midshipman. Under a cloud of steam the baby sweltered in its purple sauce, long, pallid, bloated: its lumpish, irregular surface gleamed with a heavy, unctuous light, and every here and there its pallor was broken by an outburst of turgid plums.

'I have seen more spotted babies in my time,' said Keppel, gazing upon it, 'but it should do pretty well. Hurry up with the dissection, Ransome, can't you?'

There followed a period of silent greed, and avid scraping of plates, and then the torpid revival of conversation. There was a good deal of talk about the forthcoming rearrangement of the watch-lists—for the berth had no gentlemanly inhibitions about talking shop, and little else was ever mentioned there—and a long, desultory and inconclusive wrangle between Preston and Bailey about the merits of Funchal as a port of call, a vapid conversation, since neither of them knew anything about the place whatever.

'Mr Ransome, sir,' said FitzGerald, cutting straight across it, pushing his untouched plate away and getting to his feet. 'Mr Ransome, when first I came aboard, something passed between you and me. I wish—' he paused for a second, leaning on the table, very pale—'I wish to make you the most public and unreserved apology.'

Ransome flushed as red as if he had been found picking a pocket. He looked utterly miserable. 'That's handsome,' he said at last, awkwardly getting up. '——' he said—a string of unprintable oaths—'that's very handsome,' and he took Fitz-Gerald's hand with appalling force.

6

H.M.S. *Centurion*, at sea
32° 27′ N., 18° 30′ W., off Funchal
November 2nd 1740 O.S.

'My dear Sir,' wrote Peter,

'I embrace this Opportunity of sending you my Love and
Duty by the Hands of Mr FitzGerald who is my particular
Friend and who is leaving the Ship and going Home in an
Indiaman. He is a prodigious good Fellow and a very Fine
Gentleman, but is not quite suited for a Life at Sea. He is to
have a Pair of Colours in the Company's India service, but
vows he will go there by Land, for the Sea-passage would
make him pule into a Lethergy.'

Peter thought that rather a good expression, and underlined
'Lethergy' twice.

'This is a very strange Place, with a Hill of a huge Bigness,
like Croagh Patrick, and the People are Black when they are
not White. I have not been ashore, because Mr Saunders has
stopped my Shore Leave in consequence of a Disagreement
about the Pennant Halliard. He is a prodigious fine Seaman
but rather severe, like Tiberius. But I have seen it through the
Perspective Glass and there are Vineyards in which People
labour, all up the Hill, in steps. And the People in the Bum-
boats come with Grapes and all kind of Gee-Gaws: they do
not speak English, but I have bought a Shawl for my Mother
and some Sweetmeats for my Sisters and some Madera Lace
to shew what the Foreigners imagine is Lace. I have a Flying
Fish for William and I wish it may arrive entire. I kept it

below until the other Officers complain'd of the Stench, when I gave it to Sean to preserve. He sends his best Duty and begs to be remembered to Pegeen Ban, Bridie Walsh, Fiona Colman, Norah at Ardnacoire, Maire Scanlan, Maggy, the ganger's three Daughters and some more I forget. He was flogg'd again on Thursday for reasoning with the Butcher. How he Howl'd. But he privately assur'd me when I went below with some Oyl that it was Nothing to what he had every day from his Mother, at Home.

'Mr Walter desires his best Compliments, and begs you will accept of an anker of curious old Madeira. He is very kind to me, and sometimes desires me to read a Page of Horace with him, which he means kindly I am sure and sometimes he explains the Theory of Winds. He is prodigious learned and has a great Heap of Books. He bids me remind you of the *Balliol Sausage and Jno. Barton.*

'Mr Anson is also very kind and has taken Notice of me Four times. He is a prodigious fine Seaman, better than Mr Saunders even, and the Officers and Men have a great Awe of him, though he never Rails or Curses them. No one wou'd presume to murmur when he is on the Quarter-Deck. At Dinner there was a Post-Captain who wanted to marry my Mother and wish'd to be kindly remember'd. His Name was Callis.

'We had but a tedious Passage and the Officers curs'd amazingly. Because of there being so few Upperyard-men, we cou'd never run up the Royals and Stunsails except the Wind was abaft the Beam and very small, and we have to work the Ship watch and watch, with too Few able Seamen to make up Three watches. But the Hands are growing more expert. I can hang by my Heels from the Truck of the Main-Royal, which is very diverting as you see everything Upside down and waving like a Phantasmagorio. Mr Keppel shew'd me this. He has been at Sea since he was Ten years old. And Mr Ransome who is quite Old has been at Sea since he was Eight: he is Mr Keppel's particular Friend. Nat. Bailey is another Midshipman and he bought three Apes on Shore and gave me one, which is very handsome in him. I hope to be allowed on Shore tomorrow for I have a great Mind to a Parrot. The Spaniards had smok'd our Proceedings before we weigh'd from Spithead, and their Squadron lies off this Island, a Seventy-four, a 66, a 54, a 50 and a 40, with a Patache of 20. The 74 is call'd the *Guipuscoa*, a Name I cou'd never remember to tell the Commodore. So we may be in Action soon, which pleases the Ship's Company wonderfully.

'I beg you will tell my Mother that my Shirts are Holding up to Admiration. She was much concern'd for the Collarbands. And please to take great Care in undoing the Packet, for between the Tobacco and the Box made of Shells there is a Nest of Curious Serpents and a Scorpion in a Jar of Spirits which a Seaman of my Division brought me. They are for Dermot and Hugh to share as they please. The small Sailcloth Bag is for Mother Connell.

'They are calling for me now, as the Indiaman sails on the Tide. So in Haste I send you and my Mother my dear Love and my Duty, and my Love too for all at Home.

Your affectionate Son . . .'

And he scrawled his name as the ship's boy stood waiting and an urgent cry came from the Indiaman's boat. He felt a queer, burning tightness in his throat: home had seemed so near while he was writing.

If wishes could have given him wings he would have been in the Rectory at that moment: and sitting there alone, he felt wretchedly low and unhappy. Behind him the mixed collection of midshipmen's animals stirred, grunted, scratched or cooed according to their several temperaments.

In his solitude the midshipmen's berth, usually so crowded that one had to crawl over and around the inhabitants, seemed almost uncomfortably vast. 'I never thought I would feel like this aboard a man-of-war,' said Peter in a melancholy inward voice.

After some time he raised his head from his arms and turned round. There was a wicker cage with a lonely palm-dove in it just behind him, which he had bought that morning from a boat alongside.

'Well, my dear,' he said, opening the door and holding the warm fragile little creature, whose heart beat fast against his palm, 'at least you may go where you wish.' And he carried the bird up to the gangway, where Funchal blazed in the sun. 'There,' he said, letting it fly.

Yet within three-quarters of an hour what a different face of things was seen. Peter, released by the first lieutenant (a good-hearted man, though often sorely tried), was gaping at the wonders of Funchal: his visage shone with warmth and pleasure, and in his hands he carried a small turtle, a basket of peaches, some bits of coral, a very lively representation of the martyrdom of Saint Lawrence made of volcanic rock, and a long woollen hat. The ground felt strangely firm beneath his feet after forty days at sea: already he had acquired the rolling gait and the hanging arms of a sailorman; and, with his open admiration of everything around him, he had very much the air of Jack ashore. Everything here was so very different; even the air, uncooled by the sea all round, was strange, and although its solid heat made his blue coat feel six inches thick he sniffed its unknown and foreign scents with delight. If only he had found Sean, and if only FitzGerald had been there, he would have been completely happy.

He had searched all the lowest taverns by the water-side for Sean without success: there were a great many men from the *Gloucester*, *Severn*, *Pearl* and *Wager*—the *Tryal* was still at sea in her vain search for the Spaniards—as well as all the Centurions who could be trusted ashore. They were exactly where even his short experience of the Navy had led him to suppose, busily seeing the world through the bottom of as many glasses as they could afford or contain, in a variety of very debased pot-houses: but Sean was not among them.

He met with him at last in a little square, sitting on the steps of a church with a scarlet rose behind his ear and a young woman by his side—a young woman as beautiful as an angel, though perhaps inferior in virtue.

'There you are, Sean,' said Peter, 'gallivanting as usual, I find.'

'Oh, I was not, your honour,' said Sean, removing the young woman's entwining arm. 'I was just entertaining this elegant female with reasons.'

'And is this the faith you pledged to Pegeen Ban, to say nothing of Bridie Walsh, Fiona Colman, Norah the daughter of Turlough and Helen Concannon?'

'Musha, it was all such a long time ago,' said Sean, 'and with such a world of empty sea between.'

'Pretty sailor,' said the young woman.

'And as for you, young trollop,' said Peter briskly—he had no terror of women, having so many sisters—'you go home and mind your needle. Sean, fie and for shame. Come along with me, and improve your mind by the sight of the world abroad.'

Sean came, carrying the turtle and Saint Lawrence, though with many a reluctant backward look, and presently they fell in with a party of midshipmen—Hope and Preston among them—who were persuading a mule to carry their purchases down to the shore.

'We have given him a bucket of wine,' said Hope, 'but still he won't go.'

'We have beaten him until we are quite tired,' said Preston, 'and he stands there like an image.'

'Image, is it, your honour?' said Sean. 'If I had the Portuguese penny to buy the herb I saw just now, you would see him run after me like a cricket.'

'Do you understand mules, O'Mara?' asked Preston.

'How would I not understand them, your honour, for all love? Let you give me the Portuguese penny and see.'

'Hurry, then,' said Preston, producing a coin.

'Sure 'tis just round the corner,' said Sean.

'I wish your fellow would hurry, Palafox,' said Preston, after some time.

'Eh?' said Peter, still lashing his shopping on to the mountainous load.

'O'Mara,' said Preston. 'He's gone to fetch a herb or some-thing. He understands mules.'

'Did you give him money?'

'Yes. A rial, I think it was. Why, can't you trust him with money?'

'No,' said Peter, scenting black treachery. 'Oh no, you can-not trust him with money. Nor women, of course.'

'Can you trust him with drink?'

'Well, you might leave him with a bottle; but only if you did not mind never seeing it again.'

'What can you trust him with, then?'

'You can trust him to be out of the way whenever you want him,' said Peter, 'and to tell a dozen great lies every time he says a single word.'

'Why do you keep such a desperate fellow?'

'Faith, I cannot tell. I shall turn him off, one of these days.'

'I wish he would hurry up.'

'You'll never see him again, nor your money either, the ill-looking thief.'

And indeed Sean had vanished: he was seen no more until the *Centurion* was preparing to weigh, when he was detected in the act of insinuating himself aboard through the ward-room lights, dressed in no more than a kind of depraved calico shawl. It appeared that he had been seized by the Inquisition and had been racked for maintaining the glory of the British Crown: they had also, he said, taken his clothes from him, the Portuguese penny and a sizeable quid of tobacco, scarcely chewed on at all; and they had designed to throw him to the Papal bull on the first Monday after the dark of the moon. But having deluded the Inquisition (whom he described as a so-phistical, blue-nosed rogue having one ear larger than the other and a pompous black beaver hat with the brim turned up at the side) he had launched a frail, limping child of a boat single-handed through the surf to regain the ship—a devotion to duty which would be rewarded, said Mr Saunders, with a flogging clean round the squadron the next time it occurred. And the Protestant martyr's pay was stopped until the slops should be paid for: a period which, according to Peter's calculation, should see them in latitude 117° West.

And that was a long space of distance and time, by any reckoning. Much kinder winds met them south of Madeira: not quite all that might have been hoped for, though often true enough for day after day of sailing with the royals and studding-sails set and scarcely a brace to be touched, while the leagues of southing ran sweetly along the side, two and even three in the measured hour: but almost the entire circumference of the world was yet to run, and still no more than one sleeve of Sean's jacket was yet paid for.

The midshipmen of the *Centurion* were not an unduly sensitive crew—a man-of-war does not provide an atmosphere in which delicate plants can survive, far less flourish—but they had perception enough to see that Peter was lonely without FitzGerald and kindness enough to wish it remedied. Ransome showed him the intricacies of the double-emperor knot, an appallingly difficult piece of work of no practical utility whatever, but which he alone in the berth could tie—perhaps in the whole ship's company, for he had learnt it as a little boy from a very old man who had sailed with Blake, in the days when the knot was still sometimes used by way of ornament. He would also come and sit with Peter from time to time, saying little, but being there in a large and companionable way. Bailey and Preston initiated him into their private and most exclusive rat-hunt, which held its illicit meets in the hold; and Hope taught him the noble game of chess. Another who went far out of his way to be friendly was Elliot. Elliot was a quiet, reserved fellow, somewhat older than Peter; he had been at sea since the beginning of the war, and before that he had been at a nautical school, where his natural bent for mathematics had so developed that it was said that he could be heard murmuring the table of natural cosines in his sleep. Like Peter he was a clergyman's son; but the Reverend Mr Elliot was even poorer than the Rector at Ballynasaggart, being no more than a curate: worse, he had translated Sallust, with notes, and had printed him.

Sallust is an excellent author; Mr Elliot's translation was

excellent too, and his notes were copious, judicious and learned; but the public's utter indifference to Sallust, with notes or without, had plunged the translator into a variety of miseries too complicated to relate. The result was that his creditors had clapped him into the Fleet, the prison for debtors; and there he would stay, incapable of earning a penny, until he paid his debts. It was as if they believed the poor old gentleman was malignantly hiding a secret hoard. He was not: he had paid everything he possessed; but there he would stay until death released him, as far as they were concerned, for they were as mean-spirited, ungenerous a pack of creditors as one could readily find.

So Elliot had come aboard very meagrely equipped by the grudging charity of a surly cousin, and he had been unable to buy many real necessities, because his pay, what little there was of it, went to maintain his father in the Fleet—for in the Fleet the prisoners, unlike those in common gaols, had the privilege of buying their victuals or of starving genteelly to death if they could not afford to. But, being an uncommonly ingenious creature, like so many sailors, Elliot had made himself a tolerably accurate quadrant, a pair of parallel rulers and a Gunter's scale.

'You must disregard the lower lines,' he said to Peter. 'I did not get them right at first. Take the upper reading—there's your co-tangent. Do you see?'

'No,' said Peter, having stared at the rule and his paper for some little time.

'Never mind,' said Elliot. 'Let us begin again at the beginning. Now you have your noon-reading, have you not? So, noting down the height of the sun, you turn to your tables— here. Now comes the rule—here. Do you see?'

'No,' said Peter, at last. 'I am very sorry, Elliot, but I don't.'

'I wonder how I can make it clearer,' said Elliot thoughtfully. 'Perhaps the trouble lies farther back. What is a sine?'

'It is the thing you look up in the table when you have found your angle,' said Peter.

'Yes. But I mean, what is it itself? What does the word mean?'

'Sure, I don't know at all,' said Peter. 'Do you have to?'

'Yes, you do. I will try to explain the whole basis; that's where you have gone astray, and rule-of-thumb navigation will not answer for your lieutenant's examination. I will try my father's way: he took me into the garden and showed me the steeple—we lived in a cottage then, just by the church—and asked me to find its height. Now you think of your steeple at home.'

'We haven't a steeple,' said Peter, anxiously. 'Only a little small thing for the bell.'

'Well, think of a very tall tree.'

'All right,' said Peter, frowning with concentration; 'I have that in my mind.'

'Now you are to measure the height of that tree. You cannot climb to the top. But you see the tree's shadow there on the lawn.'

'On the lawn. Very good,' said Peter.

'Then you take a stick of any length that comes to hand. We will say five feet, for example. You thrust it into the ground, quite straight upright, and push it in for a foot.'

'A foot,' said Peter, unconsciously making the gesture of one who thrusts in a stick for a foot.

'And you measure its shadow,' said Elliot, seeing the English garden with the shade of the steeple running across it as far as the red brick wall. And you find the stick's shadow is just six feet long. Then you pace out the shadow of your tree, and you find there is a hundred and twenty feet of it. So how high is the tree?'

Peter thought for a long while. 'It's a desperate tall one,' he said, doubtfully, 'to be throwing a shadow like that, unless it was late in the evening.'

'No: listen,' said Elliot, 'your stick's shadow is six feet long, and the stick's height is four feet. Your tree's shadow is a hundred and twenty feet long. Then how high is the tree?'

'Eighty feet,' said Peter, with a slow grin of intelligence spreading across his face. 'I said it was a desperate tall one.'

'That's right,' said Elliot. 'But why is it so?'

'The Rule of Three, perhaps?' suggested Peter.

'No. It is because the proportions of the triangles are the same, always. Here are your triangles . . .'

The lesson went on. Elliot was not a particularly gay companion—he had had too much of his youth battered out of him by heavy care and responsibility for that—but he understood the problem thoroughly, and he had the gift of making it comprehensible, of passing on his knowledge; which Mr Thomas had not, nor the writer of Peter's manual. Added to that he was patient, good-natured and steady: so when the *Centurion* crossed the Tropic of Cancer, Peter, who was not a stupid fellow at all, though a trifle mercurial, was aware of it by his own unaided calculation.

'There,' said Mr Thomas, with qualified approval, looking over his shoulder. 'I knew you could do it. Your former reckonings were either wanton idleness, Mr Palafox, or pure vice. If not a combination of the two. Now, gentlemen, it can hardly have escaped your notice that somewhere between the tropics lies the equinoctial line.'

'Just half-way,' said Peter, with conscious pride.

'Mr Palafox sets us all right,' said the schoolmaster. 'And that being the case, we may expect to enter the zone of equatorial calms very shortly. There, no doubt, we shall have the pleasure of towing the ship in intervals of calling all hands to trim sail; for the doldrums, young gentlemen, is the sailor's purgatory, and they will put an end to your idleness, destructive of morals and discipline alike.'

'Are they very horrible, sir?' asked Peter.

'Greasy horrible,' replied the master, with satisfaction, 'with scum floating on the sea and miasmas that rot the living flesh from off your bones.'

'Perhaps they will not be so bad,' said Keppel—for Mr Thomas was in a good humour—'After all, the Trades were not what was expected, were they, sir?'

'They will be bad enough, Mr Keppel, I assure you. I do not expect above half the midshipmen's berth to survive: oh, how sorry we shall be; and how the work of the ship will suffer.'

'But the trade winds were not steady, were they, sir? Why was that, sir?'

'You may put it down to the cursed malignity of fate if you wish, Mr Keppel. It is all part of the same misfortune that has dogged this ship from the moment she was commissioned. It began early, with the coming aboard of a bunch of midshipmen, each one more grossly ignorant of his profession than the last. I have never seen the like in five and thirty years of sea—look at Mr Bailey's fadge of a reckoning here. It is all part and parcel of the decline of the service. This modern Navy, with its fine uniforms and frills and pampering of the lower deck like cossets, does not produce midshipmen like the alert, intelligent, seamanlike youngsters—now, Mr Palafox, what's to do?'

'I was only putting on my coat, sir.'

'What do you want with a coat in this heat? Don't you see the deck quite drawn with the sun?'

'Yes, sir,' said Peter, shivering.

'Then it is great nonsense to say you are cold. However, the equator will warm you up, ha, ha. And it will comfort Mr Bailey, too. He will find it is a great comfort and a great help to his navigation to see the line drawn across the sea, with all the degrees marked plain in red.'

But the sun blaring down from the height of the sky brought no warmth into Peter for the rest of the lesson, nor for the rest of the day. The breathless hot night could not get the ice out of him, either. The next day it was worse, and so it went on as the ship ran south. For days and days he lay shivering in his hammock, with blankets piled over him. His wits went astray for most of the time, and he raved in delirium: sometimes he searched and searched through a crimson sea for the names of the Spanish ships; sometimes he worked navigational problems with endless anxiety over and over again; sometimes he was at home, but the misfortunes of Elliot's father had accompanied him, and everything was a confusion of inexplicable sorrow; sometimes he was on his journey with FitzGerald, but they never progressed, though the time raced by as they struggled vainly with a shadowy opposition of dreams; and sometimes he was standing by FitzGerald's chair, as he had done for all those smoky lamp-lit hours in the Indiaman off Funchal while FitzGerald played with the Company's officers for shocking stakes—but this time FitzGerald lost instead of winning, lost all the time, and staking all his credit and his future in one last desperate game, lost that, and turned his cold, hard gambler's face on Peter with bitter enmity. Yet now and then he was conscious, and he had a confused recollection of different events, separate in time and often with neither beginning nor end. One was the voice of the surgeon.

'So you have a calenture too, my young friend. Well, a slime-draught will set you on your feet directly. See that he has it three times a day.'

Then it was the surgeon again.

'No, sir, I am afraid the poor lad has a putrid fever—the same as most of the others on my list.'

'Is it bad, Mr Woodfall? What do you think of his state?' That was the Commodore's voice, anxious and strangely resonant.

'Well, sir—it is early to say. We have buried thirty-six, counting the three today. But he is young. However, I would not care to promise a recovery.'

'You will do all that is feasible, Mr Woodfall. If there is anything in my stores that can be of any use—wine or . . .'

Then it was the infernal noise of hammering that rang through his head and somebody told him that air-scuttles were being cut in the ship: and sometimes he heard snatches of the funeral service on deck—Mr Walter's grave voice saying '. . . and so we commit his body to the deep,' and the splash.

There were many sounds that came through—the piping of the captains up the side, hushed but excited voices speaking of a chase, the thunder of gunnery practice, often repeated, and the thousand noises of the working of the ship. Ransome's hoarse whisper, 'I tell you what, cully, if you croak, I'll rip out the flaming saw-bones' lights and cram 'em down his throat.' But most often it was Sean, talking in the soft language of their home, quietly singing the ancient songs, the weaving-chant and the rowing-song, that he had heard before he could even talk or stand.

But the sickness, the breaking head, the chasing nightmares of delirium came to an end at last; and they moved him, very weak and poorly, up out of the fetid stench and heat of the 'tween-decks to the upper-deck, where he lay in the clean morning air, swinging in his hammock under the blue sky and the white sails while the warm south-east wind sang in the rigging and the *Centurion* ran with flowing sheets westward under Capricorn. All down the waist of the ship other hammocks swung in exact time with the easy roll and pitch: not far from a quarter of the ship's company was there or still below, too sick to be moved.

'Mr Palafox, I am heartily glad to see you looking better,' said the master, appearing by his side.

'Thank you, sir,' said Peter, hurriedly removing the lemon from his mouth—both he and Sean had a passion for lemons, and had laid in a store at Madeira.

'I have often been below to see you,' said Mr Blew, 'and so has Mr Saunders. But you were in a sad way—raving like a lost soul. On one occasion you addressed the first lieutenant as an ill-faced, mangy son of a Rural Dean, and on another you asked me whether my mother knew that I was out. This was a very high pitch of delirium, Mr Palafox. But, however, your intellectuals are now restored to at least their former pitch, eh? Ha, ha.'

Peter smiled, but palely, for the good man's laugh thundered in his ear, and the horny hand patting him on the shoulder jarred him from head to foot.

'So I have brought you our position, like if you were an Admiral already,' continued the master, giving him a slip of paper.

'Thank you, sir, very much indeed,' said Peter. '24° 10′ S., 38° 52′ W. But, sir,' he cried, 'I have missed the equator. Oh, Mr Blew!'

'Dear me, yes,' said the master. 'We crossed it long ago, in about 28° West. Why, we have been in soundings these five or six days past. But never mind, my boy,' he said, seeing Peter's disappointment, 'you will certainly cross it again, if we survive the passage of the Horn.'

Mr Blew left him; the officer of the watch passed by with a kind word, and some of the men of Peter's division grinned hairily into the hammock, with signs meant to encourage him; but it was a busy time of the ship's day, and Peter had sunk into a delicious half-sleep when the cry of 'Land ho' from the mast-head galvanised him and the entire ship's company. There was an instant darting into the rigging: many of the hammocks—all, indeed, that were filled by sea-men—writhed impotently: and again the hail floated down. 'Land ho, four points—five points—on the starboard bow.'

It was six weeks since Madeira had disappeared beneath the horizon, six weeks of unbroken sea, and everybody in the ship was passionately eager to see the landfall. The quarter-deck was crowded, and even the land officers discussed the matter, earnestly peering through telescopes in as nautical a fashion as they could manage.

Very soon, unable to see anything but the backs of Marines and idlers, Peter had fretted himself into a smoking rage.

'It's Brazil,' said Keppel, running by.

'I can't *see*,' cried Peter, in a weak scream.

It appeared that Keppel had not heard, for he did not stop, and Peter fumed some more, glaring malignantly at the impervious red backs of the soldiers. But two minutes later a block rushed silently down a foot from his head and he heard Keppel's voice in the rigging. 'Make fast and sway him up,' said Keppel.

'Make fast it is,' said Ransome, hurriedly and furtively taking several turns round Peter's body to lash him into his hammock. 'For to stop you falling out, cock,' he explained in a secret wheeze at Peter's ear. 'Because why? There's a dozen hammer-heads alongside, ravening like a charity school. The bollo-sharks prefer the leeward side, for the dead 'uns,' he added, as a piece of information calculated to gratify an invalid. 'Here he comes—handsomely, now.' And Peter felt himself rise: he mounted until he reached a strange position, sloping at forty-five degrees from the horizontal with his head uppermost, and there he hung, something like a swaddled baby, placidly regarding the purple land that now stretched long across the lowest sky, more fixed than any cloud. It was neatly done, while every eye in the ship was turned elsewhere, and for a long while it remained undetected, long enough for a slight return of the fever, aided by the excitement, to make Peter's head wonderfully light, and to people the distant land with an interesting host of creeping elephants. However, one striking irregularity in the orderly row of hammocks was bound to attract unfavourable notice sooner or later.

'Who is in that hammock up there?' asked the Commodore.

'Which, sir?' came the first lieutenant's anxious voice: then much more loudly. 'Mr Palafox, what are you doing there?'

'Admiring the New World, sir,' called Peter. 'An't it pure?'

'Who presumed to raise that hammock?'

'Loving hands unseen,' cried Peter, giggling feebly. 'Nautical enterprise, cock.'

'Mr Palafox, you will hear from me.'

'Liberty for ever,' cried Peter, freeing one arm and waving it. 'Three times huzzay,' and he madly flung a half-sucked lemon straight at the quarter-deck.

'Sir,' said Mr Walter's agitated voice in the awful hush, 'sir, consider—the boy is out of his mind. Fevered, sir.'

'He'll be out of his skin directly,' said the first lieutenant.

'Mr Saunders,' said the Commodore crisply, 'I should like that hammock trimmed at once, if you please.'

The squadron lay at anchor in the harbour of Santa Catarina, or St Catherine's, as they all called it, on the analogy of St Helen's and by way of showing their independence—no truck with silly foreign names. Christmas had come and gone: a strange Christmas, with ninety-five degrees of humid heat, and a feast of boiled parrots and something that was alleged to have been a monkey. Peter was still nominally on the sick-list,

but he was sufficiently recovered to make a sad beast of himself; and in spite of the surgeon's prognostication of a tenes-
mus, his iron digestion, trained on Rectory cooking for years,
surmounted parrot without a murmur—indeed, he appeared
to thrive upon it, for after a very little while he deserted the
hospital tent and haunted the *Centurion*, where every inch of
standing rigging was being set up afresh for their voyage round
the Horn.

It was on the second day of returning to the ship that he was
the solitary witness of Ransome's joke. Ransome was in
charge of a party sending up preventer-shrouds at the mainmast. 'It's a preventer-shroud,' he explained to Peter, 'for to
prevent 'er from rolling the mast by the board.'

After some little time he looked up from his work with a
startled look, which was succeeded by a gleam of delighted
surprise. 'That was a joke,' he cried, hardly able to believe it
yet. 'I made a joke. I said, "It's a preventer-shroud, to prevent
'er from rolling her mast by the board," come heavy weather.
To prevent 'er. A preventer to prevent 'er. Do you smoke it?'

'Yes,' said Peter. 'Ha, ha.'

'Oh, I wish your mate was here,' said Ransome, 'the other
Teague, I mean—now don't get into a mother, no offence,
cully. He dearly loved a joke. I must tell the . . .'

He hurried off to tell the working-party. 'Hor, hor,' said the
working-party, but rather shortly; they did not really believe
that this flight of wit was spontaneous. They were convinced
that it had been prepared well in advance, probably from a
book; and Hairy Amos gave it as his opinion that 'Mr Ransome, though a tolerable good seaman, was trying to fly too
high, by half."

It was not only the fascination of Ransome's jokes (for
Ransome, once launched on his career, strained every limb to
make another) that drew Peter aboard, nor even the exceedingly interesting work in hand; but in fact the island was a
dismal place. There were the hospital tents, with sick and
dying men—they buried forty Centurions alone—and then in
the stifling heat, the morning fogs, the evening mosquitoes in

their clouds, followed by the nocturnal sand-flies, the baffling and sticky impenetrability of the jungle, rank unhealthy jungle hemming in the few paths; and all this did somewhat counteract the charm of the brilliant macaws in every tree, the monkeys peering down, the wonderful fruit that the few inhabitants whom the grasping and avaricious governor would allow to trade with them brought to the guarded edge of the encampment. All these things weighed heavily against the fascination of the New World—the high land of Brazil (High Brazil, they called it) could be seen from the island—and the delights of the low latitudes, like the fire-flies and the fantastic flowers: and after reflection Peter decided that he liked the Tropics, but not very much. And then again, with so much doing all around him and he feeling so very much better, he felt left out and disagreeably like a shirker.

The squadron was busy indeed. The *Tryal* was hove right down—the sloop's tall masts had been giving endless trouble—and every ship rang with the blunt sound of the caulkers' hammers; there were miles and miles of rigging to be rove, great guns to be struck down into the hold to reduce rolling, an infinity of vital tasks, quite apart from the wooding, watering and victualling of the ships. They were short-handed, as they always had been, and men were dying fast of tropical disease: everything must be done at great speed, not only to leave such an unhealthy place, and not only to reach the Horn before the onset of the austral winter, but to be at sea in the highest possible state of preparedness in case of a meeting with the Spanish squadron.

'They mount three hundred and four guns to our combined two hundred and thirty-six,' said Elliot, 'and that gives them sixty-eight more than us, quite apart from their extra weight of metal—the *Guipuscoa* has thirty-sixes in her lower tier.'

'But they are only Spaniards,' observed Peter.

'Dagoes,' said Preston.

'There you go again,' said Ransome, 'calling names. How can you be so simple? Don't you know they have been rounding the Horn and sailing the South Sea these hundred year and more, where we never been? You got to be a right seaman to do that, ain't you? It is just like these farming coves by land. They say, "Oh, it is only a parcel of Spaniards," they say. "Our men beat them, in course." So you get no thanks because it is only natural, and if you are beat because you was out-gunned and out-manned and you could not open your gun-deck ports, which we swim too low to open 'em now in a hatful of wind, and the Spaniard has a tumble-home as high as a first-rate with all his guns in play—why, then they are down on you, these City coves and these farmers, like a hundred of bricks, and call you a pitiful fellow. No. You can say whatever you like,' he continued obstinately, although no one had contradicted him, 'but the Spaniards can build ships and sail 'em and fight 'em too.'

'It stands to reason they can,' said Elliot, 'and in the wardroom they say there is a correspondence between the governor of this place and the Spaniards on the mainland: so they will know our force now, if they did not know it before; and they will take their measures accordingly.'

'You can say what you like,' repeated Ransome, shaking his head, 'but if the Spaniards can't build ships and sail 'em and fight 'em too, you may call me Jack Pudding.'

7

'WHEN THE WIND SHIFTS AGAINST THE SUN, TRUST IT NOT, FOR back twill run,' said the sailmaker's mate, squinting at the sky through the eye of his needle. 'No, Mr Palafox,' he added, 'you must put the cringle *so*, and your palm *so*. We don't do it Greenock-fashion in the Navy.'

They were on the fo'c'sle, sitting cross-legged among a vast area of canvas, and the working-party was reinforcing everything that could be reinforced. The squadron was three days out of St Catherine's, where they had worked almost without intermission; but still there was a great deal to be done, and aboard the *Centurion* at least, the 'tween-decks were still crowded with stores, and there was even less room to move than before. Some of the stores (and four hundred men eat and drink far more than a ton a day, even on Navy rations) were still on the hoof, in the form of little lumpish black cattle, whose dismal noise could be heard from far below, together with the steady nagging sound of Sean reasoning, though only verbally now, with the butcher, on the subject of glory.

' "Trust it not, for back 'twill run",' repeated Peter. 'That's poetry.'

'Aye. And it's truth too, as we shall find before the moon comes up. Now, sir, if you will kindly move your stern from the luff of this here sail, maybe we can come at it more easy.'

'You may expect bad weather,' announced Peter, entering the midshipmen's berth.

'Don't be so pompous, Teague,' said Bailey.

'Anyone would think he had invented the weather,' said Preston.

'They have so much of it in Ireland that he thinks he is part-proprietor,' said Hope.

'It rains every day there,' said Keppel.

'It does not,' cried Peter. 'Or at least, not very much. But you are a set of low, ignorant fellows, and I am resolved not to notice you. And who's been at my sea-chest? A man cannot leave anything in this berth, unless he takes it with him.'

'I did,' said Bailey. 'I have to see the Commodore, and I hadn't a clean shirt.'

'Then you ought to have turned your own inside out, as you always do for mustering.'

'Oh, what a lie!' cried Bailey, going very red. 'I never did, except that once.'

'You always do: it is very noisome, Bailey. And it was a great piece of folly to go to sea with only one shirt to your name.'

'I had two,' cried Bailey, 'and anyway it's all very well for you to talk, with all FitzGerald's dunnage and a dozen of everything. I think it is perfectly disgusting to go prancing about like a South Sea Bubble, with cambric flying in every direction. I've a month's mind to heave it all overboard, except for what the berth decides are strict necessities.'

'You and who to help you?' asked Peter, advancing with a meaning pace.

'You leave me alone,' said Bailey, moving briskly sideways. 'I am all dressed up, and washed, and I am not going through it all over again for the pleasure of giving you a beating. But you are far too well-off: it is not decent in a midshipman.'

' "Angustam, amici, pauperiem pati

Robustus acri militia puer

Condiscat," ' said Elliot, coming in, 'And I bet you cannot construe that, Palafox.'

'Certainly I can,' said Peter, who had heard it many, many times from Mr Walter—almost every time, indeed, that he had applied to that worthy man for a guinea from the small stock the chaplain held for him. 'But I do not choose to display my learning.'

'Ha, ha,' said Keppel.

'Can *you* do it?'

'I dare say,' said Keppel. 'Anyway, I lay a month's pay I can make out more words than Teague. Tip us the verse again, Elliot.' Keppel paused. 'It's Horace, I know,' he said. 'We did it at school. Angustem pauperiem, the anxious pauper. Militia, the anxious, or care-worn, *military* pauper—the midshipman, in short. Amici acri, sour friends—the other fellows in the berth. Condiscat—oh well, never mind. What do you make of it, Teague?'

Peter pushed aside the moulting ape—the one survivor of the many creatures from Madeira: Agamemnon had coped with the rest—and declaimed, 'Let the robust youth, my friends, be trained to endure pinching want in the active exercise of arms.'

'Exactly what I said,' cried Keppel: but eight bells struck away his words, and the robust youths whose watch was called hurried on deck.

Peter's was the first watch, and in the dead hours of the night it became clear that the prediction was coming true. The top-lantern was already swinging in a great and increasing arc overhead, while aft the great poop-lantern rose and fell against a darkness so close and dense that it seemed as if the black sky had come far down under the force of the wind to hem them in. It was a great hot wind from the east, gusty and full of flaws, and it came over the *Centurion*'s larboard quarter, bringing flat-long sheets of spray across the deck: they handed the topgallant-sails, and Peter, going aloft, heard the masts singing for the first time in his life. He knew all the notes of the rigging very well, but this was something new, a deep and vibrant groan that one could feel as well as dimly hear, and it was caused, he found, by the working of the masts against one another in the trestle-trees and caps: the masts themselves were alive, bending and tense in spite of the bar-tight weather-rigging.

Yet still the *Centurion* buried her lee-rails in a white line of foam, palely luminous in the dark: at six bells all hands were turned up to shorten sail again, and at eight bells Peter tumbled below more dead than alive, helped on his way by a green sea that smothered the quarter-deck waist deep.

He was soaked, but stifled with heat, and he swung himself into his hammock without taking off more than his jacket, for it was ten to one that the watch below would be piped up before very long.

'It is scarcely worth while going to sleep,' he thought, staring at the lamp as it lurched in time with his hammock.

Then, through a confused dream of drums and guns, came the sound of the middle watch coming below and Ransome's voice calling upon him to rise and shine. 'It's beginning to blow,' he said. 'Take care on deck, young Teague.'

The first thing that met Peter's eye was the white top of a wave towering over the fife-rails, and the next was the first lieutenant's irritated face.

'Mr Palafox,' he said in a voice that sounded clearly above the roar of the wind, the uninterrupted thunder of the sea and the loud harping of the mizzen shrouds, 'what do you mean by being late on deck? Go below, sir, and do not present yourself again with your hair uncombed. This is a man-of-war, not the Calais packet. I shall expect to see you again in fifteen seconds, properly dressed and brushed.'

At four bells Peter and Bailey were below again, breakfasting on a tin mug of small beer and a ship's biscuit. 'You wouldn't believe how it is blowing,' Peter told the only midshipman awake.

'Is the sun up yet?' asked Hope sleepily.

'No,' said Bailey, wringing some more sea out of his pocket. 'But you couldn't see it if it was. There's a fog you could cut with a knife.'

'And it is blowing,' said Peter, 'with a preternatural blast.'

'I wish you would shut up,' said Keppel.

'You and your preter-thingummy blasts,' said Ransome, suddenly waking up. 'Why, when I was in the *Royal Oak* off the Sound I had my pigtail blown off, and never reckoned it out of the way. Is your pigtail blew off yet?'

'No,' said Peter.

'Well, then,' said Ransome, instantly going to sleep.

On deck Peter, with the small comfort and the small beer inside him, found that the fog had whitened, and now the substance of it could be seen tearing through the rigging: so the sun had risen. But even after half an hour the drum-tight fore-topsail was still no more than a curved grey hint in the racing whiteness, and still the wall of fog enclosed the ship, sailing with it at a breakneck pace: from the dim wall to the windward the grey waves came racing faster still, curling high, sweeping with a shocking speed along the *Centurion*'s side; and all the time their tops were whipped off in long lines before them—hard water, not blowing foam, which hurled across the

126

deck and filled the air. With the rising of the sun the wind increased.

'Mr Elliot,' said the first lieutenant, 'go for'ard and see that number two is double-breeched. Mr Palafox, my compliments to the Commodore, and the wind is freshening.'

Peter's aye-aye was choked by a hissing mass of water that hit his face just as he opened his mouth: it was as if someone had flung a bucketful with great force, at very close range, and a good deal went down. He hurried up the sloping deck, scrambling under the lee of the men at the wheel, passed the sentry at the cabin door, and plunged, dripping, into the presence of the Commodore. He found the great man in a night-cap, firmly stayed fore and aft, in the act of shaving himself with a gleaming razor.

'Thank you, Mr Palafox,' said the Commodore, deftly timing his stroke to the pitch of the ship. 'My compliments to Mr Saunders, if you please, and I will be on deck in three minutes.'

Four minutes later, as the quarter-deck guns barked out the order to the invisible squadron to bring to with the larboard tacks aboard, Peter was half-way up to the fore-topsail yard, with his hands just below the heels of Matthews, the captain of the foretop, and below him the hitherto clean-swept deck was alive with men as the crew prepared to hand the topsails, bunt the main-course and bring the ship into the wind.

Handing a sail, a square-sail, consists of going out along the yard, with your feet below it on a rope slung parallel with the yard, attached to it, and called the horse; the yard comes to your middle, and when you have reached your proper place on the yard you lean over it and grapple with the sail that bellies out below you while men on deck haul on the bunt-lines and clewlines to raise the lower part of the sail up towards the yard, thus helping you to wrap the sail close to it, making all fast with the gaskets and so furling it. It sounds fairly simple; and in theory it is fairly simple; but when the sail has an area of three thousand square feet, and when huge quantities of it balloon with enormous violence into your face, nearly knocking you off your perch and quite ripping all the careful folds of canvas from under your hands (which usually means that the men on either side of you have their hard-won sail torn away too, so that they hate your vitals), and when the wind is so strong that every inch of the canvas is frantically alive, so strong that the horse tends perpetually to fly into the bunt of the sail, leaving you without a footing, why then it all becomes more complicated, particularly when everything is done in a howling fog. However, there is this compensation: if the wind is blowing hard enough you scarcely can fall off, because you are pinned to the whipping yard by its force, bent in a hair-pin's curve. Yet if it is impossible to fall to the deck, it is also very difficult to get down there by any less drastic method, because once the sail is furled the wind has a free passage, the horse is even more violently strained away towards the bowsprit, and you are held between Heaven and the sea until the wind chooses to abate or until you manage to elude it by judicious writhes and gropings inwards along the yard. What released Peter was not any diminution of the wind, nor his cramped inching towards the slings, but the movement of the ship: with immense way on her still, despite the reduction of sail, the *Centurion* turned into the eye of the wind and lay there pitching furiously, held by her reefed mizzen. In the same moment the gale, which had hitherto pinned Peter to the yard from behind, came full into his face and hurled him backwards from it; the horse also shot out to its sternward limit, and Peter, whose legs were shorter than those of the men for whom the distance between the horse and the yard had been calculated, lost his footing. He had his right hand firmly round the gasket, however, and for a moment he presented the interesting spectacle of an almost horizontal body, slightly attached to the foretopmast yard, slowly revolving about its own axis. Matthews, the man outside him, who had been waiting with what patience he could muster until Peter should reach the slings, leant inwards, grasped Peter by the hair and dragged him forward over the yard, at the same time hooking his bare foot round the horse and bringing it under Peter's searching toes: this done, and the midshipman settled, Matthews crawled bodily over him and hurried down—he had a nice bloater toasting by the galley fire, and he did not want it to get too brown, any more than he wanted to receive the stinging whack from the bos'un's rope's end which was the usual reward of being the last man on deck.

'Mr Palafox,' said the second lieutenant, 'you are not to play in the rigging. This is no time for acrobatics. And do not rub your scalp when I am speaking to you. In spite of the fog I saw you imitating an ape on the fore-topmast yard just now: there is no need to emulate the same creature on the quarter-deck. The ape, sir, is not an animal that a sea-officer should take for his model, whatever you may suppose from the manners and appearance of the midshipmen's berth.'

'What is this I hear, young man?' said Mr Walter, meeting him at four bells in the forenoon watch. 'It is said that you take advantage of the prevailing obscurity to amuse yourself aloft. I wonder at it. It might have been hoped that your recent illness would have turned your mind into a more serious course.'

'Now let there be no monkeying about in *this* watch,' said Mr Brett, at noon. 'Mr Palafox, you may take—no, not Mr Palafox. Mr Bailey, you may take a glass up and see what you can make out as the fog lifts. Mr Palafox, you may make yourself useful to Mr Randall in the shot-lockers. There you will find less to tempt you to untimely gambolling.'

'Aye-aye, sir,' said Peter, acutely aware that the Commodore, as well as two or three of the land-officers, was just behind the officer of the watch: he vanished, and far down by the well he saw nothing of the coming of the sky, nor of the reappearance of part of the squadron through the tearing veils of mist. Part of the squadron: for the *Pearl* was no longer there. The *Pearl* was gone, and no amount of scanning of the clear horizon could find the remotest trace of her. And at first the rumour, which instantly penetrated to every part of the ship, reaching the shot lockers five minutes after the fact was reported on the quarter-deck, gave out that the *Tryal* had also disappeared: but a little later it was said that she had been seen a great way to the leeward, with her mainmast gone, and that the *Gloucester* had been ordered to bear down and take her in tow.

'I hope she swims, I am sure,' said the gunner, meaning the *Pearl*, 'but there was a cruel amount of sickness in her. I saw Captain Kidd looking wholly pale when I went aboard her last. Howsoever, she should have rode it out, unless she loosed her guns, which is barely likely, seeing she has a good gunner in Mr Webb. We were shipmates in the year twenty-eight, in the *Vanguard*, ninety—the same as what they call the *Duke*, only nobody minds it. Pass me that tally, will you, Mr Palafox?'

The tally lay between two balls in a partially-filled shot-garland, and as Peter groped for it in the dim light of a bleary lantern, one of the twenty-four pound cannon-balls, impelled by the pitch of the *Centurion* in the enormous swell, rolled with a deep growl against the other, nipping Peter's finger so that tears of anguish came into his eyes and he sprang about very briskly, waving his hand and roaring.

'This is what I mean about her loosing her guns,' said Mr Randall when Peter had quietened down. 'You perceive the force of a ball rolling free for scantly a foot: now consider the force of a gun that has broke loose, and think what a whole broadside rolling free can do. And you must consider, too, that the roll is much less down here than it is on the gun-deck even, let alone the upper; for she rolls from her keelson, do you see, though she pitches regardless. But I tell you what it is, Mr Palafox,' he added, after a long pause, filled with the dull, thunderous grumbling of ball, chain and double-headed shot as the tons and tons of iron shifted gently and settled with the varying strains of the bucking sea: 'I tell you what it is,' he repeated, notching the tally. 'I did not altogether like to hear you sing out so loud over a little pinch. We did ought to remember the Spartan boy, Mr Palafox.'

This wretched fellow, this Spartan boy (a half-wit, in Peter's private judgment), had haunted the Rectory of Ballynasaggart, and had followed him aboard to appear on eight separate occasions in Mr Walter's conversation: Peter was perfectly well acquainted with him and his stupid ways; but he wished to be civil to the gunner, so with as much appearance of interest as he could summon with a handful of agony to distract him he said, 'The Spartan boy, Mr Randall?'

'He had stolen a fox, which he hid it under his gown, and when his elders were talking, the fox started to gnaw the boy.' Mr Randall made a lobster's claw of his right hand and snapped it to indicate the gnawing. 'But did he sing out, Mr Palafox? Did he cry, "——the——fox. I will rouse it out of my gown"—for they wore gowns in those days, Mr Palafox—"and dowse it overboard"? No. Not he. He sat quiet while his elders were talking and the fox gnawed through his stomach, through his liver, clean through his anatomies until it reached his heart. Which is a clear proof that you should not cry out when pinched—a trifle that happens to a gunner fifty times a day.'

Peter thought that it was a clear proof that the elder Spartans talked far too much: but after a moment's thought he decided to suppress this reflection as being disrespectful, and instead he asked, 'Would it not have done to have slipped the fox quietly out, without interrupting or saying anything?'

'It might have been more expedient,' admitted the gunner, 'but, oh goodness me, how very much less moral.'

'Why did he want the fox in the first place, Mr Randall, sir?'

'A very fair question, Mr Palafox,' said the gunner evasively. 'However, we will not go into that just now, for it scarcely would be fit. They had some very old-fashioned ways in those times, you know. Very old-fashioned, they were: and Papists, I make no doubt. When I was a boy there were some old master-gunners who always made a cross on the ball before they loaded, which was left over from the old days when they aimed their pieces at the Turks and such, and reckoned that a cross on the ball would send any Turk to hell;

131

which is all part and parcel of the same thing, do you see? Mumbo-jumbo, as you might say.'

The connexion escaped Peter: but he very distinctly remembered that every single ball that Mr Randall had handled in the many days of gunnery practice had had its little cross.

'You may reckon three degrees as sixty leagues—sixty sea-leagues, mind,' said Elliot. 'So it is roughly sixty leagues then, since we crossed the latitude of the river Plate.'

'So we are a thousand miles from St Catherine's,' said Peter, adding up the figures on his slate.

A thousand miles of sea, and some sweet sailing.

'And with this lovely southern current,' said Peter, 'we ought to reach the Horn in about the same time.'

'The *Tryal* has to be refitted first,' said Elliot.

'Yes,' said Peter, staring over the side towards the sloop, an odd, maimed object with a dwarfish jury-mast, lagging behind the *Gloucester*, which fumed at the end of the tow-rope, with every possible sail set to keep up with the squadron. 'Yes, but even so . . .' He did not finish the sentence, and although his eyes were fixed on the squadron—the *Severn* ahead of the *Centurion*, then the fat-sided *Wager* with her oddly patched foretopgallantsail, the little *Anna* pink to leeward, and last the *Gloucester* and her burden: but an empty place where the *Pearl* had sailed—he did not see them, any more than his ears consciously perceived the steadily repeated splash of the lead and the cry of the man in the channels, a cry that had run through all the watches these many days, ever since they had come into soundings again. Mr Walter stood a few feet from them, taking samples of the sandy bottom that the deep-sea line brought up on the tallow put to the lead: he was exceedingly interested in this pursuit and he kept up a continual private conversation with himself upon it. Yet neither Elliot nor Peter heard a word of it; for not only were both accustomed to the only way of finding peace in an overcrowded man-of-war, which is to shut yourself up from the perpetual outside din and jostling, but the minds of both were already away round the Horn and far upon what Peter thought of as "the other side"—the coast of Chile and Peru.

Nobody knew the contents of the Commodore's orders but himself: but although there was a great deal of variety in the squadron's conjectures this only applied to the details, and the main intention of the expedition was very clearly understood to be the harrying of the Spaniards in the Great Southern Ocean. And that, to the dullest soul aboard, meant gold. Visions of treasure filled the gun-deck, where the men swung in their close-packed hammocks: at St Catherine's tales had come aboard of Indian tribes who used gold fish-hooks, and gold to weigh down their nets, tribes where the children played at alley-tor with marbles made of gold; and the more these tales were repeated by their original hearers the more their fascinated audiences asked for more. There were tales of the Incas, shining in armour made of gold, and of the Spaniards who took all the gold away and shipped it to Old Spain in galleons every year: hundreds of these tales, many with a strong vein of truth, and all believed. The five ships' companies were all, from the ward-room to the obscurest holes where the loblolly boys had their being, in a strong and highly advanced state of greed: they all knew that a powerful Spanish force lay between them and the accomplishment of their desires, but with one accord they dismissed that as a trifling nuisance. Their fever to be at the task of loading the hold with bullion made them wonderfully attentive to their duties, and now that even the stupidest impressed ploughboy was something like a seaman, they would fairly fly aloft to make sail and increase the squadron's pace: and on the other hand, they would look pensive and discontented, if not downright mutinous, when under the impulsion of a growing wind the studdingsails and royals showed signs of carrying away and were obliged to be taken in—there never was such a crew for cracking on; and Mr Walter made himself downright unpopular by his often-expressed wish to have more time to study the ocean's floor.

'Yes,' said Elliot, as if Peter had spoken. 'I hope you may

be right. After all, it should not take long to set up a mainmast of sorts. One of our spare topmasts would answer very well. I wonder they have not done it themselves, the helpless set of lubbers.' He looked angrily at the crippled *Tryal*. 'After all, good Heavens above, she's only a sloop, and has no right to give herself such airs. Look how the *Gloucester* yaws,' he said, as the sluggish *Tryal* snatched at the tow in the long swell and made the close-hauled *Gloucester* spill her wind. 'I must say I find it hard to wait,' he continued. 'I want to fill my pockets with moidores until there is no room for my hands.' He drummed impatiently on the rail, and a flush mounted in his keen brown face. 'It is not for myself,' he added. 'I don't care a farthing candle—but there are special reasons, you know.'

Peter nodded, and he was about to speak when Ransome and Keppel came hurriedly aft towards them. Ransome was strangely pale under his tan, obviously the prey of some strong emotion.

'Has Agamemnon had them?' cried Peter.

Agamemnon, that turbulent cat, who ordinarily ruled the berth with an implacable tyranny, selecting the warmest midshipman as a bedfellow whenever Ransome was on duty and beating that midshipman whenever he moved as well as biting as hard as a dog at the first suspicion of a snore, had grown weirdly meek since St Catherine's—meeker and meeker as the signs of her approaching maternity increased. It was known, moreover, that Ransome, who fed the expectant mother with a pap-boat, dreaded the arrival and the consequent destruction of the kittens with a degree of open cowardice that would have disgraced a maiden lady. He had distinguished himself in the battle of Cape Passaro, could face a broadside yard-arm to yard-arm with the utmost composure, and had cleared the quarter-deck of a Spanish brig-of-war with no more than a belaying-pin, single-handed: but he could not drown kittens. There was no question about the drowning: the first, second, third, fourth, fifth and sixth lieutenants, all of whom had been scratched, bitten and generally maltreated and bullied by Agamemnon, were quite as firm as the chaplain, the surgeon and his mate, the carpenter, the gunner, the bo'sun and all the others in whose cabins Agamemnon had been sick. 'The animal is a menace to the well-being of the ship, and should be destroyed,' they said, 'but in all events we are determined that the breed shall not be perpetuated.'

'No, it is not that,' said Keppel. 'Go on, Ransome. Tell them.'

'You see that sloop?' said Ransome, hoarser than usual.

'Yes,' said Peter and Elliot, staring.

'Well, she's quite small.'

'All right,' said Peter. 'What of it?'

'But she's a *great* trial to the *Gloucester*. She's a great *Tryal*—oh hor, hor, hor.' Ransome could not contain himself long enough to explain the joke fully, but between writhes and gasps he did his best. 'A *great* trial—hor, hor—*Tryal*—you smoke it? Oh, my stomach. I got it out solemn, didn't I?' he wheezed to Keppel, thrusting him half-way through the neatly triced hammocks in the weather-netting. 'I said, "You see that there sloop?" and they says, "Yes, we see un," and I says—oh, hor, hor, hor *hor*.'

'That's the second I made,' he said faintly, as they supported him below. 'The first was before. It was very good, but not as good as this. Oh I hope I live to tell them all in Wapping. Oh, my stomach. Oh.'

The great bay of St Julian and the empty pampas rolling to the sea: the illimitable plain and the cold wind over it—a world almost devoid of life and bare of men except for this one brief week of intensely crowded busyness in a corner of the bay, when a tiny stretch of the enormous shore was black with men from all seven ships of the squadron, and the bowl of the sea re-echoed with the sound of hammers as the *Tryal* was put to rights. Seven ships, for the *Pearl* had rejoined. They had seen her on the same day that St Julian's had heaved up on the starboard bow, and she had fled from the approaching ships with all sail set to the royals; for only a week before she had fallen in with five Spanish men-of-war, one wearing a pennant

135

so closely modelled on the Commodore's that she had been deceived, and discovering her mistake almost too late, had escaped only by running under full sail over shoaling water—a horrible risk that the Spaniards refused to take. The second time, therefore, the *Pearl*'s first lieutenant (her captain lay at the bottom of the sea fourteen days out of St Catherine's) decided not to endanger his command, and would have vanished over the rim of the sea had not the *Severn* and the *Gloucester* been better sailors. As it was it took them hours and hours of furious cracking on before they ran her down and found her cleared for action, with all her teeth showing.

The excitement over the *Pearl* was very great; the certainty of the Spaniards' presence was more exciting still; but the necessity of working without a moment's respite in order not to be caught on shore, and in order to meet the Horn and the enemy in a well-found state, overlaid it all; and Peter, for one, came away with few distinct memories standing out from a confused impression of an immense amount of work accomplished in a very short period of time; and if he had been asked what Patagonia was like, he would have replied that it was a dry, brown, treeless, inhuman land with nothing attractive in it except the penguins on the shore—and even they were too inquisitive, always hurrying in to stand in rows among the work—a country, moreover, where the men were perpetually trying to creep away and dig for gold in the dusty grass.

But when they were at sea Peter had time for his journal again. This was not the official journal that every midshipman was required to keep, with his navigational records like a subsidiary ship's log-book, but a private account which Elliot had urged him to start, and which he had kept since latitude 28° S.

'March 5th lat 52° 32' S. When we got under way *Gloucester* fouled her anchor and after 7 guns to order her to her station, cut her cable. Her people in a horrible mother. How we laughed. But before that there was a council of war, with land-officers and all captains: we are to attack Baldavia. And

Capt. Murray of *Wager* is to have *Pearl*, Mr Cheap from *Tryal* to be capt. of *Wager*, and Mr Saunders to command *Tryal*, but he is too sick to move so Mr Saumarez holds his place, which makes Mr Brett first of *Centurion* pro. tem. He will be charm-ingly mild. We have had poor little winds, but we raised Cape Virgin Mary yesterday. It grows precious cold. Am very glad of FitzGerald's warm things. Fitted Sean into his largest pea-jacket, with canvas to make out. I left my spoon in the sand at St Julian's. Elliot says no two officers have the same longi-tude for St Julian's—some make it under 70° W. and some as high as 74° 30′. He explained about lunar observations and the chronometrical machine, which I wish they would find out, for it is impossible to be sure of your longitude without you know the time it is on the meridian of Greenwich. Though you can find your position by transits. . . .' There followed a long and creditably intelligent piece about sidereal time, lunar tables and astral navigation. Then Peter wrote, 'Mem. to tell Sean to put more lemon in the young whiskey, and to ask the sailmaker to let out my reefer. Ransome made a joke on the 2nd and is working on another now. He says he Did for Agamemnon's little cats, but we believe he has hidden them abaft the well. Preston's ape died yesterday, which is the last of them all: he grieved very much, though it was a wicked ape and never would love him. Mr Woodfall begged to dissect it, but Preston would not indulge him, saying that the ape was the better Christian by ½. All the captains came aboard of Cape Virgin Mary, in a sweet calm. Thought Mr Cheap (made post into *Wager* from *Tryal*) and Mr Saumarez looked very conscious and solemn. Hope said he pitied the poor midship-men in *Tryal* and would not be in their place for 10 l. and not for 20 l. when Mr Saunders gets better. The squadron is to sail very close as we have great hopes of falling in with the Dons, and any officer of the watch who allows his ship to be more than 2 miles from *Centurion* is to be reported to the Commo-dore. While the captains were aboard somebody blew himself up aboard the *Gloucester* and all the captains screeched out Fire and rushed off like hares. How we laughed. But it only turned out to be a little blaze of powder: and then it came on to blow and we lay to until the end of my watch. Cape Virgin Mary is the entrance of Magellan's Strait, but we are to go through the Straits Le Maire, because——'

'Scribble, scribble, scribble, Mr Palafox,' said Bailey, hurtling into the berth with his customary delicate tread, 'what an old Scribe and Pharisee you are becoming. Han't you heard of the landfall?'

Peter flung his book and his pen aside and ran on deck to join the starers. It was a dim greyness looming from a mass of cloud, much like any other landfall from the deck and at that distance, but every unoccupied man aboard gazed at it with passionate attention, for this was Tierra del Fuego, and round its farther side ran the tides of the Great South Sea, the Pacific Ocean.

After a long while Peter went below for a thick jacket and joined Ransome and Keppel in the fore-topgallant crosstrees: the squadron was standing in along the shore, and from this somewhat over-crowded eminence one could clearly see the land—more and more distinctly every minute.

'I say, it's uncommon bleak, ain't it?' said Keppel, staring at the cruel black cliffs through the rain.

'What a coast to be to the windward of,' said Ransome, 'in a strong nor-easter. I never seen a single place you could run for, all the time we been coasting here, nor a single place where you could land a boat, not if it was ever so.' He poked his telescope towards the unbroken line of surf. 'God give us sea-room on a coast like this,' he said.

'I don't know,' said Peter, turning up his collar. 'I think it looks rather like home.'

'Then you must come from a damned uncomfortable place,' said Keppel, judiciously. But the wrangle was cut short by a hail from the quarter-deck. 'Mast-head, there. What do you see on the larboard bow?'

'Nothing, sir,' bawled the mast-head. 'Only cloud and rain.'

'They are looking for Staten Island,' observed Keppel; and in a low chant he sang, 'For Staten Island ho, for Staten Island hee.'

'Deck,' hailed the look-out. 'There's something white in them clouds on the larboard bow. Three points on the larboard bow. I think it's snow,' he added in a private voice, 'for it's cold enough, I'm sure.'

As the day wore on there was no doubt about its being snow: the appalling desolation of Staten Island drew very close indeed, so that without moving from the deck one could see the towering cliffs and mountains of Tierra del Fuego on the one hand, and on the other mountains and cliffs that made the first look mild; for those of Staten Island soared black and naked up to eternal snow, with never a tree or a kindly beach to alleviate their malignity.

Rain swept across the face of Tierra del Fuego: from Staten Island a squall brought a drumming of hailstones into the sails.

The Commodore never left the quarter-deck: this was barely charted land and sea, rarely traversed by Englishmen except for a few buccaneers, and they too busy keeping afloat to make accurate observations. Beside him Mr Brett worked diligently at his easel, drawing the coast-line—a strange implement aboard a man-of-war, and a strange occupation for the acting first lieutenant. The seamen stared, and exchanged covert winks; but their respect for the Commodore kept them from despising this lady-like accomplishment, and they did no more than deplore it as a break with tradition.

At night the squadron lay to, for to all appearance the two islands were now one, joining in the distance: no strait between them could yet be found. There was a feeling of tense expectation throughout the squadron, and in the midshipmen's berth of the *Centurion* at least, a babel of conjecture, a poring over charts and a din of heated talk that went on until it was almost entirely quelled by the news that the ship's entire company would spend the night bending a complete new set of sails. Mr Brett might paint pictures at an easel; he might be gently spoken and hardly ever shout or curse; but he was an exceedingly capable officer, and those who expected to find him at all soft in the execution of his duties were horribly mistaken. He intended that the new sails should be bent that

139

night, and that night the new sails were bent.

Two minutes after eight bells in the middle watch found Peter dead asleep, worn out with struggling with an obstinate foretopmast staysail by the fugitive light of the waning moon. But the forenoon watch saw him on the quarter-deck before his time, bubbling with anticipation.

The squadron had opened the Straits Le Maire with the dawn: it was plain now, a wide and obvious gash that had been hidden before by a false fold in the land, and now the crew (a resilient body of men, as sailors must be to survive) was waiting with wholly renewed delight. The wind was fair; at the mizzen flew the signal for *Pearl* and *Tryal* to take station ahead; and after what appeared to be an interminable wait, the Commodore said, 'Very well, Mr Brett; we will make sail, if you please.'

The *Centurion* paid off before the steady east wind, half a gale and more; the hands at the braces moved as one; and she entered the Straits Le Maire.

'I never, *never* seen such a tide,' said Ransome, watching the creamy lines that snaked along the strait. 'Portland race is a gutter to this.'

The *Centurion* was racing through the strait with the wind and the tide at twelve knots. She was foul, as all the squadron was, and from a little way below the water-line to far below her keel she carried a clogging mass of weed, but now the sea was running with her with a prodigious force, and the lowering shores fled by on either hand. Now and then there were stifled cheers from the men crowding the fo'c'sle and waist, shivering but unconscious of the cold, and all looking steadfastly towards the rapidly approaching end of the strait and the open sea.

Peter begged a moment's leave and raced below to drag Sean on deck. 'Look at the sea, you omadhaun,' he said, elbowing through the men at the falls.

'Where?' cried Sean, gazing wildly into the sky.

'There, you mooncalf,' shrieked Peter. 'There. It's the Great South Sea itself, the golden ocean, and we sailing upon it, joy.'

8

WOULD THIS NIGHTMARE NEVER END? PETER SAT ON A LOCKER
in the berth instinctively braced against the prodigious roll: he
held his aching head in the crook of his arm, his forehead
against the dripping oilskin. The icy water that washed about
the deck came almost to his knees on the starboard roll, and
surged across to the other side as the *Centurion* rose again, but
Peter did not notice it—it was so usual now, and he had not
been dry these three weeks past. He slid his free hand down
to ease the familiar pain of his broken ribs, and again he asked
himself, 'Will this nightmare never end?'

It had begun so long ago, within one hour of their clearing
the Straits Le Maire, full of hope and delighted to see the
Southern Ocean. He remembered the beginning so well—
Ransome's voice saying 'Look out for squalls'—the hurried
orders, the onset of the storm from the dark north-west, and
the turning of the monstrous tide, which, dammed up by the
whole continent, had rushed them back so furiously that
before it let them go they were more than twenty miles south
and east of Staten Island, far into the Atlantic once more.

He remembered the beginning: but after that it was a succession of storms, blackness, white water and snow from the
black sky, blackness and such winds that a man must crawl,
clinging to the handlines, hardly able to breathe, to fight his
way along the sheltered waist of the ship. Wind and the perpetual cold, cold so intense that the rigging froze, so bitter that
the flying spray froze on the shrouds, and the ratlines were
round bars of ice; so fierce that every rope and line was rigid,
brittle and never to be trusted: it was a stout rope that had sent

him hurtling from just below the foretop, a rope that broke because its frozen length acted as a lever to shear it in the block. But he had been lucky: his fall had been broken on a man's shoulders before he hit the deck, and it was only the mainstay that had caught him under the heart, staving in a couple of ribs. It was nothing to what some had received: there was Davis, for example, an excellent seaman; he had gone overboard that dreadful time when they had had to wear ship without a sail set, by manning the foreshrouds so that the clinging men formed a resistance to bring her before the wind: and in the insane rolling and the tearing gale Davis had lost his hold. They had seen him swimming strongly for an endless minute, without the faintest chance of launching a boat or bearing up; and they had heard him call to them for life. Then there was Matthews, who was plucked from the ice-sheathed fore-topmast yard in the black night, when the clewlines parted and the sail was lashed to ribbons—he was just a white blur falling and a lost cry swallowed in the wind, barely audible although Peter could almost have touched him. Sommerton, Green, Aiken: so many others. And so many storms. They followed one another, with rare intervals of foggy calm, just long enough for new rigging to be sent up, new sails to be bent, enough for the ship to survive the next somehow—they followed one another so that now it was impossible to sort them out, for they had a nightmarish continuity: it was an unceasing struggle in which time itself had stopped as it stops in the worst of dreams.

'I shall try to write it down,' said Peter, dully. But somewhere in the wash and bilge his journal rocked to and fro, its pages spread and pale. Yet he had done his best to keep it up: for Elliot, only a little while before the end, had begged him to persevere. Elliot had been light-headed then, and going fast; but there had been something cruelly moving about his care for Peter's book.

It was the scurvy, of course, that had broke him down; but it was Cape Noir that killed him. It was on the thirteenth of April. 'I will write it down,' said Peter, again. The thirteenth of April, three days after they had lost the *Pearl* and the *Severn*: thirty-eight days of beating round the Horn, with rarely a sight of the sun or the moon, with a current of enormous but incalculable strength setting eastward and driving them back: yet every officer aboard reckoned their position a good ten degrees west of Tierra del Fuego, and the course was set for the north at last—north, to bring them up the Chilean coast with sea-room and to spare. Edging up to the north with reborn hope the *Centurion*, the *Gloucester*, the *Tryal*, the *Wager* and the little *Anna* pink, shattered, pumping day and night, but still capable of high ambition, sailed day after day. Elliot was already very ill by the first week of April, the teeth loosening in his jaw; he was too weak to get in or out of his hammock, but they brought him the noon-readings whenever they had them, and the dead-reckoning and the rare shots of the moon: he worked their position with Halley's compass deviations pinned up overhead and Frezier's chart beside it. He was quite certain that they were running far clear of the land, running up their northing out of the zone of perpetual storm and into the warmth: it kept him alive.

And on the thirteenth of April, one degree south of the mouth of the Strait of Magellan, and by their reckoning at least two hundred miles to the west, they were steering north-north-west with their larboard tacks aboard and a stiff gale that tore ragged cloud across the racing moon, when at two bells of the middle watch the pink's guns blazed out and right under the lee bow they saw the tremendous surf towering on Cape Noir.

The wind turned and saved them at the last minute, when they were almost in the breakers: they clawed off the shore and stood again for the south and west. But you could feel the courage leak out of the ship: the men felt dumbly that they had done all that men could do, but that it was not enough, and that the ship was accursed. For some days together the winds were fair: the crew could get some rest and even dry their quarters and eat cooked food: but it counted for nothing. The disappointment stunned them; and it killed Elliot.

They were terribly accustomed to death. Peter had seen men drop and die on the deck and had hauled them aside so that they should not impede the work; he had seen so many die: he was hardened to death. But when Elliot went over the side he stood there openly crying: he cried like a child and the tears ran down his face with the rain. It had been so important for Elliot to live; he had not wanted to die, as some of the old men did, and the very sick; and almost the last thing that ever he said was that he must cling on—'for there are special reasons, Peter, you know.'

But that was long ago. Since then they had buried one hundred and seven, for the hopelessness reinforced the scurvy, whatever the surgeon and his mate could do.

After that, what was the main happening? The turning up northwards again; then that appalling sudden storm that caught them with their topsails unhanded and ripped them to thread: no, that storm was after the one when the rest of the ships disappeared. 'I must write it down in succession,' said Peter again.

There had once been a time when it was almost impossible to write in the midshipmen's berth, when you had to take your journal into the top, either because there was physically too little space or because someone would inevitably pour the sand into the ink in a spirit of fun. But now Elliot was gone: and Hope was gone too, vanished at some moment in a furious storm when the ice blew from the sea and drew blood where it touched—no one knew exactly when or how. Keppel was lashed into his hammock, and nobody thought he would leave it. There was room enough now: and now when a midshipman came below he ate silently and fast, devouring what meagre rations and green scum was left, and flung himself into his hammock, dead until the next pipe. There was not much boyishness left in the midshipmen's berth.

'All hands on deck,' came the cry, as familiar as the unceasing clank of the pumps, and Peter lurched off his seat. From the shadows on the other side Ransome and Bailey rose like automata and they went silently on deck. It was the main-

course to be reefed and the yards braced round—a few minutes' work for a single watch in ordinary times, but now a long
and painful toil for the whole ship's company. There were no
idle hands any more, and Peter found himself tailing on to a
brace immediately behind the Commodore's French cook.
On the yard the lieutenants reefed next to the seamen, and Mr
Walter held the wheel with the schoolmaster: but for all this
reinforcement there were now no more than a dozen upper-
yardmen in a watch—a force with which no sixty-gun ship, no
twenty-gun ship, would ever have dreamed of setting sail in a
calm at home—and the simplest working of the ship was a
dangerously slow manoeuvre, which told very heavily on the
few skilled and able-bodied men.

'Listen, cully,' said Ransome quietly, drawing Peter aside
when the work was done and they were dismissed below.
'Listen, cock.' He seemed embarrassed, and Peter looked at
him stupidly. 'It's young Preston,' he said. 'I am not saying he
is frightened—not the wrong colour, you know, eh? But he is
getting low in his spirits, you understand what I mean? Needs
to be give a hand now and then, you smoke it? A cove like
you, with plenty of bottom, could bear up to him: he would
mind your signals more than mine.'

Peter nodded. He knew very well what Ransome meant.
Preston had not yet cracked under the strain, but he was
frightened through and through. They all were: men who
understand the sea, who know that their ship is slowly disinte-
grating, that she is short of food and water, that she is fantastically undermanned, burying six or seven hands a day, and that
she is in the worst seas and the most terrifying storms in the
world, are either frightened or born fools. Peter knew the
danger they were in; he knew that every time he went aloft his
life depended not only upon his own skill and diminishing
strength, but also upon the chance of a rope or a sail carrying
away, and he dreaded it. He was frightened nearly all the time;
he was frightened in his sleep, and had been for weeks and
weeks. It had never occurred to him not to perform his duty,
but he understood how it could come into one's mind to lurk

below, particularly if one's courage were undermined by the scurvy that had by now attacked almost everyone aboard in a greater or a less degree. He understood what Ransome meant.

There was only one man in the *Centurion* who seemed really unmoved. Peter had seen the Commodore anxious, very grave, perturbed; but he had never seen him afraid. He had seen a great deal of Mr Anson, too: the Commodore was rarely from the quarter-deck: whenever Peter's watch was called he found the Commodore there, usually in streaming oilskins, standing somewhat abaft the wheel. He appeared to be made of iron and oak, quite unchanging, except that he grew a little more affable as things grew even worse.

Peter had an immense respect for him, and although they did not often speak, a real affection: the Commodore held the ship together, and the officers drew strength from him. In the very worst of times there was no hint of anarchy: the routine of the ship went on in the most orderly manner that circumstances would allow. Everything that could be done was done, in a seamanlike fashion, quickly, with no thought of argument.

How long anything more could be done was another matter. This was a question that Peter asked himself several times as they cruised off the island of Socorro in the vain hope of finding some other ship of the squadron—for this was their rendezvous in case of separation. They had been cruising, if that is the right term for the staggering progress of a terribly battered vessel with barely enough hands to trim her sails, for a fortnight, and the coast off which they cruised was as inhospitable as all the rest: no hope of any landing or refreshment there. Worse, it was a rendezvous and a station that had been calculated at a time when the squadron was complete and at least adequately manned: it had not been meant for a single ship with a dying crew; but the Commodore would not be found wanting at his appointment or in his duty, and he kept his appointment by cruising there, and he thereby did his duty by taking all possible measures to reassemble his forces in order to attack the Spaniards. So without a moment's peace they cruised, with no sea-room and a terrible shore to the east in a region of westerly gales, in continual anxiety and a painfully dying expectation of their friends.

How long can it go on? thought Peter to himself, as they hurried northwards and south again between the limiting latitudes of their rendezvous, north and south again under topsails and courses—far too much sail, but being unable to lie-to with so little sea-room they were forced to carry it all, though it might very well carry away. Only a few days before the *Centurion* had been struck by lightning: it had injured five fit men who could not be spared, and Mr Brett: it had knocked Peter flat, and when Sean picked him up there was a queer long brown scar on his cheekbone. But what would once have been a nine days' wonder passed with little remark: they were surprised at nothing now, and they carried the stunned sailors below with as much phlegm as the next morning they carried eight of their comrades up from the sombre gun-deck, once so crowded, now so filled with empty bays—carried them up for the usual morning burial service.

How long could it go on? Not much longer, perhaps. But while the ship floated it would float in a naval fashion, with the log heaved regularly, the watches piped up and down, the due observations made and recorded, respect paid to the quarter-deck and the dead buried in decency.

Peter was pleased with three things. The first was that they were now in latitude 45° S., be their longitude what it might, so that even if they went down that day, still they would have rounded the Horn, which was a high point of ambition: the second was that Sean should have done so very well. He had long ago been freed from the butcher's realm—there were no beasts left to tend and the butcher was dead these many leagues to the south—and now Sean was no less a figure than the captain of the foretop. He had greatly distinguished himself by going aloft to cut away a sail that was about to destroy the yard—almost certain death—and in the uncountable subsequent storms he had played a noble part, sure-footed, very strong, skilled, and as brave as ever he was. 'Sure, admiral dear,' he said to the Commodore, on receiving a kind word in the face of the ship's company, 'I have always been quite as brave as a parish of lions—it's no virtue at all, but the blood of my people.'

The third was that Keppel was still alive. He was low, very low, and he appeared to have shrunk to the size of a child; but he kept up his spirits amazingly, and Peter hoped that if only they could make Juan Fernandez within the week—for bitterly against their heart, though forced by sickness and by dwindling stores, they were to make for the next rendezvous in the morning—then they would save him, for everybody knew that Juan Fernandez abounded with scurvy-grass and a hundred such remedies. A week was a fair allowance for the distance between Socorro and the supposed position of Juan Fernandez: but then again there was that infernal question of longitude; their charts all differed, and the island was no more than a speck in the vast Pacific.

'Look out for squalls,' said Ransome, breaking in upon his meditation. Peter looked up. 'Well, that's the queer sky of the world,' he said, looking at the strange massing of violet light in the west. 'I thought we had seen everything; but we have not, I find.' He looked quickly over his shoulder in the direction of the land, and there surely enough rose the infinitely remote white peaks of the Cordillera, far within the continent. The cruel black precipices of the coast were too far beneath the horizon to be seen, but they were there, and a great deal nearer than the mountains.

The crew were already at their stations: the order to hand the topsails came at the same time as a distant growl of thunder. Peter had time to notice a sinister trembling of the sea as he swung up the starboard foreshrouds, on the weather side: it was a trembling ripple of the surface over and above the heavy swell from the west and it travelled with an extraordinary rapidity, jarring the heavy vessel for a second as it passed.

The fore-topsail was half clewed-up. Peter was working between Sean and Sergeant Borroughs of the Marines: leaning over to re-tie the soldier's gasket he heard the flat air suck and sigh. He braced himself for the expected blow, but it came from the wrong direction. The false wind plucked him backwards like a straw; then in an instant the true wind smashed him against the yard with a greater force than he had ever known. The sail flew from its gaskets: momentarily he saw the half-flowed sheet like a bar below him and then it parted silently, the great crack lost in the all-pervading shriek of wind. The sail was a streaming mass, split in every seam, threshing with diabolical strength as it fouled the stays. Sean already had his knife at work, slicing through the earrings. Peter whipped out his own, and the canvas shot away, straight on the wind. He leant inwards to try to make the soldier understand what to do: but there was no soldier there.

In a breathing-space before the wind redoubled they reached the deck. It was a scene of shocking disorder: the gig was sprawled across the waist and the studdingsail booms lay in a criss-cross, brought somehow from the chains, while posed madly upon them all stood the top-lantern. But there was no second of time for gaping: they ran along the hand-line to the mainmast lifts, where a spray-drenched party was striking the yard to save the main-course, the only sail spread that was yet unsplit. Colonel Cracherode was on the rope in front of Peter, and his mouth opened and closed without a sound.

Mr Stapleton was by his side, pulling at his sleeve and pointing forward. Peter understood him to shout something about the bowsprit gammoning, but before the lieutenant could repeat it a green sea hurled him across the deck. Peter passed him a moment later; he was crawling on his hands and knees, reaching to lash himself to the bitts—he was very weak with scurvy, blotched and swollen. There was nothing to be done about the gammoning, nothing but the roughest makeshift: Peter took three men, cut a writhing length of stay and took what turns he could about the bowsprit and the figurehead, making all tight with capstan bars as tourniquets, lashed along the head rails. It took a long time, though it was little enough to stand the enormous strain that the bowsprit must take from the forestays: yet the Centurion's head, still with a lick of gold leaf on his helmet, was unusually solid—it might do something for the moment.

They had been somewhat under the fo'c'sle's lee, and now when they came back to the full force of the storm it seemed to be less: Peter heard the surgeon shout as he passed, 'There's life in us yet.'

The light was fading, and the wind, though still tremendous, was declining with it: yet still squalls hurled out of the darkening sky, from different directions now, and often the high scream reached its intolerable topmost pitch for minutes at a time—blasts that would lift a crouching man into the air. And now the sea that the hurricane had raised caught up with the wind, an enormous hollow sea, racing, scooped into wild irregularities by the squalls, so that the labouring ships had no even motion but ran in mad, jarring lurches—ran straight for the land, a race-horse speed under bare poles and a lee-shore white with five miles' breadth of murderous surf an unknown length of time away: half an hour, an hour perhaps; not more with this unrelenting wind.

He was by the fife-rails of the mainmast going aft when he saw it, and for a second he did not believe that what he saw racing towards him high over the starboard quarter could be a wave. It was impossible—at that height it was impossible. But his body believed it, and in the sickening moment of grace before the sea struck the ship his hands had clenched round two belaying-pins.

There was a blow, a shuddering blow like a broadside, and then he was holding on while the deep water poured over his head. She was right down on her beam ends; he could tell that, because he was clinging upwards to the ring round the mast, which was now almost flat. Would she ever get up, he wondered, or was this the end? He had time to find that he was not afraid—it did not matter very much.

With a great long roll the Centurion righted herself, water pouring from her in shining streams; righted herself, but not altogether, for her ballast and her stores had shifted, and she lay over a good two streaks to port.

'Mr Palafox,' said a voice close at hand, 'report on the foreshrouds at once, if you please.'

'Aye-aye, sir,' said Peter, automatically hurrying forward.

'Six parted, sir,' he shouted, a few moments later, 'one dead-eye broke, and two lanyards, to starboard: three shrouds broke to larboard.'

'Very good,' said the Commodore, 'Mr Bailey?'

'Five starboard shrouds gone, sir; only one to lee.'

'Mr Ransome?'

'All but one, sir, with their lanyards.'

'You know what to do,' said the Commodore, smiling at them.

They knew what to do. In this sea, with the ship rolling gunwale and gunwale, the masts could not live long, nor could any sail be set until the shrouds were stirruped and new lanyards rove. There was not a second to lose, and although they were driving furiously towards a desolate shore they flung themselves on the work, each with a party as strong as could be spared.

Peter forgot the lee-shore in five minutes: the work called for every last degree of concentration and power and skill. But as they hauled on the lanyards with the roll of the ship and the shrouds tightened steadily he felt the wind on his left side instead of his back, and looking aft he saw the mainsail rise ghostly and fill. The wind had backed into the south and they were standing clear of the land.

The next few hours saw a strange scene on the *Centurion's* deck. The chaplain and the master stood to the wheel, while every man who could move knotted rigging and bent sails—soldiers, cooks, sailors, the surgeon, the stewards, the commander himself. By dawn she was far out to sea, sailing easily, though still with a considerable list, with a stiff south-easterly breeze.

'Thank God for some sea-room,' said Ransome. 'It makes me nervous to feel the loom of the land.'

'North-west and a half north it is,' repeated the quartermaster at the wheel. They were heading for Juan Fernandez, patching, repairing, pumping, splicing and making good as well as they might while the wind and the sea were kind. The hurricane, in its final turn, had blasted them northwards on their way, and they lived on the hope of seeing that green paradise rise out of the sea ahead.

They had little else to live on, except incessant toil, for the shifting in the hold had staved seven of the very few remaining casks of biscuit and the bilge had destroyed it: most of the water, green, thick, but just drinkable, had gone the same way.

'Did he keep it down?' asked Peter.

'Yes. So far,' said Ransome softly, looking over his shoulder. 'It should do him a power of good: he shall have the rest in the night.' He spoke softly, for it would not do to let it be known that there was fresh meat in the ship, although it was no more than cat. In the cavernous holds there was not a rat left alive, and they had not been drowned but hunted down by desperately hungry men, grown more cunning and fierce than the rats. The most spectacular scar on Peter's face, the one the other side from the lightning burn, was caused by his running full tilt against a standard as he finally cornered a rat in the forepeak. And as for cats—the galley cat had gone, the various ship's cats of the hold; the kittens that Ransome had indeed hidden abaft the well had been found long ago by some of the after-guard; and it had required all his uncommon ingenuity and knowledge of hungry crews to keep Agamemnon alive until this time.

'You could do with some for yourself,' said Peter, looking at Ransome's swollen legs. Ransome grunted, but made no reply: The scurvy had begun on him at last: they knew it perfectly well in all its many forms, and there was no mistaking the swollen legs, the dull, ugly patches on Ransome's arms and the reopening of the old cutless wound on his shoulder.

'No, sir,' said Peter, in a louder voice, 'the line over the peck-brail, if you please; and then serve it.' He moved over to guide Mr Walter's hands through the intricacies of the repair.

'That is better,' said the Chaplain, picking up his prayer-book. 'Now I am afraid I must leave you: but tell me quickly,

Peter, how are you?' He looked anxiously into Peter's face: it was a thin face, drawn and grey; no longer a boy's. 'Very well, sir,' said Peter at once. 'Capital, I thank you.'

'Your gums? It always starts there.'

'Sound as a bell. And yourself, sir?'

'Well, I thank God. How I wish I could say as much for the men I must go to. Peter, I pray that we may see this island, or——' He broke off and hurried below, clinging to any hand-hold as he went, though the sea was calm. Peter shook his head as he looked after him.

'Peter, your honour,' said Sean, just behind him. 'Do you know with your learning where this island will be?'

'Certainly, Sean,' said Peter, 'sure it's no way ahead. We shall raise it tomorrow.'

'We shall raise it tomorrow in the evening maybe,' he said.

'Tomorrow, Sean, you will see it green like a jewel in the sea,' he said, trying to smile.

'Listen, Peter a gradh, will you not lie out of kindness to me? They all do be saying we are too far to the west. Let me know the truth of it for all love, my dear.'

'Wait just a little while longer, now Sean, will you then?'

'There was himself in the masthead from two bells to six.'

'I know.' Peter had seen Mr Anson come down. 'We will wait on his word, for sure he knows best.'

There was a conference of the officers going on in the stateroom at that moment, as Peter knew very well, and he knew very well what they were discussing. Their longitude was uncertain: the longitude of Juan Fernandez was uncertain. They were trying to hit on the meridian, but still they were borne westward, and by the majority of their reckonings they should have reached it before. There was a strong feeling among the officers that they had already run too far to the west, that Juan Fernandez lay behind them, and that every day's sailing bore them away from their one hope of safety. The Commodore was of another opinion: he was almost sure that he had seen land still farther to the west, although every officer maintained it was cloud: and now every hour counted.

The conference had broken up. With grave faces the offi-cers came on the quarter-deck, the Commodore last.

'Mast-head,' hailed the Commodore.

'Sir?'

'What do you make out to leeward?'

A long pause. 'Nothing, sir,' came down the slow cry. 'Open sea and no cloud.'

'Mr Saumarez,' said the Commodore, 'you will make the course due east, if you please.'

His face was expressionless. Mr Saumarez betrayed a want of ease, and Peter thought he detected a hesitation as the first lieutenant repeated the order.

'Tomorrow, Sean, at the latest. For you must understand that we are running on the parallel now, and the latitude is as sure as the sun. You will keep the men in good heart: I know you will.'

'I will that, what there are of them; but the Dear knows they are dying like bees with no winter honey.'

'Mr Palafox, relieve the mast-head. Take my glass,' said Mr Norris, leaning heavily against the conning binnacle, drum-ming his weak fingers with an agitation that he tried to con-ceal. 'You are all right aloft, are you not?' he asked privately as Peter came for the glass.

'Yes, sir. Aye-aye, sir,' said Peter, the first to the question, the second to the order, as he ran up past the foretop. It was true that he felt perfectly well, apart from an enormous tired-ness—they were never far from the edge of exhaustion—and a perpetual hunger that sometimes drove him nearly mad.

'Nothing?' he asked, settling in the crosstrees.

'No,' said Preston, sliding his leg over with an old man's caution and grasping nervously for a double handhold. 'I saw a whale blow. Nothing more.'

'Here,' said Peter, feeling in his pocket, 'eat this in the top on your way down.'

'You are a good chap, Palafox,' said Preston, snatching the

biscuit. 'Thank you very much. It's a whole one,' he said incredulously, with a corner already stuffed into his mouth.

Peter sighed and began to sweep the horizon with the telescope. It was not one he was used to, and it took him some minutes to focus and manage with ease. He stared and stared again. How could Preston possibly have missed it? A clear landfall straight ahead perhaps twelve leagues away. His hands trembled so that for a moment the objective was lost: but he steadied again: he must be trebly certain before he hailed the deck, and anxiously, with expectation hot in his throat, he scanned the far landfall. Two points it stretched on the starboard bow, two points on the larboard. No, three points, four points—it stretched north and south in one unbroken line, and that high brilliance was the snow of the mountains.

With death in his heart he hailed the deck. 'Land ho. High mountains from six points on the starboard bow to six on the larboard. Snow and high land.'

He could feel the cruel disappointment well up from the silent deck, as bitter as his own. The Commodore had been right and the officers wrong: they had missed Juan Fernandez, and this was the mainland, more than two hundred miles to the east. This was the Cordillera that sent back the sun, huge mountains of eternal snow; not the pleasant hills of Juan Fernandez. They had been wrong: they had missed by perhaps no more than an hour of sailing: and now they must beat back into a settled westerly wind, with men dying six and seven a day for want of a handful of greenstuff. How many would pay for the mistake with their lives? The ship and her whole company, in all likelihood.

'Port your helm.' He heard the order on deck, and below his sadly dangling feet the yard braced very slowly round as the *Centurion* came up into the wind.

The 30th of May; the 31st, seven men each. The 1st of June, five. The 2nd, only three. June 3rd, five, of whom one was Norman, a bo'sun's mate, fit up until a few days before. The 4th, five. The 6th, the last man of all the pensioners, and six other men. The 7th, no less than twelve; and sixteen on the 8th.

'How many men can you count in your watch, Mr Brett?' asked the Commodore.

'Ten, sir. And six can still go aloft.'

There was a howling scream at the mast-head, piercing words rushing one on the other.

'What does this mean?' cried the Commodore, with a flash in his eye.

'I beg pardon, sir,' said Peter, touching his hat. 'It is Sean O'Mara, sir. He means he sees land. A green island aswim in the sunrise, he says.'

For the first time he saw Mr Anson moved out of himself. The Commodore flung down his hat, clasped his hands for a moment, and then ran for the shrouds.

9

'MR PALAFOX, WHAT THE DEVIL DO YOU MEAN, SIR? HOW CAN you presume to answer me with, "I came as fast as I could"? Here have I been waiting six mortal minutes while you stroll about the island taking your ease in the shade. What do you mean by it? I wish you may not be growing sullen, as well as grossly obese and idle.'

'I did run, sir.'

'Don't you presume to answer me, sir,' cried the lieutenant. 'I saw you. Do you call that gasping waddle a run? Look at you—a great, blubbery, slab-sided hulk that can't reach the maintop without stopping to pant five times on the way. Oh, what a horrible greasy sight. More like one of these sea-calves than a King's officer. You have been fooling about in the cabbage palms. I know it as well as if I had seen you, so don't you dare to deny it, for I will not bear it. Get into that boat directly. It is always the same with these midshipmen—let them on shore for five minutes, and they come back disgustingly bloated and wanton.'

'My dear boy,' said Mr Walter, 'I hope you may not be taking to dissolute ways. I heard you and Keppel and Ransome hallooing and singing until three in the morning, and this is not the first time, by a very long way. The Commodore has taken notice of it more than once. He said, "How can anyone get any sleep with this infernal din going on?" Surely, this is very inconsiderate in you, Peter?'

'I am very sorry, sir. We were hunting a goat.'

'What, in the middle of the night?'

'We thought it more sporting, sir, for it was the very old billy we always shoot on Fridays: he is getting very slow in his pins.'

'Poor creature. No wonder he is getting old and nervous and slow, the way you harry him. It is a shame, I declare; and I think it but right to put you in mind of the fate of the Children of Israel, when they waxed fat and kicked.'

'Where is that——midshipman? Oh, there you are at last, Mr Palafox. You will find yourself confined to the ship if you go on like this. You are sailing pretty near the wind, I can tell you, my friend: only this morning Mr Saumarez said, "I wonder what has come into that young fellow. He was a quiet, sober, well-conducted midshipman a few months ago, apart from talking too much by half; but if he goes on at this gait he will soon have corrupted half the crew with his example." '

'Who put this goat into my bed?' asked the master, with awful quietness. 'What depraved wretch—Mr Palafox, come here. Mr Palafox. Mr Palafox—is the boy deaf?'

• • •

Mr Palafox lay on his back in the boat, his noble brow shaded by a palm-leaf hat, while Sean fished over the side. There was already a mound of fish between the thwarts, but he fished on with the fanatic intensity of one who cannot possibly pull in enough.

'There'th a thea-calf,' said Keppel, nodding lazily over the bows. He had not a tooth left in his head, and this obliged him to lisp.

'The thea-calf ho

The thea-calf hee

The thea-calf thwimming in the Thouthern Thea,' he chanted.

'Garrh,' cried Sean, furiously shaking his fist at his rival. 'The confident thief.' The sea-lion slid backwards under a wave and popped up on the other side, staring with unwearied curiosity.

'Your soul to the devil,' growled Sean, jealously switching his line over to the starboard gunwale.

'There are enough fish in the sea for everybody,' said Peter, closing his eyes.

'There are not,' said Sean. 'There are never enough fish in the sea. Those outrageous beasts eat more than is right. I have him,' he cried, jerking the line. 'Oh, if it is not the codfish of the world.'

'Then put it back. We don't want any of your common old cod. Wait for a chimney-sweeper—that's worth eating. Or else try for a crayfish. I could fancy a crayfish, I think.' Peter had grown delicate in his eating: he had a proud stomach now, very unlike the stomach that had shrieked for a weevily biscuit or the leg of a toasted rat. But it had taken some time to become so difficult: for weeks on end he had eaten everything and anything that was put before him, and had then gone out hungrily looking for more in the woods.

He had changed. Changed very much, imperceptibly day by day: but if one had looked through his journal, flicked over the pages, one would have seen the difference. The first entries dated at Juan Fernandez were concise, dry statements of position, wind and weather, anchorage, memoranda of work to be done. 'Wind at WSW½S. Warp to be carried out tomorrow. Remember foul ground extends at least 1 cable, the Spout bearing WNW by long-boat compass, West Bay and Sugarloaf points in a line. Variation 9° 53' E by my reading, 10° 1' by the master's. Keppel took 3 bowls of soup. Number 3, 7, 9, 10 and 11 to be trained round and looked to.' This referred to guns: they had found fresh traces of men on shore—broken pots, Spanish filth, fish yet undecayed—and although they had then but thirty men to fight a 60-gun ship, they had to make what preparations they could.

This kind of entry continually recurred, with the names of the men they buried—for the effects of the scurvy still killed the sickest men for three weeks after they landed. There was a happier note very early, however, when the little *Tryal* came in on June 12, sailed somehow by Captain Saunders, his second lieutenant and three men, who were all who could stand on their feet, apart from the reinforcement of Centurions who were sent as soon as the *Tryal* made her signal. But then there was the long agony of the *Gloucester*, who plied for a month and two days off the island, sometimes clearly in sight, sometimes gone for a week of unceasingly contrary winds, unable to beat up, she was so short of hands—and that in spite of the men sent from shore with fresh victuals. At length the crew of the longboat did bring her in: and in August Peter made the sombre calculation—'*Centurion* 506: 292 dead, 214 alive. *Gloucester* 374: 292 dead, 82 alive. *Tryal* 81: 42 dead, 39 alive. 961 men sailed from St Helen's in these three. 626 of them are dead. Is there any hope for *Wager, Severn,* and *Pearl* now? We could not have lasted another week at sea.' And, writing that, he remembered how they crept in towards the land; how they had let go their anchor in order not to run to the lee, and how they had not had the strength to bring it home when the wind came fair, but were held there in sight of salvation, unable to move, until the Commodore, risking all, sailed the anchor out of its bed.

Yet as the lovely, gentle weeks dropped by the entries began to be peppered with such notes as—'Bailey and I shot two sea-lions, which makes five.' 'Eight crayfish today. Preston dared me to send the biggest to the Commodore, with the compliments of the berth: which I did, by Sean.' 'A chimney-sweeper off Monkey's Key, 53 lb. and it took Ransome and me half an hour to land him. Drowned baby, in honour of Keppel's getting to the top of Admiralty Hill for the first time.' 'Ransome made a joke before dinner: Preston said we could have catched the turtle if it had been attempted to be turned—Ransome said it could not *turn* turtle, because it was a turtle already. Unable to eat, although he tried. Sent to the surgeon. Pumped. Mr Woodfall let me hold the tube. Better now, though weak.' 'The *Anna* came in. We had given her up long ago. Frightfully battered, but the crew in good shape. They sheltered up a creek they found on the main and were fed by savages. Her master makes low jokes about King's officers not to be allowed out without a master-mariner to guide their motions. He is a coarse fellow, though a capital seaman.' 'Sean commended by Mr Saumarez for his long splice on the best bower's cable, but in the evening he was rebuked for dragging one of *Gloucester*'s carpenter's mates up and down the Sugar-loaf by his pigtail—a man called O'Toole. The O'Tooles ran in King Murtagh's battle with the Danes, and are all thieves.' '*Anna*'s stores found to be much damaged, but the tobacco is safe: the men are wonderfully gratified. Sean gave me a quid to try: but I am sensibly better now.' '*Anna* surveyed. I went through her with the carpenters: very shocking indeed—14 knees broke, breast hooks gone, she is iron-sick, and I wish I may never see anything like her spirketting again. She cannot possibly go home, and is to be bought by the Commodore, broke up, and her timbers used. Her men go into *Gloucester*. Mr Gerard, her master, thought to argue with *Gloucester*'s Number One, but caught a Tartar. Lord, how we laughed.'

In the little boat there was a beautiful silence, warm, contemplative and easy: a soft breeze came off the land, green-scented, and above them a frigate-bird lay on the wind. There was the distant sound of the smiths and carpenters working on the *Gloucester*, but not furiously hard—a steady, even rhythm of normal work. The *Centurion* and the *Tryal* lay almost ready for the sea, with their yards across, tall, trim, gleaming with cleanliness, their 'tween-decks wholesome and fresh at last. Here and there, dotting the bright grass of Juan Fernandez and showing in the clearings, were the rude huts and bothies that the crews had been allowed to build and inhabit; and from many of them rose blue fingers of smoke that mounted straight before the breeze from over the high land drifted them out to sea.

'This is a wonderful place,' murmured Peter, with his eyes closed. 'I wish we could stay here for ever. Sean, this is the Tir na 'nOg, no doubt,'

'It is that, your honour, honey,' said Sean. 'And a large piece of it I shall take home for Pegeen Ban, if the island does not get there before us.'

'How will you know which gets there first? How will you know at all?'

'What are you talking about?' asked Keppel, 'with your Tir Mc Thing?'

'Why, it is an island, you know,' said Peter, 'that comes floating off the coast of our country every few years or so, and if you can reach it you stay young for ever: but it is always a great way off, and difficult to be reached. We call it the Tir na 'nOg in our language.'

> 'The Tir na 'nHo
> The Tir na 'nHee,'

sang Keppel, quietly, with an endless repetition of three notes, as he stared down through the clear water to the sun-dappled weed below.

'Proinsias Burke went there,' said Peter.

'And Conn Riordan the cithogue.'

'Ah, but he was a seal-woman's son, and therefore is not to be counted.'

'And so was Proinsias, only the other way about; for was not the seal of the stack Proinsias' own da, with a grey muzzle on him and one ear, no more?'

'It is the truth you say, Sean, and Proinsias came back after three hundred years and found his wicked old shrew of a wife lying quiet, which made him laugh, and his wolf-hound hanged by the Queen, which made him weep, and his heart broke so it did and he grew old in a day.'

'Sure I knew him myself, the old, old, the very old man, and gave him a penny as he sat in the rain with no dog for a comfort to sustain him.'

Then the silence dropped on them again, until quite suddenly Sean said, 'And how will I call the King when I see him? Will I say my lord, or your honour? For I will speak in English, for glory.'

'Sure I cannot tell,' said Peter. 'Perhaps you say Majesty. Do you know, Keppel?'

'I always call him "sir",' said Keppel, carefully dropping a crumb of bait to a vermilion fish to eat. 'Some people use the third person, but it's liable to get their tiller-lines crossed.'

'Do you often talk to him?'

'Yes,' said Keppel indifferently. 'He's my godfather,' he added.

'Oh,' said Peter: and after a pause, 'I suppose you are pretty important—important, I mean, by land?'

'No. Not a bit,' said Keppel cheerfully. 'Not unless someone knocks my brother on the head. Then it would be enter Mr Midshipman Keppel, the Queen of the May, in an ermine tippet and crimson breeches, attended at a respectful distance, by Admiral Palafox and Captain O'Mara. But why are you going to visit him?'

'And does he not owe me a gold pound for my fingers, and three for my toes?' asked Sean, who, like most of the sailors, had been cruelly bitten by the ice of the Horn. 'And will he not wish to see before ever he pays—for it is a sum to set a man up in cows for his life. The Dear knows I wish I had twice the number, like the monster at the fair, to have them froze off at the price.'

'But——' began Keppel. The flat boom of the warning gun cut off the word. 'Buoy your line. Quick. Give way,' he cried, and before the echo came back from the hill the boat was moving fast for Cumberland Bay.

There was a scene of intense, ordered activity at the anchorage, the squadron's boats hurrying from ship to shore as the men swarmed on to the beach. Already sails were being bent aboard the *Centurion*; what was wanting in her rigging and cordage was being prepared at full speed, and men were running with the capstan bars.

The look-out on the top of the island had seen a sail: she had come hull-up and then had tacked away: she was surely a Spaniard, and had perhaps seen the tents on the shore. This was the information that Peter snatched up in fragments: though some still maintained that she was the *Severn* or the *Pearl*, and some that she was the fore-runner of a squadron of force.

'Very well, Mr Saumarez,' said the Commodore, eyeing the boats that were to tow the *Centurion* out into the wind, and speaking above the scream of the fiddle on the capstan and the roar of the shanty as the anchor came home. 'It is very well indeed.'

But Peter, standing on the shore and watching the masts come into line and the white cloud break out from the yards, felt that it was all very ill. He had known that he was deep in the first lieutenant's disfavour, that sundry misdemeanours had yet to be purged; he had known that somebody had to be left with the boiling-party, but the news, coldly and sharply delivered in the midst of his glee, the news that this somebody was to be Mr Palafox and none other, had been like the sky falling in.

'Rot Mr Saumarez,' he thought, passionately stamping the sand. '——Mr Saumarez, the——lieutenant. How I hate this loathsome island.'

'Never take on, sir,' said Hairy Amos, to soothe him. 'They'll never find nothing, but sweat there and back like——'

'You hold your tongue,' cried Peter, with monstrous injustice. 'And new-reeve that tackle at once. Green, what are you gaping at? Is this a——picnic? I'll have the next man flogged who looks up from his work. Gibbering like a lot of French monkeys. Who tied this lubberly knot? Don't you know a parbuckle?'

Quite demurely the men hoisted the blubber. Since those far-off days in the Channel, Peter's voice had taken on an entirely different ring; un-selfconsciously it could make the menacing noises to which the men were accustomed—noises that were personally directed and were yet essentially impersonal: rank talking to rating, not a boy to a man. He was not much older in years, and he looked much like an ordinary boy: yet on occasion out of that boy's face could look a man old in hard experience—a disconcerting sight, but not a rare one in the Navy, where a midshipman might have been in action ten times by the age of fourteen, and have seen violent death looking straight at him in a hundred different shapes. But what was more important was that the men really liked him: they knew he understood his work: they knew how he had behaved when the wind blew strong: and he had not spent so many of his watches below bearing a hand in the indescribable squalor of the 'tween-decks—twenty or thirty fit men cannot look after two hundred sick and dying as well as work a ship through those dreadful seas—he had not done that for nothing, and they let him fulminate without resentment.

He cooled off quite soon: for it is the custom in the Navy for the officers to share in all the very nasty work—the Commodore had carried stretchers with Peter at the other end when they first unloaded the fetid sick-bay—and by the time the *Centurion*'s topgallants had disappeared, Peter, greasy from head to foot, was seen to smile.

'I sailed along of a cove once, sir,' said Hairy Amos, throwing a handful of tried-out blubber under the cauldron, 'as what lived on this here for seven months on end.'

'Did he, though?' said Peter, looking at the frittered blubber attentively.

'Yes, sir, he did, withouten lie, strike me——'

164

'You are not to swear, Amos,' said Peter.

'No, sir. Beg pardon, sir. Which he was one of these Hull whalers, and by mistake he got left with three or four mates, a hunting reindeer—a sort of flat-footed wild cow, sir—in Greenland: and they had been trying-out whale blubber, same as like we are trying-out sea-lion blubber. So when they had ate up their reindeers, and they see as how the master had abandoned them for the winter, which the winter is precious long in those parts——'

'No it ain't,' said Burrows.

'Yes it is,' said Amos.

'No it ain't,' said Burrows. 'Not alongside of the Horn, it ain't.'

'Who are you?' asked Green, who had nothing whatever to do with the discussion, and who knew perfectly well who Burrows was, having slept within eighteen inches of him throughout the commission.

'Pipe down,' cried Peter. 'Strike me——Hairy Amos, go on.'

'Which the winter in those parts is very, very long,' said Hairy Amos slowly, fixing Burrows with his eye. 'So they said, "Strike us——, we shall have to eat the fritters, what we have tried-out blubber of, these four months past." And so they did; and so they was all rescued come the summer,' concluded Amos.

'What happened next?' asked Smith.

'Nothing.'

'Well, that's a rotten yarn,' said Burrows, and the boiling-party appeared to agree.

'Hur,' cried Amos, vexed by this reception, 'which I had the honour of addressing my remarks to Mr Palafox, not to a lot of crawling longshoremen. I mean to say, my old shipmate said as how these fritters, the whale fritters, I mean, not these *here* fritters, what we are trying-out now——'

'How did your shipmate know about our fritters?' asked Burrows suspiciously. 'What call had he to go on about our fritters? They are very good fritters.'

'Not these fritters,' cried Amos, lost in the complexity, and now convicted in the eyes of the party of disloyalty to the ship, whose fritters were far better than the *Gloucester*'s fritters or the *Tryal*'s, let alone the distant fritters of some unknown Hull whaler.

'What did he say about the Greenland fritters?' asked Peter.

'He said, sir,' replied Hairy Amos impressively, 'which these was his very words, "Whale fritters," sir, "is the loathliest meat in the world." '

This was greeted by a stony silence: the men refused to be impressed by Amos's friend, or to pay him any credit; and after a while Burrows said, 'You and your fritters.'

'I only passed the remark,' mumbled Amos.

'You and your remarks,' said Burrows. 'I never heard such a tale.'

'If you know a better, Burrows,' said Peter, stirring the fire, 'you tell it.'

'Hor, hor,' cried Hairy Amos, 'that's right, sir. Fair enough, hor, hor.'

They were waiting for the sea-lion blubber to yield its oil—it was wanted to give the *Centurion* boot-hose tops—and there was nothing to do but wait, now that the casks were all neatly arranged and the next boiling of seal-lions were flayed.

Burrows scratched his head. 'Well, sir,' he said at last, 'I don't set up for to be a literary gent'—glaring at Amos—'but at least I can tell a *true* tale of what happened to me, and not to some lubber in God-knows-where, with so-called fritters or wild cows with stuns'l booms rigged fore and aft. It was in the year twenty-one—or was it twenty-two? No, it was twenty-one, without a word of lie, for it was the same year that I married Sue, a laundress then as she is now, God bless her, second door past the Lion in Thursday Street, Deptford: you can't miss it, and if you do the Lion will always send a potboy to show you the way—shirts got up directly and sailors' tarpaulins mended as well as officers' linen, by S. Burrows: and she can show you her lines, not like some people's so-called females—' another glare at Amos, who blushed and hung his wicked old hairy head. 'In the year twenty-one I shipped aboard of the *Rose*, P. Rogers master, of two hundred and forty ton, from the Pool for the Coast with a mixed cargo; and we was four days south and west of St Vincent when a Sallee rover laid us along. Well, we fought as long as we could, but they grappled us tight and come over the side yelling blue murder—a lot of nasty black men with swords, two hundred of 'em and more. So they sorts us out and puts us in rows, a-peering into our hands. And those as had horny hands they put to one side, and the rest—a few gentlemen passengers and the merchants, they drops overboard, seeing a gentleman's no sort of use—begging your pardon, sir.'

'Never mind,' said Peter, laughing as loud as the rest of the party and looking at his hands, which would certainly have kept him aboard the rover.

'Which I mean, no use in the slave-market of Sallee,' explained Burrows anxiously, 'for I am sure they are very useful for—for——'

'Navigation?' suggested Green.

'No,' said Burrows. 'Any shell-back mate can do that. For——'

'Parsons?' said Smith.

'No,' said Burrows. 'The apostles were all from the lower-deck. Not parsons.'

'Scholards?' said Amos.

'Scholards, maybe,' said Burrows, doubtfully. 'Anyhow, very useful and valuable, I am sure, for something. But not in the market of Sallee, where they carried us. And I was sold to a Jew-man named Isaac, which he was a very good master to me, and gave me my liberty when the fleet lay off Tangiers, where he lived then, having removed; which would have been handsome in a Christian or a renegado, and he was only a Jew, poor man. But he said according to his religion when you had served seven year——'

'Mr Palafox, sir?' This was a stranger, a man from the *Tryal*, and the Centurions stared at him in wooden silence, jerking their thumbs or their heads towards Peter.

'Mr Palafox, sir? Compliments of *Tryal*'s midshipmen and would be honoured to see Mr Palafox to dinner.'

'My best compliments to the *Tryal*'s midshipmen,' said Peter graciously, from amidst the oil and blubber, 'and I shall esteem myself most happy.'

'Aye-aye, sir,' said the seaman, and padded away, muttering '. . . shall esteem hisself happy, shall esteem hisself—best compliments and shall esteem. . . .'

It was difficult in fact to esteem himself very happy while the *Centurion* was at sea. Quite apart from his bitter initial disappointment, he found that he was lost without her: he had for so long identified himself with the ship. But he was not strongly miserable, either: in addition to a naturally sanguine temperament he had plenty of work (nauseating, but important), and he prided himself on the tier of casks that awaited the *Centurion*'s pleasure—a full tier placed ostentatiously near the *Gloucester*'s and *Tryal*'s and out-topping them both. The surviving midshipmen of the *Tryal*—Balthaser, Todd and Bentley—were cheerful, hospitable souls, and they invited him often. The *Gloucester*'s berth was not nearly so much to his liking, although they were perfectly civil to a guest and did more than their duty: he did not come to know them at all well, however. Captain Saunders also asked him to dine: but Captain Saunders had too recently been his first lieutenant, with the power of the high justice, the middle and the low, for Peter to rid himself of a feeling of guilt in his presence, although Captain Saunders was the most amiable of hosts—a totally different being from the Number One who had so often and so insistently mentioned Peter's shortcomings from the other side of the disciplinary table. Peter mentioned this feeling to Bentley, who laughed, and said, 'It's always like that. Did you hear about Mr Anson at Portsmouth? He went to Sir Charles with an Admiralty order for three hundred hands—flat order, no nonsense. But he had been a snotty—sounds funny, don't it, the Commodore a midshipman, ha, ha—under Sir Charles, and the Admiral (who knew about the order, you see, and wanted every man-jack for the fleet) sang out, "Mr Anson, take your hands out of your pockets this minute." Which cooked his goose without another word said.'

'It's the *Centurion*,' said Peter, positively.

'I doubt it,' said Todd.

'I tell you it is,' cried Peter. 'Look at that sprits'l tops'l—do you see the damned awkward great patch in the starboard leach? I put it there myself. There, as she rises. And t'other is a prize she has taken.'

'I doubt it,' said Todd.

'Bah,' said Peter, clapping his telescope to and darting down the hill.

'Please, sir, may I come too?' he asked, purple in the face with speed, as Mr Saunders stepped into his cutter—the signal for the sloop's captain was flying from the *Centurion*'s distant mizzen.

'Make haste, then,' said the captain, and Peter skipped into the boat as they shoved off on the wave.

The cutter pulled at racing speed, for the men were as eager to see the prize as Captain Saunders and Peter, and to hear the news: but it seemed a tedious age before the ship and the boat came together.

The grinning berth greeted Peter with a flood of wonderful details.

'Pizarro's squadron turned back at the Horn,' said Preston. 'Lost two ships.'

'And the rest battered beyond belief—all condemned, ha, ha,' said Bailey.

'And the Spaniards *were* on the island until a day or two before we came in. Only a country force, armed merchant-men, but they would have chewed us up: and there we were cursing like mad because we couldn't find it earlier.'

'We had such a chase.'

'Lost her and found her again—Mr Saumarez leaping about the main-royal truck all night.'

'Crowded on everything, including my wipe.'

'Ran her down in the evening.'

'Fired four shots.'

'And she let fly her sheets and halliards in alarm.'

'She did, really. Never seen such a sight—washing day nothing to it—royals, stuns'ls and all.'

'Loaded with silver.'

'And sugar and things—cloth.'

'Twenty-three cases of dollars, two hundredweight apiece.'

'And masses of plate.'

'And fifty-three hands—Lord, what a help they'll be.'

> 'The *Carmel* ho
> The *Carmel* hee
> Was crammed with silver.
> Tweedle dee,'

sang Keppel, coming below. 'Mr Palafox, sir,' he said with an elegant bow, 'allow me the pleasure of congratulating you on being far better off than you were last week.'

'What, do I get some?' asked Peter, looking pleased.

'Oh, yes. You get some, although you were only lounging about under the palm-trees while we ran horrible dangers afloat: there were four real six-pounders shot off, bang, bang, bang, and Bailey had a fit.'

'Where's Ransome?'

'In the prize. So is your man, watching the Dons like a hawk. Let's go and wave.'

The prize, *Nuestra Señora del Monte Carmelo*, was sailing under the *Centurion*'s lee—a handsome, high-built Spanish ship with a noble poop, upon which stood Mr Saumarez, and Ransome near him. Ransome saw them, but did not venture to signal overtly: instead he waited until the first lieutenant had walked to the weather-rail and then he slapped his pocket, nudged the air with his elbow, raised an imaginary bottle, curved his arm as one who would dance—indicating thereby that they were all on fiddler's green now, and that it was very delightful. But the humour of his gestures overcame him, and they heard a hoarse, stifled bellow float over the water, saw Mr Saumarez turn sharply and Ransome's head bend attentively to the signal-book, while hard words passed on the *Carmelo*'s poop: these appeared to wound Ransome to the heart, for when the first lieutenant had resumed his station, Ransome was seen to apply an immense spotted handkerchief to his eyes, and from time to time he was obliged to wring it dry.

Sean was at the break of the fo'c'sle, armed, and glaring now down the forehatch, now into the waist of the prize, where a few disconsolate Spanish passengers stood sadly about: he was obsessed with the idea that someone, somewhere, was hiding some yet undiscovered silver, and the impossibility of seeing all the captives at once was wearing him to a hag-ridden shadow. He saw Peter out of the corner of his eye, touched his forelock, and without ever removing his piercing gaze from a tiny yellow Spanish merchant, suspected of having moidores in the heels of his shoes, Sean laid his forefinger to the side of his nose in a very significant and portentous way.

As the *Centurion* glided into her anchorage and the cable tightened behind her, rising in a straight line from the sea and squirting water as it took up the strain, the *Tryal* stood out of the bay.

'She's for Valparaiso,' said Keppel. 'There were some other merchantmen bound there with this *Carmelo*. There was an embargo, an embargee, on all shipping until a little while ago: but then they decided that we had all sunk, ha, ha, and took it off. Little did they know that I was aboard, with my advice at the Commodore's disposal at any time of the night or day.'

The next few days witnessed scenes of unparalleled activity on Juan Fernandez as the squadron made ready for the sea: officers could be heard begging their men not to overdo it, not to strain themselves past repair—a weird sound indeed—as the water-casks, the dried cod, the innumerable stores, flew into the *Centurion*'s eager hold and the *Anna*'s guns darted aboard the *Carmelo*. A party came to Peter in the falling dusk and with tears in their eyes implored him to intercede with the first lieutenant, that they might go on by lantern-light. Sean sat on the chests of silver, great black rings round his eyes for want of sleep, foaming with rage when anyone approached. The bo'sun and a numerous party of volunteers were detected at midnight creeping about the upper rigging, improving work already passed by the rigorous first lieutenant. Hairy Amos caught his beard in a tackle, but would not have the heaving stopped on any account, preferring to lose enough to stuff a large pillow rather than delay the departure by a minute.

'Ah, dear Lord,' exclaimed Peter with a sigh, as the *Centurion* gathered way, 'how glad I am to have a deck under my feet. I was all at sea when you marooned me on the island.'

'No, you worn't,' said Ransome, frowning. 'You was ashore.'

'That was Teague's joke,' explained Keppel. 'They always make jokes like that.'

'Wheere's the joke?' asked Ransome.

'He said he was at sea when he was on land. They call it a bull: but for my part I am willing to believe that it was unconscious in this case.'

'He said he was at sea when he was on land. Oh well, hor hor,' said Ransome heavily. 'But it worn't very funny. Not as good as mine about the *Tryal*.' The disease had eaten into him, and he betrayed the uneasy jealousy of the established wit for an upstart rival: but his native good humour rallied at last and he said, 'It was quite funny, though. At sea (meaning all astray, like) when on land. Hor, hor.'

'It was a lovely island, indeed it was,' said Peter, gazing affectionately at the beach where the Gloucesters, unable to be ready as soon as the *Centurion* and the newly-armed prize, milled frantically, like ants in the distance. 'And I am very glad to have a piece of it to carry to Ireland.' He referred to an enormous mass of rock, chipped into the semblance of a map of Juan Fernandez, that encumbered the berth, together with a mouldering turtle (thought to be asleep and destined for William), a net full of shells and a palm-leaf of moderately vigorous growth. 'It was a lovely island,' he went on, 'but I am prodigious happy to leave it. Even this disgusting berth is agreeable, even its brutish inhabitants: the rude merriment of my untutored shipmates is delightful, and the artless howling of the first lieutenant is music in my ears.'

At this moment Peter felt a pair of very cold grey eyes boring into the nape of his neck. Ransome gave him a shattering nudge by way of a hint, and Keppel burst into a paroxysm of coughing.

'Young gentlemen,' said Mr Dennis. 'We are at sea.'

'Yes, sir,' they said.

'We are at sea,' repeated the lieutenant, gazing about with profound satisfaction. 'Not taking our ease like young ladies in an al fresco party.'

'Oh no, sir,' they said.

'And at sea,' said the lieutenant, with a sudden burst of ferocity, 'there is work to be done. There is discipline too. You may have heard of it somewhere. And mast-heads exist, Mr Palafox.'

Peter looked up, and unable to suppress his delight, said, 'An't it charming to see them, sir? I had almost forgot what a top-gallant looked like, all round the Horn.'

'Then you may gratify yourself with a closer inspection,' said Mr Dennis. 'Oblige me by running up there, as quick as you like.'

'Aye-aye, sir,' said Peter aloud. And in a much softer voice he added, 'All right, Old Jersey Shirt (for Mr Dennis, like Mr Saumarez, came from the Channel Islands, and was to be seen, in cold weather, in the uncouth woollen garment of the natives of Jersey), I was going there anyway. So put that in your pipe and smoke it; and don't I wish you may like it, ha, ha.'

A lovely island, thought Peter: and all the ship's company said the same. But when it remained clearly, obstinately, in sight all day, and the next and the next, there were not a few to be found who were so darkly ungrateful that they shook their fists at it while they whistled with all the force of their lungs for a wind to carry them away.

• • •

The drum-roll and the crash of the bulkheads going down as a ship clears for action is perhaps the most exciting sound in the world. The drum thundered in the *Centurion*, the officers' cabins vanished, casks lashed between the guns splashed overboard leaving white rings that ran to mingle with the wake as the *Centurion* tore through the sea towards a ship that was approaching on the opposite tack.

'A seventy-four,' said Preston, ducking under the vast spread of the starboard lower studdingsail.

'Can't see a thing,' said Bailey, hopping.

Up in his station by the larboard fo'c'sle guns Peter said, 'I can't make her out.'

'She's a stout ship,' said the gunner, standing near him. 'Five minutes now.'

'She must be a man-of-war, the way she comes down,' whispered Preston. 'She means business.'

'Unless she's a merchant who takes us for another.'

'Don't be an ass. Of course she's a man-of-war—a two-decker. A sixty-gun ship or a seventy-four.'

'Can't see a thing, head-on like this.'

'Four minutes. Three, and she is in range,' murmured the gunner to himself, narrowing his eyes against the glare.

For the long moments before the ships converged the *Centurion* was filled with a solemn hush, broken only by the song of the wind and the sea ripping by. At the guns of the upper-deck the crews crouched ready: from the gun-deck wafted the smell of the slow-match, poised glowing in the linstocks. In a second the broadside could shatter the silence: Keppel and Ransome stood with their whistles, watching Mr Brett for the signal.

'Mr Blew,' came the Commodore's voice, 'I beg you will hail her in Spanish.'

The master came racing forward to the starboard cathead. 'Qué nave?' he hailed. 'Que entregue en seguida—somos Ingleses.'

'*Tryal*'s prize,' came the answer, and as the ships swept past Peter saw Mr Hughes, first of the *Tryal*, standing on the fo'c'sle and peering somewhat nervously into the *Centurion*'s gun-ports one after the other: and as they came abreast he saw the red and gold of Spain flying below the English colours. But not a gun went off, and the *Centurion* came up into the wind, while the big Spaniard ran under her stern to lie-to in her lee.

'Well, there's still the other,' said Peter hopefully, looking away to the smaller vessel on the horizon.

'Pah,' said the gunner disgustedly. 'That's only the *Tryal* with half her masts blown off. Maniacs.' He stumped off, and a universal discontent filled the *Centurion*.

'They must have cracked on like a lot of bay-boons,' said Mr Blew angrily, 'for to carry away like that just after refitting.'

'What nasty lines she has,' said Peter, sneering at the Spanish ship. 'Just like Spillane's wagon overturned in the bog.'

'Have you seen her name?' asked Bailey. '*Arranzazu*. What despicable nonsense.'

Presently the rumour spread that the prize had carried only five thousand pounds' worth of silver, and the crew's indignation knew no bounds. The wretched *Tryal* had chased her for thirty-six hours through appalling weather (the *Centurion* had split her main-topsail in the same storm, but preferred to forget it) and had followed her throughout the length of the night guided by no more than a chink that showed through an ill-fitting cover: but the Centurions felt cheated, vexed and cantankerous, and they regarded the crew of the *Tryal* with righteous disdain—a disdain founded on different and contradictory reasons: first, the prize should never have been a prize at all, but a fighting Spaniard; secondly, if she had to be a prize at all, she ought to have been the *Centurion*'s prize; and thirdly, if the *Tryal* had taken a prize, she ought to have taken a rich one.

'And I lost a valuable basket, stowed by the hances, when the decks were cleared,' said Peter.

'They had a full ten days at sea ahead of us,' said Preston. 'That is what I call taking a mean advantage—I mean, to go careering about the sea at such a pace, and crowding on so that they carry away their main-topmast and spring all the rest, in chase of a paltry five-thousand-pounder.'

'Five thousand pounds is a sum I scorn,' said Bailey. 'They ought to think more of the service and less of prize-money,' he added.

'And do you know what?' cried Keppel, darting furiously into the berth. 'The Commodore is going to commission her as a frigate, R.N., and Sawney is to be made post into her. They are shifting *Tryal*'s guns into her at this very minute, and the sloop is to be scuttled. That's what they get for having run his Majesty's ship into a crimson wreck. Rewarded with a fine new frigate—she was a man-of-war in the Spanish service off and on—and begged to make themselves comfortable aboard—a wonderful sailer on a wind—promoted—petted. Oh, it's famous, ain't it? So now we don't even get our share of the hulk. It's pretty well, eh?' With a howl of frustrated avarice he vanished on deck.

'Oh, well,' said Peter, philosophically, 'there is still a prodigious lot of sea, and I make no doubt that it is swarming with prizes. I will bet we make a round dozen before we reach Paita.'

10

IF ANYONE HAD TAKEN PETER'S BET, PETER WOULD HAVE LOST his money: nobody did, of course, for it might have brought bad luck to the ship; but still, he would certainly have lost his money. The squadron swept the sea off Valparaiso, swept the coast of Chile, the coast and headlands of Peru; they recrossed

Capricorn with flowing sheets and a southerly gale, strung out in a wide line abreast, the *Centurion* and then the *Carmelo*, courses down to the larboard, under the command of Mr Saumarez, and beyond her, out of sight of the *Centurion* but within signalling distance of the *Carmelo*, the *Tryal's Prize* with a motley crew of black, yellow and dun, kept in apple-pie order and a miserable state of cleanliness by the men of the *Tryal*. The three ships covered an immense area of sea, a strip perhaps fifty miles wide in which nothing could pass unseen; and as they cruised in the lanes of mercantile traffic they watched with unremitting attention. But never a sail did they find.

'November 1st. 14° 2′ S. 76° 39′ W. Island Gallan bearing NNE½E 7 leagues, Morro Viejo S½E 5 miles. Wind at SSE backing S,' wrote Peter. 'No news. We took in some men from *Carmelo*, in case of a Spanish force out of Callao. Many flying fish. Sean caught a bonito from the larboard bumkin.

'November 4th. My birthday. We have been 412 days at sea now and I have more than a year's seniority. I did not like to mention it in the berth, but Mr Walter very kindly brought me a cake that he had saved from those taken in *Tryal's Prize* which Mr Saunders complimented him with. It was especially kind in him, as he cannot be trusted with sweet things—avows it himself—not even loaf sugar: has been seen hiding it under his cassock in the wardroom and Jennings swears that the Commodore's steward has to keep the Commodore's own preserves under lock and key, with the key round his neck. So seeing the cake, the berth smoked the reason, and Ransome arranged the cake in a shot-garland, with a candle—there was only room for one on the cake, a rat having trimmed it about. It was an uncommon elegant notion, but unfortunately the tallow ran in the sun, rather, and it was impossible to be relished very much, quite apart from the weevils. And they treated me to a famous rum-punch, which we drank, roaring and laughing like anything until Mr Brett sent to ask were we attempting to raise the Devil, and if so he was to be told the minute he appeared, in order to read him in at once, the ship being so short-handed. Sean gave me a comforter, 2 fathoms long, which he had knitted up out of black and purple wool found in *Tryal's Prize*. Query, how did he come by it? It will be very useful when we are out of the Tropics. Most kind and obliging in Sean.

'November 5th. 10° 36' S. 77° 41' N. Cape Barranca bearing WNW½W. Variation at noon 7° 1' S. Light variable airs at S and SW. No news. We are more than 50 days out of Juan Fernandez now, and Mr Blew says they can send an express from Valparaiso to Lima in 30 days, so by now they may know all along the coast that we are here, and may already have laid an embargo on the shipping in Peru as well as Chile. The men are still in very high spirits however, and work the ship so briskly it is a pleasure to see. Mem. to ask the sailmaker to add 2 pieces to my canvas trousers: they only come to my shins, and are painfully tight. Mem. to give Rogers a handsome present for the *Centurion* in a bottle he made me.'

It was Peter's watch below, the afternoon watch of a very warm day, not too hot, but sleepy weather. He yawned, closed his journal, and opened his Horace. The Ode about Maevius was to be prepared for Mr Walter, and he and Keppel had made a version with which they were rather pleased.

' "Mala soluta navis exit alite
Ferens olentem Maevium"—The ship with the malodorous Mr Saumarez aboard squares her yards with an unfortunate omen.

"Ut horridus utrumque verberes latus,
Auster, momento fluctibus"—Remember, O South Wind, to bang her about starboard and larboard.

"Niger rudentes Eurus, inverso mari,
Fractosque remos differat"—Let the black East, the sea having been turned upside-down, carry away her booms.'

He skipped a little to the piece the berth had particularly relished.

' "O quantos instat sudor tuis,
Tibique pallor luteus"—Oh what a sweat bedews your crew, and oh what a tallowy colour you are yourself.

"Et illa non virilis ejulatio,
Preces et adversum ad Joven"—and that effeminate wailing,
those prayers to unregarding Jove . . . extended upon the
winding shore, you shall delight the cormorants, who like that
kind of thing; and a libidinous he-goat together with a ewe-
lamb shall be a thank-offering to the tempests.'

'Unkind to the libidinous goat, however,' said Peter, closing the book. It was unkind to the first lieutenant, too; for he
had worn himself wrinkled and thin in a not unsuccessful
attempt to guide the midshipmen in the way they should
go—an uncommonly thankless task. Peter yawned again,
curled up on the locker, and in two minutes was fast asleep,
wheezing gently—whee-soo, whee-soo, in time with the long
pitch and roll of the ship. He had, deeply engrained by now,
the sailor's ability to sleep at any moment of the day or night:
he also had the naval habit of becoming instantly and wholly
awake at the least unusual sound. The thunder of Bailey's
enormous feet coming below would never have stirred him,
nor the crash of the evening gun: but a wrong note in the
rigging, the sound of the way going off the ship, would pierce
through all the disregarded clamour and rouse him at once.

The sound that brought him to his feet now, however, was
one that would have roused a sailor nine parts dead, if he were
cruising upon the Spaniards in the Pacific. 'Sail ho,' came
down from the mast-head, and as Peter reached the quarter-
deck Keppel had already flung the signal-yeoman the flags that
raced up to bid the squadron chase.

There was no need to ask where away: telescopes at the
mast-heads all converged upon some white fleck to the leeward, invisible from the deck, and the few free eyes aboard
were all trained round and fixed. Few free eyes, for the *Centurion* was crowding on sail to the height of the crew's desire,
and one cannot shake out a reef and stare at a prize for long,
however clever one may be.

'We are gaining,' said Preston. 'She's hull up already. Look at
Tryal's Prize; miles behind.'

'She has carried away her starboard main-tops'l stuns'l boom,' said Peter, swinging his glass back to the fleeing Spaniard. 'If we do the same,' he added, squinting along the yard to where the long, tapering boom bent with the thrust of the studding-sail, 'this mast will go by the board, and we shall lose her: it is only fished in the woulding.'

'I know,' said Preston. 'But that need not worry us, I mean about losing her, because if the mast goes, we shall certainly be killed, ha, ha.'

'Lord,' cried Peter, 'how she runs. We are making eight knots——'

'Nine,' said Preston.

——'Eight,' said Peter. 'And she must be making seven at the least.'

'That can't be three bells?' cried Preston aghast.

'It is, though,' said Peter, looking back at the sun. 'One more hour of light, and no moon at all.'

Three bells in the last dog watch. Four bells as Peter came down. The sun, with its maddening tropical habit of dipping at six, was nearly touching the sea: from the deck the Spaniard's hull could just be seen now, but unless she carried a mast away she would still be miles ahead by the dark, and then she would certainly tack.

The sun went down: it went suddenly down, and the night in the eastern sky swept in a huge arc towards the zenith. It was dark night on the starboard beam; a violet, momentary twilight high overboard; and on the larboard hung an orange remnant of the day. Then—you could see it move—the arc of night passed over the masts, down the bowl of the sky, to close in the uttermost west; and it was dark. Already the stars were huge and lambent: behind the *Centurion*'s stern the Southern Cross sprawled across blackness; and the dingy, patched, weather-worn sails had all turned ghostly white—the courses and part of the topsails: the others could no longer be seen except as spectral hints against the stars.

The watch below was a watch below in name only: not a man moved from the deck. At the common table and in the separate gun-deck messes the rats walked slowly about, choosing the least unpleasant biscuits: in the midshipmen's berth the burgoo steamed and grew lukewarm—it could not grow cold, for the temperature was 98° down there.

'We will have the royals off her, if you please, Mr Brett, and the stuns'ls,' said the Commodore.

The upper-yardsmen vanished in the shrouds, vague forms in the velvet night, all muttering 'Why?' and 'Eh?' within themselves.

'Sail,' cried the mast-head. 'Sail ho . . .'

'Sail hee,' whispered Keppel.

'. . . right ahead.' The look-out's voice was uncertain. This was the third hail for an imaginary ship since sundown.

'Mr Stapleton,' cried the Commodore, 'what do you find?'

'Nothing, sir,' came down after a long pause. 'I see nothing from here.'

'Quartermaster,' snapped the Commodore. The *Centurion* had yawed, a barely perceptible yaw as the helmsman tried to keep one eye on the binnacle while the other ranged over the bowsprit.

'Mr Anson, sir,' said Colonel Cracherode, to Peter's infinite relief, 'will you indulge a landsman's curiosity and allow me to ask what—to enquire whether——'

'Whether the chase has tacked, sir? It is very likely, indeed. As I conceive it, the Spaniard will have borne his helm a-weather just after sunset; and just about now he will tack again to steer for the land under a strong press of sail. That is why we are holding our course, in the hope of intercepting him on the second reach. I may very well be mistaken: but if I were the Spanish captain, that is what I should do. Mr Brett, we may take a reef in the topsails, I believe. And perhaps it would be best if you were to carry a night-glass aloft yourself.'

Mr Brett had barely reached the maintop before his voice came down, strong with excitement—surprisingly loud, 'Sail four points on the larboard bow.'

'Hands to the braces,' cried the Commodore. 'Port your helm. Clap on to that bowline there. Mr Ransome, the main tack: bear a hand.'

The *Centurion* turned smoothly to the wind: far aloft Peter and his party waited for the order, and the second it came they let fall the fore topgallantsail and raced in off the yard; it was instantly sheeted home, and under the additional thrust the *Centurion* plunged her head into her bow-wave: but this interesting sight was lost on Peter, he being wholly taken up with staring at the faint loom ahead, a hint of white in the starlight.

Twenty minutes later she was no faint hint of a half-guessed whiteness, but a ship within long gun-shot, clear and distinct.

'One,' said Mr Randall; and for the first time in his life Peter saw a gun fired in earnest. A brilliant orange tongue shot towards the chase, and for a split fragment of time the scattering of the wad could be seen in it: in the instantly succeeding darkness the yellow stab still played in his eyes, to be replaced within the second by two more blinding jets as the gunner intoned, 'Three. And five.' The *Centurion* yawed again: the starboard fo'c'sle guns beginning to bear, and they fired as they bore.

'She is forereaching us,' observed the Commodore. 'Three of canister above her tops, Mr Randall. That will discourage her upper-yardmen, I fancy. Keep it high, Mr Randall. Do not hull her upon any account.'

Now the guns in the waist spoke out, one, two, then three together.

'She has struck, sir,' reported the third lieutenant to Mr Brett, touching his hat.

'Sir, she has struck, if you please,' said Mr Brett, turning to the Commodore.

'Very good, Mr Brett. Mr Dennis will take possession and send the prisoners aboard with the utmost dispatch,' said the Commodore, turning and going below.

'Aye-aye, sir. Cutter's crew. Mr Palafox, the cutter away. Mr Bowles, serve out pistols and cutlasses. Step lively.'

Peter had never a word of Spanish, so he understood little of the submission of the Spanish captain, nor of Mr Dennis's orders to the Spanish crew in the waist of the ship: but he knew what he was there for, and as the prisoners got under way he shepherded them into the cutter, delivered them aboard the *Centurion*, and returned for more. The second time he came back with his load he had gathered enough information to whisper to Bailey in the chains, 'Only a——merchant-man with coconuts and leather—no sort of a prize.'

But the third time he came alongside the Spaniard he heard a dismal wailing and screeching aboard, an oath, and a man falling down.

'Rogers, keep the boat. T'others come along of me,' he cried and raced up with a cocked pistol tucked under his arm and a cutlass in his right hand—a tricky feat on a steep ship's side. The din came from the great cabin, and as Peter reached the deck he saw the lieutenant stagger backwards from the cabin with a scared and anxious look on his face. Three lines of blood were trickling down his cheek.

'What's the matter, sir?' cried Peter.

'It's a horrible pack of women,' said Mr Dennis, 'and they won't come out. They were hidden under beds and things, and then all swarmed out. One bit me,' he added vaguely, sucking his finger. 'Go on, Williams,' he commanded, 'rouse them out into the cutter.'

'Beg parding, sir,' said Williams, coming reluctantly into the light. 'I tried once, sir.'

'A fine sight,' cried the lieutenant, glaring round the half-circle of timid faces.

'After you, sir,' said an unseen hand in the shadow of the main-mast.

'The Commodore said "with the utmost dispatch",' muttered the lieutenant in a desperate whisper, with a wistful look at the door.

'May I have a go?' asked Peter.

'Yes, *do*,' said Mr Dennis.

Peter opened the door with a masterful swing. Three seconds later he shot out again, his ideas about women quite changed.

'Well, sir——' he began, reassembling his scattered locks, but a hail from the *Centurion* cut him short. The Commodore wished to know the reason for the delay.

'Directly, sir,' cried the distracted lieutenant.

'The fact is, sir,' said Peter in a rapid undertone, 'one of the women is—ahem—in a very interesting condition, sir. So I thought it would be barbarous to insist. A matter for the Commodore, perhaps, sir? Would you wish me to explain?'

'Make it so, Mr Palafox,' said Mr Dennis with profound relief. 'My respects, and the women being in a delicate state of health cannot be moved. Request further instructions, and venture to suggest they be indulged in the use of their quarters, for the time being.'

A splash of oars, a pause, and Peter came limping up the side again, followed by two Marines and the Spanish pilot. 'Suggestion approved, sir, if you please,' he said. 'The pilot to be allowed to keep up the women's spirits—is married to one. Sentries to stand guard together. And I am to say, sir, that the Commodore expressly orders that the women are to receive no inquietude or molestation.'

'Molestation, Mr Palafox?'

'That's it, sir. No molestation whatsoever.'

'Ha, ha, Mr Palafox?'

'Ha, ha, it is, sir.'

'Very good, Mr Palafox. And I tell you what,' added the lieutenant privately, clapping him warmly on the shoulder, 'I won't forget this, my dear fellow.'

'Oh, if you please,' cried Peter, writhing with anguish.

'What's the matter?'

'That is where she got home with the poker. Oh, sir,' he exclaimed, 'is it reasonable or just to carry a poker aboard in ten degrees south?'

'Where is that——cutter?' asked the *Centurion*.

'Brown paper, vinegar and Venice treacle, Mr Palafox,' called the lieutenant over the side, 'to be applied twice every hour.'

Dawn, sunset, dawn and another prize, a small one. The excitement subsiding, and the word passing for Peter throughout the ship.

'Ah, there you are, Mr Palafox,' said the Commodore, as Peter hurried into the great sunlit stateroom. 'Good Heavens, what have you been doing to your face?'

'I fell down, sir,' said Peter.

'Humph,' said the Commodore. 'Well, be that as it may, I have sent for you to see whether you can help us with a prisoner from this new prize. Mr Blew cannot make out his Spanish, but thinks he may be an Irishman. You understand the Irish language, I believe.'

'Yes, sir.'

'Then I beg you will address him in that tongue. Sit down here, by me. Sergeant, bring the man forward.'

'He is from the County Kerry, sir,' said Peter, after a rapid interchange in Irish. 'Won't give his name nor his parish. He is afraid of being taken up for a rebel, sir, and that his people at home will be troubled.'

'Ask him how he comes to be here.'

'He says he was brought by a great ugly—by a Marine, sir, too big for him to fight.'

'No, do not be foolish, Mr Palafox. What is the reason for his presence in these seas, the chain of events? If he was taken by the Spaniards against his will, and if he can give information about their dispositions, he will certainly not be treated as a rebel, but rewarded and carried to his own country. Will you make that clear to him?'

'Aye-aye, sir.'

'This is taking a long time, Mr Palafox,' said the Commodore.

'I beg pardon, sir. He had to be convinced of the right of King George to the Irish crown. But I think it was worth it, sir.'

'Is he convinced of it now?'

'Yes, sir.'

'So much the better. Now what can he tell us?'

'Sir, he says there are four merchant ships in the harbour of Paita and two galleys belonging to the King of Spain. He knows the town very well, having been there as a pedlar these many years: he says they are all the great thieves of the world, and they living in glory and as heavy with gold as Nebuchad-nezzar.'

'Never mind that, Mr Palafox. Ascertain the force of the defence, the disposition of the guns, and try to get an intelligible account of the town: draw a plan while he tells you.'

'Five streets down, and five streets across: and this is the fort, and here is the landing-place. And this is the church, so?'

'That is just the way of it, your honour,' said the pedlar. 'What an elegant picture it is, to be sure, as like to Saint Lawrence's grid as ever could be. And when will his lordship give me the Sassenach guineas, the pulse of my heart?'

'There are eight guns in the fort?'

'Eight, your honour, there are; besides those that lie on their sides.'

'And where is the treasure?' asked Peter suddenly, on his own.

'Why, where would it be at all but in the Customs House here on the quay?' asked the pedlar. 'The whole world knows that. It is the merchants' treasure I am speaking about, of course, for the King's treasure is in the fort, where Don Diego does be sitting counting it in the heat of the day and filing the edges off the gold pieces for his private advantage, the thief, and he the Governor of the town.'

'Here in the fort, the King's treasure?'

'In the strong fort itself.'

'So there we shall find it.'

'You will not,' said the pedlar, 'for am I not telling your honour the way the Spaniards had news of your coming this blessed Wednesday itself, and were they not hurrying the treasure inland a twelve leagues out of your way when I left Paita?'

'Oh,' said Peter. 'And the merchants' treasure also, is it gone with it?'

'It is not,' said the pedlar. 'Would the merchants trust Don Diego with a single morsel of coin? They would not. They are thieves, but not fools.'

'Is it there, so? Does it lie yet in the great house on the quay?'

'You may say that it does, your honour; and you may say it does not. For sure it is like a bird on the spring to fly in the air, and the merchants have the swift-sailing ship ready to float it away. On Saturday they charge it into her belly, and at this minute they do be laying on tallow and grease, the way she will swim the faster: for were they not beginning as I left Paita, and that not twenty hours since? And she is the great ship of the sea, to take so much within her—for it is a huge treasure, your honour, not like the King's at all which would be too small to wrap in a handkerchief without being lost now the Governor has had his way with it—and she is the bird of the sea for outrunning the wind so she is. Your honour will never ill-wish the poor pedlar, for saying your glorious ship will never reach the town in twenty-four hours, when the treasure takes wing.'

'I see,' said the Commodore, when Peter had relayed the news. 'Pass the word for Mr Brett. There is no time like the present, Mr Palafox,' he said, getting up. 'Take this man for'ard. Take my notes with you. Run through the whole account with him twice. If there is any material discrepancy report to me at once. Twenty-four hours, he said?'

In a matter of minutes later the *Centurion* was under full sail. The little crabs that lived in the long trailing mass of tropical weed on her bottom swam no more; they clung on to the barnacles and to the holes where the teredos burrowed like augers into the heart of oak and her sheathing.

Twenty-four hours, in which they prayed for the usual Spanish delay and trimmed the sails with fanatical care. The ship was alive with rumours, for the Irish pedlar was at large, having passed the most rigorous examination, and through Sean and the other Irishmen he made known the glories of the poetic imagination. He had confined himself to the truth with Peter—he was terribly frightened then—but now he was no longer under that unnatural constraint.

Twenty-four hours, in which the slightest variation in the wind was noted with anxious attention: for there was no man aboard who supposed that a foul ship, well over a year at sea, could catch one with a newly tallowed bottom, however great the zeal of the sailors.

In spite of the sharks there was an eager press of volunteers to be lowered over the side with weights on their feet and an axe to cut away some of the growth. This meant being half-keel-hauled, and keel-hauling, next to death or being flogged through the fleet (which was much the same thing) was the most dreaded of punishments: yet they flocked up for it, and during a horrible hour of dead calm they actually managed to hack a certain amount of the worst and longest away. But the Commodore stopped it when Dog-faced Joe and Boscawen were both brought up unconscious, with blood in their ears—stopped it much against the will of the crew, who were quite happy to sacrifice Dog-faced Joe, and even against the faint protests of the reviving Joe himself.

It was a period of such sustained excitement that yesterday's prize, *Nuestra Señora del Carmen*—carried by the armed boats under Mr Brett in a flat calm—was quite forgotten, and it was with some difficulty that the look-outs could keep their minds to the task of searching the horizon for the *Gloucester's* topsails; for they were coming now to the rendezvous.

'You will take sixty men, including the Spanish guides, Mr Brett. They are to be reliable men, who will neither get drunk nor run out of hand—if indeed the ship's company can possibly provide such a number,' said the Commodore, not sounding very hopeful about this. 'And you will land here——' pointing at the map.

'Aye-aye, sir.'

'Now let us go into the question of the men. There is Williams, who is a Nonconformist deacon at home, and . . .'

'You can't go in that rig,' whispered Peter to Keppel. He whispered in the dark—the whole ship whispered, although they lay fifteen miles from the shore.

'Yes, I can,' said Keppel, pulling a villainous little jockey-cap further down on his skull—his bald skull, for he had lost all his hair at Juan Fernandez—'I promised my Ma. It's lined with steel, and she made the velvet bows herself.'

'Silence there. Mr Ransome, have you mustered your men?'

'Yes, sir. All present and correct.'

'Lower away. Handsomely, now.' A volley of sibilant, half-whispered oaths crushed a wretched hand who had tripped and rattled a grating.

'Shove off. Give way.'

Peter sat back in the stern-sheets: he was trembling with excitement and tension, and he realised that it would be stupid not to try to relax during the long pull for the shore. He sat back and breathed easy: and in another minute he found that he was trembling again so that his larboard pistol made a little chattering sound against the hilt of his dirk.

Behind them the *Centurion* had already vanished: not a light showed on board. And between them and the ship came the two pinnaces, one from the *Tryal's Prize*, pulling very quietly after the barge.

'Take it easy. Stroke, pull long and easy,' said Mr Brett. 'We have plenty of time. This is not a race.'

It was a long pull in the dark. At one time Peter actually found that he had dozed, lulled by the steady and perfectly regular dip and heave of the oars.

'Oh, sir,' he said, waking up.

'Quiet. I have seen them,' said Mr Brett, not unkindly. Before them, low and twinkling over the water lay a necklace of light, the lights of Paita.

'Steady, now. Steady,' whispered the lieutenant. 'Lie on your oars. Mr Andrews,' he hailed quietly.

'Sir?' came the answer from the *Tryal's* pinnace.

'Mr Ransome?'

'Here, sir.' Ransome's hoarse whisper carried over the water from the darkness a boat's length away.

'You both have your bearings? The fort is one point on the larboard bow now, and the church is five. And you follow my wake in any event.'

'Aye-aye, sir,' from the pinnaces, low and intense.

'Give way.'

The lights were spread widely now: growing nearer, they twinkled no more. Nearer. And nearer. On the larboard, the shadowy form of a tall ship: was it the ship designed to carry away the treasure? There was no telling from the pedlar's 'the vast swimming castle, with a vast number of trees'. There was no telling: and they were seven hours late. Another ship and this one lit up.

A hail startled the night: it caught Peter's breath in his throat. The hail repeated, more loudly still; and voices aboard. Lights flashing on the deck of the Spaniard, shouts and splashing of oars. 'Los Ingleses, los Ingleses, los perros Ingleses,' bawled at the top of his voice by the captain, and the noise of boats making fast for the shore.

'Pull now, pull, you sons of bitches,' roared the lieutenant, standing half-upright in the sheets. 'Pull. In. Out. In. Out. *Pull.*' Behind them came Andrews' shouting and Ransome's, lurid and hearty. The long strange shape of a moored galley shot by to starboard. Lights in the fort, lights running along the rampart. 'Pull,' cried Mr Brett. A flash, a bang and a deep rumbling whiffle just overhead: another double flash that lit up the fort and showed soldiers, momentarily fixed in movement. Then the crash on the shingle sent Peter nose downwards on the thwarts. Several people walked over him: but he was up and ashore. Already the men were formed, and he darted into his place. Something hit a stone bollard beside him and howled off into the darkness, and again the sky lit up with a crimson flash as the fortress guns went off.

'Follow the lantern,' shouted Mr Brett. 'Double up, now.'

They ploughed over fifty yards of beach, and a salvo from the fort hurled itself into the sand they had just left.

Now they were in a street, sheltered from the cross-fire, and Mr Brett was ranging his forces. 'Mr Andrews, carry on according to plan. Mr Ransome, form the same line as us,' he said, shoving Hairy Amos and Sean back into the rank. 'Any man who breaks the line will be flogged. Sing out as much as you like, but keep your stations. Light the torches—bear a hand, now. Williams and Tyson, bang on those drums. Carry on. Three cheers for the King.'

The earth-shaking cheer that followed this and the tremendous tattoo on the drums, the flaring torches, the uninterrupted bellowing of the sailors gave the impression of a multitude of enemies surging straight out of Hell. A straggling volley met them in the square, but the appalling yell of the Centurions, their instant and accurate return, cleared the Governor's house from in front while the shrieking Tryals hurled themselves into it from the back.

'Mr Ransome, stay here,' said Mr Brett in the square, silent except for the distant noise of the townsmen's flight. 'Keep this Spaniard. Secure the Governor if he is to be found—the guide will know him. Mr Andrews, we will proceed to the fort.'

A single shot came from the roof of the Governor's house. There was a loud and musical ping, and Peter saw Keppel sitting on the ground, holding his head.

'Clear that roof,' cried Ransome in a voice of thunder through the furious roar of the Centurions; and as Peter's file marched off he saw Keppel stagger to his feet.

'That is the main gate, sir,' said the wretched guide, fast to the coxswain by a line round his middle. They were crouched under the shelter of a tumble-down wall, and over their heads the gun-embrasures stood ominous and clear, with a drift of smoke still wafting from them. The moment they left the wall they would be in point-blank range.

'Mr Andrews, I am going to attempt the gun-ports to larboard. You will open fire and howl and create a diversion to starboard: if you can gain a footing, well and good. If not, keep up a fire at the slits and embrasures until you hear my whistle. Rogers, come here. You see that hole? You run for it when I give the word, and—who's the next strongest?—Walton, you unship that Spaniard. Here, make him fast to this ring, and attend to what I say. Rogers will make you a back: you will clap on to the edge of that hole, that gun-port. We will come up over your shoulders. Understood? Mr Palafox, you and your party will do the same the next hole down. Now understand this: Centurions are silent, Tryals howl like the devil. Centurions to port, Tryals to starboard. Wait for my signal. One, two, three, go.'

With a roaring and bellowing behind him and the flash and crackle of musket-fire, Peter raced across the open ground, with Sean slowing to let him keep up. He had time to think, 'If they don't fire this minute they won't be able to fire at all,' and then he was swarming up Thomson's back while Sean's war-shriek rang from the battlement above him. He could not reach, his nails scraped on the stone. Sean's hand grasped his, heaved him up. Sean was fleeting over the gun-platform in the light of a single lantern: he was hurtling straight for an advancing body of men with his cutlass up and with the rest of Peter's party behind him. Sean sprang on his man with a terrible cry, missed his head, gripped his throat, dashed the hilt of his cutlass into his face, bore him down and hissed into his ear would he have his throat cut now or surrender?

The man, black in the face and unable to speak, kicked Sean in the stomach and Sean shortened his cutlass to put him to rest.

'Stop teasing the man,' said Peter peevishly, pulling Sean by the arm. 'Let him alone, can't you?' Another kick from the infuriated bo'sun's mate dislodged Sean: but this was the only angry blow struck in the action, for the fort was deserted and its defenders were still just to be seen hurrying urgently away.

Mr Brett blew his whistle. 'Strike their colours,' he said, passing the coxswain the Union flag to be hoisted.

'No offence, joy?' asked Sean, tenderly dusting the bo'sun's mate's collar.

'Not the least in the world, cock,' said the bo'sun's mate, spitting blood.

'Mr Palafox,' said the lieutenant, 'you know where you are?'

'Yes, sir,' said Peter, taking his bearings from the main gate of the fort.

192

'Then go at once to the Customs House. Kill anyone there at the least resistance. If the treasure is still there fire this rocket. If not, this one. Cox'n, give Mr Palafox the rockets. Take four men. I shall follow when the fort is secured. Understood?'

'Aye-aye, sir. Sean, Davis, Brown, Thomson.'

He raced from the fort, across the side of the square, down the long, empty street, turned right towards the place they had landed, and there along the wall of the broad building that he knew was the Customs House he saw a small group of men staggering with a chest. 'Ahoo,' he roared, banging his pistol in the air.

'Ahoo,' roared Sean, and, 'Ahoo,' bellowed the remaining three. The men dropped their burden and fled madly.

'This is it,' cried Peter. 'Kick in that door.'

The men hurled themselves against it. It was open, however, and they shot furiously into the Customs House. The solitary Negro in it turned grey, dropped his lantern and plunged out of a window.

Peter stared round in the light of the guttering candle. Row upon row of chests lined the walls, stood piled on the floor.

'Here,' he said, grabbing Sean's cutlass and prising open a lid. 'It's all right,' he cried, as the glint of the steel flashed back from the silver and gold. 'Now come on,' he said, 'get that other chest in from the road. Brown, drop that,' he snapped. 'Jump to it. Heave. Heave-ho.' he cried, straining at the handle of the chest in the street. 'Dear Lord, but it's heavy.'

' 'Tis heavy, Peter a cuishle,' said Sean, picking it up, 'but sure it'll go hard if I don't have Tim Colman's field and a bull. You have not forgot the rocket, sir, dear, I am sure?'

'I have not,' said Peter. 'Where's the flint and the steel? Oh your soul to the devil,' he cried as the flint refused its office again. 'Now,' he said, priming his empty pistol with powder. There was an instant flash, a glow, and a second later the rocket soared up to burst, in a red star that illuminated the five upturned faces, eager and tense, and told the fort and the squadron that the treasure of Paita was taken.

1 1

PAITA LAY SEVEN HUNDRED MILES AWAY, FAR DOWN UNDER THE equator, far south of the great bay of Panama: seven hundred miles and three weeks of sailing to the south. The inhabitants of that arid and slatey town were building up their smoke-blackened walls of mud, dredging inefficiently for the sunk merchant-ships and galleys, rejecting, with ill-concealed con-tempt, the Governor's explanation of the powerful reasons that had led him to stand outside the town with a numerous body of cavalry while the British sailors, fantastically dressed up in looted periwigs, laced coats and mantillas, joyously toiled day after day, carrying the heavy chests of silver to the boats that plied incessantly from ship to shore.

The said tars, now no more than a vivid and evil memory (and yet not such an evil memory either, for there had been no shadow of personal outrage or brutality; and the released prisoners from the prizes spread far and wide their account of the Commodore's humanity—one ecclesiastic, a Jesuit who had messed with Mr Walter, even going so far as to state that the salvation of heretics was not wholly inconceivable)—no more than a memory in Paita, were now variously disposed about the island of Quibo. It had been a trying passage, with contrary winds, tremendous, suffocating heat and appalling downpours of equatorial rain that had rushed through the *Centurion*'s sun-dried decks to render every single thing within her wet, warm and, within twelve hours or so, resolutely mouldy. A tedious, long and uncomfortable voyage, and even at the end, when they had at last found Quibo—madly out of position on the charts—a foul wind had kept them standing off and on, and had forced the *Gloucester*, always an unfortunate ship, away to the leeward and over the horizon. But the men's leaping high spirits had never flagged: there was not a man aboard who did not know to within a hundredweight or so the amount of the treasure that lay behind new bulkheads far below the waterline; there was not one of them who had not become an ardent calculator, a finished arithmetician; and even the lowest rating knew himself to be worth fifty pounds or more—an exhilarating sum for a sailorman.

The exceedingly important business of filling the ship's watercasks was nearly finished—a doubly urgent task, for Paita had yielded barely a hogshead, there being never a spring in the town—and it had been done easily with a sweet stream running directly at hand. Now there was some time for liberty ashore, and the end of the island resounded with the sailors' holiday. Sean, unmindful of his future as turtle-herd in chief, was passionately hurrying up and down in the blinding glare of the sun, turning the creatures as they hauled up on the sand. In another part of the island the assembled carpenter's mates stood on tiptoe around an enormous alligator while Mr de Courcy Bourke, a Negro from Paita who, by a very remarkable coincidence, had known Mr Saumarez on the Jamaica station, and who had escaped with several other slaves from the Spaniards during the attack, skipped to and fro in front of the alligator's nose. With a sudden terrifying rapidity the alligator charged for the twentieth time, snapping with a force that would have severed a topsail yard: Mr de Courcy Bourke leapt over the alligator's upper jaw and stood poised on its scaly back. The carpenter's mates scattered, shrieking with laughter: one fell, touched by the alligator's lashing tail, and he would have ended his days at Quibo if Mr de Courcy Bourke, knowing in the ways of alligators, had not slid forward, with his gleaming black arms in a muzzle that prevented the huge jaws from opening.

Off shore a large and pertinacious group of seamen groped perpetually among the oyster-beds for the pearls they never managed to find, possibly because they opened the wrong sort of shell. Solitary, on a black rock in a gloomy shadow, Hairy Amos slowly extracted a sea-urchin's spines from his horny foot. Amos, alone among the liberty men, did not sing: behind his beard he did not even smile. Hairy Amos was sad. He was the one Centurion who had got drunk ashore—blind drunk, drunk to such an extent that only the heat of the burning town had aroused him. This had been publicly, and unfavourably, mentioned by the Commodore himself during an address to the men, designed at once to commend the good conduct of the landing-party and to allay the frightful outbreak of wrangling between the men ordered ashore and the unfortunate who, left behind, had been deprived of their chance of making a booty. The Commodore had appeased the really dangerous tumult by insisting on fair shares all round: he had thrown in his own on the heap on the deck as a token. But he had also publicly rebuked hairy Amos, and this weighed on Amos's soul. Even Dog-faced Joe, that walking sponge, had refrained; but not Amos, the squadron's hairy shame.

A manta the size of a billiard-table planed out of the sea and fell with a slap like a mainsail taken aback. 'Overgrown flat-fish,' said Amos, 'I hope you stove in your stomach.'

A dazzling flight of brilliant macaws passed over his head to join the parrots and parakeets in the *Carmel*'s rigging. 'Nasty dirty birds,' observed Amos. 'Always fouling the deck for poor sailormen. Yelling and bawling like——bo'suns.'

'Well, if you insist,' said Mr Walter, accepting a cake, 'perhaps I could manage another.' Peter had sacked a pastry-cook's shop in Paita for the chaplain, but already the mound was very much less—almost gone.

'This is the kind I like best,' said Mr Walter, holding up a spherical blob of marzipan about the size of an egg, with nine kernels stuck all over it and a piece of crystallised melon concealed within. 'It has just a *little* more unction than the square sort, I believe. But, as I was saying, the Acapulco

galleon is not to be considered as a merchant vessel. It belongs
to the King of Spain and wears the royal colours at the main:
its officers are King's officers, and the merchants are only
permitted to ship their bales by grace. It is a privilege that the
merchants prize very highly, for this is the only way they can
trade with the Orient—no other ships but the annual galleon
are allowed, and they keep the secret of their navigation so
close that there are no interlopers.'

'So in this one ship they carry all their commerce, sir?' said
Peter, thoughtfully.

'Just so. Gold and silver from Mexico to the Orient: then
from Manilla in the Spanish Philippines, where the Oriental
merchants gather, all the spices and silk that the silver has
bought, come back to Acapulco. And I have heard it said, by
trustworthy men'—sinking his voice—'that the Acapulco
ship carried a million pieces of eight.'

'A million, sir?' cried Peter.

'A million,' repeated Mr Walter.

'A million, Sean,' said Peter.

'What is a million, your honour, dear?'

'A thousand thousands, so it is. And you may reckon four
shillings and ninepence for a piece of eight—or you may say
a crown to be easy in your reckoning.'

'May I so, Peter gradh? Sure, a crown's a lovely thing,' said
Sean, whistling vacantly.

'Come now, Sean, don't be stupid, I beg. Think of a thousand crowns, and then all that heap a thousand times repeated.'

'Why, indeed your honour, that is a thought beyond my
power, like counting the waves between this land and home.'

'Dunderhead,' cried Peter warmly, moved by Sean's indifference. 'I will bring it down to your brutish incomprehension. It is two hundred and fifty thousand pounds. Your share
would be a clear five hundred golden guineas.'

'Five hundred pounds for me,' whispered Sean, turning
pale. 'And did you say for me, your honour, dear? Why, there

has never been five hundred whole pounds in Ballynasaggart in the history of the world. It would buy the parish, joy. And do these false thieves of Spaniards be keeping my five hundred pounds in their old ship?'

'Quietly now. Do not bellow, Sean.'

'Where is this ship, Peter, tell me true?' cried Sean, pinning Peter's arm.

'She is somewhere between this and the East,' replied Peter, pleased at having so powerfully attentive an audience.

'So we must rush over that old mountainy New World,' said Sean, gazing eastwards to Panama. 'The Dear knows it will be the weary road with all that silver on our backs, but what is a mountain, and what is the load at all——'

'Wisha, it is not that way, Sean, my dear,' said Peter. 'The East is in the west here, because the world is a ball, and we the other side of it.'

'For shame, now, your honour,' said Sean reproachfully, still staring across the sea. 'To make game of a poor ignorant fellow (though he may be as rich as Squire David, with fifty bright pounds of his own) is no sport at all for your father's son.'

'But the world *is* round,' said Peter.

'It is not,' said Sean. 'How can you say such a wicked thing? Fie.'

'But it *is*,' cried Peter, 'and if we go on, we shall come back to where we began.'

'Of course we shall,' replied Sean, 'but that is because it is shaped like a cheese. You may go *round*, as Loegaire did: but you may not go up or down for ever, or you will fall off the ends, as Maire nic Phiarais did and we ourselves almost when we went too far south of the Horn. The whole world knows that. But for all love let us not be gossiping like a pair of old cats in the sun—where is she for sure, this beautiful ship?'

'By now,' said Peter, considering, 'she may be somewhere between 150 and 140 degrees of longitude west.'

'Then why do you sit there, man alive?' cried Sean. 'Why do we squander the minutes? Why?' he cried springing to his feet, 'do we let those false yellow dogs gloat over my five hundred pounds—and your honour's share, too, which is far greater, as justice demands, for are you not the learned man of the ocean sea? Why do we sit admiring the turtles? Come, we will tell the Commodore how it is the way we must sail on the instant.'

'Time enough, time enough: be easy. If himself'—nodding towards the quarter-deck, where the Commodore stood deep in thought—'does not know, who does, will you tell me at all? Sure, it has been in his mind since Juan Fernandez.'

'And is there time, so, your honour? asked Sean anxiously. 'They will not give us the slip, the thieves, in some odd hole of the sea?'

'Time enough, Sean. Listen, while I tell you. They have this ship, have they not? This one ship every year, that must go from Acapulco to Manilla, and from there back again with the wealth of the East.'

'The East in the west.'

'Will you hold your tongue, now?'

'I will not, Peter a gradh, for I am burning with joy.'

'And from Manilla she sails in the month of July to come to Acapulco by January or February as may be, for the way is long, Sean, nigh on ten thousand miles, and the Spaniards will lie-to at night: then in March she turns back again for Manilla, and on that course she has more favouring winds.'

'In January or February she comes?'

'She does. So you understand that we have time enough to make our northing at leisure, the way it is December now, and the tenth day of December, no more, and no distance at all lies between us and the harbour of Acapulco where she must pass—barely a fortnight of sailing, for we shall find the trade wind to carry us up a few days from here. There is time in galore—time enough and to spare.'

'Will you not touch on wood when you say such a thing, Peter dear? No, that is not wood, but the bone of a sea-lion. Touch wood, will you not? Five hundred pounds is a great solemn thing.'

'What are you doing with the sea-lion's tush? And why is it brown?'

'I am making a line of teeth for Mr Keppel, and I have browned it the way I can see how I must work. But I wish you had touched to wood the first time, so I do.'

'Well, I am touching wood now, an't I. And yet there is less need, for she cannot know a word of our being here: which is quite as well, for she is a galleon the size of a first-rate, and she mounts a wonderful number of guns, as well as a thousand men clear to fight them, and we with no more than three hundred and thirty, counting the *Gloucester* and *Tryal's Prize*.'

'I spit on their men,' cried Sean. 'I spit on their thousand men for a mock; and I spit in the Golden Ocean to bring us good luck.'

'Who has spat on the deck?' inquired a thunderous voice below them (for they were in the maintop). 'Where is that man who has presumed to spit on the deck? Where is the ship's corporal? Bring me the name of that renegade swab.'

Time and to spare. A million pieces of eight. Time and enough. The words ran to and fro in the ship, and never a group of men could be found talking without the word Acapulco in the mouth of each one. There was not one head in the ship that did not carry the muster complete—the roll of the ship's company with each man's rating set down. But here arose an infinity of argument, strong, heated words, dissension, and even oaths, alas; for upon each man's rating depended his share of the prize; and in the squadron, with its terrible list of mortality, there was scarcely a hand who was not filling another man's place. It was so from top to bottom: the original first lieutenant was now captain of the *Tryal's Prize*; his replacement, Mr Saumarez, commanded the *Carmelo*: and at the other end, one of the original butchers, a man of some education and a fearless hand with a knife, was now an acting, unpaid surgeon's mate; while Prout, entered as an ordinary trumpeter, had performed the duties of yeoman of the powder-room a twelve-month since, which put him, in his opinion, in the much smaller class of those who, like the midshipmen, shared one eighth of the whole, instead of the quarter share that had to be split among the whole mass of the generality—seamen, able and ordinary, the quarter-gunners, the carpenter's crew, the stewards, the swabbers and the rest.

They argued and wrangled by day and by night, and the Commodore's clerk, an anxious, harried, conscientious recorder, received garrulous and circumstantial deputations from every category in the ship until he found his papers were increasing upon him until there was no more room for himself to turn in the miserable hole where he lived: whereupon he shut up his door with a double lock and gave himself up to silent despair.

They wrangled at work and they wrangled at rest: but as December drew on, torrid, wet, full of squalls, the watches below grew somewhat quieter—they were too tired to keep awake in their hammocks, for the squadron was meeting with bad weather, storms from the north, dead, sweltering calms when the boats towed the ships and they creeping over the glassy sea only to have the cruelly hard-won miles snatched away when the next wind blew them back: contrary winds, maddening and frustrating contrary winds.

Time enough and to spare. The tenth parallel passed unwillingly under the keel at Christmas, and Cape Corrientes, that vital spot, still lay seven hundred miles to the north.

'Christmas Day,' wrote Peter, '10° 1' N. 103° W. We are all in a great taking. She has been known to arrive by January 10th. All day in the boats again—quite fagged out now. Hardly hold pen.'

'She' of course meant the Acapulco galleon: that golden ship needed no name.

'Sir,' said Bailey, in the open doorway of Mr Walter's cabin with Preston behind him, 'may we come in, if you please, when you are at leisure, to be explained to about the theory of winds?'

'You may command me at this very moment,' said the chaplain, closing his book. 'Sit down, Mr Bailey, I beg. Mr

Preston will find room on that trunk. Now as to winds—and I suppose that you have the trade winds in mind, like the rest of us—we read in the Learned Job Ludolphus, book three, chapter one . . .'

'The Commodore's compliments to Mr Ransome, Mr Keppel and Mr Palafox, and he would be honoured by their company at dinner,' said the Commodore's steward.

'Eh?' said Keppel, still deaf from his bang at Paita.

'Commodore—dinner,' bawled Ransome, whom Keppel could always understand.

'Oh. Compliments—respectful compliments, Wright—most happy. I say, Wright, what will be for pudding?'

'What a carnal object you are, Keppel,' said Peter.

'I did not,' cried Keppel; 'I only asked what was for pudding.'

'That's what I said,' roared Peter.

'No. That would be Wednesday,' replied Keppel. 'Come on, Wright, what's for pudding?'

'Sir, it is a sort of French muffin in rum.'

'French muffin,' said Ransome, relaying the words.

'Eh?'

'Muffin. French. In rum.'

'Oh. Good. I tell you what, Wright, you must tell Froggy that there will be really important guests today—connoisseurs, you know—and that he had better exert all his powers. Tell him, Wright, not to be near with the pudding, whatever he does.'

'What's the matter, Ransome?' asked Peter, when the steward had gone.

'Sooner face a broadside any day of the week,' said Ransome, more hoarsely than usual, 'or grapple a fire-ship. You can't drop your fork when you're alongside of a fire-ship. He means it very kind, I am sure: but I wish he would not.'

'Never mind it, Ransome,' said Peter; 'there won't be anyone else, I dare say; and if there is, we will back you up. You will enjoy it when you get there.'

'Last time I upset a chair,' said Ransome nervously, 'and one of the land-officers was stern-fast to it, with a little china cup in his hand.'

'Well, gentlemen,' said Mr Anson, sipping his port, 'I admire your good breeding. I have had the pleasure of your company all through dinner, and I have not once heard the name of Acapulco.'

It was a tradition at these entertainments (which the Commodore tried to make less awful, but which nevertheless were very serious delights for the junior officers, and for poor Ransome an unmitigated torment)—it was a tradition that none of the ship's affairs should be discussed: the theory was that they were a group meeting voluntarily in a social manner—by land, as it were, or as passengers—and although the theory of equality remained wholly theoretical for the midshipmen face to face with their Jovian commander, still they never talked shop, but either remained perfectly mute, or cudgelled out some neutral kind of remark. So these direct words from the Commodore sent a galvanic thrill through his guests: even Keppel heard plainly.

They stared at the Commodore, regardless of manners, and the Commodore smiled back at them, three intent faces, alert and waiting. He looked at them. They were brown, thin and scarred, and in spite of their civilised surroundings and their decorum they had a fierce, almost buccaneering air that was not wholly counteracted by their sober uniforms. Peter, for one, though dressed in his best—the purple and fine linen reserved for high days—had grown so that his powerful, horny hands stood five inches from their cuffs, and his tightly imprisoned arms and shoulders imposed a dangerous strain on the seams sewn in distant Gosport; his one remaining good shirt had lost a button just after the turtle was removed, and now he could breathe; while below the table the extreme tension of his breeches prevented him from ever bending his legs, and he had grave doubts about rising again. Ransome was better off, having done growing; but even his coat had been soaked in his chest round the Horn, dried in the blazing sun of Chile, soaked again on the equator and covered with mildew; so it showed forth but a faint likeness of its once glorious form. And Keppel, though the best equipped of them all, presented a spectacle that would have made his mother turn grey, had she not been bald, and therefore obliged to wear an auburn wig of which she complained in the summer as being disagreeably warm: for he had shrunk with the scurvy and his little wizened face looked preternaturally old; like his mama, he had no hair at all, having moulted in his recovery; but he wore no wig. However, Sean's kindness had replaced his teeth, which now shone in a fixed and criminal grin that had nothing to do with the rest of his face. He had put them in for the first time today, in honour of the occasion, and the sight had turned the Commodore pale. He had said nothing, of course, but it was observed that he sent the first dish away untouched, and when he subsequently addressed Keppel—'Mr Keppel, may I help you to a little calipash? Or do you prefer the calipee?—Mr Keppel, you would oblige me by putting the pudding out of its misery: it would be a sad shame to send it away unfinished'—he looked not directly at that unlovely midshipman, but slightly to one side of him.

'Acapulco,' repeated the Commodore. 'I will give you the toast of Acapulco. For, gentlemen, I will not disguise the fact that this is at the very heart of our expedition. This is where we can hit the Spaniard the hardest: so let us drink to Acapulco and a happy encounter.'

They might drink; but drinking, however zealously, could not command a wind. Nor could the ancient practice of whistling, nor yet the scrupulous avoidance of any unlucky act or word. There were some Indians aboard, and Negroes; and from odd recesses of the ship, arose the thin, acrid fumes of Aztec and Mayan magic fires, to mingle with the weird, half-heard beating of a Voodoo drum somewhere in the forepeak: Sean was discovered burning a candle before a portable saint, the property of one of the Catholic Irishmen—Peter, quite outraged, sent the apostate away with a flea in his ear; and remained to offer a candle himself. Mr Walter preached with uncommon vehemence upon the text 'I praise the Lord who directs my hands to the spoil' to a wonderfully attentive congregation on the last Sunday in December.

Yet the precious days flew by. December had gone. Twelfth Night found the *Centurion* and her consorts wallowing in the trough of an eastern swell, with not a breath of air to fill the sails as they flapped drearily overhead; and the current was drifting them away to the south.

But even foul winds have an end, and calms; and on January 10th Peter could write. 'It *is* the trade wind at last. It has been steady now since the middle watch. The north-easter carried us up just far enough, as Mr Blew said it would.'

And still a week later, '12° 50′ N. 32′ W. The blessed wind holds true. We have barely trimmed a sail all day, and this makes four in a row.'

Then, 'January 26th. 18° 4′ N. 118° W. Wind steady at WSW. We are north of Acapulco and in her track. Just before I came below the course was altered to SE½E, which the men hearing they cheered until they were checked, for they understood that we were standing in for Acapulco now. We may yet be in time, if only we make a good landfall and the Spanish pilots are to be relied upon. It is said they are not to be trusted, but sure they will not dare to deceive the Commodore. There is time enough: but I wish I had never said so aloud. Mr W. complains to the Commodore about sorcerers and Papists.'

'There is time enough, for sure,' said Mr Brett to Mr Dennis.

'Of course there is,' replied Mr Dennis.

'I have heard tell,' said the bo'sun to his mates, 'that she often does not get into port until well on in February.'

'In such a very long voyage,' observed the surgeon, 'it is inevitable that there should be delays; and when we consider that the vessel is conducted by Spaniards—well, all I can say is, that I shall be very much surprised to see her before the month of March.'

'I have it from Mr Blew, who had come directly from

talking with the older Spanish captain,' said Mr Stapleton, 'that they hardly ever set their to'garns'ls for months on end—forbidden by the regulations, apparently, whenever the wind is more than the lightest air.'

'What do you mean with your "wish it was only Christmas now"?' asked the temporary, acting, unpaid armourer, advancing upon the Able Seaman Wills with strong displeasure. 'What do you mean by it? What does it matter if Christmas *is* passed? You ugly great swab. It's Jonahs like you that bring bad luck. There's *plenty* of time. Take that!'

'That's right,' said his approving mates; 'you scrag him, Nobby, the dismal crow.'

'There is time, time enough still: time and to spare.' The ship's company told one another this with emphatic conviction as January wore away and February grew. They kept up their spirits, in spite of the utterly maddening coast, where every high land, every cape, every island was hailed by the Spanish and Indian captives as the sure sign of Acapulco— endless promises of the harbour tomorrow. They kept up their spirits; but after three disappointments the prisoners had to be kept under a double guard, or the men would have destroyed them. It was impossible to say whether the captive pilots were malignantly cunning or merely inefficient to the point of lunacy; but in either case the men wanted their blood.

The squadron was spread abroad in a wide-searching net, and not a signal passed between them without raising a wild flurry of hope aboard every ship. Throughout every minute of the day and night the keenest eyes in the world scanned the huge round of the sea: but still the days went by, and still the blue emptiness deferred their hopes.

'February 12th. 12° 30′ N. 112° 14′ W. Light airs at W veering N. The barge is sent away again to run down the coast, with orders to discover the harbour and not to be seen—Mr Dennis and Ransome. They should be back tomorrow or the next day, if the Spanish captain is to be believed, for we raised a headland bearing ESE 12 leagues that he swore was the true landfall. I took him to the masthead to view it, by Mr Brett's orders: had a month's mind to tumble him off. If we find that the galleon has got in, I shall: and Keppel will cut his throat. We find it hard to wait till tomorrow.'

But if Peter found one day's waiting hard, he, in common with the entire squadron, found two, three and four days' waiting harder still. Yet four days did not see the barge back again: it was a full week before their intense anxiety and suspense found relief.

At four bells in the forenoon watch the look-out reported a sail.

'Lug-sail, sir,' he answered the deck. 'It might be the barge.'

'Mr Palafox, take up your glass, if you please,' said the Commodore; and a very few minutes later Peter hailed. 'Deck, sir. It is the barge. She's broke out the private signal. Now she's making another.'

'What is it, Mr Palafox?' This was the Commodore's voice in the waiting silence.

A long pause, while Peter made doubly sure. 'It is the blue ensign reversed, sir,' he reported in a toneless voice.

He did not hurry down. The bearer of ill news is an unwelcome figure. The blue ensign reversed meant that the galleon was already in; that she lay under the hundred guns of the castle in Acapulco harbour; and that they had lost their chance of the wealth of the East.

They had not been unprepared: the frustrating hours, stretching to days, weeks and months of irretrievable delay had gnawed into their confidence. Yet the absolute confirmation of the worst was a blow whose stunning force was proportionate to the brilliance of their golden hopes; and they took it hard—very hard.

'What a glum, perishing berthful of swabs you are, to be sure,' said Ransome, who, fresh from a week in an open boat, was shovelling down turtle hash with a cheerfulness that scarcely endeared him to his companions.

'Oh, shut up, you crow,' said Peter.

'Stow it,' said Bailey.

'What did he say?' asked Keppel, cupping his frost-bitten ear.

'He said we were gloomy,' bawled Preston.

'——him, and his——blue ensign, reversed,' said Keppel.

'Well, strike me,' cried Ransome, 'this is a fine, 'micable welcome for a cove with good news, brought three hundred miles, most of it pulling—hard tack and damned little water all the way.'

'What good news?' asked Peter, with a sudden renewal of interest.

'Crush me if I tell you now,' replied Ransome, sulkily. 'Pass the soup. And take your great thumb out of it.'

'He hasn't got any news,' said Preston.

'Oh, an't I?' cried Ransome, rising at once. 'Didn't you see them blackamoors what we took?'

'Yes,' said the berth, somewhat agog, but not very much.

'Well, we took 'em by night in Acapulco harbour.'

'What of it?'

'What of it? Ah, what of it?' said Ransome. 'Ay, what indeed?' Once Ransome had become oracular there was nothing to be done: no threats, no kind words would affect his obstinacy then, and they all knew it. They plied him with food, and waited.

'. . . so the third day we open the right harbour at last,' he said, smiling now and replete. 'And in the night we come paddling soft in the dark for Acapulco, which is a long town in the bottom of a bay, a good harbour as we judged. And under the loom of an island we see this canoe with the black-amoors fishing over the side. So we bears away for their light and takes 'em up, and Mr Dennis asks 'em what they know. And they tell him four things. One, the galleon is in. Two, there was a garrison on that island guarding the harbour until three days before, which they must have took us if they had still been there. Three, that the Governor withdrew the red-coats, because why? Because he reckoned that the squadron was not in these parts any more. Four, that the Governor give out by proclamation that the galleon would sail as usual on the 14th March, and the merchants were to hold themselves ready. And I will tell you something else,' said Ransome, looking round the half-circle of fascinated listeners with a gleam of fierce satisfaction in his kind, weather-beaten face. 'We missed her on the way in, and that was a bitter hard stroke: but bound from Manilla to Acapulco she carries merchandise, which we would a' had to carry home again with all the risks of spoiling and being done down by the landsmen, for the Spaniards won't ransom a cargo, not if it rains——'

'Brass cats?' suggested Bailey.

'Brass cats *and* dogs,' said Ransom, 'which we know very well, to our cost. Besides, she is the size of a first-rate, and there would not be room for half her stuff aboard us and the *Gloucester*, not with our own stores in the holds. But mark me,' he said, bringing his fist into his hand, 'when she is bound *for* Manilla, she carries nothing but silver and gold. That stows away. That don't take room. We rouses the ballast over the side and puts gold in its place. Lord love your heart, there's no better ballast nor gold.'

When the Commodore laid down their stations on the chart, the tracing looked very like a fan, an open fan with spokes. The handpiece, the conjunction of the spokes, was Acapulco, where the galleon lay, and radiating from this spot ran five lines, each fifteen leagues long. The first terminated in the *Carmelo*; the second in the *Centurion*, three leagues on *Carmelo*'s starboard beam; then, at the same interval, the *Tryal's Prize*, the *Gloucester* and the *Carmen*—a curve of ships that made the fan's periphery. Between them the ships covered some seventy miles of sea, and with incessant vigilance they kept watch day after day, while the *Centurion*'s cutter and the *Gloucester*'s lay inshore, four leagues off by day, close in at night, to signal the first movement of the galleon.

The galleon herself was an intimately familiar shape to Peter: he, with Mr Dennis and the cutter's crew, stared at her with the most unwinking concentration throughout the night. Spaniards, in general, are not early risers, but on the other hand, they never seem willing to go to bed at all, and often the cutter's crew could see the galleon plain by the lights of Aca-pulco for most of the hours of darkness. At other times their night-trained eyes, aided by the gleam of the stars, pierced through the warm, velvety blackness (it was always dead calm inshore by night) to make her out as she lay moored to two enormous trees, deep within the gun-ringed harbour. She was difficult to see, for the little island and the Punto del Griso shut the harbour's mouth, and only by creeping along the north-eastern shore of Acapulco bay, well within the castle's range, could they get more than a stern-on glimpse. Yet every night they saw her, and every night Peter, with a strong night-glass, made out all the features of her massive build: he knew her very well.

The fourteenth day of March was the day she was to sail. The Governor had proclaimed it by a drum throughout the town: and there was not a man afloat who did not trust in the Governor's promptitude—nor was there a soul so dull that he could not reckon the difference between New Style and Old, the Julian calendar and the Gregorian, which made the Span-ish March 14th fall on the English 3rd. If the expedition had done nothing else, it had at least produced a crew of ready-reckoners: men who before could barely count beyond ten, nor tell the time upon a clock, could now without a moment's hesitation convert seven hundred and ninety-three thousand pieces of eight into guineas and then work out a hundred and seventy-third share of it.

So on the third of March, Old Style, there was a watching and an expectancy aboard the squadron and the boats that can rarely have been paralleled in the long record of naval vigils—an expectancy so great that Peter, gasping under the unrelent-ing sun in the little overcrowded boat, tried to slacken his own share in it. It seemed to him unlucky to hope with such positive and utter confidence. It seemed to him that somehow it must warn the Spaniards—that they must feel uneasily aware of the tension and of the concentrated, singly-focused, unremitting glare of so many eyes.

For his part he tried to throw doubt into his mind. There were the three missing Negroes to arouse suspicion in Acapulco: there was the possibility of the squadron's topsails having been seen from the high land that floated always on their horizon, the mountains behind the town. And yet, in spite of all his caution, his heart beat so that he could hardly breathe as the pure dawn came up over Mexico on the appointed day: it beat high at noon, when the pitiless heat drove straight down on to the unheeding cutter's crew: but it was filled with choking bitterness when at last the laggard sun dipped in a crimson blaze below the western sea.

He was armed against disappointment, but not strongly armed enough. Like nearly all his shipmates, he still had a violent belief that the galleon would sail—that delays must always occur—that the Negroes were mistaken—a thousand logical reasons, and some that were not logical at all: he felt that she *must* sail because they had all worked so hard—they had cleaned the ships' bottoms, they had brought the squadron to the highest pitch of readiness with devoted toil, they had sacrificed some of their prizes to concentrate their force, they had worked like galley-slaves, and they had deserved the galleon. So she must come—she must.

He felt this very strongly, even after the squadron, terribly short of water, had stood off and on, rigidly in station, for still another twenty days, during which Passion Week had come and gone (that brought a fresh jet of confidence, for no Spanish ship would stir in Passion Week) and still the sea was bare. He felt it even to the last moment, when the stormy season was coming fast, and when it was clear that the squadron could not keep the sea without fresh water: in his mind, his intellect, it was plain that the galleon had been warned and would not sail; and yet when he heard the final order, 'We will make sail, if you please, Mr Brett: the course north-east,' he turned away from the quarter-deck with a feeling in his heart like death.

12

'WHERE'S MY JOURNAL?' ASKED PETER.

He could get no answer, but he persisted, angrily, and at length Wilson said carelessly over his shoulder, 'You don't mean that book with the green cover, do you?'

'Yes, I do.'

'Oh well, I dare say that is the one we chucked out. You did chuck a book of some sort out of this young fellow's place, did you not, Hill?'

'Where is it?' cried Peter.

'Overboard, of course,' said Wilson, 'and that is where you will find yourself if you don't stop your noise. Hill, your deal.'

Peter hesitated, glaring at Wilson's wide back: then he turned and ran on deck. He went into the foretop. He had intended to go much farther aloft, but in the top he paused for breath, leaning wearily against the stock of the pattarero, and he decided to stay there.

'The swabs,' he exclaimed, with hot indignation, 'the infamous swabs.' He clenched his fist; then let it go. Only a little while back and he would not have borne it: but now he felt so utterly unlike himself—uneasy, apprehensive; as if his courage were watered. Yet still he would take it up with them when he went down, he assured himself. Nervously he looked over his shoulder at the main-staysail. 'If that goes on pulling like that,' he thought, 'it will start the mast again. I am sure the crack is growing.' This was the horrible fissure in the *Centurion*'s foremast that had been discovered and strongly fished by the carpenters a few days after they had finally sunk the mountains of Acapulco behind them at the beginning of their western voyage for China, the whole width of the greatest ocean in the world, with a storm that had crippled the *Gloucester* to start them on their way.

He would certainly resent it openly and force an explanation: but not today, perhaps. He was feeling like a jelly-fish today.

What an odious thing to do, to throw his journal overboard. So needlessly cruel—such an unkind, hard thing to do. There had been a great deal in that journal, everything from their arrival at Chequetan for water for their great westward voyage—Chequetan, where he had finished the first volume with a lively account of Mr Walter and the electrical fish, the torpedo—right up to the burning of the *Gloucester* in latitude 12° 17' N. and longitude 151° 30' E.

These two, Wilson and Hill, together with Pollock, were midshipmen from the *Gloucester*, and in them and the other officers of that ship Peter had caught a glimpse—more than a glimpse by now—of another kind of naval life. He had guessed, from what little he had seen aboard the other ships of the squadron, the ships that were not commanded by Mr Anson's own lieutenants, and from the tales of the other midshipmen who, like Ransome, had served under many captains, that the *Centurion* was a happy ship and that he was unusually fortunate in starting his career aboard her: but how exceptionally happy a ship she was he had not realised until these newcomers had settled down in the berth. They were all senior to Peter, who was indeed the most junior present; and Wilson and Hill, finding Peter's quarters more to their liking than their own, had moved in without ceremony. But it was not only that—that was a question of seniority, and there was no arguing with the prescriptive rights of the service—not only that, nor principally that: they also imported a brutal kind of horse-play. They picked on their fellow-Gloucester Pollock, a small, frightened fellow who had been their butt since St Helen's, and they showed every intention of making life a misery for Peter, Bailey and Preston too. They drove the hands very hard, with a delight in being unpleasant that was a revelation to Peter—an attitude that was faithfully reflected in the behaviour of the *Gloucester*'s crew, who were an awkward lot of men, unwilling except in strong emergency, brutalised, accustomed to frequent floggings, and withdrawn from human contact with their officers. The midshipmen of the *Gloucester*, in this respect, showed some of the qualities of their captain and his lieutenants, exactly as the *Centurion*'s berth bore witness to Mr Anson. It was not that Wilson and Hill were downright blackguards; but they had been brought up in a tradition of hard, loud-mouthed coarseness, severity to the men, and loutish practical jokes of whose cruelty they were largely unaware, together with a wearisome striving for dominance, for being cock of the walk, that apparently never slackened.

They were good seamen, and courageous (qualities which are certainly to be found with a taste for bullying, whatever moral tales may say), but the attributes upon which they chiefly valued themselves were those which made them most disagreeable as companions and to the world in general. The *Centurion*'s berth was not, and never had been, an abode of plaster saints: they bellowed and swore at one another and at the men, but their language—their meaning, rather—was essentially different from the *Gloucester*'s filthiness; and above all, the berth had hitherto been an essentially friendly place, with plenty of fooling about in it, but no domineering whatsoever.

Wilson and Hill, then, were not yet downright blackguards: for example, they had never intended to throw Peter's journal overboard—it had flown through the open port by misadvertence—and they were ashamed, though too ill-bred to bring themselves to apologise: but they were nasty fellows to have about, very much nastier than they knew. Not blackguards yet, though if they survived and carried on in the same way, it seemed that they might very well develop into specimens of the slave-driver captain, that horrible, sometimes half-mad figure that stained the naval record for too long, and made some ships a floating hell. *If* they survived—that was a proviso with a real meaning; for apart from the perpetual dangers of the sea, officers of that stamp had a way of disappearing in the night. Men will only stand so much: and the kind of men produced by that kind of discipline have been known to turn to their own wild sense of justice in the dark.

Hitherto they had steered clear of Ransome and Keppel; but from what little Pollock had to say, Bailey, Preston and young Balthaser of the *Tryal* looked upon the future with misgiving. Peter should have bitten hard at their first attempt, but he had not: he had fumbled the first and best occasion, hesitating like a hen crossing the road.

'I don't know what come over you, Teague,' said Ransome, afterwards. 'You wouldn't have suffered a half of that hazing from us.'

'Well, you said yourself that we ought to do the civil, and let them settle down and find their feet. You talked about guests, and so on.'

'That's right, cully,' said Ransome, scratching his head. 'I did say that.' He was a very unquarrelsome fellow: he valued peace in the berth very highly. He had, all his life, been accustomed to the roughest brand of humour, so the newcomers' baboonery had offended him less. He also despised the kind of senior midshipman who was always using his superiority, and, in addition, he was used to seeing each man take his own part. But, on the other hand, he now felt obscurely that these fellows were 'swinging their weight about too much, by half'.

'Would you like for me to shove in my oar?' he asked doubtfully, after a long pause.

'No, thank you,' replied Peter crisply. 'I can look after myself if they want any kind of trouble. But thank you all the same, Ransome.'

It was all very well to say that, reflected Peter now, sitting down in the top: but how to cope with the situation was another matter entirely. Gross, over-fed, under-bred bumpkins. If he had spoken out when he ought there would have

215

been no question of losing his journal: it would never have come to that point.

There had been such a lot in that private log. He had looked forward to reading it to them at home. But perhaps he could patch it together—thread that narrative back into a line. It began on the surf-bound Mexican coast, five thousand sea-miles behind them, where they burnt the *Tryal's Prize* and the *Carmelo* and watered the ships. Then there was the anxious cruise off Acapulco again for the cutter, left there as a scout in the unlikely chance of the galleon's weighing. The cutter with Mr Hughes of the *Tryal*, Sean, and four of the best seamen the *Centurion* could find. The waiting for the cutter and the days passing, dropping by, hope fading, the stormy season just at hand, and no cutter: Spanish prisoners sent into Acapulco to the Governor, promising the release of all the rest if the cutter's crew (taken, perhaps) were given up. Then the sight of the cutter itself, not taken by the Spaniards but beaten off stations by currents and winds, yet capable of finding its way back after forty-three days on the hostile sea, half the time without water—an astonishing feat of seamanship that had nearly cost the crew their lives. Poor Sean: as they handed him up the side he was so thin that Peter could carry him with ease.

Then came the account of the storm: then of the strange calm and the terrible swell that had rolled *Gloucester's* main and foretopmast by the board, only a few hours after twenty Centurions had been sent to help them send it up. No. He had it wrong. First, in June, the *Gloucester* had lost her mainmast, at the same time that the *Centurion's* foremast had been sprung: that was during those seven long weeks when they were hunting for the north-east trades. It was after they had found them at last that this western hurricane came on, dismantling the *Gloucester*, who already had no more than a jury mainmast, and so hobbled along, keeping them back while the scurvy broke out again. And it was then that the flat calm came, with that unbelievable swell. It was then that the leak began, too. He could hear the pumps now, a noise that never

216

stopped all round the clock. They had searched and searched, but they never could find the source of the leak, and still the water poured in at the stem, deep down. Only a dry-dock would let them come at it, and there was no dry-dock for five thousand miles. Even now, running with a strong following wind, she made a desperate amount: what would she do beating up into a big hollow sea?

The *Gloucester* had been in a terrible way, unmanageable in the sea, with her people—the whole ship's company—pumping with no rest at all for twenty-four hours. And Captain Mitchel had come over to report seven feet of water in the hold, increasing every hour, her upper works shattered and appalling damage below, with much less than half her company fit to keep afloat. Peter remembered his grey face, almost inhuman with drawn-out care.

They had just managed to get the bullion out of her, after transferring the sick, but scarcely a barrel of stores.

Then they had burnt her; and her guns fired one by one: the fire reached the magazine, and she went up in a crimson flash filled with black falling timbers that splashed hissing in the sea, and there was nothing of *Gloucester* but a dark pall of smoke that followed the *Centurion* as she ploughed her single furrow across the Pacific, alone now, the only ship on the enormous sea. One ship of the whole beautiful squadron, and she undermanned, sickly and leaking, with an uncharted ocean to cross.

And there were so many other things in these four months past—the bonitos, the turtles and dolphins, the wide-winged sea-birds and the strange weed on the sea; the new faces aboard, the *Tryal*'s officers, Mr Saunders back again—Captain Saunders now—the *Gloucester*'s rigid and gloomy commander, the new hands, some with fascinating tales of the East, Paulus the Dutchman from Java, Widjoo the Malay, the cheerful black men and their songs. He would forget it all.

Suddenly he remembered the happenings of one day with extraordinary clarity: and on reflection it seemed to him that that was the day that marked the beginning—the beginning of the time when everything had gone wrong for him.

They had picked up the trade wind, and they were running under topsails alone, for the *Gloucester* delayed them: but at least they were making a steady four knots, and had been, day after day: and he felt uncommonly cheerful. On that particular day he stepped on deck at three bells in the afternoon watch, and Mr Saumarez, turning in his steady pacing on the quarter-deck, happened to ask him what it was that he carried—an ordinary question, nothing in the disciplinary line, but prompted by normal curiosity.

'It is a serpent, sir,' said Peter, 'and I am going to ask the smith to repair this hole, if you please.'

'A serpent, is it?' said the first lieutenant, turning the spiral tube in his hands. 'A kind of musical instrument?'

'No, sir,' said Peter, in all innocence. 'No, sir. We use it for making our whiskey.'

'What is whiskey?' asked Mr Saumarez. The drink was barely known in England, and not at all in the Channel Islands, the first lieutenant's home.

'It is a sort of Irish cordial, sir,' said Peter.

'I see. Very well, Mr Palafox,' said Mr Saumarez. 'Carry on.'

'Thank you, sir,' said Peter, taking back the serpent. Then in an evil moment he added, 'We call it uishge beatha at home—the water of life.'

'Eh?' cried Mr Saumarez, when Peter had gone a few steps. 'You do not mean aqua vitae, I trust? Not eau de vie? You are not speaking of ardent spirits, for Heaven's sake?'

'I don't think it is the same thing at all, sir,' said Peter, doubtfully. 'But it is rather strong when it is very new.'

'Bring the stuff to my cabin, Mr Palafox,' said Mr Saumarez in an official voice.

'Pah,' he said, gasping. 'This is raw spirit. Is this an ill-timed joke, Mr Palafox?'

'No, sir,' quavered Peter, aghast at the lieutenant's angry expression. 'It is only our morning draught.'

'Do you mean to tell me that you have dared to brew, to

distil, this poison here in the ship?—actually aboard the *Centurion?*'

'Yes, sir.'

'And drink it daily?'

'Yes, sir, if you please.'

The first lieutenant stared at Peter with incredulous horror for a moment, and then, in a sterner manner than Peter had ever known, settled down to a searching enquiry.

Peter and Sean had distilled their whiskey regularly from St Helen's on. Finding the quality and the price equally disagreeable in Portsmouth they had laid in a stock of barley and had malted it as occasion required. It was not very good, although Sean had brought a bottle of Ballynasaggart water from Bridget's well, which made the best whiskey in Ireland, and they always kept a little of the old to mix with the new in order that there should always be some true Irish water in the barrel; so to ameliorate their brew they had added fresh lemons at Madeira. No, he replied, they had never made any secret of their proceedings. It was thought to be medicine, he supposed. No, he had never given any to the hands, except Shaughnessy, Hanlon, Lyons, Burke and Donohue, who were the only Irishmen left. The others did not like it, although it was good for them—would not touch it.

What had he to say for himself? Was sorry that he had done wrong—had not intended to commit a crime—was persuaded that it had recovered Keppel in the last stages of scurvy before Juan Fernandez—had fed it to him with a spoon. But Keppel was not to blame: Peter had obliged him to take it. No, he had not read all the Admiralty regulations—did not know the penalty for such an act—was amazed to hear it, and very sorry. Had no more to say in excuse—they always did it at home—drank up a cupful on rising against the damp of the air—had not been aware that he was criminally debauching the crew, undermining discipline, setting dreadful example—knew that drunkenness was a sin—begged pardon, but was never drunken himself—no, did not think that he was a degenerate sot.

'You still do not seem to realise the enormity of the offence,' said Mr Saumarez. 'Are you not aware, Mr Palafox, that this is a court-martial business, and that I shall be obliged to report it to the Commodore?' Mr Saumarez was not fooling: this was not the frightening noise of an angry first lieutenant blowing up an errant midshipman—noise and little more: it was very serious and Mr Saumarez was not enjoying his inquisition in the least.

Peter had not known—would not have contravened the regulation—would never offend again—hoped that Mr Saumarez would overlook it this time.

'No. I am sorry, but that is impossible. You must go to your quarters and not leave them until you are sent for.'

Then the shattering interview with the Commodore, flanked by the first lieutenant, Mr Woodfall and the Chaplain. The Commodore as stern as Mr Saumarez—'Are you aware, Mr Palafox, that I am in doubt whether it is not my duty to disrate you? To withdraw the officer's privileges which you so grossly abused and turn you before the mast, where you can be more strictly supervised as an irresponsible and dangerous person?'

Mr Walter's anxious, kindly intervention: 'Not an evil boy at heart, nor very dissipated—may yet be reclaimed—the fault lay more in the bibulous nation than in the individual.'

A helpful word from the surgeon: 'The liquor might have some medicinal value in skilled hands—should never have been administered to Keppel—nonsense to pretend that it had cured him: much more likely responsible for the loss of his hair—but in a proper exhibition and dosage, might very reasonably be supposed to have some antiscorbutic powers.'

Mr Saumarez' just but unflattering report of Peter's maritime value: 'Attentive to his duty, though apt to talk far too much and boast—to advise his superiors—to frequent the fo'c'sle too much—to make too much noise—to argue. Had sometimes been found below and asleep when he should have been on deck—had never been visibly drunk—had behaved creditably on such and such occasions (some very trying)—

discreditably on such and such other occasions (mostly foolish). Had some seamanlike qualities: apart from this fantastic history, had committed none but venial crimes. Witness, had he not known of the distillation, would certainly have said that Mr Palafox was worth retaining for the good of the service.'

The Commodore's summing-up: detestation of drunkenness—spirits abroad in a ship more dangerous than naked powder—disappointment in Peter—total lack of responsibility, discrimination, common sense—awful consequences to be expected if everybody behaved in the same manner—ship a floating Bedlam. A captain's powers aboard—their remarkable extent—midshipmen not commissioned officers—liable to be disrated, sent into lower-deck, flogged, discharged at next port, abandoned to own devices. An awful pause: then his decision: distilling to stop for ever—implements confiscated—the illegal liquor impounded for medical use. The uncommon leniency prompted solely by Mr Saumarez' report and Commodore's own observation of good behaviour in certain crises: but no further indulgence to be expected. Any relapse would lead to instant application of prescribed penalties and end of naval career. Then such a wigging about responsible conduct, behaviour expected of a King's officer and use of mother-wit: it reduced Peter to a lower state than the worst wrath of the Horn; it wrung unwilling, shameful tears out of him, which no terror or privation could have done; and when at last he was dismissed he went away with such a load of disapprobation weighing on him that he never seemed to have recovered his cheerfulness from that day to this.

Yes. From that dreadful afternoon onwards the journal had contained many sad and despondent entries—not only the personal account of additional and onerous duties by way of punishment, nor marks of favour withdrawn; not only the grievous trouble that he had brought down on poor Sean; but accounts of contrary winds, continual pumping, steadily increasing difficulties with the over-strained, worn-out rigging; and worse still, the scurvy. Everything seemed to date from that time, as if that had been a signal for misfortune to begin.

The scurvy. It had started within a surprisingly short time after their departure from Mexico, long before it could ordinarily have been expected. Had their deep disappointment something to do with it? It grew in spite of fresh fish caught over the side, turtles kept healthy and alive from Quibo, often-renewed rainwater, and the livestock that they still had from Paita: it was contrary to all experience, and it was even more discouraging than it had been round the Horn.

It spread and spread; and although they were now running off their westing at a steady five knots, almost the last entry that Peter had was a calculation of the possibility of their reaching Asia before the western monsoon set in, if they went on losing men at the present rate—a calculation which had no encouraging result.

Scurvy. Peter had seen it in all its disguises: he was dreadfully familiar with it. It was surprising, therefore, that he had not recognised it in himself, that he should not have realised the cause of his perpetual tiredness, the lethargy that oppressed him at this very moment in the foretop, the continual indwelling anxiety that made what would ordinarily have appeared a trifling risk swell into an awful, impending disaster— the same morbid timorousness that he had seen in so many men before—in Preston, for example, and many more besides. Peter was sick, and very sick: but he did not know it.

'However,' he said to himself, 'I must tackle this business. I will do it, certainly. Perhaps at dinner, tomorrow.'

It was a somewhat moody and silent dinner in the midshipmen's berth: but when it was over Hill began to stir himself in quest of amusement. He nudged Wilson and said, 'By the way, young Palafox, what is the name of your little sister?'

Peter leant back in his seat and looked at him for a moment. 'Listen, Hill,' he said quietly. 'I have not said this before, because you were new in the berth. But you will have to find another tone when you speak to me. You understand what I mean, do you not? No, no,' he cried as Hill started up. 'No:

we don't want any theatrical display at all. You can stop that at once.' Into his tired voice there had sprung the authentic quarter-deck rasp, unconscious, unemphatic and convincing. Hill sat down, staring.

'And I will have a word with you, Wilson,' said Peter with contained ferocity. 'You have been picking on O'Mara. You will find yourself in very serious trouble if you go on. You know quite well what I mean. And I am not talking about the way you make a vulgar nuisance of yourself in this berth, either.'

Wilson's ugly face was squinting with anger. 'Lousy young coxcomb,' he blurted out.

'Stow that,' whispered Ransome. 'Stow it, I say. I am senior here, cully, and I am going to tell you something. You and your mate come it too strong, see? You can pipe down, like Palafox says. This is a good berth,' he said, looking affectionately round the hideous, cheese-shaped, awkward enclosure, whose low beams were studded with little bits of his scalp where he had banged his head these two years past. 'This is a good berth, and we have had some good jokes in it: but you ain't going to come it so strong any more. Because why? Because I won't have it, that's why. Palafox spoke very well.'

'I entirely agree with Palafox,' said Keppel, looking from Wilson to Hill with frigid distaste. 'You have mistaken the tone. And if you are to be here for the rest of the commission, I suggest that you should change it.'

'That's right,' said Bailey: and from the rest of the berth there arose a solid, unspectacular, unanimous manifestation of public opinion. But Peter did not hear it: he went slowly on deck, feeling so strange that he hardly knew where he was; and when he reached the gangway he fell down with a force that stunned the senses out of his head.

'Tinian Island, September 3rd,' wrote Peter, propping the new journal up on his knee. 'This is a wonderful place, very like Juan Fernandez, only more so. I got up this morning—they were arming the cables—gackled 7 fathom from the service with roundings of hawser, on account of the coral. But I came out in very large interesting spots or blodges and was obliged to be carried back by Ransome and Sean. I have been much carried about (like a heathen image) for the benefit of the air; but never so grandly as coming ashore, when the Commodore took one end of my hammock and Captain Saunders the other. P. Palafox, 1st Lord of the Admiralty. I told Ransome that: Lord, how we laughed.

'We came in a week ago, and it was touch and go whether we should fetch the island, they say, only I was in a sorts of stupid amazement then and did not know what was carrying on for a great while. It is a beautiful place, with melons, oranges, limes, lemons, coconuts, a curious large fruit we eat for bread, and flat squashing fruit and many others and an amazing plenty of wild cattle which the Spaniards had come to make jerked beef of when we surprised them. They had already bucanned, or jerked, a great deal and built huts, which is very delightful for us. Poor souls, they thought we were the galleon, for the Commodore was exceedingly deep, and beguiled them with the Manilla ship's signals, and they pulled out to greet us. They had come in a bark from Guam, a pretty little thing, and none of them got off to give the alarm. I have been eating since noon, and it is now about four: but, however, I could wish that Sean would hurry with some more of the flat yellow kind of fruit.'

'There, your honour, dear,' said Sean, bending as he came loaded under the lintel, 'and I found a new patch of melons, with an old cross-looking sow making a beast of herself, like the Lord Lieutenant in the middle of them all.'

'Thank you very much, Sean,' said Peter. 'Why, here is a new fruit entirely,' he said, holding up a guava.

'Is it good, the creature?' asked Sean, solicitously proffering a freshly split coconut brimming with milk. Peter nodded, speechless with guava, and reached with his free hand for more. Like the rest of the invalids, he had an almost insatiable appetite for fruit. The fit men, some seventy out of the combined crew, had an equal desire for meat; and as this beautiful island overflowed with both, the two sections of the community were equally content.

'I had a strange dream, a strange dream indeed,' said Sean, watching Peter with marked satisfaction as he attacked another guava still. Peter nodded, to show that he was attending, and Sean went on, 'A strange dream it was, and a waking dream too. For it was before the sunrise, when I was walking alone on the shore and wondering was there ever a turtle in these parts for you to be pecking. And while I was wondering, and turning the question about, I walked by the shore: and so walking I dreamt I heard a curlew call, and there I was at home, by the lake of the Two Mists with the birds flying, heartbroken. Sure, Peter, I thought the day of my death had come.'

'Sean,' cried Peter, starting up, 'you'll never say that? And myself lying here with the curlew's cry in my ears before dawn?'

'God between us and evil,' said Sean.

'Let Him shield us from the dread,' said Peter, and they fell silent. The light of the sun coming in at the open door had a sinister gleam in it now, like moonlight that had been heated. Peter set down his unfinished guava and looked into the shadows.

'Hallo, pale Palafox,' said Keppel, thrusting his plain face through the window. 'Can you take solid food yet—why, what's the matter? Anyone would think you had seen a ghost. Not worse, are you?'

'Lord, no,' said Peter, recovering; 'I am very well—only you came so quietly it surprised me. And then your face, you know, Keppel, is horribly plain.'

'What a lot of room you have to talk, my flower,' said Keppel. 'Hallo, O'Mara. Is he really well, do you think?'

'The Dear knows I hope so, your honour,' said Sean, rather quietly.

'Well what about meat?'

'No beef or mutton, Mr Woodfall says,' said Peter, with an invalid's solemnity.

'Well, this an't beef,' said Keppel, rummaging in his bag. 'And it an't mutton, either,' he said, handing a curlew in through the window. 'Strike me,' he exclaimed, 'what is the matter with both of you? Don't you eat curlew in Ireland? It's a capital dish, skinned, *not* plucked, and broiled. It should have been a brace of teal, but I missed them, and brought the curlew down instead.'

'Are there curlews alive, then?' asked Peter, faintly.

'Of course there are, booby,' said Keppel, quite put out. 'What an unaccountable fellow you are, Palafox. You can hardly walk up by that pond without shoving your way through parcels of curlews, millions of curlews in swarms. And duck. Good afternoon, sir.'

'Good afternoon,' said Mr Brett, hurrying in. 'Better, Palafox? Taking nourishment, I see'—glancing at the monstrous pile of stones, pips, and fruit skins. 'Excellent. But dear me, we shall have to straighten this out. The Commodore is coming. Mr Keppel, bear a hand, if you please. That pillow-case. Hair-brush. O'Mara, pass the towel—you have Mr Stapleton's leave to be here, I trust?'

'Oh sir,' cried Sean, with a tear in his eye, 'and would I ever quit my duty without the lieutenant's good word?'

'Hm,' said Mr Brett. 'Well, take that bucket and swab him down. I want him shining in forty-five seconds. Mr Keppel, hold the pillow case open.'

One minute later the Commodore walked in, accompanied by the surgeon. His eye fell with approval on the apple-pie order—Peter's sheet squared with geometrical nicety, and the patient himself in a high state of polish, if somewhat breathless and worn.

'I hope you are feeling better, Mr Palafox,' he said kindly.

'Thank you very much sir,' said Peter, sitting rigidly up; 'I am exceedingly well.'

'I am happy to hear you say so,' said the Commodore, with a smile. 'But I hear that you joined the ship without permission this morning. That will not do: it may have an adverse effect, eh, Mr Woodfall?'

'Yes, sir,' said the surgeon. 'Show me your tongue.' This was to Peter, and it was said rather sharply, for Peter was not Mr Woodfall's favourite patient. Some weeks back he had been persuaded by Sean—and thinly-veiled threats of murder had formed part of the persuasion—to dose Peter with acidulated whiskey: and the patient had eventually presumed to recover. 'However,' he said reluctantly, having peered down Peter's gullet (for he was a just man, and kind when not vexed in his professional capacity), 'I find no relapse. Still no beef or mutton: but I think we may proceed to a little swine's flesh, gently seethed; and we may perform light duty the day after tomorrow.'

'Very good,' said the Commodore. 'We can do with all our really capable officers,' he added, to Peter's inexpressible gratification. 'And here, Mr Palafox, is a trifling book that may help you to pass the time between meals. It was among the poor purser's dunnage, and I beg you will keep it, if it amuses you at all.'

'You are very good, sir,' cried Peter, red with pleasure, 'and I am extremely grateful for your attention.'

'Listen to this, Sean,' he said, five minutes later. ' "What said the fellow to the chandler that had a gross of candles stolen from him? Take not your loss to heart, friend; no question but they will be brought to light." '

'Ha, ha,' said Sean. 'What kind of a book may it be?'

'It is called,' said Peter, turning to the title-page, 'The New Help to Discourse, or, Wit and Mirth, intermix'd with more serious Matters, consisting of Pleasant, Philosophical, Physical, Historical, Moral and Political Questions and Answers: with Proverbs, Epitaphs, Epigrams, Riddles, Poesies, Rules for Behaviour, etc., with several Wonders, and Varieties: particularly, A concise History of the Kings of England. Together with Directions for the true Knowledge of several Matters concerning Astronomy, Holy-Days, and Husbandry, in a plain method. By W. W., gent.'

'Sure it's a great deal to be in such a little small book,' said

Sean. 'What a learned man Mr W. W., gent., must have been, your honour, dear. And does it tell you how to behave, so?'

'It does. Listen to this—"Cast not your eyes upon others trenchers, nor fix them wishfully upon the meat on the table. Put not your meat to your mouth with your knife in your hand, which is clownish. Cleanse not your teeth with the table-cloth or napkin, or with your fingers; but if others do it, let it be done with a toothpick. Gnaw not your nails——" '

He broke off, and looking out through the door, he hailed, 'Ransome, ahoy.'

'Ahoy,' answered Ransome. 'Can't stop a minute, cully,' he said hoarsely, pausing on the threshold. 'I got to get the casks run up. How are you, cock?'

'Famous,' said Peter. 'But just lie-to for a second and read this.'

Frowning heavily over the book, Ransome slowly wheezed out, ' "One being much abused by a miller, the fellow at last told him, that he thought there was nothing more valiant than the collar of a miller's shirt; and being asked the reason, answered, Because every morning it had a thief by the neck." '

A profound silence followed. Then Ransome's frown could be seen to dissolve; his face became more and more suffused, and a slow grin spread broad and delighted. A strangled gasping began. 'Oh, hor hor hor,' he went. 'The thief, hor, hor, is the *miller*, the cove he's a-talking to. Do you smoke it? I didn't hardly get there all at once. The collar, do you see, goes round the miller's throat, hor, hor. Ain't it deep? Did you understand it, O'Mara?'

'No, your honour,' said Sean, very obligingly. 'It was too deep for me.'

'Oh, it *is* plaguey deep,' said Ransome; 'but stand by, and I will make it plain. There is this fellow, you see, what the miller is blackguarding and calling out of his name: so he says, "Which I always heard tell a miller's shirt was the bravest thing in the world," says he. "Why so?" asks the miller, suspicious. "Because why?" says this first cove, the one the miller was blackguarding so. "Because why?" says he; "for because it has a thief (meaning the miller, you understand me—he means the miller is a thief; because in his trade the miller steals the flour. Which is true), because it has a thief by the neck every morning. Do you smoke it now? When the miller puts on his shirt, he means, the collar gets a thief (that is, the miller) by the throat. Or put it this way . . .'

'What about those casks, Ransome?' asked Peter, seven labourous jokes later.

'Damn 'em,' said Ransome, with his bright blue eyes starting out of his head. 'Hark to this one. "A fellow going in the dark, held out his arms to defend his face; coming to the door—oh Lord, I can't go on, hor, hor, hor—coming to the door, he ran his nose against the edge of it, whereupon he cried out—oh, I'll never get it out, hor, hor—cried out, Hey, day, what's the matter, my nose was short enough just now, and is it in so short a time grown longer than my arms?" '

'Mr Ransome, sir,' said a ship's boy, darting in. 'First Lieutenant's compliments and would like to see you *at once.*'

'Oh,' said Ransome, his enormous grin fading. 'Oh. Thankee. Well, it was worth it.'

'Ransome. Hey, Ransome,' shrieked Peter after his flying back. 'The book. You've taken the book—you've taken . . . The devil lie in your plate, you false dog. Did you ever see such a thing, Sean? To rob a palsied comrade, Sean? Is it not the black shame of the world?'

'Though slow in appearance, your honour, dear, Mr Ransome has a wonderful presence of mind,' said Sean, in some admiration.

Light duty began on Wednesday, in the sweet dawn of the day; and Peter, strongly reinforced by a little swine's flesh (the greater part of a sucking-pig—the creature having indeed been a little swine), was already bounding about the deck. Like nearly all the invalids at Tinian he had recovered with astonishing speed.

Light duty consisted of moving all the forward guns aft, to get the *Centurion* by the stern, in order that the carpenters could come at the leak. Peter had been busy: somewhat too busy, as the following harsh words revealed. 'No. Not a parbuckle,' cried Mr Stapleton. 'I said straight through the fair-leads, didn't I? Why will you always improve on your orders, Mr Palafox?'

'But sir, don't you think——'

'No, I do not. You do what you are told, and leave the thinking to me. You start off by advising me to run a tackle to the capstan, and now you—confound your impertinence. There are some midshipmen who will never have the decency to lie down and die, whatever the circumstances. Because they are born to be hanged, no doubt,' added the lieutenant darkly. 'And don't stand there smirking. Rouse out the hawser as I said, and look lively.'

One by one the heavy guns rumbled aft, preceded with anxious care by the hands who would have the task of holy-stoning out the ridges made by their wheels in the deck. Slowly the Centurion himself, the figure-head, rose to turn his battered, but irredeemably insipid, simper to the lower sky, and the carpenter's crew swarmed down to her cut-water and stem.

'We brought her by the stern,' wrote Peter, 'and the carpenters worked until three bells. Rolled the guns back—hot work with the tide making and a swell setting E. The leak started at once. Moved guns aft again. Carpenters worked harder. Guns for'ard: leaks worse. Crew vexed with carpenters. We are to try again tomorrow. Ransome hides when off duty, and can be heard laughing like a whale in the woods.

'September 14th. The Commodore is not well and is come ashore at last to sleep: the men much put about, but Mr Walter assures me it is not grave—Mr Anson would stay aboard to see everything done, and his steward could not bring him to eat anything but a biscuit in his hand while there was any work forward. But the land and fresh provisions will recover him, everybody says; and Mr W. explained that the land counteracts the gross humours of the sea. Ransome still lurking, in a sort of perpetual slow fit. Leak botched up within-board; carpenters abhorred by all, and blamed. We are to have a whole day's liberty.'

Keppel, Bailey, Preston, Balthasar of the *Tryal*, and Peter stood looking at the small Spanish bark: at their heels ranged a pack of nondescript, vaguely hound-like dogs, brought from the Spanish garrison of Guam by the prisoners for the purpose of hunting the wild cattle of Tinian, and fallen upon by the *Centurion*'s people with that brisk and determined compulsion to domesticate everything from alligators to apes which characterises a man-of-war's man in all latitudes. The dogs, at first dismayed and appalled, now responded with unbounded and indeed embarrassing affection.

'She's a pretty little craft,' said Keppel. 'About fifteen ton.'

'Trim lines,' observed Preston.

'Bah,' said Peter. 'Don't you see the burke from her plashing-strake to her pawdle? How do you suppose she could ever lie close to the wind with a prowlburke like that? It is the way she could never come within six points of it. It stares you straight in the eye, that horrible prowlburke.'

'It is not so plain from where I stand,' said Keppel, after a moment's silence, 'but I see what you mean.'

'It is their country build, I dare say,' said Bailey.

'Not what we are used to,' said Preston, shaking his head.

Balthasar said nothing; but when they moved off in a cloud of eagerly whining dogs, he lingered behind, gazing at the bark. After a while he caught Peter up, and begging him to stop for a moment, he said, 'It is very stupid of me, I am sure, Palafox, but please would you tell me what you meant? I thought I understood most of the parts of a ship, but'—he glanced down to see that nobody heard—'I somehow do not remember the prowlburke, nor its effect on sailing close to the wind. And if they were to ask me at the lieutenant's examination, why, Lord, I should be properly posed.'

'They won't,' said Peter, with a grin, 'for it don't exist. I made it up. And they never smoked it, ha, ha. Prowlburke and pawdle, oh Lord, what stuff.'

'What a fellow you are, Palafox,' said Balthasar, staring very hard.

'Tace is Latin for a candlestick,' said Peter, looking uncom-

231

monly sly. 'Mum is the word, you follow me? We will invent some more.'

'But why?' asked Balthasar, still far behind.

'Why?' asked Peter. 'Do you know what those swabs did when I first joined? I was as green as could be, and when they sent me to the gunner for a couple of fathoms of right thin firing line, I went like a lamb. And when they told me to tell that to the Marines, I trotted off to the nearest redcoat and told him. There was no end to it. Wasn't it the same when you first went aboard?'

'Yes,' said Balthasar, going pink, 'it was. They made me— never mind. We must certainly invent something more, and I will back you up.'

'The glooming-pot bowse,' said Peter.

'The praliday-hankins,' cried Balthasar.

'But don't go and overdo it,' said Peter, his confidence in Balthasar's discretion beginning to wane.

'Come on, you slugs,' shouted Keppel, a great way off; 'we've got a boar in this bush. Loo into him then,' he shrieked to the reluctant dogs. 'Loo into him, break him and tear him. Come on, my hero,' he cried as Peter came snorting up the hill. 'We've got a boar in this bush. Come and get him out for us.'

'In there?' cried Peter.

'Yes, thrashing around—no, don't go in, you flaming idiot, he'll rip you to pieces. Hold him. God help us, he's gone in. Oh——' This gasping cry was forced out of Keppel by a blow that flung him on his back, the furious barge of an enormous wild sow that exploded out of the bush with Peter attached to her tail.

'What . . . do . . . you want . . . me to . . . do with it?' roared Peter, in jerks, scudding madly along with the pig.

'Hang on,' cried Bailey, fleeting over the lea. 'Think of the hams.'

'Never let go,' howled Preston, just keeping up.

'Work up to windward,' said Keppel, drawing ahead of the dogs with a prodigious burst, 'and as soon as I see daylight between you, I'll fire.'

'No,' cried Peter, 'you mustn't . . . she's . . . very much . . . in pup.'

'Cast her off, then,' said Keppel. But as Peter let the tail slip through his hand the sow whipped round with astonishing agility, and foaming with rage she rushed upon her pursuers. The tide changed on the instant, and now, scouring the grassy plain with feet that twinkled in the sun, Keppel headed the urgent rout. Immediately behind him came Bailey, whose laboured gasps persuaded Keppel that the sow was on his back: then came a mixed flight of midshipmen, running with the utmost perseverance, then the dogs, mute with alarm, and then the gravid, persecuting sow, with glaring, crimson eyes, skimming over the flowery turf, the embodiment of pallid fury.

Peter sat before his open book, refreshing his powerful mind with beef. He wiped his fingers, dipped his pen (an albatross plume) and wrote: 'September 22nd. Variable airs all day. W and WSW. Mr Blew was quite mistaken when he said that the moon would bring a change. The new moon was on the 18th, and since then we have had nothing but a small gale ESE½E. Which is just as well, since this is the foulest ground that can be imagined—coral rocks like razors even in 50 fathom water. Though indeed we are safe enough now, having gackled with the fire-grapnel chains; which is a prodigious example of caution. Mr Blew is almost recovered and grows wonderfully cantankerous, which we are all very glad to see, his former meekness being against nature. I also sat with Crooke (of the fore-top) and Carlow, who are in a fair way. The coopers are still very sick, however, which makes watering tedious slow. I desired Hume to show me how to fashion a cask, but he said the cooper's mystery needs 7 years. I borrowed his tools though, and mean to attempt a barrel tomorrow. Mem. to warn Balthasar against flying too high: drooling board-prittle is coming it too much; and the pussif tasset can hardly be attempted to be believed. But so far it succeeds to admiration, and it is a pure joy to see them conning their manuals. I have thought of——' But this valuable contribution was lost in a sea of ink: a sudden gust had overset the inkhorn, and now it ruffled the pages in wild disorder.

'Bah,' cried Peter, flinging a handful of sand over the mess and darting out to look at the sky. It looked much the same, a deep, luminous blue, with a few white clouds sailing on the perpetual course of the trades. Far down in the north-east a low bank of dullness promised them their usual refreshing evening shower. On the beach of coral sand, white, tinged with the most delicate pink, the usual surf beat in its long, steady rhythm. The coconut palms stood, bowing graciously after the gust, and their fronds made a gentle clattering over the deep boom of the surf. In the bay the *Centurion* rode with an easy lift and peck to her best bower on the incoming tide: everything looked perfectly normal—a sea-born paradise. But Peter was not the only one to be staring at the sky; there were several seamen on the shore, looking up; and heads popped out of the huts and the storehouse. 'I don't know, I'm sure,' said the master after a deliberate inspection. 'Will there be wind?' he asked in Spanish, addressing one of the native prisoners, who was moodily pounding a crab in a bowl. The brown man glanced at the sky, drew up his shoulders and spread his hands in a gesture that he had caught from the Spaniards. 'Damned heathen,' muttered Mr Blew, and retired into his shelter, stubbing the ground crossly with his stick.

'Easy with that barrel there,' cried Peter, seeing a couple of hands bouncing a small cask on a mound out of mere lightness of heart. 'There you——swabs, you've sprung the chime-hoop. Quartermaster,' he said sharply to a man who came hurrying out of the palms. 'You are supposed to be in charge, and here's a cask staved.'

'Which it was a very old one, sir,' said the culprit.

'They are all very old ones,' said Peter, 'and that's no reason why you should bang them about. Get on with your work in a responsible manner: and the next man I see with sand in his hair will find himself on the defaulters' list.' For by way of varying their toil several of the men had been standing on their heads in the sand.

. . .

'Mr Keppel,' said the second lieutenant, 'you understand the management of hounds, I believe?'

'Yes, sir,' said Keppel, without a blush.

'Then you will take a party to the high part of the island behind the look-out point and secure as many beeves as is practicable. The utmost economy of powder will be observed, Mr Keppel.'

'Aye-aye, sir.'

'The armourer will serve out four muskets, flintlock; three pikes, boarding; six knives, skinning; for all of which you will sign. You will draw on the local supplies of dogs and proceed with the utmost despatch. You may take seven men: and you may also secure a reasonable number of swine for the ward-room. Very, very great care will be taken to ensure the good eating qualities of the ward-room swine, Mr Keppel.'

'Aye-aye, sir. May I make a suggestion, sir?'

'If it is to the point, Mr Keppel.'

'Palafox is an eminent hand with a hog, sir, if you please.'

'Very well. Make it so, Mr Keppel. Have you any observations to make on the equipment?'

'Yes, sir. A horn, hunting, is required for signalling to the pack.'

'The service makes no provision for horns, hunting, Mr Keppel. A little seamanlike ingenuity will enable you to cope with the difficulty.'

A couple of hours later the wild cattle of Tinian were on the move. Urged by the weird shrilling of a bo'sun's pipe, the motley pack herded them in little groups past an ambush where the best shots in the *Centurion* (and there were many to choose from, the crew having been continually schooled in the use of fire-arms) picked off the handsomest beasts.

'This beats lifting the landlord's deer,' said Burrell.

The half-gypsy poacher Soames, from Winchester gaol, replied with his dark, lop-sided grin: he rarely spoke; but after a minute he said, 'I miss the keepers. It's hardly natural, like.'

'That young cock knows how to handle the dogs,' said Dray.

'But he's lifting them off of the line,' objected Burrell,

listening to Keppel's 'Hoick, hoick, get along for'ard,' and the excited yelping far down the hill.

'Ain't he taking advantage of the wind?' said Dray. 'Don't you see as how it is backing? Don't you know them beasts won't ever come anigh these dead 'uns upwind of 'em?'

The poacher nodded. 'He's a fly cove,' he said, with strong approval. 'I wouldn't mind going out with him in the New Forest. You don't know nothing, Henry Burrell,' he added. 'Can't you see the wind come round two points already?'

'It'll blow up dirty tonight,' said Burrell, to change the injurious topic.

'Never you mind if it'll blow up dirty or not, Henry Burrell,' said his shipmates. 'You attend to your duty and stop arguing.'

But the unlucky Burrell was right. The wind backed, turned round again, fairly boxing the compass, and a little before sunset a howling squall, solidly loaded with rain, threatened to carry away the roofs of the trim orderly booths that the hunting-party had erected in a convenient dell.

'What?' shrieked Peter, double-lashing the ridge-pole with a twist of sinuous creeper.

'I said it was beginning to blow,' roared Keppel, in a lull.

'That's right,' said Peter, but his words were lost in an almighty bellow of thunder.

'What?' asked Keppel, at the top of his voice.

'That's right,' repeated Peter.

'What is?'

'Never mind,' said Peter, flapping his hand. Conversation was really impossible, and they sat in the doorway, watching the almost incessant play of the lightning and the fantastic drive of the tropical rain. For two feet from the ground the sodden earth rebounded, a kind of low haze of liquid mud: the air between the flashing plummets of rain was filled with atomised water, heavy and wet in their breath. Everywhere there was noise, a vast, omnipresent bass drumming and the high, varying shriek of the wind.

'There must be a powerful great surf running down there,'

said Peter, tasting salt on his lips. 'What a good thing we gackled the cables.'

Keppel roared something, probably to the same effect, but all Peter could make out was the word "off-shore", and before Keppel could repeat it their attention was diverted by a coconut, which came through the roof with the force of a cannonball and smashed against the flank of a pig.

While Peter rapidly fished the broken branch and staunched some of the inpour of rain, Keppel dragged the damaged pig to one side, carefully erased the inscription "Midshipmen's Mess" and by the blue light of the lightning he wrote "Wardroom Swine" in store-keeper's chalk. Then he crept through the mud to the two other booths, where the men had stopped up every possible ventilation, had lit a little fire and had already accumulated a solid fug of tobacco-smoke, wet seaman, wet dog, and the smell of a villainous brew over the fire. He made them prop up a well-nourished beast and lie with their heads sheltered under it—there was no point in trying to shift, for they were already two hundred yards from the nearest palms—and then crawled back to do the same in the officers' hut.

The water rose steadily; and a little after midnight their roof left them bodily, in one movement, like a card. But it was not cold, and they were tolerably accustomed to moisture: they even slept in snatches, for the slaughtered prey made charming soft lying, and they were both heavily bloated with animal food.

They slept enough, in all events, to be lively and brisk when the dawn came up. The wind had gone, and the absence of its noise—greater by far on land than at sea—made everything seem very strange. Indeed, the scene was strange enough apart from that. Everywhere everything about them was a green wreck: everything that could be battered down had been battered down, even to the smallest blade of grass. Branches lay tossed in the wildest confusion: the strong trees stood bare and stripped above the flattened undergrowth. Three dogs and a large white bird lay dead in the stream that now poured by the huts, struck down by the storm. A few yards away a black furrow showed where the lightning had ripped open the earth. With the rising of the sun a gentle steam mounted all over the destroyed vegetation: and from every point came the unaccustomed purling of streams.

'Here's a pretty howdy-do,' observed Keppel. 'We shall have to cut out a path down to the bay.'

'Things have come to an elegant pass when we have to hunt pigs for the wardroom and then hack a road to carry them back,' said Peter. 'I propose that we go down and come back with a larger party. After breakfast.'

Keppel, too, was on fire to see the ship: he hesitated: but he was in charge. 'No,' he said. 'Dray, bend a line to that bough. We must make a sledge. Mr Palafox, you will take the compass, if you please, and mark out the shortest line with Burrell and Hobbs. Look alive there, Dray: rig a cross-piece abaft the runner—here, give it to me.'

It was a long, steaming task hauling the carcasses down. The men had to be held in from lurking up into the remaining trees to get an earlier view of the bay, for they too were very anxious for the ship: but they worked hard under Keppel's impulsion, and for the last few hundred yards, before the woods gave way to the sand, they needed no urging. They fairly ran away with the sledge and burst out of the trees.

There was the beach, the wide bay still roaring with surf: but there was no ship in the bay. No ship out at sea. There was no sign of the *Centurion* on the jagged horizon; no sign at all but her distracted people standing in black, silent groups on the edge of the sea.

13

'NO, MR PALAFOX,' SAID THE COMMODORE, 'I TELL YOU again, do *not* push the saw. Pull, and let me pull.'

'Aye-aye, sir,' said Peter, acutely conscious of the sharp eye piercing up at him. The eye was almost all that was to be seen of Mr Anson, who was covered with sawdust: he had chosen the least enviable place, that of bottom-sawyer in the stifling saw-pit, and even he was beginning to feel the heat.

'Give way, now,' he said, more kindly. 'Easy does it.'

'Pull,' said Peter to himself. 'Pull. Not push.' Four times in the last hour his zeal had led him to aid the Commodore's long heave by a thrust of his own, and each time the whipping, ten-foot, double-handed saw had bent and bound in the cut. 'Pull, pull, pull,' he said, timing his work to the feel of the invisible Commodore. It was quite true: handsomely did it, not brute force. The cut advanced, the dust flew down in even clouds, the long plank divided smoothly from the palm-tree's bole.

'One hundred more will do it,' thought Peter, pulling steadily. 'And that will make thirty-seven foot this afternoon.'

Another two days might see all the timbers cut, and then they could begin the building of the sides. Already the little Spanish bark lay neatly divided into two, waiting in her dry-dock for the transformation that would enable her to carry a hundred and thirteen men over the remaining two thousand miles of Pacific Ocean. They were going to lengthen her—to make a thirty-nine ton vessel of a fifteen-tonner—to the highest degree that her beam would stand, and already the work was well in hand.

At the ninetieth cut Keppel and a one-eyed hand appeared, waited for the plank to leaf away, and hurried off with it like ants.

' 'Vast sawing,' said the Commodore. 'I must clear my foothold.' He scooped away the hill of sawdust, shook a cloud of it from his head and collar, blew his nose, spat on his hands, and the sawing recommenced.

Through the even, pulsating hum of the saw Peter could hear the din of the hammers by the forge. They must nearly have finished the iron-work by now, if the hand-made bellows were still working. As regularly as a machine Peter pulled on the saw: automatically he kept his eye fixed on the scored mark by his feet: his body was absorbed in the rhythm of the work, but his mind ran free. Behind him there was the distant crash of a tree. 'That will be the big one Mr Dennis marked,' he thought, with satisfaction.

What a difference these twenty days had seen. Three weeks ago, or nearly, the island had been a place of black despair. The *Centurion* had vanished: she had driven in the night, with an off-shore hurricane, reefs to the lee, her guns unsecured, her yards on deck, and scarcely a hundred men aboard—many of them incapable of heavy duty—to work her in that annihilating sea. She had foundered with all hands: that was the sure opinion of most. Foundered within an hour of parting her cables: and that was the verdict of deeply experienced seamen. A few were sanguine enough to hope that she might have driven clear; but the most hopeful could not tell how she was ever to beat up to the island again against the prevailing wind with such a wretched crew and in such a condition as the hurricane must have left her—it being supposed that she swam at all. And when, in the succeeding days and weeks, no miracle occurred—no suddenly reborn *Centurion* appeared in the bay—the sanguine party admitted that they were wrong.

They had been very bad, those early days. In spite of the wonderful refreshment of Tinian, many of the hands, especially the older men, had already taken about as much as flesh and blood could stand. It did not seem that they could face up to this new blow. There was even a time when the very fabric of naval existence appeared to be on the edge of carrying away—when the discipline of the remaining ship's company was no longer an unquestioned certainty. Even in such an excellent crew sea-lawyers were not lacking, and they spread the tale that the officers' commissions were lost with the ship, and that their authority now therefore lapsed on land—that every man was free to do as he chose.

But the Commodore had dealt with that: after his address to the assembled men—one of his very rare addresses, for he was not a loquacious commander—there had been no further breath of mutiny; and although the men had at first confronted their seemingly impossible task with no more than apathetic obedience, Mr Anson's certainty, his immense prestige among them, their affection for him, and the example of his cheerful, indefatigable industry had worked an extraordinary change.

'The hands will not be driven,' he had directed at the council of the officers. 'They will be shown. These are good men: they need encouragement, not hard words. I need not add,' he had concluded, dismissing the supposition with a smile—'I need not add that the officers will show no sign of despondency at any time whatever.'

Of course, he had been right. No seaman who had sailed under Mr Anson was going to stand idly by, watching him labour without lending a hand: and on a much smaller scale, no men of Peter's watch and division would show a grudging heart when Peter was struggling with the task of warping the bark up to the rollers that were to carry her into the as yet non-existent dry-dock. In a few days the men were wholly recalled to their duty. Without adequate ropes or tackle they ran the bark up the beach by an ingenious system of levers and palm-trunks. They sawed her in half: they remade cordage, improvised an entire forge, adapted, new-fashioned, and reworked old iron, turned themselves from sailors into shipwrights.

The officers would show no despondency. No, they

showed none: but there was none who understood his profession who did not have secret misgivings about cramming a hundred and thirteen men into a thirty-nine-ton bark together with provisions for two thousand miles of sailing. They knew what miserable charts they had ashore: they knew that their only compass was a trifling toy found in the Spanish boat: they knew that they had not a single navigational instrument among them. They showed no despondency: Peter, in the intervals of heavy labour, did not dare to repeat even to himself the forbidding calculations that he had made: but although for his part he worked as hard as ever he could, he was unable to find any gaiety in his heart, even now, three weeks after the catastrophe; for Sean had been aboard the ship when she had driven—Sean, as well as many other friends and people dear to him: Ransome, Mr Walter, Bailey, Mr Brett, half the men with whom he had been through so much; and there was the dear ship herself, the good, brave *Centurion*, a living thing for a sailorman.

'Please, sir, Mr Dyer's duty, and may he have the sectional drawing of the upper-futtock riders?' This was a ship's boy, panting with haste and heat.

'They are on my desk, Mr Palafox—stay, I know exactly where they are.' The Commodore hurried out of the saw-pit and the choking dust. 'You may come with me, Mr Palafox. We have earned a breather.'

The Commodore's tent stood on a beautiful stretch of turf overlooking the anchorage, by a strange, overgrown avenue of pillars, the open temple of the former inhabitants, a gentle race who had worshipped there before the Spaniards had taken them all away to die of homesickness and despair in another land. Near the tent a spring bubbled up to make a little pond, sweet and clear. The Commodore flung his hat aside and knelt on the grass. 'Come on,' he said, plunging his head and shoulders into the water and gasping with the freshness. 'This will make you twice the man.'

Peter needed no second invitation. The delicious coolness ran all over him, and, as Mr Anson said, he got up twice the man. He was shaking the water out of his ears when he saw the Commodore staring fixedly beyond him. He turned. Those blue breeches belonged to Gordon, the lieutenant of the Marines. The blue breeches flew down the slope, vanishing and reappearing among the trees: they emerged on to the open grass. The owner was roaring in broken gasps as he came.

'The Spaniards,' thought Peter, with an icy chill.

'Hawp, hawp,' bawled the soldier, running even faster. He was before them; a sketchy salute, punctiliously returned, a wildly pointing hand.

'Control yourself, Mr Gordon,' said the Commodore sharply.

'The ship,' laboured out the gasping soldier. 'The ship. She's—coming in.'

What a day it was. Tools were thrown aside in utter disregard of order and arrangement. All up and down the wide shore blazed huge fires with roasting pigs and cattle for the half-starved crew. A babel of talk went up to the sky as the returned survivors told their shipmates the history of the last three weeks: and as they sat, every mess faced straight to the sea, in lines—they could not take their eyes from the *Centurion* as she rode, remarkably trim and ship-shape, on the easy swell.

'. . . carried on trailing the sheet-anchor with two cables an end . . .'

'. . . jears broke when we was a-swaying up the main yard . . .'

'. . . black men worked like good 'uns, didn't you, Sambo? But the Indians were terrified and amazed . . .'

'. . . parson nearly burst hisself at the capstan. Twenty-one hours bringing the anchor home—not a second's rest . . .'

'. . . driving and perishing on the outrageous billows while you swabs was laughing and talking on shore, a-picking of fruit . . .'

'We was not, Henry Burrell. We turned to and built . . .'

'Without so much as a halfpenny brad . . .'

'Made augers . . .'

'Made saws . . .'

'No compass, which Mr Brett had took it aboard . . .'

'No quadrant, till Hairy Amos kicked one up in the sand and didn't know what it was until Mr Palafox tore it out of his hand, roaring, like . . .'

'Which Joe Welling found vanes to fit 'un in an old drawer thrown away . . .'

'Laid her keel . . .'

'All the liquor gone with the ship . . .'

'And the tobacco . . .'

'Slainte, Sean my dear,' said Peter, raising his glass.

'Slainte, Peter a gradh,' replied Sean, engulfing the comforting punch. 'And so, your honour,' he continued, wiping his mouth with the back of his hand and sighing with relaxation, 'the first lieutenant said, "O'Mara, what shall we do? Oh let me have your counsel and aid, if you please." So I replied, "The first thing to do, Mr Saumarez dear, is to brail up at once."'

'Did you indeed, Sean? Well, it was excellent advice, since it brought back the ship.'

'Sure, I did no more than my duty in sustaining the poor man with my wisdom,' said Sean, 'the way you would have lost all your prize money if the ship had not swum, and myself my own sweet fifty pounds.'

'Why, so I should,' cried Peter, charmed with the new thought, 'and now it has come back, joy. The Dear knows I had forgot it entirely. But by my soul it's welcome back, so it is. Now, Sean, do not exceed with the punch, I entreat, for I must go along and have a word with Mr Walter and Ransome, and ask Mr Brett how he does.'

'Sure civility is the pearl of elegant breeding,' said Sean, briskly refilling his glass, 'and I will treat my messmates to the rest of the bowl.'

'You were a good, kind island to me,' said Peter, nodding to Tinian out of the open port, 'but may I be struck crimson and purple for ever if I wish to see you again, or anything at all like your foul bottom.'

He had some call to be bitter, they had taken an infinity of precautions to secure the ship: they had hurried stores and water aboard: they had swept and swept for the lost anchors, but in vain: and the third day after the ship had come in, a sudden wind, blowing with the running tide wrenched the anchor out of its hold in the brittle coral, and the men on shore saw her driving again. They rushed for the boats, and the Commodore sent the barge racing back for them. But Peter and Ransome, with a strong party of men, had been well inland after cattle, and when they had come back to the shore they found no ship, nor a single living soul on the sand.

It is true that this was not so desperate a case as it had been before: there was the barge left for them, instruments, hurried instructions, a chart; but it had been quite discouraging at first.

However, the knowledge that they could build—for they had done it already—and the lively example of Mr Anson's way of tackling difficulties had kept them in tolerable spirits. They had instantly set about reuniting the little bark, quite large enough for the few who were left and very much handier in her original shape.

They were actually rattling down her shrouds when the *Centurion* reappeared: Peter and Ransome had worked out their course for Macao, and although they were very pleased to see the ship again, it was not wholly without regret that they abandoned the glory of an independent command and the certain assumption that they would reach Macao first, to the unspeakable amazement of the *Centurion* when she should arrive.

'A very creditable piece of work, Mr Ransome,' the Commodore had said, fixing the bark with his telescope. 'To have done so much in five days is more than I could have expected, even in much more senior officers. You have done exceedingly well.'

'Hor,' said Ransome, mauve with gratification, 'Palafox done it mostly, sir.'

'I am sure Mr Palafox behaved very well,' said the Commodore.

'I beg pardon, sir,' said Peter, 'but I suppose you could not spare a moment to have a look at her?'

'No, Mr Palafox,' said the Commodore firmly. 'I have a deck under my feet: and not even the pleasure of overlooking your work—I can see from here that she is admirably joined—will induce me to leave the ship. Not even the pleasure of seeing the place where we sawed—you remember?—will take me ashore.'

Yes: she had come back. They had finished their watering in one prodigious, continual outpour of energy, much hampered by the want of the long-boat (destroyed at the *Centurion*'s first driving), but spurred on by the dread of a fresh capful of wind, and they with one anchor on such a foul bottom.

And now it was done. Full of bucanned beef, salted pork, fresh water, wood, and, for the moment, fresh fruit in abundance, she was standing out for the open sea. All around him the familiar pattern of naval life was taking shape again. The lift and roll of the ship had awakened his sea-legs: the sound of holystoning the deck filled his mind with peace. At eight bells he would form part of the watch: Mr Saumarez would have something rude to say to him, no doubt: he was at home again, and it was delightful.

'A hundred and fifty-seven miles and one third, in twenty-four hours,' said Peter.

'Mr Bailey?' asked the master.

'I have the same answer, sir,' said that wily young man.

'Very good. That is correct,' said Mr Blew. 'And that, I may tell you, is a remarkable figure for a ship that has been in tropical waters so long, and has never seen a dockyard in two years, six weeks, and one day.'

They were sitting, the navigation class and Mr Blew, under the break of the quarter-deck. They had been discussing some particularly fine points to do with the transit of Venus, and

Mr Blew had got somewhat out of his depth—a predicament from which he had saved himself by a sudden reversion to dead-reckoning.

'And what is more, young gentlemen,' he continued, 'I believe that we shall log one hundred and sixty tomorrow.' They nodded in solemn agreement, for although this seemed an outrageous figure, they had but to stand up to feel the force of the following wind, steady, warm, continuous, with never a hint of slack air. Not indeed that one among them could not gauge the exact strength of the wind by the tight curve of the sails—she was under plain sail only, for she could carry no more—and the line of the flowing sheets.

They fell into a contemplative silence. The steady sound of the pumps, the grind and splash of water, was there to remind them of the old leak up under the stem, but they paid no attention. The big following sea that sent the *Centurion*'s figure-head into the foam at regular one-minute intervals sent enough water into her to keep the pumps going watch and watch; but they were flying along with a prosperous gale, and the charms of the Orient lay all before them. Neither Mr Blew nor his class paid heed to the pumps.

'November 4th. 22° N. 119° 17' W. Wind strong and steady at E. It is my birthday again and we sighted Formosa for certain, which pleased the crew uncommon. No latitude at noon because of low cloud yesterday, so what we saw was Formosa and *not* Botel Tobago Xima. Course now WNW. This is my 3rd birthday at sea: Sean gave me another comforter, which there is not room in the berth to measure exactly. Mr Walter some excellent guavas, preserved. The berth was going to have a spread, but Ransome and I are bid to the wardroom to dine. Mem. to ask Ransome——'

'Are you ready, cock?' hailed Ransome, six inches away.

'Yes, pretty well. Don't I look it?'

'Well, cully,' said Ransome, having surveyed him with care, 'I dare say it's the best rig that can be managed. But if I was to see you at home, I'd say, "That perishing——must be down on his luck. Because why? Because he's been a-prigging of the clothes off a scarecrow." '

'Well——your eyes,' returned Peter, 'perhaps I am no tailor's dummy, but who showed you how to use a double-whip saw on Tinian?'

'Who thought of getting the timber-heads under a purchase first?' said Ransome, very warmly; and pursuing his advantage he wheezed, 'And who banged Joe Pride's hand with a hammer so often every time he drove a trennel that poor Joe came to me with tears in his eyes a-begging to be put to any other work, which he could not bear the wild look in Mr Palafox's eye every time he clapped on to a hammer any more?'

'Who worked out a course that led through the middle of Borneo? And who had to correct it?'

'Never mind,' said Ransome, reddening to the ears. 'Who thought of a tackle from the big palm-tree——'

'Wrangle, wrangle, wrangle,' said Keppel. 'Anyone would think you had built the Ark between you. Shut up.'

'Young gentlemen,' said the steward, 'the officers is almost all in the wardroom.'

'Come on,' cried Ransome, and they sped aft. This willingness on Ransome's part, this positive eagerness to dine elsewhere, was something new and strange. But social intercourse held no terrors for Ransome now. They were scarcely seated in the overcrowded wardroom—crammed now with the *Gloucester*'s lieutenants, surgeon and purser as well as the *Tryal*'s—they were hardly in their places before Ransome, with anticipatory delight shining in his countenance, addressed the first lieutenant in the following words: 'What reply was made to him, sir, that said, he did not use to give the wall to every coxcomb?'

'Why, Mr Ransome,' said the first lieutenant, poising his knife above the loin of pork and thinking tolerably hard, 'I dare say it was "Tack, you——, or I will ram you," or perhaps something downright impolite.'

'Sir,' said Ransome, swelling visibly, 'the reply was, "But *I* do, sir," and so the fellow gave him the wall.'

The wardroom found this richly humorous, and until the first remove Ransome sat in silent satisfaction, neither gnawing his nails, fixing his eyes wishfully on others' trenchers, nor cleansing his teeth with the table-cloth: then he stunned the *Tryal*'s surgeon by asking, 'How many bones are there in a perfect man?'

'How many bones? Well, let me see,' began the surgeon, looking anxiously at Mr Woodfall.

'The bones which do support our earthly tower,
Are numbered four hundred and eighty-fower,'

stated Ransome firmly.

'You came out very strong at dinner, Ransome,' said Peter, as they cooled off on deck after the wardroom's punch.

'Pretty strong,' admitted Ransome complacently. 'Did you watch Parson Walter when I axed him, "Who was the first man that publicly writ of the Antipodes?"'

'And the one about the custom of certain Greeks.'

'But it worn't as good as when the Commodore invited me and Balthasar, and I brought out the piece about the King of Sweden.'

'Ransome,' said Peter, 'where is that book?'

'Hor,' said Ransome, going red, 'I'll give it back by and by. It is out of the way just now. I don't know if I could put my hand on it, exactly.' Ransome was a wretchedly inefficient liar: not only did he look utterly shifty, but he also clasped both hands to his bosom.

'I believe it is under your shirt,' said Peter.

'No, it an't,' cried Ransome, hurrying blindly away.

'It is no good hiding yourself there,' said Peter, arriving some time later in the berth, where Ransome was making a dismal attempt at hiding himself behind Keppel and the equally stunted midshipman Pollock, from the *Gloucester*. 'You give it up directly, Ransome.'

'Which I don't know where it is,' said Ransome, illogically and uselessly huddling himself into a smaller compass.

'I do,' said Keppel, in an awful voice. 'It is abaft the gloom-ing-pot bowse.'

'Oh,' said Peter, changing colour and recoiling a step. He looked hurriedly for Balthasar, and saw him, trussed up under the beam in a hammock, gagged and bound and already painted ochre from head to foot.

'No,' cried Peter, finding his retreat cut off and backing against the jear-capstan casing. 'You can't do that to me. It's my birthday.'

'Can't we?' said Bailey, with a wicked grin.

'You and your prowlburke,' said Preston, hissing.

'And us combing through the manual for the plashing-strake.'

'No,' shrieked Peter as they closed in upon him. 'No. I've got to go on deck. . . .'

'What is this shocking noise about?' asked Mr Saumarez.

'If you please sir,' said Keppel, 'we are painting Mr Palafox blue.'

'What a stupid blunder,' cried the first lieutenant. 'Don't you know that green is the proper emblem? Come, come; mix yellow with your blue and you will have green—the only correct colour. When will you begin to realise that you *must* think before you act?'

The dawn came up pale and grey: the *Centurion* had been lying-to all night, for they were in soundings, and it was al-most certain that the dull blur seen on the larboard beam some time ago was the Asian continent.

Peter, with a good deal of green lingering about his person and a vile temper in his heart, was peering into the fog, from time to time making petulant and ineffectual motions towards fanning it away.

'It *is*,' he said, as a low, dim shape wafted by, and the cackling increased.

'It can't be,' said Bailey. 'It's birds.'

'It is,' repeated Peter, and hurrying to the officer of the watch he saluted and said, 'Report a number of small-craft under the bows, sir.'

'How many, Mr Palafox?'

'Oh, perhaps a thousand, sir,' answered Peter carelessly.

'Mr Palafox,' said Mr Brett with a frown.

'Beg pardon, sir,' said Peter.

Yet as the mist lifted it showed that a thousand was many too few. There were four, five, even six thousand sampans abroad on the sea, and every minute of the growing day revealed more. The quiet grey water was covered with them, all round the ship as far as the eye could reach, and with unwearying industry their crews fished over the side, all talking at once in a high, small, incessant gabble that filled the entirety of the air.

They fished, looking neither to the right nor the left. They took no notice of the *Centurion* whatever, and the wondering crew had the weird impression that this was a dream in which they themselves were no more than floating shadows.

Hails, many times repeated, wreathed smiles from the quarter-deck, the cry of a pilot in all the many languages that the *Centurion* could muster, silver coins displayed, gold, all left the myriad fishermen unmoved. They neither heard nor saw: they fished.

'Lower away the cutter,' ordered the Commodore. And when the cutter returned, 'What have you learned, Mr Palafox?' he asked.

'Nothing, sir,' replied Peter. 'The craft only answered "Bah" in Chinese.'

'What is the Chinese for Bah, Mr Palafox?'

'Bah, sir, begging your pardon.'

'Hm,' said the Commodore, looking at him hard before he turned away. 'Sampan ahoy,' he hailed, 'Pilot-o?'

Peter looked quickly at Keppel: he detected a tremor, but no sound emerged.

'Pilot-ee?' continued the Commodore. 'Macao? Savvy?'

'The irritating creatures,' muttered Mr Walter, hanging over the rail in a quiet fume. 'I should like to bang their heads together.'

'Ram one of the——, and take up her people: that will make 'em attend,' said Peter to no one in particular, and rather more loudly than he had intended.

Peter had already been struck by lightning: but that was a tame affair in comparison with the sudden blast of the Commodore's displeasure. And when he was half-way up to the mast-head he was desired to come down again to hear some reflections upon loquacity—undesirable in midshipmen; his manners—susceptible of improvement; his status in the ship—remarkably low; oaths in general—abhorrent to the Commodore; oaths by the young in particular—disgusting, unmanly, ill-bred. And all this delivered within a few yards of Peter's messmates, who could not hear a word officially and who stood with glazed expressions staring out to sea, but who would have been a good deal more than human if they had not treasured up some of the more forcible expressions for subsequent use.

It was a thoroughly exasperating day. They sailed slowly through a horde of utterly indifferent Chinese: from his height Peter saw innumerable efforts made from the quarter-deck to enlist even the faintest show of interest, and all in vain. Gradually the quarter-deck grew hoarser and more vexed: more and more of Peter's colleagues joined him.

'Here, cully,' whispered Ransome, as yet unscathed. 'I brought you a bite of pork to pass the time.'

'Thankee, cock,' said Peter, his ill-temper dissipating all at once. 'I was clemmed with hunger. Is that Keppel at the mizzen?'

'Yes. I fed him just now. He laughed when Mr Dennis dropped his glass.'

'And Bailey and Preston at the main?'

'Yes. Mr S. said they looked pleased with theirselves.'

'Little Pollock on the jib-boom?'

'Giggled, I believe.'

'It's a hard life, Ransome.'

'A very hard life, cock.'

'Will we ever get a pilot, do you think?'

'Commodore swears he'll sail through the damned channel with the boats sounding every inch.'

'Swears, does he?'

'Something chronic.'

'I hope we get a pilot, Ransome. Shore-leave, eh?'

'Hor, hor, cully. Shore-leave, hor, and don't we wish we may get it?'

And so the day passed, and the next, and the day after. Always the interminable dream-like procession of dumb, deaf, impassive Chinese faces, the ship lying-to all night, creeping along by day, and the crew frantic with impatience and frustration.

They passed Pedro Blanco and the charted reefs: they passed reefs uncharted, and hovered on the edge of shoaling water. They were actually reaving the channel with the cutter sounding ahead before they elicited the faintest interest in an Oriental face. But this face was keenly interested: together with its owner it came racing over the sea, ran up the side with seamanlike rapidity, saluted the quarter-deck, and was instantly divined to be that long-awaited sight, the visage of a China pilot. The bargain was struck at once: the pilot took up his post and conned the ship with strange squeaking cries and effective gestures, and regarded, with veiled triumph, the disappointment of his rivals, who now came in profusion, carrying certificates (many ribald, some serious) from Portuguese, Dutch and English master-mariners, but all too late.

Nearer and nearer came the shore. An outward-bound Dutchman had already passed them in Macao road, dipping his ensign as he went.

'I thought it would be yellow,' said Sean, staring at the land.

'Not this,' said Peter, reassuring him; 'this is Macao, which is Portuguese, *That* is China, on the other side.'

'Macao,' said the pilot. 'Very jolly. Very nice. Very, very nice. Oh yes.'

'Show a leg,' said Bailey, hurrying from his lurking-place. 'He's just coming on deck.'

'Shore-leave?' said Mr Saumarez, gazing about. 'Why, confound your impertinence, we have not even laid a hand to the anchors yet. Quartermaster, get that party for'ard at once. Mr

Keppel, stand by at the cathead. Look alive, slow-bellies. Are those men asleep? Mr Palafox, take your hands out of your pockets this minute. Shore-leave, forsooth . . .'

To the Revd. Mr Palafox,
Ballynasaggart Rectory,   Macao, in China
Co. Galway.   December 21st, 1742 O.S.

'My dear Sir,' wrote Peter,

'By Mr Walter's kindness I may send my Love and Duty from this Side of the World, for we have reach'd this Port, and he is to go Home in one of the Merchantmen which resort hither for the China Trade. Some other Officers go with him, chief of whom is Capt. Saunders, formerly our First, but now made Post, and charg'd with the Commodore's despatches to the Admiralty. These will be made Public (or what Part of 'em is fit for the Public Gaze) in the Gazette, and to them I will leave the Task of recounting our Voyage: for otherwise, upon my Word, I shou'd be hard put to begin. William cou'd encompass it, I am sure, or Homer or Virgil; but I was never an Eminent Hand with a Pen, and I know that even the Commodore has been coop'd up these three days together with his Clerk, compiling his Letter to their Lordships. However, I have noted down particular Occurrences in a Commonplace Book, and with that to refresh my Memory, I hope to carry you (in Figure) in a total Circumnavigation of the Terraqueous Globe when I reach home. This (God willing) shou'd be in a few months after Mr Walter, for we have but to careen and refit, and then we weigh for Batavia and so round by the Cape—the beaten track of the Indiamen and perfectly charted and known. Our Expedition is done. It is not fit that I should give particular News of it in a private Letter, before the Despatches are known, but I may say that we have not accomplish'd all that the World might have hop'd, yet still we have done something, and at least we are come to this Place, where no Man-of-war has been before us.

'We had but an uncomfortable time of it round the Horn,

as was to be expected; but we were entirely recover'd at Juan Fernandez. Then we had some charming sailing, in our Cruise on the Spaniards: a brush or two, some Success and some Disappointment, in the usual Mixture; and so, after some Difficulties that it wou'd be tedious to relate, we cross'd the Pacific Ocean—surely a strangely nam'd Sea.

'As for China, I despair of giving you an Image of the Country. But Mr Brett, our 2nd Lieutenant, has in the Most Obliging Manner, given me some capital Drawings made on the Spot, and these, together with some trifling Presents (which I beg your kind Acceptance of) will tell you more than if I puzzled my Wits clean through the Watch. The little wicker Parcel is fill'd with Tea, which is a China Drink, and much taken by the grand People in England, they say. The country way of making it is to put some in a Pot and dash scalding water upon it. A tolerably large Handful will answer for a Pot. It is said to invigorate the Fancy and strengthen the Nerves: I cannot say I find this effect in myself, but this may be either brutish Insensibility or the result of Hard Tack, Junk and dried Pease as a 2 years' Diet. I have put Labels on the other Presents, to shew what they are and for Whom: they are small, but Mr Walter is already deep-laden and I wou'd not impose upon his Good-Nature—though indeed he has a wonderful Store of it and supported us much, in fair Weather and Foul.

'As for myself, I am in Health and as strong as a Horse. How I hope that Placidus is perfectly well, and that his near Fore-foot is no longer so Tender. Sean, too, is as strong as a Horse and has his Health entire, apart from some Fingers and Toes, which came off by reason of the cold in the high latitudes South. He desires his best Duty and all his Respects. He is a steady, excellent Fellow and much esteem'd by the whole Company. He is Captain of the Foretop, and the Commodore ask'd me privately cou'd he read and write? Which may mean that he designs him for a Warrant.

'Now, Sir, with my dear Love to my Mother and you and to my Brothers and Sisters as well as to all who remember me kindly, I will close up this Letter. I am asham'd it is such a sad scrubby Epistle, but I will make it up by Spinning my Yarn, as the sailormen say, by the side of a good Turf fire, in my own place at Home.'

He signed, folded, and looked up into the face of Pollock, on the other side of the narrow table. Pollock's mouth was open, and he was gazing vacantly into the air. 'You will have to be pretty brisk if you want your letter to go in the *Walpole*,' said Peter, catching his eye.

'I don't know what to say,' said Pollock. 'It is such a long time,' he added, in a very low and doleful voice.

'Cheer up, young codger,' said Peter. 'Come, this will never do. They all say what a roaring blade you are—you mustn't give way, you know.'

'Do they, Palafox, indeed?'

'Sure, strike me——if they don't. There now, dash away. Can't you begin?'

'No,' said Pollock, relapsing again.

'Would you like my beginning? It's pretty good.'

'Oh yes, if you please.'

'All right. What's your establishment at home? I only ask to make it square.'

'There's my mother, and Sue.'

'Capital. "My dear Madam," ' Peter began, adapting his letter while Pollock scribbled busily after him. '. . . we'll leave Placidus out: and Sean: but you can have a drawing if you would like it, and leave Mr Brett in. Needn't mention *Gloucester*'s mishaps—just say you've been transferred—only worry them else. You're as strong as a horse, an't you? Good: make it so. No brothers? Cut out brothers. I suppose you don't have turf at home. No? Put in sea-coals or wood, as the case may be. There. Sand the blot. That's as handsome a letter as the soul could desire. No, don't seal it—that wouldn't be civil to Captain Saunders, who carries it. Fold again. Sling it over, and I will take it with mine.'

'What an amazingly good fellow you are, Palafox,' said Pollock. 'I am extremely obliged for your——' but Peter was gone.

• • •

On the bank of the Pearl River, with its back to the teeming city of Canton, a Chinese sage contemplated the innumerable sampans and junks. By his side his grandson, a sharp child of six winters, tended a caged cricket and gambolled in the mud—a child destined, it may be added, for a public death by boiling just forty years on.

'Grandpapa,' said the fledgling gallows-bird, 'I see two sumptuous palanquins approaching in the distance.'

'Are they officials?' asked the sage, turning quickly and peering through his spectacles.

'I cannot tell, being so young in years,' piped the child. 'They are not *very* sumptuous palanquins, for although they are ornate to a high degree, the hangings are somewhat tawdry.'

'They are not sumptuous at all,' said the sage, as the palanquins drew near. 'They are crude, vulgar, essentially modern palanquins; metricious palanquins: yet I have been put to the trouble of presenting a benignant aspect, in case they might be mandarins, by your unconsidered remarks.'

'There is a foreign devil marching by the nearest palanquin, grandpapa.'

'A barbarian, my child. The educated man does not say "foreign devil".'

'A barbarian, grandpapa. Pray, grandpapa, tell me about the barbarians?'

'They are engendered by the apes of the farther western deserted regions, and by certain unclean spirits of those parts, my child: they are covered with hair, but they are capable of a rude speech for their simple communications among themselves: and they have, from the supernatural side of their ancestry, a curious ability to travel in very large sea-going machines, which waft them up and down. They first had the happiness of finding the Celestial Empire in the reign of Sun Chi, when it was reported that they were capable of domestication and responsive to kindness; and it was ordered that they should be regarded as neutral monsters of the third class, neither benign nor malignant, to be officially preserved as curiosities and allowed suitable nourishment, but to be shunned by unauthorised persons.'

'What is suitable nourishment for a monster of the third class, if you please, grandpapa?'

'A small brick of a very hard farinaceous substance will sustain one for a week,' replied the sage. 'They are not costly to maintain: but neither are they pleasant, having the hairiness of the one parent joined to the intractability of the other, together with the unbelievable lack of polish of both, doubled.'

'The monster in the second palanquin has no hair at all,' reported the child, returning through the crowd.

'Then it is one of the Smooth Southern Monsters,' said the sage sharply, 'and so much the worse.'

'And pray, grandpapa, why does the monster perpetually chant "Palanquin ho, palanquin hee"?'

'It is an abortive attempt at speaking the human language,' said the sage.

'Does it want its brick of farinaceous substance, or is the monster in pain, grandpapa?'

'Not in half as much pain as you will be in a minute if you do not stop asking damn-fool questions,' cried the exasperated sage. 'Leave the foreign devils alone, can't you? And mind your own business. You will certainly come to a bad end if you go on like this, you very disagreeable little beast.' With those ominous words the sage turned his face to the river, and took no further interest in the proceedings whatever.

And this, in its way, was typical of the *Centurion*'s dealings with the Chinese. The root of the trouble lay, perhaps, in that polished nation's disregard for the military character: in a land where the fighting man was officially rated as "equal, but perceptibly inferior, to the remover of impurities from the public thoroughfares, fifth class", and popularly as almost indistinguishable from a hired assassin; in a land, moreover, to which no ship of the Royal Navy had hitherto penetrated, the Commodore found it extraordinarily difficult to have due respect paid to his master's flag, and even (in spite of the good offices of the Portuguese and the well-meant but inept intervention of the East India Company's men) to provide his ship with her daily necessities, let alone the refit that she needed so badly. Obstruction from the lower officials, continual delays, false promises and misunderstandings kept the *Centurion* in Macao for a time that seemed never-ending and perfectly intolerable to her officers; and even when the Commodore, overriding the pusillanimous merchant's advice, cut the red-tape by a direct and forceful approach to the Viceroy himself in Canton, the work carried on with maddening deliberation.

Maddening, that is, for the commander and the senior officers: the crew, the midshipmen's berth, and the younger lieutenants, were charmed with their long run ashore. Now that the ship was in her berth, refitting at last, with a horde of very able, if dilatory, Chinese caulkers thumping away at her bottom and sides, while smiths hammered and blew, and shipwrights wrought, the more volatile part of her company scattered abroad to add to the gaiety of Macao, Kowloon and Canton, where, for all the official Chinese reserve, and despite their status as monsters, neutral, third class, they found congenial places of entertainment and convivial souls.

Peter was particularly fortunate in making friends with some East India Company cadets, two of whom had a working acquaintance with Cantonese and all a profound knowledge of the haunts where foreigners were welcomed and fed to the bursting-point. There were also a few daring young Chinese of the mercantile class who invited him out; and at other times he scoured the countryside with Keppel and Sean in pursuit of the outraged Chinese fox. He thought China was quite lovely; and in common with all his messmates he did not mind how long they were delayed, if only his pay could be made to last out.

This was a proviso of some importance. Two years' pay, even at a midshipman's meagre rate, had at first appeared an inexhaustible sum; but appearances are notoriously deceptive, and by February an outbreak of borrowing began in the midshipmen's berth. By March there was no more to borrow, and everybody was deeply in debt to everyone else: the entire communal purse had been entrusted to Keppel to run its chance at the fan-tan table of the Teahouse of Joyous Surprises. For one dazzling moment it had swollen to three times its size, then it vanished quite away, leaving seven anguished paupers behind it. A round-robin to the Commodore, a determined frontal attack upon him after dinner, had both failed to move him an inch from his position: the prize-money was not to be touched: thrift was a quality to be cultivated, and in no profession was it more important than theirs: they were to regard their prize-money as a nest-egg, a sheet-anchor: he was sorry to find that they had already dissipated their pay, which was ample for all reasonable needs—far more, indeed, than he as a midshipman had ever dreamed of possessing: but here were ten guineas, which they might change with the comprador, and he hoped they would not contract expensive tastes, most unsuitable in a naval career.

Ten guineas was a handsome contribution: but still the *Centurion* lay up, and somehow the guineas dribbled away. Presently small articles of personal clothing began to go over the side into bum-boats or the local equivalent; the personal loot of Paita had preceded them, and quadrants, parallel rulers and protractors followed. The more tender-hearted wardroom officers were attacked; and Peter, for one, did not scorn to pillage the gundeck.

'March 17th,' he wrote, 'I believe Sean is hiding two pieces of eight. I distinctly heard something rattle when he pretended to be called away before I could pin him. Mem. Mr Brett, one and ninepence. Mem. to see if Slimebound Lee Hee will change Balthasar's groat with a hole in it. Can I do without my reefer?'

'Certainly I can,' he answered, aloud. 'The course home never goes above 35° S., and therefore must be perfectly warm, all the way.'

The reefer-jacket went over the side, and he thoughtfully added Ransome's as well, thus saving him the trouble of making a decision. Yet still no way of discovering any considerable supply could be found, and on April 3rd he wrote, 'We only wandered about Macao today, as glum as gib cats.'

It was a thinly-equipped berth, therefore, that stood in the waist of the ship or on the quarter-deck as the parting salute to the Portuguese fort boomed over Macao road and the *Centurion* filled to stand out to sea on April 6th. Thinly-equipped, but well furnished with animal spirits: the ship was in noble condition; her rigging was a joy to behold; her silent pumps gleamed with paint that would surely rest undisturbed between here and the Channel; ready in the braces, mingled with the Centurions, stood a good score of fresh hands, experienced able seamen, Dutch and East-India lascars. She was homeward bound, and as she came about she ran through her stays with an easy confident glide—tallow below and never a speck of foul weed—that promised a beautiful run.

They had not done all they had intended: that was true; for luck had been against them, and the secrecy of their expedition had been a farce. But they had come round the Horn, where no ship had been able to follow them and live: they had cruised on the Spaniards in a sea where the Spaniards had felt themselves utterly safe: they had destroyed an immense value of enemy shipping and merchandise—infinitely more than they carried in prize-money, for they had sunk, burnt, and destroyed, according to their orders. And they had sacked Paita. They had done this at a terrible cost to themselves: and even now they were to beat against the monsoon to Batavia. But the first was past and the second was yet to come, and for the moment they were reaching upon a fair wind, with a clean, stout ship under them; and above all, they were homeward bound.

14

'ALL HANDS ON DECK. ALL HANDS ON DECK.' THE CRY AND THE insistent pipes rang through the ship.

'What the devil's the matter now?' asked Peter, rolling sleepily out of his hammock. 'Hands to punishment?'

'Commodore—addressing the crew,' cried Hill as he flew from the berth.

Peter shot up on deck, and blinking in the sunlight ranged himself in his due place on the quarter-deck.

'What on earth . . .?' he thought, screwing up his eyes. They were only a few days out of Macao, not far out of soundings yet: nothing could have happened to warrant such a portentous assembly.

A great silence filled the ship as the last scurrying hand nipped into his place. Two hundred and twenty-five pairs of eyes were fixed on the Commodore from the main-deck: nineteen pairs from the quarter-deck. Only the quartermasters looked forward, as they steered the *Centurion* on the easy, sighing wind.

Mr Anson withstood this fire and cross-fire of eyes with complete equanimity. He waited for a moment after the total silence had fallen, and then in a voice that could be heard very distinctly, he said, 'Men. We are going to try again for the Acapulco ship. Quiet, there. I have withheld this news until we were at sea, because now no foolish babbler can destroy his shipmates' chances. The galleon sails in March from Acapulco for Manilla. You know that. She raises Cape Espiritu Santo in the Philippines between the first week in June and the end of the month, New Style. If all hands attend to their duty we shall reach the station in time. This year there may be two ships, because we shut them up last time. Now there may be some of you who have heard the stories they put about concerning the galleon—that she is a tall ship, with a great crew and sides so thick that they are proof against shot. They *are* tall ships: they may carry fifty guns or more: and they may have five or six hundred men but they are *not* proof against shot. It you engage them a great way off, if you have no taste for closing, why then your shot may not pierce. But,' said the Commodore, and a slight flush mounted into his face, 'if you behave as I am accustomed to see you behave, we shall engage her, or the two of them, and I give you my word that it shall be so close that one shot will drive not through one side, but both. And if you are the men I believe you are, we shall sink her or take her.'

The cheer crashed out like a broadside. Three cheers that rocked the *Centurion* from keelson to truck, then a vast disorderly cheering that went on and on.

'That will do,' said the Commodore. 'Dismiss the men, if you please, Mr Saumarez. The course is due east.'

Due east the *Centurion* flew. In the morning she was flying still, her bowsprit right in the eye of the rising sun: and the wind held fair.

'We must not be too sanguine,' said Peter, trying to master his hands as he straightened the chart.

'No. We had high hopes before, and they was dashed cruel hard,' said Ransome. 'We must not raise 'em too high.'

But even as they spoke they knew it was no good. The ship was alive with excitement: all the disappointed longings, swallowed down with a sailor's hard-learnt philosophy, had sprung into brilliant life, as strong and stronger than ever: the ship was blazing with expectation—and they were part of the ship. They might talk as much as they pleased, but in their hearts there was a bubbling ferment that would not be kept down.

Never had the Commodore spoken with such certainty.

Always, before Acapulco, there had been caution, reserve: this time he had said, 'I will bring you to the station where she must pass: if you have spirit enough, we shall take her.' He had certainly acquired some secret intelligence in Canton or Macao: he knew that she would sail: and he had given nothing away—the whole crew had been convinced that they were bound for Batavia; everybody on shore had been so unquestioningly certain of it that at this very moment, in the clerk's cabin, there lay bags of mail for Batavia.

Eastward, eastward, and south about Formosa. 'May 5th. 21° 57′ N., Bashee Islands bearing SSE 20 leagues. Botel Tobago Xima 7 leagues N. So the Bashees were 25 leagues too much to the W. on the chart: corrected it.' These observations were of the first importance in navigation, and the Commodore was not, for one minute, going to allow such opportunities to pass: and as the observations were also of the greatest assistance in bringing them to their station in time, every man aboard capable of making them wielded the instruments with passionate zeal.

Glory and a million pieces of eight depended on their efficiency: for this was the galleon bound for Manilla, and her cargo was solid silver and gold.

Efficiency was their ambition and their watchword. Even in the highest days before Acapulco, Peter had never seen men race up the rigging or fling themselves to the braces with such instant, intelligent speed. It was as if their hopes had come to life five times reinforced by long rest. And at the guns the crews practised with indefatigable care: if a shot went wild there was no need for any officer's reproof; the gun's crew would be as down as if each man had lost five guineas, and the captain would look wretchedly ashamed. With so small a ship's company there could not be men enough to fight all the guns: they were divided into gangs of ten on the main-deck, twelve on the gun-deck—two loaders to each gun, and the rest to run from one port to another. They practised continually, so that no words were needed, and the heavy guns ran in and out with silent, astonishing speed.

The sharpshooters, the men with small-arms in the tops, brought themselves to a degree of perfection that would have made a musketry instructor gasp. They were a band of thirty, carefully picked by a long series of competitions, followed with breathless interest by the entire crew: within this band rank and rating went by the board, for a steady hand and eye might be found in any man, irrespective of his degree; and some of the most skilled specialists—warrant officers and their mates—found themselves under the iron rule of Gyppo Soames. For two years past the pipe of All hands to witness punishment had primarily meant that Gyppo was going to cop it again; and the rolling drum's chief duty had been to drown the poacher's anguish. But now what a change was here: Soames neat, clean, a conscientious, exemplary tyrant—a most respectable man indeed. And for that matter, the *Centurion*'s defaulters' list showed an unnatural blankness from the day of the Commodore's address: it was marred only once, in May, by the record of a furious battle between Hairy Amos and Henry Burrell, able seamen of the starboard watch, for the possession of a musket named Old Noll, allegedly superior to all but Gyppo Soames' Dead-Reckoner.

'May 15th. No latitude at noon. Logged 71 leagues, course SW 17 hours, SW½W 7 hours. A glorious run after yesterday's and the day before's head-wind and dying airs. Topmen fired upon a pewter plate (old) veered out on a 20 fathom line: 30 holes in it at first volley: praised by Commodore. Mem. Cape Espiritu Santo shows as one knob, three little knobs, one knob, then a headland bearing NNE 1 mile to the sea.

'May 17th. Terrible day of calm. Boats away to tow—how much lighter she is—but still am quite fagged out. It is the anxiety, not the exercise. 4 miles logged. Slight current setting E½N however, a great comfort.'

'May 18th. Half-gale at N and NNW. Crew rejoiced. Carried away larboard main-topgallant studdingsail boom: rigged out another and made good in 7 minutes 45 seconds. Sean begged I would explain plain rule of thumb navigation. Spent all watches below at mast-head watching for Cape. Mem. one knob, three clustered knobs, one knob, headland: must be on starboard bow. Later: wind dying in gusts—much anxiety.'

'May 19th. 11° 53' N. 3° 46' E. of Botel Tobago Xima. A prodigious run. We may do it yet.'

'May 20th. Beautiful gale throughout middle watch and forenoon. Raised Cape at noon. I saw it at the same moment as Wilson, whatever he may say, SSW 11 leagues—knob, 3 knobs, knob, on starboard bow. Instantly tacked and struck topgallants, because of the sentinels they post there for the galleon, with beacons. Cape Espiritu Santo is in 12° 40' N. precisely and 4° E. of Botel Tobago Xima: all our reckonings agree. This is May 31st, their style, and 3 days before the Acapulco ship has ever made the Cape. We are to cruise between 12° 50' N. and 13° 5'. Crew in most amazing high spirits. Must get some sleep, not having turned in these four watches together.'

'May 31st. Gunnery practice. Some elegant shots. Number 7 and 10 lower tier still a little slow, being mostly ship's boys. Longboat lashed alongside, in readiness. Mem. shot-garland no. 4 is a little worn.'

'June 3rd. Keeping station. This is June 14th N.S. We grow somewhat uneasy. Sorcery beginning again. Lascars very sly about their sacrifice to Pulay Wooloo—a god of their parts, I find. Gave them a Canton hen. Wish them luck. I had a horrible dream that we were blown off station: I wish it may not be an omen.'

'June 5th. Keeping station. Guns firing all day as usual. The black men's guns won the prize. How they gleam, when heated. Mulberry lost his little finger running up no. 36: said "Damn um," and laughed heartily. Tomorrow is the height of their time—the most usual day—16th, their style.'

'June 11th. Cruising still. An anxious week, but anxiety allayed because of fresh breezes at W. and WSW., which must keep her back. Men have little time for anxiety, being as busy as bats. Scene between Commodore and Sean. Mr Anson wanted mutton: Sean said No, only two China sheep left, and begged pardon, but one must be kept for Commodore to celebrate victory and one to sustain Spanish captain in defeat. Commodore still wanted mutton, however: Sean grew dogged—was told obstinate, pigheaded; asked if he wished to be flogged? Unmoved. Commodore went aft, muttering.'

'June 12th. Accident with no. 41. Overheated—kicked at the charge—turned, damaging trunnion. Beautiful repair by Aston, goldsmith by trade. Ransome sleep-walked with a cutlass. We pray earnestly for head-winds, which will be fair for the galleon. Weed beginning to grow.'

'June 13th. Prayers answered. Fresh breezes and ½ gale E. and NE. Mulberry says it is his god—nonsense. Lascars look uncommon knowing, but say nothing. Gunnery, small-arms; very strict lookout.'

'June 16th. A shocking thing has occurred. We were confident that we were on station 15 leagues off the cape, but at dawn we found it looming at a bare 7 leagues, the tide having set prodigious strong. Clawed off with all haste: but have our topsails been seen? *Gloucester*'s were, off Acapulco. If their sentinels were awake they could already have sent one of those amazing swift outrigger canoes beyond us already, in the dark, as an aviso to the galleon.'

'June 18th. Backing and filling in one patch of weed all day. Anxiety very painful. Could she have passed us in the night, days ago? Ship filled with rumours.'

'June 19th—30 their style and the last day of the month. Can hardly bear it any more. Commodore keeps the deck. Unable to sleep or eat. If she don't come within 48 hours it is all up.'

Worn and irritable from lack of rest, Peter came off duty at the end of the middle watch. It was four in the morning. He could not face small beer and biscuit, nor the unending guess and conjecture of the berth. He moved slowly up to the foretop in the grey light of the declining moon: the dew was wet under his hands, and the rigging fiddle-string tight. The *Centurion* lay head-on to the Pacific surge, and remotely before her the stars shone low. It was now the morning watch, and somewhere beyond the rim of the sea the sun would have risen. Peter made a quick calculation: yes, the first rays would be coming green through the woods in Tinian now. They would be lighting the blackened keel of the bark they had burnt: and the dawn would be racing westward at an inconceivable speed. Soon—in an hour and a half or thereabouts—it would have covered the whole tract of sea that had taken them so long to pass, and it would put out the stars.

They were growing a little paler already. Yes, he thought, shifting a leg cramped with sitting and moving up to the topmast-head to loosen it out, yes, they are much paler already, and the small three in a line have almost gone.

That star, he thought: I cannot place it. He called the astronomical atlas into his mind: but no, he said again, I do not make it out.

'Oh, strike me,' he whispered aloud, with something like horror (yet not horror, either) in the sound of his throat. 'It can't be . . .'

The star had not paled. Nor had it risen at all, like those few that could yet be seen: and there was *no* star in that quarter, nor any planet at all.

With a long swooping rush he slid down the back-stay. 'I beg pardon, sir,' he said in a low voice to Mr Dennis, the officer of the morning watch. 'But I believe there may be a ship's light one point on the larboard bow. I am not sure, sir.'

The third lieutenant's face froze in attention. Without a word he vanished aloft: he was back; he gripped Peter's hand, shook it briefly, made a dash towards the Commodore's cabin, checked himself and said, 'No. You may go—compliments, of course—say I confirm.'

'Mr Dennis's compliments, sir,' said Peter, addressing the wide-awake eyes that gleamed from the cot, 'and there is a top-light at south-east.'

'Very good, Mr Bailey—no, Mr Palafox, I see. I will be on deck directly.'

It was impossible to say how the news had spread: but even

before the Commodore had stepped from his cabin the men were appearing in the dimness from every part of the ship. The entire watch below was on deck, waiting and waiting: silently waiting and staring aloft towards the mast-head.

And when at last, with the sun, there came the wonderful cry from aloft it was not a surprise, but a confirmation—a profoundly satisfying confirmation, received with a deep, sighing growl.

She had long been stripped for action. There was little to do, and that little was done in seven minutes: now they were to wait. Yet before the galley fires were doused Mr Anson ordered a hot dinner: all hands would eat it, he said, or be sent below during the whole of the action.

With polished mess kids they watched him anxiously. Satisfied, he ordered the fires to be doused, and five minutes later the drumroll, tan tarara tan, filled all the ship. Clear for action: and action stations.

Peter, moved by some strange impulse—which was shared by all the rest, he noted, although not a word had been said—darted below for his best uniform. With the drum still thundering in his ears he took his place on the quarter-deck. Colours came with the rising sun, and gold and blue the Commodore stood at the windward rail: gold and blue, Mr Saumarez stood at the lee with the second and fifth lieutenants beside him: plain blue the master, conning the ship behind the wheel: red the officers of the Marines. Peter, Keppel and Preston were on the quarter-deck. The other officers were in their stations about the ship: the surgeon in the cockpit, ready: Ransome and Bailey with Mr Norris and Mr Stapleton in the gun-deck, ready; Mr Smith of the *Gloucester* and Hill on the fo'c'sle (he had replaced Peter at the guns by seniority); Balthasar and Mr Hughes in the waist, ready; Mr Wood of the *Tryal* at the quarter-guns.

Far, far over the sea she came, the familiar shape that Peter had seen so often in that distant Mexican bay by night. He knew every line but one, a dark cross like a royal, and yet not a royal, high above the white sails. 'It is the crucifix,' he realised, with a strange thrill in his heart. 'The cross that the Spaniards sail under in enemy seas.'

'She is clewing up her topgallants,' he said to himself. 'She holds to her course, bearing down. She means to engage.' And he found that the noise that he heard was his heart. He glanced quickly at the impassive faces to see if anyone else had noticed it too.

'Quite the size of a first-rate,' he said, continuing his interior monologue. 'We shall have the weather-gage in ten minutes, if she holds on her course. Then she cannot escape.'

'Mr Saumarez,' said the Commodore, 'we will hale on the wind half a point.'

'One league,' said Peter, as the swift patter of feet died away. Everything had been long foreseen: there was nothing to do but to wait. His duty was to wait through the increasing tension: he was there, like the others on the quarter-deck, to second the Commodore at an instant's notice—to be there for any emergency.

'She is bringing-to,' said Peter as the galleon began the movement. She lay there, a beautiful ship, brought-to under topsails, with her head to the north: and as her fore-topsail spilled the wind the royal standard of Spain broke out at the main-topgallant mast-head, a puff of smoke appeared in her side, and a little later the deep cry of the challenging gun reached the *Centurion*.

Between them a squall of rain drifted and turned. Peter saw the Spanish sails shiver, and then she was lost. A few warm drops fell on his cheek. The squall passed: and there she lay still, waiting for them; and her gun-ports were open.

'I think we may show them our colours,' observed the Commodore, looking at his watch. Keppel and the signal-yeoman sprang into motion. The ensign, the broad pennant, the Union flag appeared on the instant.

'They have not cleared yet,' continued Peter. Something was going over the side of the galleon. Might he look with his glass? Would it be proper? No. He could see now, anyway. It was a cow or a bullock. Another. They were throwing their stores overboard to clear the guns.

'Pass the word for the gunner,' said the Commodore. 'Mr Randall, can you fetch her with the chasers?'

'Yes, sir.'

'Make it so, Mr Gunner. The chasers alone. You will lay them yourself, Mr Gunner: no other gun will fire until the order is given. You will disturb her people at their work, Mr Gunner.'

'Aye-aye, sir.'

Boom, went the larboard chaser, and Peter strained for the pitch of the shot. Splash, splash again, and the third bounce must have struck her abaft the mizzen shrouds. A hoarse murmur ran through the ship, drowned by the crash of the starboard gun. That wetted them, thought Peter: and at the same minute he saw smoke from the galleon's stern. Three plumes of water appeared ahead of the ship on either bow, and a spent Spanish ball made a hollow thud somewhere forward.

'In topgallantsails,' said the Commodore, just raising his voice above the sighing of the wind in the rigging. The upper-yard men raced silently aloft, and at the halliards and clew-lines the hands worked in perfect co-operation, without a word: for the first time in his sea-career Peter heard the weather-clew and its block slap up against the lowered yard, a hundred and fifty feet above his head.

'Fore and maincourse,' said the Commodore, after a pause in which the starboard bow-chaser fired again—the fall of the shot unseen. He meant to close under topsails and mizzen alone, with the *Centurion*'s decks clear fore and aft. She still had a great deal of way upon her, and the gun-crews below could hear the gurgling run of the water racing along her side just under the sills of their open ports.

The *Centurion* was ranging up alongside the galleon, ap-proaching her larboard quarter to run up under her lee, so that she might not fall off before the wind and escape. The Spaniard's immense poop and her broad, gilded stern-gallery could now be seen plainly, and the faces of men. The range was closing fast.

'The sprits'l yard fore and aft, if you please, Mr Saumarez.

271

Tops, there. You may fire with the first gun. Mr Brett, the guns may fire as they bear,' said the Commodore, looking at his watch again and noting time and position on a slate. A hole appeared in the foretop-sail and the Spanish stern-chasers barked out again.

Spaniards were busy on their spritsail yard. 'And they are doing the same,' said Peter, 'as if they meant to board *us*. Damn their impertinence. Spirited, though.'

Now the broad sea between them was a lane, a lane that narrowed with each heart-beat. Nearer and nearer the Spaniard was just keeping steerage-way, keeping the wind on her starboard quarter, waiting for the *Centurion*. The two ships were almost on parallel courses now: the *Centurion* had already crossed the galleon's wake diagonally, and she was racing up with the white water tearing at her stem.

Closer still, and closer fast. 'Hands to the braces,' cried Mr Saumarez a second before the *Centurion*'s bowsprit ran under the galleon's lee. The rest of his order was lost: as the *Centurion*'s bows passed the galleon's stern-ports the Spanish broadside thundered out. But already the topsails were backed, and the way came off the ship.

They were side by side within close pistol-range, moving, but without any appearance of movement, for they moved together. Between them lay a dense night of smoke, pierced with innumerable scarlet-orange jets and shaken by the hellish roaring, the metallic bellowing of guns. The *Centurion* fired continuously: the galleon in broadsides, slow, measured, all-embracing thunderbursts of sound and smoke and fire.

One, that had swept the bowsprit and head. Two, on the roll and too high. 'This is it,' said Peter in a whisper. Three. The whole smoke-bank lit up with a roar like the falling sky, and an enormous jarring blow struck the *Centurion* full.

The Commodore was shouting: the first lieutenant vanished: the main-topsail yard came round a trifle. Glancing up Peter saw the flashing of the muskets and swivel-guns in the tops; but he heard nothing.

Four. The fourth broadside. He had been waiting for it. Mr

Blew was down. In the waist a gun was over and its crew struggling madly. The Commodore was beckoning. 'My compliments to Mr Norris and we are going to run up. For'ard guns to be traversed.'

'Aye-aye, sir.'

Peter dashed by the sentry at the hatch, raced along the gundeck, gave his message, shouting through the heavy swathes of inward smoke; dashed back. Mr Anson was standing with his hands clasped behind him, with his back to the galleon, looking keenly up into the sails. Mr Blew was gone. There was blood on Preston's cheek.

Five. And between Keppel's head and Peter's passed a great hum and a hot blast of air. Keppel said something inaudible and winked: Peter blew his nose.

A gust of wind rolled the smoke slanting across the deck, starboard quarter to larboard bow. He saw the Spanish quarter-deck on his right hand, high, and the officers standing there: he could see their faces, dark, unmoved—swords, laced uniforms, long wigs. A young fellow was looking straight into his face. Clear in an instant's lull between the *Centurion*'s guns came a snapping volley from the tops: the young Spaniard fell, disappearing behind the rail.

Now the *Centurion* was ranging up along the Spaniard's side. The sixth broadside. And seven. A ball struck the quarter-deck. Where it had touched there was a deep furrow. Eight. Something rang on metal and he was down, staring at his foot. A six-inch splinter quivered in the heel of his shoe, which lay in the lee-scuppers—his foot untouched. 'Dear me,' he thought. As he wrenched the splinter and the heel away he had a moment's glimpse of Sean carrying a man below.

Nine was coming. Wait for it, he said. Then nine. There was a terrible screaming somewhere forward, and a block with a great serpent of rope fell on the quarter-deck. 'Preston. Palafox. Attend to that.'

For the tenth and eleventh broadsides they were in the mizzen rigging, knotting and making fast. He saw the Spanish deck, aswarm with men, and the officer who gave the signal for the guns. The Spanish tops, almost empty except for a few in the maintop. One of them fired at him as the *Centurion*'s mizzen came abreast of him. On the Spanish quarter-deck there were not many officers now. Their ensign had gone; but it had been scorched by gunfire, not struck.

'Down with your helm. Brace up sharp. Forestays'l,' cried the Commodore. One more broadside, a deep and wounding broadside, fired at the bottom of the roll into the *Centurion*'s gun-deck, and then the *Centurion* had forged ahead, out of the galleon's lee, to lie on her larboard bow, with every gun traversed in the wide ports and bearing, while the Spaniard's broadside thundered into the empty air.

On the galleon's side a red glow showed amid the smoke. Then it was a sheet of flame blazing and racing all along. The mats in her boarding-netting were on fire. Her guns slackened. High Spanish voices could be heard. 'If we fall aboard her,' thought Peter, 'that will be very bad.' He glanced along the hammocks in their own netting. They were soaked, of course. The sanded deck was running with water, and the pumps were rimmed with full buckets. But the cordage was dry. And there was powder in the open magazines.

'Fending poles,' ordered the Commodore. 'Stuns'l booms. There. Stand by.' But before the order could be carried out the flaming mass went by the board, hissing in the sea.

It was a different note from the galleon now. Not a full broadside any more, but the crack of the chasers alone and the few fo'c'sle guns that could bear. The *Centurion* was firing her whole starboard double tier in an unending thunder, and the sound of cheers ran through the din. And once again Peter could distinguish the crackle of the muskets in the tops.

He could see the frightful damage in the galleon. The wind tore the smoke, and there were officers running between the guns. Four ports forward had gone. Amidships two guns lay asprawl. Only four men held the quarter-deck, and as he looked one sank to his hands and knees. The *Centurion* was firing grape, and the murderous hail swept the galleon's deck: the unceasing deadly fire from the tops rained down.

'But he's no fool,' said Peter, seeing the galleon's yards brace round.

'Ball,' cried the Commodore, touching Peter's arm.

Peter tore limping with one heel below. As he passed on the order the roar of the Spanish lower tier swallowed up his words. He pointed to the twenty-four pound balls by the nearest gun. 'Hot work,' said the lieutenant, grinning savagely out at the smoke-blackened galleon's side through the shattered port of number 51—dismounted, but efficiently secured.

Going on deck Peter was stopped by men carried down to the cockpit, then by the racing stream of powder-boys. He reached the deck exactly in time of the galleon's fire, the broadside once again. Then he was on his back and his mouth was full of blood. He could not see—only a redness before his eyes. But it is nothing, he said, shaking his head and crawling up. A splinter had hit his mouth and forehead, but only flatwise. He mopped away the blood and took his place on the quarter-deck. Preston was no longer there. It was bloody underfoot.

'All right?' cried Mr Saumarez, peering into his face. Peter nodded.

'Graze,' he shouted.

Now the galleon had come up and turned to the wind. They were side by side again, and although the Spaniard's upper guns fired slow and few, her lower tier gave a crushing broadside yet, steady and determined.

'Edge her closer,' said Mr Anson to the wheel.

Yard-arm to yard-arm now: and the sky sent back the roaring of the guns. The galleon's main-deck had men running. Peter could see a scuffle in the hatchway: an officer pistolled a man.

The freshening wind tore the smoke fast away, and where three midship ports were knocked into a gaping hole he could see into her lower-deck. An officer was there beating at the gun-crew with his sword.

Forward three of the galleon's guns fired together: then a

pause, a long pause. Two more guns, and three: all went home. Gordon of the Marines threw up his arms, moved two jerking steps and fell across the rail. A longer pause from the Spaniard: then two more guns, lonely, fore and amidships.

Now it was the *Centurion* alone, firing without cease, the jetting flame and smoke and iron. 'Tops there. Tops,' hailed the Commodore in a tremendous voice above it all. 'Tops. 'Vast firing.'

On the galleon's deserted main-deck, darting, dodging for cover among the shattered boats and spars and guns, leaping over the piled-up dead, a single figure raced for the windward rigging. He reached the maintop.

At the main-topgallant mast-head the royal colours of Spain jerked, poised again for an instant, streaming in the wind, and then ran down, faster and faster, down in a dizzying flight down, struck down to the empty deck.

'Mr Saumarez,' said the Commodore in the uncanny silence. 'You will pull across in the longboat, if you please, and take possession of the galleon.'

15

'June 21st, 1743,' wrote Peter, with singular precision, '12° 40′ N. Cape Espiritu Santo bearing WSW. 6 leagues. Yesterday we took His Catholic Majesty's galleon *Nuestra Señora de Cobadonga* after a brisk engagement lasting about 2½ hours. The Spaniards behaved very well: their admiral and 67 killed, 84 wounded—152 casualties out of a crew of 550. We lost Corless and Windrow, seamen, killed; Mr Norris and 16 wounded—19 casualties out of a crew of 227, counting me. She mounted 42 carriage guns, 28 patereros in her gunnels and a 4 pounder in each of her tops. She carried 1,313,843 pieces of eight and 35,682 ounces of virgin silver and plate, which is a hundred thousand pounds more than we hoped for. We were like to have lost her and ourselves, however, by the ship taking fire just abaft the open powder-room. Mr Brett whispered it to the Commodore when he came aft to congratulate him on the victory: but we put it out without fuss. Sean behaved exceedingly well—because, says he, hurling himself wet upon the fire and rolling it out (though his head was in the powder itself) I will not be choused out of my glory for all the devils in hell. Poor Preston got stunned by a block. I was bowled over by a bit of a splinter. Keppel lost his best teeth, by gaping: they dropped out and were smashed by the next broadside. We are all somewhat deaf, but uncommon cheerful.'

Uncommon cheerful: indeed they were, in spite of the prodigious amount of work to be done, knotting, splicing and making good the battering the ship had received, as well as keeping the galleon afloat (she had a hundred and fifty shot, many of them clean through both sides of her, as the Commodore had promised, and between wind and water), getting her into sailing-trim—for it was impossible to transfer so great a weight of treasure on the high seas, and the galleon was to sail to China with the *Centurion*, as a post ship, R.N., with Mr Saumarez in command and a scratch crew to guard a multitude of prisoners who vastly outnumbered their captors— resentful prisoners who had supposed that they were surrendering to a ship of force, not a skeleton crew.

Uncommon cheerful, although immediately after the action Peter, Keppel and Pollock came down with a violent attack of the mumps, and yet could not be excused duty for a moment, but must keep their watches, armed to the teeth in case of surprise.

Uncommon cheerful in Macao again, and merrier still on the long, easy voyage through the Sunda straits—a single pause at Prince's Island for gentle exercise, water and new

277

varieties of fruit—and thence, with uneventful, easy sailing across the Indian Ocean, round the Cape of Good Hope, where their gaiety was increased by a large reinforcement of Dutch seamen. These men were permitted to do nearly all the work of the ship while the Centurions wandered about advising, watching and encouraging them—that is, whenever the Centurions could be prised away from their uncountable papers of sums and calculations, their precise estimates of their wealth and their varied plans for disposing of the same.

Uncommon cheerful through the South Atlantic, waving happily to St Helena as they flew past with a fresh breeze astern: outrageous cheerful when, after an incredibly rapid voyage up through the tropics, they reached the western forties and learned from an outward-bound English ship that they were at war with France: quite off their heads with delight when, after creeping through the chops of the Channel in a dense fog, they found that they had passed straight through the middle of the French fleet itself.

Uncommon cheerful. But not so Sean: not so Bosun's Mate O'Mara in his new glazed hat. Black care and a crushing weight of responsibility had descended upon him from the moment Mr Saumarez had beckoned him to the poop of the galleon, where the blood still ran with the send of the sea and the smell of powder drifted up from the shattered deck. He had one million, three hundred and thirteen thousand, eight hundred and forty-three pieces of eight to guard, besides the raw silver, the gold bars, the plate, the treasure of Paita and the bullion from the other prizes: and he intended to finish the voyage with precisely one million, three hundred and thirteen thousand, eight hundred and forty-three pieces of eight, as well as the rest. Yet he had only two eyes, and sometimes he had to close them. It was dreadful. When he slept (which was seldom) it was embowered in the clinking canvas sacks, far down in the airless hold, surrounded by a choice armoury of razors, pistols, cutlasses and a mighty axe.

In China he never went ashore unless Ransome would relieve him. Ransome was the only man aboard that he would wholly trust. Peter was not allowed beyond the threshold: Mr Brett Sean could not abide—'He does be laying a great compliment upon his speech, the creature: and his granddam was the serpent himself,'—this was because Mr Brett rarely swore at him; a most suspicious circumstance. Even the Commodore could only win the most grudging admittance, and then Sean's anxious breath was upon his neck every minute. Any warrant officer, petty officer or rating was shot at, without distinction or warning; and after a while they gave up coming down to ask Sean how he did.

The peace of the South China Sea, the tranquil breadth of the Indian Ocean eased his lot: but the recruitment of the Dutchmen in Africa was a sore trial to Sean. They were obviously thieves, raparees, transported felons: he could tell by their furtive expressions and their evil little small eyes—hell-spawn, to the last ill-shaped mother's son.

Then there was the landing, a perfect torment: and after that the culmination, the Centurions' march to London, through Westminster, past St James's, where the King beheld them, and quite through the City to the Tower, with drums beating, colours flying the galleon's battle-singed honours and the *Centurion*'s old faded ensign, and the crew, white, brown, yellow, black and mulatto, dressed in their best and with idiot grins permanently fixed, marching by the thirty-two enormous creaking wagons of treasure, the officers at their head with swords drawn and gleaming. Sean smiled, though wanly, at King George II; but the close-packed citizens reawakened his ire. The false thieves stood there cheering the way they would have him believe they would not touch a spoke of a wagon if he took his eyes off them. But Sean was not to be deceived by the serpents of London: he knew all about them, the criminal toads, and he glared unceasingly from side to side, with his cutlass ready and poised.

Into the White Tower they came, and the clash of the portcullis was music to Sean. The Lieutenant of the Tower and the beefeaters met with his total approval—cautious, discreet men, who understood the value of locks—and as the last chest passed into their keeping, behind huge iron bars and twenty-five feet of stone, the weight of a million and a half silver pieces fell from his soul, which expanded, breathed for the first time in twelve months and fourteen days, and uttered its relief in a shriek that made the beefeaters turn deathly pale.

With his own money, however, Sean was singularly unconcerned. He carried it about, with inconsequential levity, in his side-pocket—for it was mostly in Bank of England notes. He was so illogically carefree, indeed, that Peter confiscated five hundred pounds of it until he should be in a better frame of mind, and allowed him only a pocketful of gold, which he instantly spent, and came borrowing groats at a time.

The effect on Peter was as different as it could very well be. He had been—the mumps aside—as cheerful as a cargo of grigs from Cape Espiritu Santo to Spithead and from Portsmouth to London. But the Admiralty behaved in a pretty handsome way, for once since its inception. It was slow in rewarding the Commodore, and some time passed before he found himself a peer, rear-admiral of the blue and a sea-lord; but it actually paid the Dutch sailors and sent them home with a gratuity, refrained from instantly pressing the returned Centurions, and expedited the paying out of the spoil. For Peter, attending at the office of the prize-court with the rest of the midshipmen's berth, it was an awful moment when the clerk handed him a draft for one thousand, three hundred and seventy-eight pounds, four shillings and twopence halfpenny. And it was a still more awful moment (for gold is more real than any paper) when the cashier at the Bank of England casually scooped the last shovelful of guineas off the scales, tipped them into the sack and then, grunting, pushed the load across the counter.

It was a solemn task conveying this ponderous bag across London to Keppel's father's house. It was a solemn business sitting with it in the stage-coach to Holyhead, although it was lighter by then, for the enlargement of poor Elliot's father from the Fleet had cost a good round sum—not nearly so round as it would have been, however, if Lord Albermarle's man of business had not taken the matter in hand, buying up the unhappy curate's debts at five shillings in the pound. This had been a wonderfully fortunate affair, because not only had Mr Anson come home to find one of the livings on his estate vacant, but Elliot's sisters, who lived with their father in the Fleet, just managing to keep him in victuals by working fourteen hours a day at a milliner's, were able to advise Peter in the article of Paris bonnets (which came across the water, war or no war) and ribbons, mantuas, pelisses, mittens, caps. From their new vicarage in Wiltshire, they sent up, by express, a bonnet for Mrs Palafox, a bonnet for each of Peter's sisters—stupendous confections a good yard high, with birds, lace, fruit and unexpected flowers, as worn by the ladies of St James's—in addition to the first three eggs their new hen had ever laid, and a guileless infant trout the first-fruit of their father's eager rod.

A solemn business, the carrying it aboard the packet. So solemn that Peter scarcely noticed the hearty battle in which Sean was seized by the press-gang and had to be rescued from the few survivors of the group.

'What the devil do you think you are doing with a *Centurion*'s petty-officer?' he had snarled at the astonished midshipman in charge. 'Who the——are you, you miserable little sloop's snotty? What's your seniority? Speak up. I thought so. You say sir when you speak to me. Cox'n, release that man. Strike me, you perishing lot of longshore half-baked slime-bound swabs, don't you know a man-of-war's man when you see one?'

'*Centurion?*' gasped the midshipman, 'I beg pardon, sir.'

'*Centurion?*' murmured the press-gang. 'Cor, love a duck.'

A solemn business, carrying it off the packet on to Irish soil: equally grave, the cunning burial of the main bag under the floorboards of the little cart.

'You can't have that horse,' whined Peter for the third time, as Sean paraded a noble animal before him on Merchant's Quay.

'Crush me,' said Sean, spitting into the Liffey, 'and how will they know we are the glorious heroes of the world if we are not mounted up on high-bred horses?'

'Never mind,' said Peter doggedly. 'You take that creature (which is spavined anyhow) right back again, and bring the little ass.'

'I will not. Upon my soul I will not. To ride behind a little small ass is a fate I will not abide. Listen, your honour, honey, let me buy the pompous horse out of my own, will you, sir dear? There now, Peter a gradh, we will ride in triumph, and glory over the Leinstermen, will we not? and you will buy a laced coat, sure? And never go home in that horrible old blue, the way it never got well from the mildew in Paita?'

'No,' said Peter.

'Listen——'

'I will not. Sean, bring me the ass.'

'And is it an ass, Peter a gradh?' said Sean, with a real tear in his eye, 'And they putting the mock on us from Dublin to Ballynasaggart? I have not deserved it, your honour.'

'Oh, well . . .' said Peter, and they compromised on a sort of an elderly horse; but at least it had a leg at each corner, and it drew the little cart and its load of bonnets, ribbon, a large piece of Juan Fernandez, eight green parrots, one fruit bat (torpid) from Sunda, two terrapins (thought to be alive), one shivering ape, some crocodile's teeth, a curious Chinese tree, a porcelain pagoda, a keepsake from Miss Anne Elliot (in Peter's own bosom—but the cart also carried him) a Cape Hottentot's drum, a small dolphin in an advanced state of decay, and a large number of hideous shawls, besides miscellaneous objects of doubtful charm or utility; and a very handy ballast of gold. The horse drew the cart briskly across Ireland, stopping by night in small, uncouth uncostly shebeens, whatever Sean might say, with his gaze fixed longingly on magnificent inns where the coaches stood, and the gold rattling in his pocket—for Peter had yielded up a note to be changed, now that Sean was under his eye.

The motive for this rigid economy was plain. Peter had sworn by his soul that he would put one thousand guineas, and not one tin farthing less, into his father's own hands. For this was a sum that would exactly double the Reverend Mr Palafox's stipend, when put in the Funds; it would dower his daughters and it would send William to the longed-for Trinity College. There was no longer much of a margin; but come what may, he was not going to spoil the glorious roundness, and he plodded doggedly into the County Roscommon with Sean whining, hopelessly now, by his side.

It was a fair day in the Connaught summer when they reached the Plain of the Two Mists, where the curlews wept in desolation over their heads. That is to say, it was well above freezing, and the rain only dripped slowly from Sean's round, glazed hat.

'In five minutes more we shall see the Connveagh bog, so we shall,' observed Peter.

'The old bog itself, thanks be to God.'

'I thank Him,' said Peter, taking off his hat.

'Do you see the cloud lift on Cruachan? Two points on the starboard bow, sir, dear.'

'I do. Give way now,' he called to the horse. It was a partially nautical horse, having served in the Marines, and it gave way nobly.

Silent on the green road, its hoofs; silent the wheels as they traced their long ridge in the mud.

'There's Joseph Noonan's cabin,' said Peter softly. 'And I see the ash-trees of home.'

'There's Pegeen Ban admiring the world.'

'It's herself is taking the air, standing on the bog with her milking-stool under her arm.'

'Good day, young woman, and God's blessing to you.'

'May the dear God love you, sailormen, and would you have seen a small obstinate cow creeping over the bog? Why, your soul to the devil, Sean! Why, Sean dear, I hardly knew you. And Peter! Oh, what have they done to your poor face, all banged with guns? And Sean honey, your ears, and have you them lost? Oh, Sean, what a strange hat you have on. Oh, Sean, I hardly knew you,' cried Pegeen, shedding tears. 'And are you come from the wars far away? Poor things, in the little small cart,' she said compassionately. 'And myself calling after you to bring the King of Spain's old crown, so I did.'

'Well, Pegeen acuishle,' said Peter, leaning down to reach in his sea-chest, 'here it is. I will not say,' he said, looking at the circle of gold—a votive offering from Paita and a piece of private loot—'I will not say that it is his very best crown, not his holiday crown. But there,' he said putting it on Pegeen's sweet head and giving her a resounding kiss on the cheek, 'it was the best I could do, the time being short and the wars so cruel.'

'Oh Peter, the glory of Connaught you are,' said Pegeen, hugging him breathless and turning at once to see her crowned head in a puddle.

'So am I,' cried Sean. 'I am a gorgeous hero too, Pegeen Ban,' and he flung up a handful of guineas that fell again with the rain.

' 'Vast heaving,' said Peter to the maritime horse. 'Sean, cast off the starboard shackling-block. Bear a hand, now.' For in the soft distance he had seen a twinkle of white in the ash-trees of the Rectory garden. It was his smallest sister, who had been clambering up there to look for him these five weeks gone, since the news that the ship had been signalled came into the West: now she had fallen a yard, and was held by her powerful pinafore and one pigtail uncoiled. She was inverted, and it was the flailing about of her petticoats as she kicked that provided the twinkle afar.

'Cast off, man, will you?' he repeated in a quarter-deck roar.

'I will not,' cried Sean, madly embracing the horse.

'Fie, Sean, for shame,' said Peter, nipping out of the cart. 'You audacious reptile.'

'Four years I have obeyed,' continued Sean, skipping and pointing his toe, 'and now the joy of disobeying an officer is more than my heart can withstand.'

'Now Sean, my dear, will you cast off this horse, for it's the way I want to ride home with speed?'

'For shame, Sean O'Mara, to answer him so. To disobey

284

orders, your soul to the devil. When you marry me, Sean, that never will do.'

'For to please you, Peter, my dear, I will,' said Sean, buckling to. 'And the back of my hand to you, Pegeen Ban; and I may marry somebody else. But I am not obeying to order, your honour, for you see, I am casting off by the larboard.'

'Sean, you are to marry me,' cried Pegeen, gripping her stool.

'Sure, I *may*,' began Sean. But their courtship was lost to Peter as he leapt on the horse with a shriek and urged it wildly over the bog. Away on the other end of the road a far shape had appeared. Placidus galloping, with his master up, pounding the turf like a three-year-old. Mr Palafox's cassock flying out in the wind: then William and Dermot, aprons white on his sisters, the others behind and they running like hares.

'Give way,' cried Peter, restraining a powerful impulse to tack, for the wind was in his face. 'Give way,' leaping the horse by will-power over a line of turf in the road.

He flashed past the cross-roads and Noonan's low cabin.

'Welcome, Peter,' they called. 'Welcome home from the sea.'

'Welcome home from the Golden Ocean,' all waving. 'Welcome home from the Golden Sea.'

And he was down from his horse and running to greet them. 'Welcome home, Peter darling. Welcome home from the sea.'